BRIGHTER THE LIGHT

By

Susan M Cowley

Edited by John Parker

BRIGHTER THE LIGHT

BRIGHTER THE LIGHT

April 1946

The fight was over. Not that any blows had been exchanged, and the only ones who had caused a fuss were her and her little girl. A crying baby though can make enough noise to wake the dead. Margaret certainly had. Audrey felt sure she had known exactly what she was doing, but her daughter's wailing, a frightened and desperate pleading with her mother, began to make her change her mind. Audrey felt the blood draining from her face, the hot beads of perspiration on her cheeks turning to ice. She felt suddenly cold, and racked with the most guilt and shame. Passers-by were looking; staring at her as if she had committed some ghastly crime. She clutched her side and moaned silently: they *know*, the *whole world knows what I have done.* She stood on the steps of St Angelina's Adoption Agency in a daze.

It was as if a bomb had dropped and killed her, except by some devilish, cruel trick she could still see and hear and think; the thinking was the worst, the most terrible, unceasing torture: to be condemned to *remember* what she had done.

Having decided to give her baby away, she had, she only realised now, made absolutely no plans about what to do afterwards. The surrendering of her child had seemed so shocking; both in the anticipation and the act itself that it was if she had somehow assumed her own life would end in that same, appalling, earth shattering moment. Little Margaret had bawled so desperately when the nurses took her, slowly, but firmly, from Audrey's shaking arms. Her plaintive cries, echoing down the long, gloomy corridor as the two strangers walked away with her, had torn at her mother's heart like sharpened stakes.

It was then that Audrey had rebelled, woken up, realised the awful, full significance of what she had blundered into.

—

3

She had run down the corridor, shouting at the nurses, telling them it had all been a mistake - she did not want to give her daughter up forever, only for a while, until she was back on her feet, until she could cope again....but not forever, no, no, no...! Two more nurses had quickly appeared.

They spoke to Audrey, gently, reasonably, in low, modulated voices, one on either side of her, taking her arms, guiding her, reminding her; she had signed the adoption papers, it was legal and binding, they had an obligation now, a legal duty, a moral duty.

A child's welfare was at stake. Their words were hypnotic, they were sympathetic, they understood. They smiled. One said, 'God's will be done.' Then somehow she was back at the front door of the building. The door opened and she was on the outside again. 'God's will be done,' the nurse repeated. The heavy wooden door had slammed shut. She had hammered on it, called out, pleaded, begged, torn at the paintwork till her fingernails were broken and bleeding. But no one heard her; no one came.

Audrey walked slowly, unsteadily, but in what direction she did not know. Her feet felt like boulders, huge weights which she was obliged to drag for evermore, her burden; her penance now for all eternity. She thought: 'perhaps I should kill myself now; my beloved Martin is dead, my best friend is dead, my parents have disowned me and I am almost penniless; my baby girl was all I had in the world, and now, in the hope she may have a chance of a decent life in this pitiless world I have given her away. What reason is there for me to go on living?'

She wandered the streets aimlessly, bumping into people and lampposts, oblivious to trams, cars or bicycles, unaware of where she was, the overcast Liverpool sky mirroring her dark and ominous mood. Then something made her look up; the dull street had been momentarily brightened by a flash of lightning zigzagging across the rooftops.

A few seconds later came a rumble of thunder and large raindrops began to spot the pavement.

The thunder and lightning broke Audrey's trance. A torrential downpour noticeably gathering force, all along the street people were diving into shops or breaking into a run to seek shelter. Turning up her coat collar Audrey followed a group of giggling girls up some nearby steps and through a pair of large double doors.

Looking round her eyes opened wide as she realised she had sought refuge in the lobby of Liverpool's imposing Grand Hotel. Here she and Martin had spent their wonderful night together, their last night, the last time she saw him. Tears brimmed in her eyes and she thought she might fall to the floor, fall and never get up again; 'what better place to die' she thought, 'where my darling and I were together last.'

She looked towards the staircase, where the magnificent, magical Christmas tree had stood that night. On the wall was a poster, proclaiming an appeal by a charitable organisation for the underprivileged, calling for donations and for people to come and work for them in this worthy cause and on the desk beneath it were leaflets. Audrey picked up a leaflet, printed at the bottom was a London address. She read the words again then put it into her handbag.

The thunderstorm cleared as rapidly as it had begun. Audrey left the Grand Hotel to find the sky now a brilliant blue, the air refreshed and clean, and the atmosphere in the streets vibrant. She made her way towards Lime Street Station, walking with determination now, her destination London and the offices of the Regent Trust.

CHAPTER ONE

July 1945

Mary Lawson looked nervously at the calendar hanging on the chimneybreast. It was the 9th of July 1945; the day had finally come. She sighed heavily. Her appointment at the hospital was for two o'clock. Would the riddle then finally be solved? She wondered, hoped feared, all at the same time. It wasn't as if she and Joe hadn't been trying for a baby, and for a long time, even before the war. So why had nothing happened?

Mary and Joe had met at Blackpool in the summer of 1937. She had been on the Co-operative girls' outing, and Joe was doing some electrical maintenance work on the fun fair.

That particular day though, he'd changed out of his overalls, put on a double breasted suit and taken himself off to the Tower Ballroom for the afternoon tea-dance, just as Mary and her Co-op cronies were piling in and taking over the tables. An argument over a spilt cup of tea had catapulted the young couple together, and by the third waltz, under the spell of Begin the Beguine, and the envious glances of Mary's friends, they had fallen head over heels in love, and vowed that nothing would keep them apart.

Mary Jacobs came from a small village on the Wirral peninsular, Joe from the heart of Liverpool. After the first rapturous embrace, an obstacle to their liaison had arisen; Mary's parents had disapproved.

"He's from across the water, a ruffian shouldn't wonder," was the curt summing up of their only daughter's intended.
Joe's mother had felt the same way: "Too posh for us lad, meet someone of your own kind."

Joe dug his heels in. Mary *was* his kind, he insisted. He wanted more than Liverpool was offering, and nothing was going to stop him having it, in the shape of his beautiful Mary. She was after all only a short ferry ride across the Mersey, a very small price to ensure their love continued to blossom.

Following his heart across the Mersey paid off, and he and Mary were married in a year. The decision to settle near Mary's parents was abruptly overturned. Two weeks after the wedding Mr and Mrs Jacobs had both killed in a train crash while on holiday in Wales. Joe had tried to comfort her but Mary was inconsolable; her Mother and Father meant everything to her. With no family now it was agreed that it would make more sense to move to Joe's side of the water, with his family in Liverpool.

Work was hard to come by, and Joe had by this time landed a good job on the docks, while Mary could transfer to the big Co-operative department store in the city. They would live with Joe's mother until they could afford their own home and start a family, which, Mary assumed, would not be long in coming.

Six months later they had moved from Beverly Street, the cramped two up two down terrace of Mary's mother-in-law Ethel Lawson, to a similar property a few streets away in Portland Terrace. The house was small though comfortable, but Joe wanted more.

Then of course, the dark shadow of war had intervened and Joe was called up. Ever the optimist though, he was not going to let Adolf Hitler stand in the way of his plans.

"When this war's over Mary, when we've thrashed the Jerries once and for all and I'm home for good, we'll have a place of our own and a football team of kids, you'll see."

That pronouncement had been made on Joe's last visit home. Mary still laughed at the recollection but increasingly now there also a quiet tear or two.

The war had been over for two months yet Joe's unit had still not been demobilised, and she was missing him terribly. Was there some reason he had not come home she wondered? Was he hurt? He had made no mention of anything untoward in his last letter. Had he begun to despair that the 'football team' had as yet showed no sign of appearing?

"I wish you were here Joe" She took his photograph from the mantelpiece and gazed fondly at the beaming, handsome face. "I'm so scared love," she said aloud, "scared for you, for us."

Just seeing his face reassured her. Joe always looked on the bright side, and so must I, thought Mary. At that moment there came a loud knock at the front door.

"That'll be your mother," she sighed, carefully placing Joe's picture back in pride of place.

Mary opened the door. Without so much as a hello or a good morning, Ethel Lawson stepped over the threshold.

"It's not right!" she proclaimed, pushing past Mary and blustering her way through the hall and into the kitchen. "Not by a long way..." Her voice carried through the whole house. "But I suppose it's better for you to have someone to share the bad news with."

Mary sighed and closed the door. Why had she let this pessimistic, overbearing woman force her into taking her along to the hospital?

"Would you like some tea Mother?" Mary asked filling the kettle,

"Oh child, how can you drink tea at a time like this?" Ethel began crying now, a sort of dramatic, self-conscious wailing, dabbing her eyes with a freshly laundered handkerchief. "I'll have two sugars."

Mary smiled and put her arm around the older woman's shoulder. It must be hard for her to think that she may never be a grandma, she thought.

"Not much else to do Mother, but have a cup of tea and hope for the best." Mary replied, "At least until I've had the results. Let's not jump the gun eh?"

Ethel whined again. "To think our Joe's never going to be a father. What would old ma' Rutter think?"

Mary hung her head. Along with the awful, inner emptiness if it turned out she really couldn't have children, was the prospect of some people's attitudes - the sneering, cutting remarks, the whispered derision, and worst of all the fake sympathy; she could almost hear them already: 'not a complete woman that one, can't have children, poor love...'

The kettle whistling on the gas ring mercifully drowned out the voices in her head. She picked up the tea cloth, wrapped it around the handle and removed it from the stove. Pouring the steaming water into the large brown teapot she thought again of Joe. Suppose Ethel was right, and he could never be a father? Apart from her, she knew it was all he had ever really wanted. And if her worst fears were realised, her mother-in-law would make their lives a misery, forever telling Joe that if only he married some other girl, a "healthy" girl, it would never have happened.

"Oh well," she sighed stirring the tealeaves around. "We'll have to work that out between us. As I say, things might not be as black as we're painting them - that's the whole point of going to see the doctor."

She poured the hot strong tea into two matching china cups, the ones that only came out when Ethel visited and carried them on the souvenir wooden tray from Blackpool that was a wedding present into the sitting room.

"Brews up Ethel," she said. "Let's have it in the living room, and then we'll have to go if we're going to get to the hospital on time."

Doctor Prescott read the notes on his desk while Mary and her mother-in-law sat rigid. Mary watched the doctor's expression intently. After a seemingly interminable minute had ticked away, he took off his glasses and sat back in his chair looking at the two women.

"Well?" bristled Ethel, as if addressing a delinquent boy who had been caught doing something he shouldn't.

"The results of the last test we conducted have not changed the diagnosis..." began the doctor.

"What's that in plain English?" snapped Ethel.

"Mother, let the doctor explain," pleaded Mary.

"The plain fact of the matter is Mrs Lawson," continued Doctor Prescott looking at Mary, "that you will never be able to have children naturally..."

"I knew it!" said Ethel. She then took out her hanky and dabbed her eyes. Mary gripped the cold metal sides of the chair. For a second she did not take in what he had said then it hit her with a great thud, his words resounding in her ears.

"You mean," she said in a very quiet voice, "I can never be a mother?"

"Not necessarily Mrs Lawson." He smiled kindly. "This diagnosis confirms that you won't be able to have any of your own, biologically speaking."

"But what other way is there?"

"Well, have you and your husband thought about adoption? There are so many children in need of a happy home."

"Adoption?" exclaimed Ethel open mouthed as if the doctor had suddenly begun speaking a foreign language.

Mary looked bewildered, on the verge of tears. "We've never considered such a thing doctor, not in our family – it's never been heard of." Then she thought: but there's never been anyone who couldn't have children.

She said, "Adoption, well…Joe's not got his demob orders yet, but I could talk to him about it I suppose but…"

Doctor Prescott reached into a drawer and handed Mary a calling card.

"This is an adoption agency, not just any - they have a better class of children," he said with some pride.

Hearing this Ethel lowered her hanky and looked at the card with interest.

Mary read the name out loud "St Angelina's Adoption Agency." She and Ethel looked at one another. "I'll have to talk it over with Joe of course…this is all still such a shock, I knew it could be bad news today of course but …"

"I knew exactly what was coming." said Ethel in a superior tone.

They all stood up. Doctor Prescott took Mary's hand in his. "If your husband loves you, he will understand you know."

Mary smiled feebly. "Yes, he does, and I hope he'll understand doctor, who knows."

Outside in the corridor Mary turned to her mother-in-law. "Oh Ethel, I'm so sorry." With tears in her eyes now she braced herself for a torrent of criticism, or at the very least some bitter remark.

The older lady seemed hesitant, torn between her natural instinct for unashamed reproach and the constraints of ordinary human empathy. The scales, as Mary expected, tilted resoundingly to the former.

"I feel for you luvvie, I really do" she sighed. "But let's face it Joe's not going to be happy is he, and what's folk going to think?"

Mary stiffened then bit her lip and brushed away her tears. Looking her mother-in-law straight in the eye she said, "Well, you know what they say about clouds and silver linings Ethel?"

Ethel, struggling again to contain her demon tongue, replied, "I suppose some good might come of this – but for the life of me I can't think what."

CHAPTER TWO

With a weary sigh Mary took off her coat and hung it on the peg in the hallway. After her early shift at the large Co-operative department store in the city centre she was looking forward to a meat pie and a strong cup of tea, as strong at least as rations would allow.

Although the war had now been over for four months, a return to normal life seemed slow in coming. Her Joe was still away and she ached for him. His brief letters revealed he was somewhere in the Pacific, where, unlike Europe the war had not ended with VE day; now he and his 'oppos' were 'mopping up' as he put it. It looked unlikely he would be home for Christmas either. How many was that they had missed now?

Mary's longing to see her husband was of course much tempered by the news she would have to break to him; even it if she thought it might reach him, she hadn't dared mention it in a letter. It was now three months since the doctor's diagnosis, and though apprehensive, she desperately wanted to talk to Joe, to tell him face to face that the likelihood of their having children was almost non-existent – to share her sadness, and comfort him in what would unquestionably be his.

But she wanted too to cheer him with the possibilities this opened up to them, encourage him, facile as it sounded, 'to look on the bright side'. They now knew the 'natural' route was all but closed to them. But they had wanted a child in their lives, a little one to love and watch grow for so long; now they could go ahead and make that happen. Mary still had the card the doctor had given her, an introduction to St Angelina's Adoption Agency. She recalled his accompanying words: "A better class of children."

How would Joe take to a child that was not his own? Her mother-in-law Ethel had continued to make her feelings about the matter plain.

"Don't you go thinking about that idea again Mary," she had remarked recently on noticing the St Angelina's card tucked behind the mantelpiece clock. "Not of our blood you hear – and that would never do."

"Oh it would never do would it?" Mary mouthed mockingly to herself as she cupped her hands round the warm teacup. "Not for Ethel Lawson and her kin."

But her Joe was different, she reasoned, not as pretentious as his mother; no side had Joe. In fact he was nothing like her, thank God. They would talk, just the two of them, he would listen and together they would make the right decision - for them, never mind relations, neighbours or Uncle Tom Cobbley.

Resolving to talk to Joe strictly on his own when he returned, she lifted her eyes to the photograph on the mantelpiece and smiled fondly at her beloved. "God keep you safe my love," she whispered kissing his face. "And bring you back to me soon."

"It's going to be a good year this next one," Ethel Lawson predicted tipsily. "1946 – a year to remember I'd say."

"Let 1945 go first Ethel," her sister Ginny remarked gingerly, sipping the home made damson gin with a face as frosty as the icicles hanging from the drainpipes outside. "A week left of it and we're still on rations, remember."

"How could I forget Ginny? You tell me every week – not too much of this and very little of that and I doubt none at all of the other where you're concerned!"

Frank, Ginny's henpecked husband stifled a surreptitious little laugh and suffered in return a wrathful, withering glance from his wife.

"I just wish Joe was home," Mary sighed pouring out hot if weak tea into a delicate bluebell patterned teacup and saucer and handing it to Frank. "I miss him so much."

"He'll be here soon enough," Ethel said darkly. "Then you'll have to tell him about…" She narrowed her eyes portentously, "you know what."

Ginny shot Mary a look of mischievous curiosity, while Frank poured the tea out of his cup and into the saucer and began blowing noisily on the steaming liquid to cool it.

Ginny glared at her husband. "Don't give him your best crockery Mary," she sniffed haughtily. "He doesn't appreciate bone china."

Mary smiled at Frank who had now put the offending articles down on the table. She drew in a deep breath and stared at Ethel. This time, she thought, the woman had gone too far; she was not going to let anyone think she was afraid to talk about 'you know what' least of all her interfering mother-in-law.

"You mean about our not being able to have children, and that we might think about adoption?"

Ginny's eyes opened wide. She sat bolt upright.

"You can't do that Mary Lawson!" she exclaimed. "Take on someone else's child? It's, it's – well – it's unthinkable. Me and Frank couldn't have children, could we Frank but we never gave – *that sort of thing* - any consideration did we?"
Frank lowered his eyes and focused his attention on the green and yellow tissue paper Christmas hat that had fallen onto his knee.

"Then maybe you should have Ginny," Mary replied heatedly. "And instead of thinking about yourself for a change, given some poor child a decent life. And before you say it," she was getting into her stride now, "I don't care what old ma Rutter would have to say - I don't really care for her opinion, or anyone's for that matter."

Now rounding on her mother-in-law she went on, "Maybe Joe should have married one of your kind like you were always telling him Ethel - and don't bother to deny it, I've heard you with my own ears."

Ethel and Ginny both stared her, bristling with indignation, visibly mustering their outraged retaliation. But Mary was taking no prisoners today.

"So," she said folding her arms decisively, "when you've both finished giving me advice as well as drinking my sherry and eating my food I think it's about time you got yourselves out from under my roof!" Her outburst over Mary ran from the room and up the stairs, slamming the bedroom door behind her. She fell on the bed sobbing as if her heart would break. Well she had certainly said her piece now where Ginny and Ethel were concerned. But in time they would get over it, and if not and it turned out she had burnt her bridges, then so be it. Sometimes things just had to be said, regardless of the consequences.

She thought again of Joe and wished he were with her right now. Her friend who understood her, Joe would know how she felt and be on her side against those two witches. She picked up a framed photo from the bedside table; it was of her and Joe together at Blackpool. They were both of them happy and smiling - full of love for each other and hope for the future. She kissed his face. "Maybe your mother's right love," she whispered tenderly. "Next year will be a good year - but for you and me. Dear God it needs to be, for all our sakes. Please be home soon, I'm praying for it."

14

It was the morning of the 2nd of January 1946 when the laden troop ship pulled into Liverpool docks. As the huge chains clanked against the quayside and the steel gangways were dropped, Corporal Joseph Lawson of the Royal Artillery heaved his kit bag onto his shoulder.

Providing armed support to the Allied supply ships in the Far East over the past two years he had seen plenty of action; arduous nerve- racking voyages with the ever-present threat of the Japanese Kamikaze planes. Two of his close mates assigned to another vessel had perished in one such attack, and Joe's mood throughout the voyage home had been sombre; he was glad to be alive, but the sorrow at the loss of such fine young men – just two among the very many – was as abiding within him as any physical scar or lump of shrapnel beneath his flesh.

As the familiar sights and sounds of the docks washed over his senses Joe's spirits rallied; in a couple of day's time he would be de-mobbed, and back in his own home, swapping his cramped hammock for a plump feather bed, and the loving arms of his Mary.

What a fortunate man he was – lucky to have survived, and lucky to have such a good, true and beautiful woman as his wife. Mary would never cheat on him, he knew so with absolute certainty – not like some of the poor blokes who had received 'Dear John' letters – 'Sorry dear –met someone else…' or '…come home quick – your wife's pregnant.'
He had seen good mates of his visibly crumble as they read such painful tidings. Though he had feared death many a time while away, he had never feared a 'Dear John' letter. Mary was the best.

Now the war was over they would start making plans - a good job for him, a house of their own and at long last a family; they'd both agreed, a football team would do, and why not. Joe imagined the cheerful noise and banter of children's voices about the house, the joyful chaos of a big family. He recalled that Mary in her last letter has said something about some hospital tests, but she had reassured him everything would be all right, and if his Mary said it, it was cast iron proof of the matter. Hearing his sergeant bellow the order to disembark, drowning out the mournful-glad cries of the seagulls circling the harbour, Joe fell in with his comrades lining the ship's rail.

Down on the dockside, sharing jokes and calling out to one another the lads piled into the waiting army trucks, which as soon as they were full began to move off through the busy docks and out along the road towards the barracks. In the back of Joe's lorry a private struck up a verse of 'Inky Pinky Parle Vous', which soon became a loud and hearty chorus.

They passed the distinctive Tate and Lyle vans chugging to and fro laden with huge sacks of sugar, billowing hot steam from their rooftop exhaust pipes while the glowing ashes fell into the metal trays attached below the vehicles. Joe smiled as he saw them, likewise at the huge, dignified dray horses and carts bearing all manner of exotic and wonderful goods from the docks to the rows of nearby warehouses. These familiar sights he had seen and taken for granted for most of his life. Yet now, they seemed so much more meaningful and important to him, like the pleasure of meeting old friends after a long time apart. He was coming home.

"Mary." Mr Bryant the departmental head called from the office window, "telephone"

Mary rushed up the wooden staircase and opened the door.

"For me Mr Bryant - who is it?"

"He didn't say," the manger replied. "Just that it was urgent. But may I remind you that personal calls are not permitted, if this should become a habit…"

Ignoring him Mary took the receiver from the desk. "Hello, Mary Lawson speaking."

"It's me Mary!" the voice at the other end said, "I'm coming home."

"Joe!" Her face lit up with joy. "Is it really you? Oh Joe, thank god…when does your ship get in?" She was breathless, a bundle of relief excitement and nerves.

"It's in - I'm on British soil now, up at the barracks. Another two days till de-mob, be home for dinner."

"I can't believe it, oh Joe I'm so glad – I've got so much to tell you."

"Like what?" Joe asked.

"Oh nothing – I mean everything." She laughed nervously. "I'll get something nice on the go for you – so Thursday yeah? Oh Joe, I can't believe I'm really talking to you after all this time…"

The line went dead. Mr Bryant took the receiver from her hand.

"That's enough idle chatter Mrs Lawson," he said removing his finger from the button and replacing it with the receiver. "Now if you want to keep your job, I suggest you get back to work."

"Yes Mr Bryant." Mary closed the office door and ran quickly back down the stairs to her post on the drapery floor.

"You look happy," remarked Hilda Green as she eyed Mary, grinning from ear to ear and humming a little tune begin tidying the shirts in the wooden cabinets with a degree of enthusiasm hitherto unseen.

"Joe's coming home," she almost giggled, "in a couple of days. He's coming home!"

"Oh I am glad for you girl," Hilda smiled. "Safely home at last, that is good news."

"Yes, he's one of the lucky ones and …" Mary stopped mid sentence. "I'm so sorry Hilda," she said lowering her voice respectfully. "I forgot about Reg."

"Don't be sorry pet. Reg died doing what he was good at – flying aircraft. He wouldn't want other folk to wear long faces on his account, and he'd be glad your Joe was coming home. And what's more," Hilda rubbed the small bump in her stomach, "I've got this little one on the way - something to remember him by. And Reg will be looking down on us both and giving his blessing with a glad heart." She lifted her eyes heavenwards.

"Oh Hilda you have such faith, you're such a genuinely *good* person."

Mary left the pile of shirts and came and put her arms around her friend. It would be hard going for her bringing up a child on her own. She shed a small silent tear. Hilda had lost her man but had a child on the way, while her own fate was the opposite. 'I am so very fortunate in that.' thought Mary. She could only hope and pray that her Joe would see it the same way.

CHAPTER THREE

"Nice piece of shin beef Mrs Lawson," Bill Benson the butcher remarked handing Mary the greaseproof paper package. "Taken most of your ration that has" He peered at her over the counter, hoping she would not demur now over the extravagant purchase.

"Joe's home today," Mary smiled, placing the parcel carefully in her wicker basket where it nestled among the three small carrots, a cabbage, an onion and a few potatoes she had had just bought in the greengrocers.

She had taken the day off from the Co-op and got up even earlier than usual to clean the house from top to bottom, polishing the windows with newspaper and vinegar till they positively sparkled. Then armed with her ration book she had caught the bus into town to gather the ingredients for her husband's favourite meal of roast beef and two veg, or three if you counted the onion and potatoes.

Her heart swelled with love at the thought of him inhaling the mouth-watering aroma of slowly roasting beef, the crisp, succulent golden brown potatoes, prepared 'as only you know how my angel.' Joe had always recited these words to her in the early days, with a peck on the cheek and a fond squeeze of her waist as they sat down to their Sunday dinner in those magical, seemingly far distant days before the war. Now those days would come again; her Joe was coming home to her.

"He's a lucky man your husband," smiled the butcher. "And I'm not just talking about your cooking Mary Lawson." He gave her a playful wink.

Mary felt herself blushing slightly. "Get away with you Bill Benson, what would your wife say?"

"Nothing" he laughed "she'd just take the frying pan to me - actions speak louder than words!"

"Take your money" Mary said feigning annoyance, "before I decide to have a word with her then."

On the bus home Mary gazed dreamily out at the terraced streets of Liverpool as they passed by. How would life be now, day-to-day with Joe home again she wondered?

At first she had missed him so much, not just his affectionate companionship, but all the practical things he had taken care of and she had felt quite helpless at first and thought she would never be able to cope on her own. But necessity being a great teacher, the little jobs that Joe normally did so well - the dripping tap, blocked drains, even getting in the coal for the fire - she eventually learned to manage by herself, or got someone in.

But there was more to a man than a pair of strong arms around the house; and what Mary had pined for most was those same arms wrapped around her, holding her, loving her through the long, lonely nights.

Her mates at the Co-op had been welcome company during the day, but when work was done she had come home to solitude. Ethel had visited on a few occasions in the evening for a bite to eat or a cup of tea, but away from the shop the two of them had little in common.

She and Joe had always had always had so much in common, like soul mates from the day they met. But time had passed, Joe had been to war. She had heard of other girls looking forward eagerly to their husband's return only to find themselves like strangers all over again. Then of course, there was the 'news' she had to break to him. She gave a little shiver.

"You all right pet?"

Mary looked up to see the clippie smiling down at her. "Oh yes, thank you, just felt a bit queasy for a minute that's all – a two penny please." She held out the coins.

The clippie turned the handle of her machine and handed her a ticket. "It's a bumpy old bus this – gives me the collie-wobbles some days. Or, excuse my prying, but maybe you've a little bump of your own pet?" She smiled indulgently and raised her eyebrows.

"No…" began Mary.

"Oh well there's plenty of time yet, young girl like you. I remember my first one, I couldn't keep anything down of a morning for three whole months…she's coming up to fifteen now bless her…"

Mary tried to smile politely, but the effort proving too much she turned her face once more to the window and as the bus sped on, began with great concentration to count the chimney pots.

Her stop was coming up. She rang the bell, took her shopping basket and alighted. The sun was shining now, lighting up the rooftops and cobbles, and lifting her spirits once more.

"You got a visitor Mary Lawson." Mary's neighbour Violet Duxbury, who had been energetically donkey stoning her doorstep looked up and grinned.

"Who is it?" Mary asked as she turned the key in the lock.

"You'll find out soon enough." The old woman laughed, plunged her scrubbing brush into a bucket of murky water and attacked the step with renewed gusto.

"Nosey parker," Mary muttered as she turned her key in the door. "Hello?" She called out as she stepped into the hall. "Ethel, is that you?"

To her annoyance her mother-in-law still had a key to house. She sniffed the air, which smelt of tobacco smoke. "Ethel is that you," she repeated, "who's there – hello...?" Suddenly the door to the kitchen opened.

"Hello y'self, Mary Lawson. Where've you been all my life?"

There in front of her, large as life and twice as handsome, one hand in the trouser pocket of a neatly pressed double breasted de-mob suit, the other casually holding a Players cigarette stood Joe.

"Joe!" she exclaimed, "you're early...I..."

"Shall I go out again and come back later?" His lean cheeks, tanned by a thousand and one hours on the deck of a battleship in the oriental sun creased in a broad grin.

"Oh Joe!" Breathless with joy and relief Mary dropped her wicker basket and ran into his arms, nestling her head tightly against his chest. Her Joe was really home. All the doubt and uncertainty that had clouded her mood on the bus home vanished. Against the faint ticking of the kitchen clock they stood there almost motionless for a full minute, locked in each other's arms, Mary ever so often emitting a deep sigh of peaceful satisfaction at finally being able to inhale the redolent, unforgettable aroma of her husband.

Finally Joe spoke again, the deep, familiar masculine tone making Mary quiver with pleasure. "There, there my love, together again eh, and no one shall put us asunder as the good book sayeth. I've been looking forward to this moment all the way from the docks."

"Only since the docks?"

"I meant outward bound!"

Mary smiled and a little tear, which had been forming in the corner of her eye, now rolled down her cheek. Then she remembered her 'news'- the dark and perhaps hazardous chasm which lay between them. Dare she mention it before dinner, and risk spoiling the pleasure of this moment? Or was it better to get it over with? This is ridiculous, she thought rallying herself, I'm talking like a condemned person – Joe loves me, he'll be disappointed but he'll not let it come between us.

She said, "Have you seen your mother yet?"

"No came straight home." He looked into her eyes. "It's been a long time Mary. How about you and me warm that bed up?"

Gathering her in his arms he carried her silently upstairs and setting her down on the bed said softly, "Undress for me."

Mary felt a strange frisson of shyness and excitation as she slowly unhooked her dress and let it fall, then removed her underclothes. She had never done this kind of thing before, she and Joe having both been so modest in their intimacy. She felt suddenly daring now. Joe gazed at her nakedness, drinking in her feminine curves.

Mary felt no shame, rather a pride and exquisite pleasure at revealing herself to him. Joe made love to her with an intensity and passion she had never known before. Afterwards, as they lay in repose side by side Mary thought: maybe this is the moment. I must say it now, before Ethel lets it slip. Joe would never forgive me for that, for holding out on him. He seemed to sense her anxiety. "What's troubling you love?"

Mary gave a timid smile. "Can't keep anything from you, eh Joe?"

He got up from the bed and lit a cigarette. "Well, what is it?"

She sighed heavily. "Oh Joe - I just don't know how to tell you."

Joe ran his fingers through his hair. In a sudden flood of alarm he wondered: is it my turn to be a 'Dear John' now after all?

"Come on Mary spit it out - you've found someone else – oh please God don't tell me you're pregnant!"

"What?" Mary looked at him incredulously. "How could think such a thing - why would I do that?"

He looked away. "I don't know, I'm...I'm sorry," he stammered. "It's just this damn war – it's done terrible things, and it makes you think them too. It's been a long time Mary – a woman might get lonely..."

"Of course I've been lonely Joe," Mary interrupted, staring at him wide-eyed, hurt. "But I've been lonely for you – no-one else."

He turned towards her again. "Then what is it you have to tell me? Are you unwell?"

"No – not as such."

"What do you mean – Mary what is it?"

"I wish...that we...that I...was...going to have a baby..." she began, her words faltering as her eyes filled with tears. "But the fact of the matter is Joe..."

"Yes?"

"I can't have children."

For a moment Joe stood perfectly still. Then he came towards her and sat on the bed. He took her hands in his. "That's alright Mary," he said quietly. "It'll be different now. We'll be settled again. It'll happen you'll see." He smiled. "We might just have made it happen."

Mary gulped. "No Joe, you don't understand. It's not a matter of trying. The doctor says I can't have children - ever. I'm so very sorry."

Joe stared at her for what seemed a long time. Then without saying a word he pulled on his trousers and shirt and walked quickly from the bedroom slamming the bedroom behind him. A few seconds later, Mary heard the front door closing.

"Did you know about Mary?" demanded Joe as soon as his mother opened the door. He pushed passed her into the living room.

"Well that's a nice way to greet your mother after a year away I must say," said Ethel following her son. Joe was pacing the living room agitatedly. "For crying out loud sit down son and let me get you some tea."

"Did you know?" Joe repeated slamming his hand on the gate-leg table.

Ethel nodded. "I went with her to the doctor - she's just as upset as you - not a complete woman some might say."

"And we all know who that might be Mother," Joe said with bitterness. "You and Ginny - vipers the pair of you" He collapsed into the floral patterned armchair and sunk his head in his hands. "Oh Ma what are we going to do?"

"Said you should have married your own kind son." said Ethel. "But she is my kind Ma, that's the whole point, I love her - but oh, not having kids..." He nursed his temples despairingly.

Ethel sat on the arm of the chair and gave his knee a sympathetic rub. "Oh dear, what a welcome home this is for you lad. Stay here with me then I can look after you. We'll be alright."

Joe sat deep in thought for a moment. "I suppose it might come to that Ma. Me and Mary finished?" He took a long breath. "A family means everything, it's what I've always wanted – it's what most folk have a right to expect. And if I'm to do that, I'll have to find someone else to..." He broke off as the full significance of such a prospect hit him. "But I love her Ma"...it's her I want – I mean, I don't suppose kids are everything..."

"What rubbish!" Ethel scolded him, "a marriage without children?" "Ginny's got none – her and Frank are alright."

"Cause she tells folk they are," laughed Ethel dryly. "If truth be known they're both miserable as sin but they're stuck with each other. You don't want that now do you now love."
Joe looked sullen. "Suppose not," he sighed. "But Ma, what am I going to do, how can I leave Mary?"

"Listen to me, I knew she wasn't right for you from the moment I set eyes on her – la-di-dah ways and now this soft idea she's got into her head - not blood I said and don't you forget it..." Ethel broke off suddenly.

Joe stared at his mother. "What idea? Is there something you're not telling me Ma"?"

"Oh you'd best ask her," Ethel blustered. "Not my place to go poking my nose in."

Joe stood up, "All right, there's something been going on I can tell. I'm going to sort this out." As he strode down the hallway there was a knock at the door. He opened it.

"Mary! – I..." Seeing his wife's beautiful, tearstained face he immediately softened.

"Can I come in Joe?" said Mary quietly. "We have to talk."

He nodded and she followed him into the kitchen. "Sit down." He indicated the armchair.

"What's she doing here?" Ethel sneered. "Don't you think you've done enough harm my girl?"

Mary retaliated. "How do you think I feel?" she said hotly, "with all the nasty remarks from you and Ginny, and the rest of the world when they find out. Yes! Mary Lawson the woman who can't have children, her poor husband – putting up with that. Send it to the Echo why don't you - let's get it over and done with." She turned to her husband. "Oh what's the point of talking Joe," she sighed wearily. "She's already poisoned your mind shouldn't wonder." She strode to the door but Joe grabbed her arm.

"Don't go." he whispered intently.

She shrugged him off. "I can't help it Joe, I want children, more than anything but I can't have them and that's that. If you want me, and you want to talk about the alternatives come home – if not, - " She closed the door behind her.

Joe stood in the hallway, his thoughts sunk in misery. He loved his wife dearly but could he really be content with a childless marriage? He opened the door again and watched her walking away down the street. Silently he called her name. He wanted to go after her, tell her how much he loved her, how sorry he was for causing her this pain, but somehow he couldn't, wouldn't; how could he when he was in such turmoil himself? .

Slowly he closed the door. Mary had given him time to think, but for how long? He would have to make a decision soon, and be it right or wrong he would have to live with it.

CHAPTER FOUR

As she sat on the crowded bus into work the next morning Mary felt more alone and wretched than at any time in her life. It was as if her whole life had fallen apart overnight. Even during the dark days of the war when Joe was away, the knowledge of his love had kept her going. Now she realised how much that love had been the cornerstone of her world. Was it still in place? If so it was feeling distinctly shaky. Perhaps, she tried to console herself, this awful inability to have children was a test of their love; but what a cruel one!

She had not slept a wink during the night, and when the first shards of daylight had crept through the curtains she had wanted more than anything to curl up under the blankets and finally doze off dreamily. But exhausted as she was, with Joe not there beside her it would have been hard.

"You look fair whacked!" Hilda grinned impishly as the two friends sat in the canteen on their morning break. "I take it Joe's well and truly settled back in then."

Mary was sat with her head resting in her hands, her elbows on the table. 'Yeah, he came home,' she said in a small, frail voice. She rubbed her eyes and then her face began to pucker.

"What's wrong?" asked Hilda. "Did I speak out of turn?" Holding back the tears Mary replied, "Oh - we had a row, no not a row …I told him…." All the heated emotion of the previous night rose up inside her again, and her words became a choking sob.

"There, there love," Hilda comforted her. "Can't be as bad as all that."

"But it is Hilda," wailed Mary into her teacup. "He's left me."

Hilda looked incensed. "Met someone else has he? Oh this damn war - that's what to blame!"

"It's not the war Hilda…"

"Then it's him – oh men!"

"No, it's me. You see, I can't have children, I told Joe yesterday and he left… he's gone to his mother's…"

"The selfish bugger!" cried Hilda at the top of her voice, prompting a sudden hush in the canteen and several heads to turn.

Hilda rounded on them, "All right get on with your brew you lot this is a private conversation."

There was a ripple of laughter at this from some of the cheekier elements before the hum of general chatter resumed.

Turning back to Mary and lowering her voice Hilda said, "Seriously love, you're better off without him if he thinks like that."

"He doesn't," Mary protested, 'at least I'm sure he doesn't deep down - if the truth's known Joe's a good man and he just needs time, but it's his mother, Ethel, she'll poison his mind if he stays with her."

A look of desperation came over Mary's features now. 'You see I went to see him last night, at her place, and she's already started on him with her wicked sniping." She bowed her head and began sobbing again.

Hearing the commotion and seeing the prying faces in the canteen looking round once more, Mr Bryant got up from his table and made his way over.

"Quick pet," said Hilda, "dry your eyes." She slipped Mary a clean handkerchief. "Here comes the boss."

Mr Bryant stood by them and peered over his spectacles.

"Mrs Lawson," he said officiously, "may I suggest you and Mrs Green take your 'problem' to the ladies' rest room, and leave your fellow employees, and myself, to enjoy our tea break uninterrupted by vulgar and noisome outbursts of emotion. Alternatively please take a day's leave. Unpaid."

Pointedly avoiding the supervisor's gaze, Hilda said, "Come on Mary let's get back on the floor, there's a funny smell round here all of a sudden? Have you noticed it Mr Bryant? But then I suppose you wouldn't would you?"

As they got up to leave Mr Bryant, his face pinched with suppressed rage muttered. "Not in that state Mrs Lawson if you please."

"Oh I'll be fine now, thank you Mr Bryant, please don't trouble yourself." Mary dabbed her eyes.

"No, don't trouble yourself Mr Bryant," Hilda repeated with heavy sarcasm. "We can manage quite well without you thank you very much." She linked arms with her friend and they walked out of the canteen, Hilda savouring the now admiring glances of the other staff.

When they were back behind the counter Hilda said, "It'll all work out for the best pet, whichever way you'll see."

Mary gave a forlorn smile. "Thanks Hilda, I know you're right - one way or another."

The day had been a long one. Having poured her heart out in the canteen over morning tea break Mary had tried to put on a brave face on, pushing Joe to the back of her mind as best she could. A stream of pleasant, chatty customers had helped. At five-thirty on the dot, ignoring Mr Bryant's beady-eyed looks and checking of his watch, she had promptly cashed up and said goodnight to Hilda. Alighting from the bus her thoughts returned inevitably to her heart's desire: would Joe be waiting for her at the house?

Opening the front door she had her answer at once, for though the weather was not cold the atmosphere was chilly; it was the absence of love. Shivering as she hung her coat in the hall and went in to light a fire, Mary tried to take command of her feelings. Maybe this is it now she thought - the end of things for Joe and me. Well if that was so she would have to make the best of it. If he really had made his bed elsewhere he would have to lie down on it, and she would do the same, however hard that might seem. Yes, it was no good crying over spilt milk, no good at all. There were plenty of things she could do with herself in this life she told herself as she broke up some sticks for kindling and shook the coalscuttle. Yes, plenty of things - without Joe, or any other man, or children come to that. Her bravado lasted till she had got the fire going; as the wood spat and crackled into life she slumped into the armchair and quietly wept.

For three days Joe had listened to his mother's nagging, snide remarks. "She's talking of adopting Joe. Have you heard the like? Not our blood son."

Sat at the kitchen table Ethel Lawson, oracle and layer-down of the law, set her jaw firm. "Don't be taken in with her fancy talk, you can't take on someone else's unwanted bastard. That's what most of them are you know, in them adoption places – bastards, born on the wrong side of the sheets, bastards one and all, and blood will always out mark my words…"

Even as Joe listened to the stream of invective he knew what she was doing to him, which was slowly, remorselessly poisoning his thoughts. Oh yes, his mother was good at that sort of thing, he had seen her do it to others; she was a past mistress.

By the third day he had had enough. He left the house early, hopped astride his old pushbike and made his way down to the docks. Joe had seen on his way in on the troop ship that the place had taken a proper battering from the air raids, with many of the warehouses and quays reduced to rubble. Pedalling along the approach road now he was heartened to see scaffolding going up, and to hear the cheerful whistle of builders and the rumble of wheelbarrows; the great job or restoring the city of Liverpool's greatest asset, and with it the morale of her inhabitants was underway.

Leaning his bike up against a wall, Joe sat on a pile of bricks and took out the bread and cheese he had brought from his mother's kitchen. The fresh air and sunshine and watching the bustling activity was a welcome change from her endless slander and condemnation of others, but Joe's thoughts now focused more than ever on Mary.

He had been harsh with her he realised that now. He should have listened – after all, as she said, the fact they couldn't have children wasn't her fault. Why did folk always have to look for someone to blame? It didn't make sense, any more if she was born with one arm, or a gammy leg – it was bad luck but uncharitable to take it out anyone, least of all the person suffering the misfortune.

What had he been thinking? He had married Mary in sickness and in health, for better, for worse. All right now here was the worse, but the good had been very good and maybe would be again. He realised he loved her so very much, and no matter what his mother said he couldn't be without her. He resolved to go back home that very moment and ask her forgiveness; no matter what the future held, they would see it through together. The decision made, he took out his pocket watch and seeing that it was twelve noon remembered that Mary would be at work. This made him feel guilty; children or no children, as a man he should be providing for his wife, not letting her go out to work all hours god sent – like any woman her place was looking after the home, and being able to take a pride in it.

Nearby stood Joe's old place of work from before the war, the large, looming Tate and Lyle warehouse, which surprisingly had survived the German bombers largely intact. Finishing his bread and cheese Joe got back on his bicycle and pedalled over to see if Mr Pringle the works manager was still there. He was pleased to find several of his old mates already reinstated after their demob, and there were warm greetings and handshakes all round as he entered the warehouse.

Mr Pringle was there too. "You're in luck lad," he beamed when Joe put in his request. "You'd be very welcome to you old job back. Not forgotten how to do a bit of sparking have you?"

"Like riding a bike sir," grinned Joe slapping the saddle of his bicycle. "You never forget."

The two men shook hands and Joe agreed to report for work the very next morning. Feeling suddenly full of optimism and joy now, he went straightway across the road and into the Crown and Anchor. Imbibing the rich aroma of ale and tobacco he was soon supping a foaming pint and engaged in animated conversation with a crowd of the dock lads and builders, sharing their stories of the war, tales of heartbreak and bittersweet comedy, of commiseration and hopes for a better world. Joe laughed and drank along with them, reflecting on his good fortune – he had not only his health and a wonderful wife, but now a job and pay packet to look forward to.

As the ale and the hearty male bonhomie warmed his spirits his thoughts opened out. He began to see things more clearly, see the assumptions he had been making, and that these assumptions could be, in fact almost certainly were mistaken: firstly, that children had to be of your own flesh and blood to be 'yours', and secondly that his mother was the source of all wisdom and the fount of worldly knowledge.

The former notion was a struggle to throw off but Joe could feel himself coming round to the idea of adopting a child, in fact it was giving him a sort of happy glow right now. As for his mother, she could go hang, in a manner of speaking. He was his own man, and would chart his own destiny – no woman would decide his life for him, none except his dear good wife.

Joe drained his glass and ordered another pint, grinning from ear to ear at the thought of his mother's expression when he told her what for and the smile on Mary's face when he came home to her, and of all the love that awaited him there.

CHAPTER FIVE

April 1946

The lunchtime post had come early that Friday. Joe sat at the kitchen table and gripped the official-looking brown envelope with both hands, staring intently at the sender's address on the back. Yes this was it, all right, the letter that could change their lives. It was what Mary had been waiting eagerly for since the moment he had agreed they should go ahead and try to adopt.

For Joe the decision had not been an easy one. After his euphoric change of heart in the pub and his joyful return to his wife, the sober realities of the matter had still to be reckoned with, weighed up, discussed. He and Mary had discussed it all right – and agonised and argued into the small hours some nights. Joe saw so many 'what ifs' - what if the baby proved 'difficult'? What if it grew up and people started gossiping, and it got to hear rumours, malicious ones even, about its family? What would they say, how could they explain? Would it want to find its real parents? Worst of all, would the child resent Joe and Mary, hate them even?

They talked all these fears and anxieties through, Joe trying to tell himself he was in fact over-thinking the situation. In principle he agreed that to adopt was the best thing, a wonderful thing, to give a child a home, and their love. Yes, they must simply act in good faith, Mary told him, out of love, and must continue to do so whatever hurdles or hiccups might arise in the months or years ahead. If there were dilemmas and hardships and moments of intense heartache, in the end there would be much happiness; that was the stuff of family life. She had shown him the card for St Angelina's adoption agency, and assured him they had all the qualities, material and emotional, required to provide a child with a loving and good home. Joe did his best to keep his qualms at bay, to come to terms with what they were about to do. His mother would always maintain that bringing up a child not of his own flesh and blood was not right, but he must not let her influence him. He had 'seen the light' that night in the pub; that he loved Mary and missed her dreadfully when they had been apart, and without her his life was lonely and incomplete. He had vowed they would never be separated again, not even for a day, and certainly not due to his mother's influence. If adopting was the only way they could stay together, then so be it.

Joe peered at the postmark on the letter: Thursday 25ᵗʰ April – that was yesterday; St Angelina's had acted swiftly, Mary having only telephoned them a couple of days ago.

Perhaps they had a child already waiting? Who could abandon a child, he wondered, when he and Mary had so desperately yearned for one? Perhaps its parents had been cruel or neglectful, or perhaps they were dead – there were so many orphans. These thoughts brought a lump to Joe's throat; he hoped with all his heart he had enough love to give this little person who, sooner than they had expected perhaps, was about to enter their lives.

He looked at the mantel clock. It was half past one – Mary would be home from work in half an hour. With a heavy heart and mixed feeling he put the unopened envelope on the kitchen table; she could have the surprise.

"Got some sausages for tea Joe," Mary's voice rang out from the hallway, "We'll have some chips with them." She opened the kitchen door. Joe sat at the kitchen table, and poured a cup of tea for her from the freshly brewed pot. "Here you are love" he smiled putting the cup next to the letter.

She put the shopping basket on the table and was about to pick up the cup when she saw the letter.

"Well, open it." Joe said to her, "Put us out of our misery,"

Mary looked at Joe then back to the envelope and quickly opened it.

"It's from the adoption agency Joe."

"I know that love. It's on the back of the envelope."

"Sorry, I'm all of a fluster…"

"Calm down and tell us what they say."

"They want to see us tomorrow at two o'clock."

"What else?"

Mary shook her head. "Nothing, just that they want to discuss adoption." Her eyes were luminous with anticipation. With a shaking hand she passed the letter to her husband. "This is it Joe, We're going to have a family."

"Now Mary, don't build your hopes up, they only want to see us."

Mary grabbed his hand, "But it's a start Joe," she said excitedly, "It's a start."

As they turned the corner the old grey Victorian building that housed the St Angelina's Adoption Agency loomed above them. Mary looked up, wondering how many hopeful young women had made this journey before her. Then, more painfully she remembered the many who must have come not seeking a child, but to give one up.

As they mounted the stone steps she clutched Joe's hand tightly. He reached forward and tugged on the bell pull. They stood in silence till after a few seconds the heavy oak door creaked open.

"Mr & Mrs Lawson?" The smartly dressed young woman gave Mary a comforting smile. "I'm Ruby. Come inside, Dr Evans is waiting for you."

They followed her down a long wood panelled corridor.

"Mr & Mrs Lawson Doctor" Ruby said shepherding them into a spacious room.

At a large desk by a long window sat a woman probably in her mid thirties, wearing a smart floral dress and horn-rimmed glasses. She lowered her spectacles now and looked Joe and Mary up and down in a discreet but authoritative way.

"Do sit down," she said indicating to two chairs in front of the desk "Could you arrange some tea Ruby?" Ruby nodded, smiled at Mary and Joe then closed the door.

Mary gazed around her. The ceiling seemed immensely high, the cream painted plasterwork bordered with ornate coving and cameo designs of fauns and shepherds standing out in bold relief. From the centrepiece hung a majestic glass chandelier, illuminating the room in myriad tiny patterns, throwing a soft magical light over the oak panelled walls, while leaving dark corners here and there, mysterious recesses which neither sun nor artificial light could it seemed penetrate. A fire burned brightly in the grate, but offered no apparent warmth or cosiness. From a gilt-framed oil portrait above the mantle, the face of a stern Victorian patrician looked imperiously out. The face glowered down, watching her, judging her, it seemed to Mary.

"Thank you for coming here today," Dr Evans said opening a manila folder and studying the contents. "I wanted to speak to you both, to meet you face to face. And see if you are suitable people to take care of one of our children."

" 'Course we are" Joe said rather abruptly, "Nothing wrong with us."

33

Dr Evans smiled and nodded. It seemed a non-committal gesture. "I see from the file Mrs Lawson that you cannot have children naturally and that is why you were recommended to us…."

"Did you say we've been recommended to you?" Mary interrupted, exchanging a baffled look with her husband.

Dr Evans nodded. "Yes, Doctor Prescott, he has made the recommendation in your case."

"But, I don't get it, I mean, I contacted you."

"That's right," said Dr Evans patiently, "we cannot contact a prospective adopter directly. Now a recommendation has been made its my job to follow it up, by meeting you. Which is why we're all here today, as I explained."

She looked at Joe and Mary in turn as if to make sure they understood. Though still looking unsure, they shrugged and made vague murmurs of assent.

Dr Evans leaned forward across the desk. "So, tell me why you think you would be good parents"

There was a slightly awkward pause. Mary could hear Joe breathing hard. She hoped he wasn't going to say something out of place. Joe took her hand. "Because we're good people," he said. "I've a good job – and well, and it would make Mary happy."

Dr Evans nodded. "Of course. But how do you feel Mr Lawson?"

Joe looked uncomfortable. What was the right answer to that one? And he was not used to being asked rather intimate questions, especially not by a stranger, and a woman at that.

He took a deep breath. "I'll be honest Doctor, when Mary told me she couldn't have kids I was upset. Like so many lads I'd been fighting a war for six years and all I wanted when I came home was a family."

"Of course," said Dr Evans again. Joe shifted uncomfortably in his seat. "The fact is, if you must know, I left her over it. More fool me I realised later." He spread out his hands imploringly. "I listened to my mother you see, and much as we care for them, our relatives don't always know best. I realised what I was missing. After all it wasn't Mary's fault she couldn't bring it about, just nature taking a funny course. Now we're back together and that's how it's going to stay.

34

So if adopting makes her happy, and me of course, then that's what we have to do, adopt and give a kid – um, I mean a child, a good home." Joe wagged his finger towards Dr Evans, "And let me tell you Doctor it will want for nothing. Nothing."

Dr Evans sat back in her chair. "I'm sure of that Mr Lawson. Well there are one or two forms to fill in, and then we can start to make a decision."

"A decision, today you mean?" Mary said. She looked at Joe, her eyes ablaze with excitement.

Just then the door opened and Ruby entered carrying a tea tray. She placed it on a side table, poured the tea into china cups and handed them to Mary and Joe.

"Thank you Ruby," said Dr. Evans. "Now while you're having tea you can look through these." She handed them each a form. "Please answer the questions and don't leave anything off. You'll find writing implements on my desk. I will leave you alone for a moment, you may wish to talk privately to one another." She got up and followed Ruby out of the door.

"Oh Joe, isn't it thrilling?" Mary squeezed his arm enthusiastically. She took a gulp of her tea and peered at the forms. "Oh but listen to this," she read aloud, "please enter your weekly wages, the age of child you are seeking and what sex - and here look, it says: you must agree to the child's anonymity, and must have no contact with the birth mother."

"Well it has to be that way love," said Joe. "I mean imagine if the mother changed her mind, wanted her kid back..."

"It wouldn't be her child," interjected Mary hotly. "She couldn't do that, it would be ours - I would be the mother...!"

"Exactly," said Joe patting her arm in a placatory gesture. "That's why they put that. I expect they get the birth mothers to sign something similar."

"The poor loves though," said Mary sadly. "To have to give away your baby."

"Maybe some of them want to."

"Who'd want to?"

"You'd be surprised, hard hearted some people. Anyway let's not think about that it's not what we're here for, let's fill these blessed forms in and get out of this place. It gives me the creeps."

A few minutes later the door opened and Dr Evans reappeared.

"How are you getting on?" she smiled.

"Finished Doctor thank you." Joe held out the completed forms to Doctor Evans who ran her eye carefully over them.

"That seems to be all in order," she said, "thank you."

"Well Doctor, what's the answer?" Mary was sitting up eagerly.

"To what?"

"Have we passed everything, are we approved, or whatever we have to be – to adopt a child. You did say we'd know today didn't you?"

"Today?" Dr Evans looked surprised. "Goodness me, no Mrs Lawson, not today. This is just the first step. Like all applicants your application will need to be scrutinised closely, and then your case will have to be discussed at length with the board of governors. We don't give out children just like that."

CHAPTER SIX

It was almost two weeks before the next letter from St Angelina's landed on Joe and Mary's doormat. Mary had waited anxiously checking each morning at 7 o'clock before she left for the Co-op, then scouring the hall on her return home in case the postman had been late or a letter had blown into a corner. On the Saturday morning of the second week, there it was, hanging halfway through the letterbox as she came downstairs. She was glad she wasn't going to work that day. She opened the letter with trembling fingers, and read:

Dear Mr & Mrs Lawson.

Further to our meeting at St Angelina's we are pleased to inform you that you have in principle been accepted to adopt a child. This will of course be subject to your accommodation meeting our minimum requirements for hygiene and facilities. We have arranged for our senior nurse to visit you at 12noon on Saturday 23rd March to inspect your home. On the proviso that it meets with her approval she will then discuss the necessary arrangements yourself and your husband.

Yours Sincerely,

Dr Gwyneth Evans

Re-reading the letter Mary gave a sudden gasp, "The 23rd - oh heck that's today! Talk about short notice - Joe!" She yelled up the stairs, "Joe we're going to have a baby, a child, a family! Oh I can't believe its really going to happen!"

With tears of joy and excitement she half ran half fell up the stairs, tripping over her dressing gown in her agitation and shouting repeatedly to husband. "Joe, we've got to get this place cleaned up and quick...Joe we're going to be parents...I can't believe it!"

"This place gives me the creeps" Joe shivered, gripping Mary's hand as they mounted the stone steps.

"You said that the last time we came."

"Well it still gives me the creeps."

Mary laughed and brushed some stray hairs from Joe's demob suit. She said, "Now ring that bell."

"Why do I always have to ring the bell?"

"It'll help calm your nerves."

"I'm not nervous," protested Joe. "I'm just worried you're jumping the gun again."

"Well we passed the test on the house with flying colours," pointed out Mary. "In fact the nurse said it was one of the nicest homes she'd been to."

"She probably says that to everyone."

"Well they've not asked us to come here a second time for nothing have they?"

Joe, about to remark that perhaps this latest summons to St. Angelina's was to tell them politely that they would not after all be allowed to adopt, looked at his wife's eager, animated face and thought better of it. Instead he did as he was told and rang the bell. Ruby quickly appeared.

"Mr & Mrs Lawson," Mary said handing her the note that the nurse had given them on conclusion of the home visit. "To see Dr Evans again."

Ruby smiled, "She's expecting you. Would you like tea?"

Joe shook his head but Mary nodded, "We'd love a cuppa thanks."

Dr Evans greeted them warmly and this time shook their hands. Joe thought: that's strange; this could be the big let down, brace yourself Mary, but he said nothing and smiled politely back at the doctor.

"Sit down please."

Mary put her handbag on the floor and removed her gloves. Joe's right she thought, this place is creepy. Avoiding the gaze of the stern patrician in the oil painting, she looked down at her shoes, and crossed and uncrossed her legs several times in quick repetition.

Dr Evans opened the file and after glancing down at the notes for a moment looked up at the couple.

"Well," she said brightly, "the day has finally arrived for you."

Mary smiled nervously. Joe remained silent. He hated the doctor's patronising tone and wanted desperately to say: well is that a yes or a no?

Dr Evans consulted her notes again. "I see your preference is for a baby boy, is that correct."

Mary nodded, "Yes." She nudged Joe. "That's what we agreed wasn't it?" Joe gave a sort of grunt.

Doctor Evans took off her spectacles. "I must ask again Mr Lawson; are you quite sure about adopting a child? From your expression I have to say you look – well frankly - terrified."

Joe sat as if in a trance, Mary looking at him imploringly. The tension was broken as the door opened and Ruby came in with the tea.

Covered by the rattle of the cups and saucers Joe found his voice. "Eh? Well, ah, I'm sure Doctor yes… I've never had much to do with children, before but I'll learn, and I'm a quick learner, you have to be in the army. It was the waiting that got me you see. Coming here the first time, filling in the forms, then that nurse coming to our house to weigh us up, and now another grilling…"

"Hardly that Mr Lawson."

"Well in a manner of speaking…"

"We have to be sure, you understand," said Dr Evans. "*You* have to be sure. Three weeks is time enough for a couple to change their minds."

"Mary wants a child Doctor…I want a child, we can give it a good home… with plenty of love." Joe's tone was warmer now, his words carrying conviction.

Dr Evans sat for a moment and tapped her spectacles on the desk. Mary gave a little despairing sigh.

Finally the doctor smiled. "Very well," she said, "You've convinced me young man." She closed the folder decisively. "Now let's go and see the children."

Hearing these words Mary reached out impulsively and squeezed Joe's arm, her face lit up in a broad smile. Joe lowered his head and patted her hand.

They followed the doctor down a long corridor till arriving at a door with a window at the top. Mary gripped Joe's hand.

Opening the door Dr Evans ushered them into a large room.

"Mr & Mrs Lawson" she announced to a nurse sitting at a small and meticulously clean looking desk.

Looking down the room Mary gasped. Three long rows of cots stretched from the door to the far end, where through a large church-like arched window a grey, mid morning light was filtering in through the clouds. In the cots, young children, babies to toddlers, all dressed in identical cream flannelette nightclothes were laying, sleeping, standing at the bars or romping. Throughout the room there was a soft cacophony of gurgling, keening and occasional crying.

"I'll leave you with Nurse Yardley," said Dr Evans. "And I'll see you before you leave."

Nurse Yardley, immaculate in her starched uniform and with an air of brisk efficiency, smiled at them. Gesturing them to follow her towards the rows of cots she said, "Take it nice and slowly, it's a big decision. The boys are on the right and girls on the left."

They made their way down the line, Mary's gaze tentative, looking almost timidly at the little occupant of each cot, as if fearful of intruding, provoking tears, worry, alarm, or, perhaps worst of all, hope. Seeing the curious, often anxious faces staring back at her she felt close to tears. Every single one of these children needed a home, to be taken care of, but most of all they needed love. She had an abundance of that, she knew it; she felt a sudden, desperate craving to gather each of these little mites in her loving arms and hold them to her, take them and love them and tell them everything was going to be all right, that they were safe and secure and loved, loved, loved…

This was an agony she had not prepared for; that from all these innocent little children she had to choose just one; the thought of the others she would have to leave behind now cut her like a knife, blotting out the joy and hope and optimism she had been anticipating from this moment for so long.

"Are you all right Mrs Lawson?" Nurse Yardley had stopped and was looking at her sympathetically. She had seen this before, her expression suggested; she knew exactly what Mary was feeling and thinking; the shock, the pain, the terrible act, the burden, of having to *choose*.

Mary nodded, swaying slightly. Joe took her arm. "Like the nurse says, take it slow Mary."

"I'm all right," murmured Mary. "Let's carry on."

They walked a little further down the rows. Though they had agreed on a boy Mary was now peering cautiously at the baby girls too, some whimpering, some crying at full throttle, and some fast asleep. The sleep of angels, she thought; they are so *beautiful,* so innocent...

"I want to leave Joe," she gasped suddenly. "It's too much for me. I can't do this, I can't take just one, don't you see."

"I know love, I understand, it's hard, and sad to see all these kiddies little faces but they'll be soon couples just like us for the other children – isn't that right nurse?"

Nurse Yardley nodded. "We have people just like you coming in all the time. Everyone has to make a choice, and as your husband says its not easy. It's not like picking out new furniture after all."

Mary knew the nurse's assurances were just to placate her. She had heard all about orphanages, about the children who languished in them for years, never knowing a loving home. She thought: if ever I am rich I will come back and take all these children, buy up this place and be mother to every one of these precious little ones, give them the love and the place in life they deserve....

Nurse Yardley interrupted her thoughts, "Come back tomorrow if you wish. It's a big decision and if you need more time - "

Joe nodded. "I think we will nurse, she can't do this today, and neither can I – these poor kiddies, they're all just so...vulnerable...maybe the whole idea was a mistake..." Joe's emotions were getting the better of him too now. He bit his lip and looked down at the floor.

Just then the sun came out from behind the clouds and blazed through the big arched window, casting a brilliant light across the room. Caught in the sudden glare Mary lowered her head. Looking up again her gaze fell upon a little girl. The child was sat up in her cot, her face bathed in the sunshine. Drawn by the light she now turned to peer intently out of the window. In her tiny hands she clutched a worn and ragged teddy bear.

Without speaking Mary walked towards the cot. As she drew closer she realised the child was very quietly crying.

"Hello sweetheart," said Mary softly. The little girl stopped crying and looked up at her. Mary bent down and gently gathered her into her arms. "There, that's better isn't it?" she whispered tenderly. "No need to cry now little one."

The child burrowed her head deep in the softness of Mary's shoulder. She then emerged and began, shyly yet with a curious intensity, to study Mary's features.

Nurse Yardley said, "This little girl has been here three weeks.
Her mother left her with us, difficult circumstances, couldn't cope any longer I'm afraid. The poor little mite's been so unhappy."

Mary said tremulously, "How old is she?"

"Nine months," replied the nurse.

Mary felt the warmth of the child's body against her own, both of them seeming to relax, to grow steadily calmer as the contact was maintained. Now and again the little girl would give a quiet whimper.

"There, there," cooed Mary, patting her back gently. "Joe, come here," she said, rocking the child in her arms. "What do you think?"

Joe reached out and tickled the little girl's chin. She promptly smiled.

"Well I never," exclaimed Nurse Yardley. "That's the first time I've seen her do that!"

Joe repeated the tickle, which this time produced an audible giggle. The little girl then coyly hid her face. Suddenly she wrapped her arms tightly around Mary's neck. Mary felt her heart soar, tears pricking the corners of her eyes.

Joe was smiling too now, and broadly. "Well, if we're to keep those smiles of yours coming," he said in a playful voice as he pinched the little girl's cheek, "I think we'd best take you home, don't you young lady?"

Mary turned to Nurse Yardley, and with the tears now streaming down her face and her voice cracked with emotion said, "Please, does she...does she have, a name?"

"Yes dear," said the nurse, "she's called Margaret."

CHAPTER SEVEN

April 1946

"Wake up Miss, end of the line."

The guard shook Audrey's shoulder gently. "Come on dear, I've finished me shift and I wanna get 'ome before midnight you know. And unless you want to go all the way back up the line to Crewe in five minutes time I should get off if I were you."

"Hmm?" Audrey stirred and rubbed her eyes. She glanced around the compartment. She was the only passenger. Her memory returned with a jolt and she sat up.

"Oh...so sorry," she mumbled. "Forgive me I must have dozed off." She fumbled for her handbag and straightened out her crumpled coat. "Where are we please?"

"Euston Miss, end of the line. This one goes out again in five – correction - " he looked at his pocket watch, "four minutes."

"Is this London?" There was a note of trepidation in her voice. She turned to the window and peered out. The station seemed vast, the platforms stretching on forever, the dingy smoke-filled air an echoing cacophony of booming announcements, slamming doors, shunting engines and shouting porters. All around people were hurrying this way and that. Passengers were starting to board the train now.

"Your first time in the big city Miss?" the porter asked. Audrey nodded.

"Where you headin'?"

"Headin?" she frowned

The guard smiled. "Yeah headin' - goin' - got an address?"

Audrey rummaged in her handbag, found the folded piece of paper and handed it to him.

"The Regent Trust?" he read. "That's that charity for the homeless. In need of it are we?" he smiled at her quizzically.

"Certainly not," replied Audrey indignantly, primping her coat again. "I've er...been offered a position with their organisation - I'm a trained nurse you understand."

43

"Oh, I see young lady." The guard looked her up and down then handed her back the slip of paper. "Hmm, you'll be wanting directions then. It's a long walk to the east end my dear. You could take a taxi if you can afford it - otherwise get the number 65 bus, stops on the Euston Road outside the station here, that'll take you to Butter Lane. Ask directions when you get there." Audrey thanked the guard as he held the carriage door open for her.

She handed her 'one way' train ticket to the man at the barrier and a moment later emerged onto a bustling thoroughfare. It was early evening now, and the fading light, combined with a swirling fog that had begun to descend made for a chaotic, disorientating scene.

The London rush hour was in full swing, office workers in bowler hats with briefcases and furled umbrellas, men in overalls and flat caps carrying tool bags, typists in twin sets and heels all jostling for space on the pavement. Audrey gasped, not knowing which way to turn. It was if she had been plunged into a human whirlpool, engulfing her and robbing her of all sense of place or direction.

People seemed to be moving every which way, jumping from taxis and buses then pushing their way through to catch their train home, streaming from the station and underground to join the long queues at the bus stops. Others wove their way circuitously through the crowd to buy papers from the newsstands, or hot chestnuts from the street vendors. Several were trying to cross the busy wide road, dodging in and out of the cars and buses grinding their way along in the fading light.

Fighting her way through the throng, barged repeatedly by anonymous elbows, her shins scraped by swinging bags and umbrellas, Audrey joined a long line of people waiting at one of the bus stops. One by one the red double-deckers drove slowly up, disgorged their passengers and immediately took on fresh human cargo, the conductors doing their best to maintain order and safety. "One at a time please one at a time, where's the fire mate, one at a time…hold tight please, hold tight now!" And with a 'ding-ding' the laden buses would pull away again.

Audrey strained into the fog to read the bus numbers. There was no sign of the 65. For all she knew she could be at the wrong bus stop, she couldn't get near enough to see any kind of timetable. Already feeling lost and bewildered she now began to panic. She might wait here all night and then what? She was alone in London with no idea where she was going.

"What number do you want dearie?"

Audrey turned to see a middle-aged woman in a headscarf smiling at her.

"Oh – thank you," said Audrey, "the 65 – to Butter Lane, its in the east end I think…"

"Here it comes now – best of luck."

Sure enough the number 65 had just arrived at the stop. Audrey was carried towards the bus by a sea of bodies all clambering aboard. The lower deck was already full by the time she got on. "Seats on top!" shouted a perky young conductress in her ear.

Finding a seat next to a window on the upper deck she peered out, entranced by the myriad lights that now glimmered all around though the gloom and fog as the bus jerked away and began to plough it's way in the gathering dusk towards Tottenham Court Road.

"Any more fares please! Where to lady?" the conductress enquired.

"I…don't… quite… know" Audrey stuttered,

"You're not the first. Better make up your mind though sweetheart, I got all these passengers to see to."

"Butter Lane?" Wasn't that what the guard had told her?

"That'll be a ha'ppeny." The conductress cranked the handle of the machine strapped round her neck and handed Audrey a ticket. Searching in her purse she found a halfpenny piece and handed it to the girl.

"Would you tell me when I have to get off please?"

The clippie smiled, "Of course dearie, I'll give you a nudge."

As the bus made its creaking stop-start journey Audrey tried to make sense of the day's events. Her head was a blur of confused thoughts and emotions. She realised she had boarded the train in Liverpool without any clear idea why, other than that she wanted desperately to get away, run away from her past and somehow lose herself, forget that the self she had inhabited previously had ever existed. Had her impulse been a foolish one she wondered?

The train journey seemed a million years ago now, and the only memory that remained painfully clear and strong was Margaret. Audrey's heart ached; how ever could she have given her child, her beautiful little girl away? But what choice had she had? The little money she had in her purse from the sale of her engagement ring wouldn't last very long, and she knew she had to get a job of some sort. Seeing the poster for the London headquarters of the Regent Trust was what had prompted this sudden flight – a flight from all the old familiar painful surroundings, a flight from her self, if that were ever possible. She shut her eyes tight and tried to make the thoughts of Margaret go away, go away, go away....

She pressed her face to the window and studied the passing scenes through the fog with a grim fascination. London she knew had suffered greatly in Blitz and the evidence was there to see. Every so often in a row of houses, illuminated insipidly by the street lights she would see an empty space with a pile of rubble at the bottom, the adjoining properties windowless and on the brink of collapse, the scarred walls bearing the sad remains of fireplaces, broken floorboards, remnants of furniture, lost and broken lives.

On and on the bus went, spewing out and replenishing passengers at every stop – along Tottenham Court Road, Long Acre, Charing Cross Station, Fleet Street, the great dome of St Paul's, up at which Audrey craned her neck in awe, on through the City, Old Street and into Shoreditch. It was here that the clippie rang the bell and shouted up, "Lady up top wanted Butter Lane, 'ere's your stop!"

Audrey thanked the girl and alighted from the bus. The streets here were busy too, but in a drabber, more tired sort of way. "Can you tell me where the Regent Trust is please," she asked a man selling newspapers.

"Right over there, madam." He pointed across the road to an dark, gloomy alleyway.

Number 54, Butter Lane was a grey, unfriendly looking rundown three story Victorian monstrosity of a building, which matched its surroundings. The arched doorway, set between a pair of elongated windows had at one time been finished in dark green gloss paint, which was now largely peeled away to expose the rotting timber beneath. Displayed in each window was a large poster proclaiming The Regent Trust.

Standing on tiptoe on the pavement Audrey peered in through one of the grimy panes. The place was in darkness, save for what appeared to be a faint light shining from the rear of the property, till she realised this was the reflection of the street lamp in the window. She shivered; the night was becoming a cold one, a chill breeze blowing along the alleyway whipping discarded newspapers into a small frenzy then letting them float gently back to the pavement, repeating the action again and again.

With an unsettling feeling of being watched Audrey tried the door. It seemed to be locked. She lifted the knocker and let it drop. The sound fell dead. Unlike the main street where the buses ran, the alleyway was deserted, and save for the tumbling newspapers, ominously quiet.

"Someone please answer," she whimpered. As she peered again through the window she saw a shadowy figure approaching from within. Audrey drew back in alarm. With a creak the door opened, and in the half-light what looked like a young woman appeared. In her hand was an old fashioned lantern lit by a candle.

"Can I help you?"

Audrey did not answer, could only stare at the young woman, whom, in the glimmer of the lantern she saw to be about her own age. She had a shock of bright red hair, and the biggest welcoming smile Audrey had seen in a while.

"Dry your eyes love," she said ushering Audrey inside and down a narrow corridor, the lantern casting sinister looking shadows on the peeling walls. They arrived in a more brightly lit room, what appeared to be a kitchen of sorts.

"Sit yourself down," said the young woman indicating a crude wooden bench. "I'm Nellie, Nellie Chidlow, now let's get you a nice hot cup of tea. Milk and sugar?"

Audrey nodded. Nellie picked up a large brown enamel teapot from the gas stove, poured some steaming tea into a chipped mug and handed it to Audrey.

"So what are you doing down here this time of night? Did the nuns send you – got into trouble or what?"

Audrey wrapped her hands around the mug and sipped the sweet tea gratefully. Oh what have I done she thought woefully, what is this strange, terrifying place I have come to? "I've done a very silly thing ..." She broke off and began to cry again.

"There, there love, it can't be as bad as all that." Nellie put an arm around Audrey's shoulder and handed her a crumpled handkerchief.

Audrey dabbed at her eyes then opened her handbag and gave Nellie the leaflet. "I came down here to work, I'm a nurse but stupidly thought that I could just turn up and everything would be alright..."

"So where are you staying?"

"I haven't arranged anything..." She began to cry again.

Nellie took her hand and held it tight, "Running away dearie? London's the place to be... can get lost in the good old smoke. What's your name?"

"Audrey," she replied,

Nellie smiled "Well Audrey, don't you worry your head none, I'll find you a bed 'ere for the night, then we'll have a good old chat in the morning?"

Audrey followed Nellie up a side staircase and into a large room. The room was full of ragged looking people, women and men, children, some chattering noisily, some half asleep, some arguing and cursing irritably. Rows of canvas army type beds were packed close together. Along with little piles of old clothes and bits of rubbish scattered about the place was a damp, unpleasant odour of stale sweat and strong drink.

"Here's yours." Nellie pointed to one of the canvas beds in the middle of one of the long rows. "Try to get some shut eye darlin' and I'll see you in the morning. Matron will be here then and we'll have a chat with her. And keep your handbag safe, tuck it under your pillow never know whose in here." She turned to one half drunk, bickering couple and snarled,

"Aye there you two good for nothings, there's a lady 'ere wants to get a bit o' rest – so turn it down or you'll both be back on them streets." The pair leered back at her rheumy-eyed and slumped down on their beds.

Audrey thanked Nellie and lowered herself tentatively onto the canvas bed, which tilted precariously. She looked pityingly around at the still noisy, squalid scene, the angry, vacant, hopeless expressions on the half starved faces, the bodies carrying them wizened and ageing before their time. On the far wall a large, rusting clock face with half the numbers missing told 7 pm.

With tears of bitter remorse in her eyes, and utter desolation in her heart, Audrey thought of the sweet preciousness, the absolute priceless nature of what she had left behind, and how she had thought that after that, indeed up until a few short hours ago, her life could not possibly get any worse. Yet in the hell she had now unwittingly chosen for herself, it appeared to have done just that.

CHAPTER EIGHT

"Open up Audrey." Nellie rapped hard on the toilet door, "You can't stay in here, there's folk waitin'...."

"Been in there ages," a woman grumbled from the queue, "Selfish cow...not a thought for anyone else."

"There are four other cubicles Daisy," Nellie said. "Try using one of them."

"Not bloomin' likely!" Daisy grimaced, "Old Bert's, been in them and you know what he's got!"

Nellie shook her head and knocked hard again on the door. "Come on Miss, open up - oh good evening Matron." Along the line of impatient people Nellie saw Matron Stringer striding towards her.

"What on earth is going on?" she snapped.

"It's Audrey, the young woman who came in earlier," Nellie replied, "she's in here, won't come out and can't get no answer from her. Are you all right in there Miss?" She rapped hard on the door again, amid further grumbling along the line.

"Break down the door if she's taken queer."

"Yeah, take it off the hinges."

"Come on let's drag her out – by the hair if we have to..."

Matron Stringer marched forward. "Are you all right in there?" she enquired sternly. There came a muted affirmation from within. "Then open this door, *now*, or I shall be obliged to call the..."

At that moment there was the click of a bolt and the toilet door swung open. Audrey, clutching her handbag, emerged. She looked pale and drawn.

"I'm so sorry," she said faintly, "didn't want to cause any bother..." She swayed then lurched suddenly forward. Nellie and Matron Stringer caught her by the arms and guided her to a chair.

"Take some deep breaths dearie," Nellie said holding Audrey's head between her knees, "that's it...that's it..."

Audrey breathed deeper and deeper, gasping desperately for air. "Oh dear," she panted, "my head is pounding so, and my stomach, I think I'm going to..."

"Get her to the sink Nellie," Matron ordered.

Bent over the sink Audrey heaved violently. Attempting to right herself her face looked utterly drained, and she appeared to be fading into unconsciousness.

"No - you're not going anywhere love, promise me," Nellie guided her back to the chair. "Stay with us...."

Matron leaned over and placed a wet flannel on Audrey's forehead. The coldness seemed to bring her round, and she gave a soft murmur of appreciation. The entire toilet queue, having apparently forgotten their urgent need for the cubicle, now stood sombre and entranced, as if waiting for a sign, something to tell them whether or not this obviously once elegant young woman who had so mysteriously come amongst them, was going to live or die.

"That's it now," Nellie stroked Audrey's cheek. "There, there...bit better now are we?"

Audrey inhaled and sighed out a long, slow breath. "I'm sorry," she said, "I don't feel well."

This provoked toothless, though sympathetic laughter among the onlookers. "We can see that!" Even Nellie grinned, if partly with relief that she hadn't 'lost one', not yet at any rate. "No you don't look very well to be honest with you duck – a bit green round the gills."

Matron Stringer leaned over again and examined Audrey's face. "Um," she pursed her lips, "I think its best we have her taken to the hospital Nellie."

"What? Oh no please..." Audrey's voice was filled with trepidation. With an effort she lifted her head and looked pleadingly at the matron. "I can't go to hospital, please, I mustn't, I need to work...."

The older woman smiled kindly and patted Audrey's arm. " I know you do my dear, but let's get you well first."

The hospital wing was a complete and refreshing contrast to the grubby, sordid room Audrey had just left. After following Nellie slowly up the stone staircase, along a brightly lit corridor and through a pair of swing doors at the end, she entered a properly appointed medical ward: airy and smart and clinically clean, the floor scrubbed and gleaming and not a speck of dust to be seen; the odour of ether and disinfectant she found almost pleasantly welcoming. Two nurses, their crisply starched, pristine uniforms rustling softly, were moving from bed to bed administering medication, care and words of firm but kind encouragement to the patients. Noticing Nellie, one of them broke off from her duties and came over.

"What do you want Chidlow?" she asked in a sharp, superior tone.

"Brought her to you," Nellie replied equally caustic.

The nurse gave Audrey a discerning look.

"All right," she said guiding Audrey towards a freshly made bed, with spotlessly laundered sheets. "Well don't hang around gawping," she snapped imperiously at Nellie, "get back to your lot where you belong."

"I'll see you later dearie," Nellie shouted from the door as the other nurse ushered her out. "And don't let them boss you about." She paused briefly to poke her tongue out at 'them' before flouncing out.

"I'm Nurse Townsend" the first nurse said and handed Audrey a starched white linen nightdress. "Put this on and I'll be with you in a minute."

Audrey closed the curtains around the bed and began to undress. How thin she had become, she thought as she smoothed out the nightdress and caught her protruding hipbones.

The curtains opened. "Did they feed you downstairs?" Nurse Townsend asked with a measure of derision.

"Yes… no… Nellie gave me a cup of tea."

Nurse Townsend sniffed haughtily. "Thought not, when did you last eat?"

Audrey tried to remember, "Yesterday maybe…not really sure,"

The nurse tutted, "No wonder you're all skin and bone and no strength. I'll bring you some cheese sandwiches and a cup of tea then get some rest. Come on get straight in we don't want you catching cold as well."

Nurse Townsend went off and Audrey obeyed her orders and slipped between the sheets. Almost immediately Nurse Townsend's colleague, a younger woman appeared.

"I'm doing as I'm told, all covered up in bed," Audrey smiled at her. "Though I must say it does feel beautifully warm up here on the ward. And so very clean and efficient, my old Matron in Liverpool would be most approving, and she was the most frightful dragon, though I shouldn't say it. "

"Oh they like us to look the part up here all right," replied the young nurse as she tucked in the bed vigorously. "Not like what goes on down below." She looked at Audrey and tapped the side of her nose mysteriously. "Between you and me," she said quietly, "you were lucky you had a turn and got sent up here dear, otherwise - "

"Otherwise what?" asked Audrey. "It's pretty awful for the poor souls down there, but then I suppose resources are very stretched, and the Regent Trust have to do what they can for people."

"That's one way of putting it," replied the nurse with a wry look.

"Surely you're not implying there's something shady…"

"Nurse Withers!"

The young woman jumped to attention as the curtain was flung back. Nurse Townsend, a tray of sandwiches and tea in her hands glowered at her subordinate. "There are other patients requiring attention," she said icily.

Nurse Withers slid silently out.

"Forgive me," said Nurse Townsend to Audrey setting the tray down on the bedside table. "Some of these young girls have a habit of gossiping, and making up stories too I'm afraid. Poor things have little or no education you understand. I see a lot of young women in here, and I can tell you're a young lady that's been well brought up, taught manners and what's right and wrong."

"Well I…" began Audrey uncertainly.

"And I can see I've no need to tell you to ignore such ramblings. Ignorance is a curse, but with some there's little you can do to eradicate it, wouldn't you agree, Miss…" Nurse Townsend turned gimlet-like eyes on her new patient. "I'm sorry," she said, "I didn't catch your name?"

"Audrey – just…call me Audrey."

Left alone Audrey tucked in with relish to the tray of sandwiches and tea. After finishing every crumb on the plate and draining her teacup she stretched her legs out, welcoming the clean, cool crispness of the cotton sheets against her skin. She sighed heavily; how tired she had become. Though a chink in the curtain she could read the wall clock: 11 pm. It was so very peaceful up here, she reflected again, after the mayhem of downstairs. No one arguing or singing or shouting out; only the gentle hum of the air vents and the occasional soft padding of the nurses' feet on up and down the ward.

What had Nurse Withers meant by 'what goes on downstairs'? Silly gossip she supposed, as Nurse Townsend had said. Audrey's eyelids drooped and closed and a moment later she was sound asleep.

"Good Morning young lady!" The forthright voice reverberated in her ears. Audrey sat bolt upright, "Where am I?" she said aloud to herself Then she saw Matron Stringer stood at the foot of the bed.

"Are you feeling better?" she asked, the trace of a smile on her lips.

Audrey nodded. "Thank you, yes I am Matron."

"I've been speaking to Nellie about you."

"About me?"

"Yes," said the Matron. "She tells me you are a trained nurse."

"Oh –well yes I was…"

"And that you are looking for work."

"Yes, yes I would like a job." Audrey straightened her hair, ran a hand over her sleep-crumpled face. "I need a job Matron – desperately if I'm honest – but I'm a hard worker…"

"Really?" The Matron looked at her suspiciously. "Then tell me, why have you travelled all the way here to London? I know full well there are ample positions in the hospitals in Liverpool. Isn't that where you told us you came from?"

The Matron came round the side of bed and peered over her glasses at Audrey. "So why the exodus, the sudden flight hundreds of miles? What is it exactly, young lady, that you are running away from?"

Audrey took a deep breath. 'Where do I start?' she thought

As if reading her mind Matron Stringer said, "The beginning is usually a good place my dear."

"Hello dearie!" Nellie barged cheerily through the ward doors. "Here's your glad rags back, all laundered and lovely." She laid Audrey's clothes neatly on the bed, with a bar of soap and a hairbrush. "Washroom's down the end of the ward. Oh and Matron wants to see you in her office when you're ready. Don't keep her waiting." She winked at Audrey, "very punctual is Matron, and likes others to be the same."

After washing and dressing Audrey a little more restored. The previous day's nourishment and a good night's sleep had also played their part. Nellie looked her up and down. "Oh I say that's better dearie, " she smiled, "Like a new pin."

Audrey returned to smile. "I do feel better," she said.

"Ready to face Stringer then?"

Audrey nodded. Nellie beamed at her, and linking arms with her, marched her out of the ward to the Matron's office. Nellie knocked on the door.

"Come in."

"Audrey, to see you Ma-am." Nellie guided her charge to the chair in front of the Matron's desk.

"Thank you Nellie – oh could you stay please?"

Nellie nodded, closed the door and sat in a chair against the rear wall.

"Now Audrey," began the Matron, after our discussion yesterday I have asked to see to make a suggestion, one I believe will be in your best interests."

"Oh don't say you think I should go back to Liverpool, please, I can't, I couldn't bear it…" began Audrey anxiously.

The matron held up her hand to forestall the flurry. "On the contrary young lady, I wish to offer you a position – a nursing position."

Audrey's concerned expression turned to one of eager excitement. "Really? Do you really mean it…but where would I live…?"

"I'm offering you a job with the Regent Trust. Didn't you tell me yesterday that was what you were hoping for, what you came to London for?"

"Yes but after what I told you I thought…."

"Young lady, I judge people on what I believe they are capable of, not what circumstances or mistakes may have led them into difficulty. Are you prepared to work as hard as you say you are?"

Audrey nodded eagerly. "Harder Matron, harder, I promise."

"Very well you can start in two days time. We'll find you a room, Nellie will help you." The matron beckoned to Nellie to come forward. "And she will get you kitted out with uniform and help you complete the usual forms." Audrey thanked her profusely as Nellie led her out.

"Where are we going now?" Audrey asked as Nellie took her arm again and headed full tilt down the staircase towards the front door she had come in through less than twenty-four hours previously.

"To get your lodgings sorted out duck, there's a room next to mine just come empty and if we hurry it might not have gone. Come on look lively…"

The three storey run down terraced house in the middle of the row in Drayton Terrace, and not therefore dissimilar to all the properties in the street. It was Saturday afternoon and boys and girls of all ages were playing noisily outside while mothers stood beside prams or with babies in their arms and gossiped.

Six well-worn stone steps led up to a faded red front door. Audrey followed Nellie, picking her way carefully between five small grubby children sprawled on the steps. Audrey stared at the only girl in the group. She was sat on the top step playing with a wooden clothes peg that had been covered in an old ragged doll's dress. All of a sudden the little girl hurled the peg down the steps and began to cry. Audrey picked it up and offered it to her. Refusing or too timid to take the doll from her, the child yelled even more loudly.

"Leave her alone!" yelled a strident voice from an upstairs window, making Audrey jump in alarm. "Get off with yaw…."

Audrey looked up to see a young woman with bleached hair, her features contorted in rage leaning dangerously out of the window.

"I'm sorry," Audrey called nervously, dropping the doll next to the child. The child grabbed the doll then jabbed her tongue out at Audrey and ran off down the steps and into the street.

"Shut up Lucy Norris!" Nellie shouted to the woman at the window "Come on Audrey take no notice, that one's probably on the drink again. Take more water with it you silly cow!"

Inside, the once grand house was as dilapidated as its exterior. In one of the ground floor rooms Audrey heard raised voices, a couple arguing, shouted insults and ear-splitting bitter screeching filling the dank air. Across the hallway by contrast came the melodiously haunting sound of a clarinet, its measured notes defying the raucous argument like a padre reading a sermon in the middle of a battlefield, oblivious of the noise and shrapnel flying around.

Nellie knocked on the first door. "Mrs Goldstein are you in there?"

The door opened and an amply built woman appeared, her headscarf tied at the front with a large bow and a wash-worn, faded multi coloured apron which, like its owner, had seen better days.

"What you want Nellie Chidlow?" she barked. "And before you asks I ain't lettin' you off the rent *this* week."

"Is the room next to me still free;" Nellie asked ignoring the older woman's scathing insinuation, "My friend needs somewhere to stay."

"Another one from the refuge is it?" Mrs Goldstein said, scrutinising Audrey intently. Audrey didn't move, she felt suddenly uncomfortable; that she had recklessly put her life in the hands of strangers. After all what did she know of Nellie, or Matron Stringer for that matter, and now this awful seedy boarding house and this aggressive, hard-faced harridan? She had the sense, not for the first time, of things spiralling out of her control.

"She's a nurse Mrs Goldstein – same as me."

"That right girl?" Mrs Goldstein directed the question to Audrey.

"Yes, that's right – I am a nurse." Audrey spoke as boldly as she could.

"Bit la-di-dah ain't ya lady," Mrs Goldstein grinned, "Better mind our Ps and Qs round this one Nellie."

"And I'll watch my Ps and Qs around you Mrs Goldstein." Audrey retorted. "Now, do you have a room for me or not?" Give as good you get, she thought to herself.

Mrs Goldstein's caustic smile chilled Audrey. All her bravado seemed to evaporate and she felt herself shrivelling under the woman's gaze. Then Mrs Goldstein threw back her head in a full-throated laugh – it was a laugh case-hardened and tempered by a lifetime of battling dishonest tenants, poke-nose officials, grinding poverty, her violent, errant husband and the onslaught of several years of gin and Woodbines.

"I like you missy," she roared, "got guts ain't you! Half a crown a week, paid every Thursday, two weeks in advance."

Audrey opened her purse and gave the woman five shillings. Mrs Goldstein's hand closed around the coins like a great claw, and she put her other hand into her apron pocket and took out a key.

"Keep the place tidy mind," Mrs Goldstein ordered as she handed Audrey the key. "And no men. Those are the rules. Nellie you make sure she stick by them or else – out." She jabbed her thumb towards the front door to underline the warning.

"You won't have any trouble from me Mrs Goldstein," Audrey replied opening the door. "Now if you don't mind I'd like to get acquainted with my new abode."

This remark prompted a renewed and louder burst of hacking laughter from Mrs. Goldstein as she padded off down the corridor, to the discordant accompaniment of the harp music and the quarrelling voices still vying with one another to be heard.

Audrey, followed by Nellie, entered the room and glanced briefly around. Crossing to the window opposite she took out her hanky and rubbed at the grimy glass. Looking out through the little porthole she saw below her a communal courtyard. The daylight filtering down from the high rooftops showed lines of washing strung across the enclosed space and children playing hopscotch on the flagstones; every now and then a small figure would dart in or out of one of the dark recesses of the buildings in a game of chase or follow my leader.

She turned and surveyed the room in more detail. The furnishings were cheap and basic, and like the windowpanes showed little evidence of having been cleaned in recent months, perhaps years. The iron bedstead, the chest of drawers with cracked mirror on top, the framed faded embroidery of verses from the scriptures and much of the unvarnished floorboards were visibly thick with dust.

"Well duck, what do you think of your new home?" asked Nellie.

Audrey smiled wanly, "Well…it's not Whindolls Road but -" She broke off, reluctant to sound ungrateful.

"More like something else eh?" cackled Nellie. "No, it ain't Buckingham Palace duck I'll give you that. But you wait there, I'll be back in a minute."

Audrey felt a lump rise in her throat at the memory of her childhood home; how much had happened to her since those innocent days; Martin gone, then poor Molly and Joe, the awful severing with her family, and then little Margaret…oh dear, no, she thought, most of all I must not think of Margaret, not now….

With an effort she returned her attention to her surroundings. In the middle of the room stood a sturdy square wooden table covered with a red chenille cloth and flanked by two rickety looking padded upright chairs. At the far end a matching red chenille curtain hung across the room from the fireplace to the opposite wall. Looking behind the curtain she found a small kitchenette; a gas cooker and a small sink in the corner, both covered in a greasy film.

"Here we are Audrey," Nellie had returned, bearing a metal bucket containing bottles of bleach, polish, a bottle of vinegar, rags, newspaper, and dusters and two aprons. Drawing aside the kitchenette curtain with gusto she began filling the bucket. "There's no hot water but I'll make a start on the window and you do battle with that sink, you'll need this." She handed Audrey an apron.

The two girls set to work, Nellie warbling a cheerful rendition of 'When I'm Cleaning Windows' as she perched out on the sill and scrubbed vigorously at the panes with the scrunched up newspaper doused in vinegar.

"My you're bringing them up a treat Nellie," said Audrey appreciatively as the sun's rays streamed into the room.

"Not doing so bad yourself girl – don't think the enamel on that sink's seen daylight since the Blitz!"

Audrey laughed. "It's rather a nice sink too underneath."

"Just like some people," chuckled Nellie, "you know, 'orrible on the outside, but when you get to know 'em, hearts o' gold."

"Were you referring to Mrs Goldstein by any chance," smiled Audrey.

"Ah now she's one of a kind," said Nellie wringing out the sodden newspaper into the bucket. She lowered her voice, "they do say she's a fence of course."

"A fence?"

"Receiver 'o stolen goods." Nellie mouthed the words almost silently. "But you never heard that from me, mind." She touched her sealed lips.

"Oh, right, no. I won't breathe a word," said Audrey.

Within half an hour the room had been transformed; the windowpanes sparkled, likewise the mirror, though this did now accentuate the black line of the crack that ran down the centre. All the surfaces had been dusted and polished, and the sink and cooker were spotless and gleaming. Once the floorboards had been swept Nellie went and fetched a spare rug from her own room and laid it down by the bed.

"Save you getting cold feet when you get up of a morning duck," smiled Nellie. "I'll be off now, I'll look in tomorrow see how you're settling in. I'm just down the 'all second door if you need anything. Ta-tar for now."

"Thanks Nellie, thank you for everything."

Audrey sat down heavily on the bed, tired again now after her domestic exertions. It was quiet in the courtyard now, the children having been called in for tea. Her thoughts turned to Mother Sarah; she must write to the old lady she decided, and soon, but not yet, she had to think hard about what to say. Then she thought of dear Molly – Moll would be horrified to see the mess she had allowed herself to get in. Nellie's kindness reminded her of Molly. "I miss you desperately Moll" she said aloud, "I hope we meet in heaven one day – if they'll still have me of course which I doubt." She could almost hear Molly's response: don't be so daft you've got to carry on regardless Aud – what doesn't kill you makes you stronger. Yes, we'll meet again, Vera Lynn told us didn't she!

Audrey smiled wistfully; if there were such things as ghosts or angels, which there could well be, Molly would be up there organising them that was for sure.

—

She took out her purse and emptied it out on the eiderdown. She counted what was left from selling Martin's ring. There wasn't much, just a few coppers and a shilling, enough to buy a meal in the workman's café.

If she had not met Martin she would not have shared his sweet tender love, "Better to have loved and lost..." how true that was. She had loved, been loved, and nothing could take those precious memories away. Maybe one day she would find her little girl again, meet her perhaps but that was for the future.

Now it was time to move on, to begin again. Life, her life, her new life was about to start. But there were still invisible threads still drawing her to the past. Now was the time to cut them.

Taking a pen and paper from the draw she began to write. 'Dear Mother Sarah...

CHAPTER NINE

Mother Sarah folded the letter and put it in the envelope. She stared again at the London postmark.

"Well at least I know she's alright," she sighed aloud, "but no mention of the little one. Wonder what that means? Oh the poor little mite...?" The old lady's anguished thoughts were interrupted, by a loud knocking at the front door.

"Hello Sarah, only me!" It was the big booming voice of Monty.

"She's written," cried Sarah opening the door and waving the envelope in Monty's face, "At last, she's got in touch."

"Audrey? I told you she would, after all she's only been gone a week."

"I've been worried sick," Sarah said. "Anything could have happened to her."

"Well, where is she then?" Monty asked.

"London!" Sarah exclaimed.

"London?" echoed Monty awestruck his eyes widening, his expression as if Sarah had said 'Timbuktu' or 'The North Pole.'

"No address though. She's got a job she says, working for some homeless charity, but no mention of little Margaret. Oh Monty what was she thinking going off like that - she'd have been all right here muddling along with us so she would." Sarah shook her head in sorrow.

"London," intoned Monty again.

"I fear for her Monty, I really do, and for little Margaret, what if we never see her again Mont?" And with that she began to cry quietly.

"There, there," said Monty, "London eh, well, well, well – they say as how London's full of thieves and rogues..."

"Oh don't...! Mother Sarah's gentle tears became full-blown wailing.

Monty put his big arms around her. "There, there Sarah, it might all turn out right in the end, let's hope and pray for them eh? I'm sure they're not all thieves and rogues in London, there must be some good kind people down there too. Let's ask the good Lord to send them Audrey's way, and little Margaret's, come on."

Comforting the old lady Monty closed his eyes in silent prayer, even as the ominous clouds that spelt out 'London' in all its lurid horrors and dangers, grew ever darker in his thoughts.

It was three weeks later when Mother Sarah, returning from her weekly shopping trip saw the two smartly attired rather official looking women stood on the doorstep of 112 Jericho Road. They were talking to the new resident Betty Sumner.

"I'm telling you, I don't know where she is," Betty was saying insistently. "I don't even know who you're talking about. Like I said I've just moved in."

"Can *I* help?" Sarah asked, "Who are you looking for?"

The two ladies turned to her inquisitively. "Miss Audrey Stephenson, do you know where she is?" the older of the two women asked.

Mother Sarah eyed the pair suspiciously, "Who wants to know?" she asked. The women looked briefly at one another, then at the tenant of 112 Jericho Road who remained with arms folded on the step, now looking interested to know more.

"Might I enquire do you live nearby?" the second woman asked Mother Sarah. Sarah nodded. "Good," said the woman briskly, "then can we go to your home, it is a private and rather sensitive business."

Mother Sarah, biding her curiosity led them to her house, invited them in and settled them into the front room.

"Now then," she said bringing in a tray of tea and home made shortbread biscuits, "What's all this about Audrey?" She poured out the tea and handed a cup and saucer to each woman.

The older lady cleared her throat. "I'm Miss Quinn and this is my colleague Miss Jenkins." The younger woman smiled. "We are from St Angelina's adoption agency and we…"

"So that's where she took her," Sarah interrupted snapping a biscuit in two with undue force.

"So you do know Miss Stephenson," said Miss Quinn.

"Of course," said Mother Sarah sadly, "I thought she might give her little Margaret up for adoption but I never believed she'd go through with it, a lovely little girl she was, no trouble at all."

"Quite," said Miss Quinn, "and Margaret is precisely the reason we are here. We wish to find Miss Stephenson."

"I've had a letter from her, but no address for her, the postmark's London."

"May I see it please?"

"Of course, if it'll help you find Audrey and give her Margaret back, of course." Mother Sarah's face lit up. "There's always a bed for them both here, you must tell Audrey that, oh it would be lovely to have them both, mother and child reunited, I can put a cot in the little room, Monty can give it a lick of paint..."

"I'm afraid that's not quite the situation," interrupted Miss Quinn, "Strictly speaking Audrey discharged her right to bring up the child when she left her in our care."

"Rights my foot," exclaimed Mother Sarah, "a mother's rights is what counts, what's in her heart."

She pressed a hand meaningfully to her breast. "She was in a terrible state when she left her little one with you, her chap was killed in the war, her best friend died in an accident, and her family disowned her and not a brass farthing to live on. Is it any wonder she felt she had to do the right thing by her child in the hope of giving her a better life? You can't punish a young girl for that now, and you can't keep a mother from her child, it's the cruellest wickedest thing anyone could do to two human beings!"

Mother Sarah's passionate outpouring was greeted with sympathetic nods and murmurs from the two women. There was a pause in which Mother Sarah breathed heavily and looked at them in silent appeal. Then Miss Jenkins said, "Well in some cases of adoption a mother can and does claim their child back yes..."

"I'm glad to hear it!" said Sarah triumphantly. "So Audrey's wants to take Margaret back, oh joy of joys...!" She clapped her hands, her face wreathed in smiles. "But hang about, you said you were looking for *her.*"

"That's right," said Miss Jenkins, "You see Margaret *is* wanted..."

"Of course, no-one takes the place of a child's mother..."

"But by someone else," continued Miss Jenkins.

"What? Someone...else...?"

At this point Miss Quinn took up her briefcase and opened it. She drew out a sheaf of papers. "There is a married couple who wish to legally adopt Margaret, but first we require absolute confirmation from Miss Stephenson that she is willing to finally give the child up."

Mother Sarah gasped. "She will never do it, never - her little Margaret in the arms of strangers? No never."

"But remember, she gave Margaret to us," pointed out Miss Jenkins gently. "And much as we cherish and care for the children entrusted to us, a proper family home with two loving parents is by far the best..."

"But they won't be Margaret's parents," objected Mother Sarah, tears in her eyes now, "that's the whole point – Audrey's her mother, and she loves her, oh dear me -"

"We're sorry to upset you," said Miss Quinn, offering Mother Sarah her handkerchief. "You were obviously close to Audrey, and the child?"

"Brought her into the world," sniffed Mother Sarah, "the first one to see her little smile. And now...oh dear me - "

"Believe me, we only want what's best for everyone," said Miss Quinn, "Audrey and her child, that's why we're so anxious to trace her, you do understand?"

Mother Sarah nodded. "You're only doing your duty, I can see that, and I respect you for it; forgive my taking on so, but as you say, I feel for Audrey and the babe as if they were me own."

"Not at all," said Miss Quinn, "I can see you are a person of fine feelings and a keen sense of what's right; we will endeavour as I say to do what's best within our powers for all concerned. We must take up no more of your time Mrs...?"

"It's no trouble, and I'm Sarah – they call me Mother Sarah on Jericho Road, thank you." She passed Miss Jenkins back her handkerchief.

"Well Sarah, thank you, for voicing your concerns to us, and if you should hear word of Audrey perhaps you would be good enough to contact us at this address." She handed Mother Sarah a card. "And if you could find that letter – thank you. I have to say that if after exhausting all our lines of enquiry we are still unable to locate Miss Stephenson, I am afraid we may have no choice but to proceed with granting the adoption of her daughter in any case. Good day to you."

After Miss Quinn and Miss Jenkins had gone Mother Sarah sat at the kitchen table and read Audrey's letter again. It had been a strange and unfortunate time for all of them; maybe Audrey had done what she thought was right after all. And now maybe it was going to turn right.

"Let's hope they find you." She said as she folded the letter and placed it back in the bureau. "For both your sakes."

CHAPTER TEN

May 1946

"Time don't half fly when you're 'avin' fun," Nellie declared loudly, eyeing the large clock on the wall of the ward as she poured out a second cup of tea for herself and Audrey. "Half the shift gone already and we still got the bloomin' beds to make, 'pardon my French."

"Have we got time for another cup?" asked Audrey anxiously.

"Yeah go on, the cup that cheers, we'll work faster on it when we start again."

Audrey sipped more of the strong brown liquid gratefully. "You're right about time flying Nellie, it's a month today since I arrived here."

Nellie did a quick sum in her head. "Do you know I believe it is duck, now how many bed pans is that you've emptied? I must say you look a lot better than when you turned up here," she chuckled, "Oh what a state you were in that evening, locking yourself in the how's-your father, remember that?"

"How could I forget it?" said Audrey, "but do you know what, the work here's been hard, the hardest I've done I think, but the company's done wonders for me."

"You like working with crazy Nell then do you duck?"

Audrey smiled, "Let's just say you certainly know how to cheer a girl up."

"Look if you can't have a laugh and a joke, life's not worth living, that's what I always say."

Audrey and Nellie, chalk and cheese, had indeed become firm friends in the weeks since Audrey had begun at the Oliver Regent Hospital. Though they didn't usually work together, today one of the regular ward nurses was off sick and Nellie had been asked to take her shift, much to the annoyance of Nurse Townsend. At that moment the door of the kitchen opened abruptly.

"I thought as much!" Nurse Townsend stood there glowering at them. "What on earth do you think you are doing?" she demanded.

"What's it look like Gladys?" Nellie replied holding up her cup "Want one?"

"Nurse Townsend, who considered it the height of insolence for a junior nurse to call her by her first name – which was precisely why Nellie had done so – breathed hard, her anger and indignation making her body quiver. "Tea breaks are to be taken only at permitted times, and this is not one of them." She jabbed her finger towards the clock.

"Never mind Glad, wet your whistle now you're here, I'm sure we can squeeze one out…"

"I want nothing from you Chidlow," fumed Nurse Townsend, "but your obedience on this ward, or preferably your absence from it – who was it gave you permission to fill in on this shift?"

"If you must know it was Matron," replied Nellie in a deliberately casual tone.

This provoked even more fuming and quivering from the senior nurse to the point where it looked as if she might well combust at any moment. "Then get back to work," she snapped, there's the beds still to be made."

"We know what we have to do Gladys," volunteered Audrey in an attempt to ease the tension. "Why don't you join us for some tea, just for two minutes, you look as if you could do with a break yourself."

Her reasonable tone seemed to stoke Nurse Townsend's fury further. Directing blazing eyes towards Audrey she looked about to speak, but instead turned on her heel and marched out slamming the door.

Nellie promptly erupted with laughter.

"What's got into her?" Audrey asked innocently.

"It's called getting your knickers in a twist…"

Struggling to contain her hysteria, Nellie clutched her sides and sat up. She took a few mouthfuls of tea and composed herself. "No the thing is Aud I know I shouldn't but I enjoy winding her up and having a laugh at her cos, well," she looked more serious now, "the old cow doesn't like me you see, she looks down on me."

"I can see that, but why?" Audrey asked. "You're as good as her, any day."

"Not in her books and all because," she went on, a note of sorrow in her voice now, "all because - "

"Because what?"

Nellie sighed. "Listen I'm going to see my family tonight, want to come?"

Audrey, bewildered by the change of subject stared at Nellie. "Family – why, where are they, I mean where do they live?" She waited for some further explanation. But Nellie said no more and rising from the table went to the sink and began washing up the crockery noisily.

After a few seconds Audrey said, "I'd love to come with you Nellie – your family won't mind will they?"

Nellie folded the teacloth and hung it neatly over the drainer. "Not a bit Audrey," she smiled, "they'll like you. Come on, let's get the beds made, else we'll be in more trouble with bossy breeches."

"Where exactly are we going?" Audrey asked in great curiosity as they boarded the number 18 bus on the corner of Drayton Terrace.

"Wait and see," Nellie laughed. "Soon be there."

In fact it was over half an hour before Nellie nudged Audrey to indicate they had arrived. The bus had in any case come to a standstill and the driver had turned off the engine. "Hampstead Heath, Jack Straw's Castle," the clippie announced, last stop, this is where we turn round."

"Is there really a castle here," asked Audrey as she jumped down, "and who's Jack Straw?"

Nellie pointed to a painted sign hanging above the door of an inn. "That's the name of the pub."

"Oh, are we meeting your family there?"

"No, they won't have my sort of folk in there Aud."

"Why on earth not?"

Nellie did not reply but led Audrey along the lane till they came to a gateway. There were lots of other people around now, coming in and out, young men with their sweethearts, families and a great many laughing and excited children.

Audrey asked, "What's that sound?" A plangent, tinkling strain was drifting from the field beyond the gateway.

"The hurdy-gurdy," said Nellie. She pointed to nearby tree on the side of which was nailed a poster proclaiming:

CHIDLOW'S FANTASTICAL FAIRGROUND
THE BEST OF THE BEST,
ENJOYMENT
FOR ONE AND ALL
3 DAYS ONLY

"A funfair!" cried Audrey, "how marvellous – oh Nellie I don't suppose we have time to take a look before we meet your family?"

Nellie grinned and took her arm. "Come on missy, all will soon be revealed."

They joined the throng of people and made their way into the field where by a patch of woodland stood a dense cluster of tents, caravans, attractions and awnings decked out in gay colourful patterns. The hurdy-gurdy music grew louder as they approached and a man was calling out, "Roll up, roll up, this way ladies and gentlemen, boys and girls, try your luck on the lucky dip, knock off a coconut and win yourself a prize, ring the bell with the big hammer gents and make your missus proud."

There was now a growing hubbub all around as the crowd swelled and the noise of the hurdy-gurdy was overlaid by another sound, the loud hiss and grind of the carousel's steam engine starting up.

Audrey's eyes lit up with excitement as she spied the beautiful painted horses dip and rise on their merry way around, their riders young and old clinging on for dear life or whooping with joyful abandon as the pace quickened, the vaunting melody carrying far out across the fields.

"Fancy a spin Aud?" shouted Nellie over the now deafening cacophony of machinery, music, voices and laughter all around.

"I'd love to," shouted Audrey in reply, "but we really mustn't keep you family waiting."

"Come on then, follow me."

Audrey, bemused, followed Nellie as she made her way not back towards the lane, but further on into the heart of the fairground, weaving through the sea of milling bodies, past colourful sideshows and stalls selling gewgaws and fancy gifts, goldfish in glass jars for a penny, candyfloss, toffee apples, boiled sweets and ice creams, china plates, coconut shies and penny arcades, each and every stallholder proclaiming their offering 'the finest in all the world...!'

They came now upon the huge Ferris wheel and beside it the swing boats lurching high back and forth, and beside them the airplanes fastened by chains to great metallic arms that arced and swooped across the twilight sky, their occupants screaming in terrified delight. Music seemed to coming from all directions, shot through with the strident invocations of the fairground barkers: "Don't be shy lady, roll up, roll up, and prepare to be amazed...!"

Audrey was transfixed at every turn, agog with curiosity and drinking in every glorious, colourful, exotic detail.

"Anyone would think you never been to a fairground before," Nellie laughed.

"I haven't," confided Audrey. "Mother would never let me go to them. I always so wanted to – my friend Molly and I always planned to find one secretly one day, but we never made it."

"Well, you've made it now."

"I'll say!" laughed Audrey, as at that moment they heard the giant bell being rung with the giant hammer.

Audrey was amazed how everyone seemed to know Nellie and greeted her with smiles, and fondness. A man on stilts with a big bow tie bent down and placed a kiss on the top of her head, wobbling slightly but steadying himself with the help of Audrey's shoulder. Introduced, he greeted Audrey with the same warmth and enthusiasm, as did all the other stallholders.

Some were a little more than friendly. "Whoa, like your friend Nell!" called out one young man after another as they came up and made ogling eyes at Audrey, "Bit of all right that one!"

Audrey was blushing to the very roots of her black hair. Nellie shooed the boys away with a friendly slap, and guiding Audrey towards a row of caravans, lorries and tethered horses on the perimeter of the fairground announced, "Here we are, home sweet home."

"You live here!" Audrey exclaimed as they headed for a big red and green wooden built caravan sat beneath the low hanging bows of an old oak tree.

"That's right, a fairground girl born and bred," replied Nellie proudly.

"So that's why everyone knows you!"

Spotlessly ironed white net curtains tied back with bright red bows graced the four small windows of the caravan and from the tin chimney puffed neat little curls of grey smoke.

Nellie climbed the set of uneven well-worn wooden steps and opened the door. "Hello Mum, Dad - I've brought my friend with me."

Audrey followed her inside.

"Nice to meet you." Nellie's mother, a leathery-faced woman in a voluminous floral dress shook Audrey warmly by the hand.

"Likewise young lady." Mr Chidlow, who was even more leathery faced than his wife, rose from the chair. "Sit down and make yourself comfortable, Nellie put that kettle on, I've got a few minutes yet."

"Working tonight dad?" Nellie asked putting a battered tin kettle onto the stove.

"I am that lass, doing the late shift, for young Davy – got a girlfriend..." he whispered loudly.

Audrey sat on a chair next to the door and gazed around the snug cosy interior of the caravan. Oil lamps hung from the curving roof and the walls decorated with fancy coloured plates and pictures, with gleaming horse brasses in lustrous polished leather straps set on either side of the black cast iron stove. The stove emitted a warm orangey-red glow, reflecting off the horse brasses and shining ornaments decked around. It seemed to Audrey most enchanting, a place of magic, a sort of magician's den, where untold mysteries of long ago lived in daily communion with its inhabitants, and where dreams were woven.

"So what they call you love?" Mr Chidlow asked breaking into her spellbound reverie.

"My name is Audrey."

"Speaks right this one Nell." Mr Chidlow nodded, his smile warm, his approval genuine. "Where you from lass, it ain't round here."

"I'm from Crosslands near Liverpool," she replied

"Long way from home then..."

"She's a nurse Dad, with me at the trust and she's..." Nellie stopped mid sentence.

Just then from outside came the pleading voice of a young child. "Mummy, Mummy, Mummy..." Suddenly the caravan door flew open.

"Whillan!" Nellie beamed and held her arms wide. "I wondered where you were."

A little boy came bounding up the steps into the caravan and straight into Nellie's outstretched arms. She scooped him up affectionately. "Oh I've missed you little man!" she exclaimed holding him tightly to her.

"Miss you mummy," the child murmured burrowing his head into her neck.

"Ooh he's run me ragged Nell I tell you...oh dear me..."

An elderly lady, breathing heavily had now appeared in the doorway.

"Come in and take the weight off Granny," Nellie said. "Meet Audrey, she's my friend."

Audrey rose and offered the old lady her seat.

"No, no thank you don't disturb yourself my girl," said Granny Chidlow, "I'll sit by the stove."

"Got her name on, that chair," chuckled Mr Chidlow

"Now Whillan," said Nellie, "I want you to meet my friend."

"Hello missus." Whillan said.

"Hello Whillan," replied Audrey offering him a big smile. "I'm very pleased to make your acquaintance." Then she mouthed discreetly to Nellie, "I never knew you had a child."

"That's 'cause I never told you," Nellie winked, setting Whillan down on his Granny's knee. "Now I'll mash that tea."

Audrey now took a good look at the little boy. His hair was a mass of tight black curls and his skin a dark shade of brown.

"He's four this year," Nellie said. "Mum and Dad look after him so I can work." Lowering her voice she added, "And before you ask I ain't seen his father for years, he was gone before Will was born."

"Gone – you mean he just upped and left you?" asked Audrey outraged.

Nellie sighed. "Oh no, it wasn't like that, he was taken away I'm afraid."

"Taken?" Audrey sat up in horror now.

"The MPs, the Military Police, they came for him, dragged him from me, I couldn't stop them, and I never saw him again. No letters, no contact, nothing, I don't know what happened to him." She stirred the teapot noisily then dropped the spoon with a clatter. "He could be dead now for all I know."

"Oh don't say that Nell," Mrs Chidlow said pleadingly, "I've told you, one day he'll come for you and Will, I'm sure of that."

Nellie shook her head resignedly. "It's four years Mum; he won't be back now."

"You're his wife, and he loved you, you'll see one day…"

"And meantime Whillan's all right with us, " Mr Chidlow said, "Half cast they call him, 'cause of the colour of his skin. Fits in well with us fairground folk, don't you boy." He ruffled Whillan's hair fondly.

Audrey stared thoughtfully at Nellie. "Was he an American soldier then?"

Nellie nodded. "Met him here at the fair, we fell for each other straightaway, like I'd known him all me life. The colour of his skin didn't bother me, he was my fella and I loved him." She gave a deep sigh. "But not everyone understood. See the coloured soldiers were treated bad, all right to fight and die for their country but weren't supposed to have the same fun as the white soldiers." She wagged her finger emphatically, "If they so much as mixed with the local women – the white women, they was put on a charge, and usually got beaten up too by the other yanks."

"Their so-called comrades," interjected Mr Chidlow shaking his head in disgust.

"So it was dead risky, but Curtis always found a way to see me. We courted in secret, got married in secret and were doing ok till one day he got shopped."

"Shopped?" said Audrey looking puzzled.

"Betrayed," said Mr Chidlow.

"Goodness, who by?"

"His mate was seeing Gladys Townsend," Nellie said

"Our Gladys Townsend?" Audrey asked

Nellie nodded, "The very same, she was a barmaid at the Jack Straw then, before she got her high and mighty job at the hospital, always was a stuck-up cow, and of course he soon dumped her, so out of spite she went and told the American sergeant that the feller had forced him self upon her. Curtis's so-called mate, to try and save himself from what was coming told his sergeant about all the other black soldiers who were seeing white women in the area."

Audrey put her hand to her mouth. "Including you and Curtis."

Nellie nodded. "The next night they came for Curtis. Our lads on the fairground gave the MPs a taste of their own medicine mind you, but in the end they had Curtis away."

"Oh Nellie I'm so sorry," said Audrey reaching out a hand to her friend's arm.

"Well maybe I was stupid to believe it could ever work out between me and Curtis, but I married him and I got Whillan and that can't be a bad thing. What I don't need is anyone sitting in judgment on me, I get enough from Gladys at work."

"I'm not Gladys Nellie."

Nellie smiled, "No you're not thank goodness."

"I've told her to speak up for herself," Granny Chidlow said looking straight at Audrey. "She ain't done nothing wrong, she was married after all, not like some of 'em, those Yankee boys who promised everything, got what they wanted and left the women holding the babbies, fancy believing their tales though, I don't know...."

Audrey swooned suddenly as if someone had just stabbed her in the heart. Granny Chidlow might almost but be talking about her. She felt a nausea rising within her; Martin too had made a promise, promised to come back, to marry her, but he hadn't. But what was she saying, it wasn't the same at all, Martin had died, given his life for his country, he hadn't abandoned her like the rogues Granny Chidlow was talking about, how could the confusion even enter her head...Then Audrey suddenly became aware that Granny Chidlow was staring straight towards her, her eyes glazed as if seeing something else, connected to Audrey, yet far, far away...

Granny Chidlow was still speaking, "...And I'll tell you this, some of the GIs who courted the English girls weren't fussy about the stories they told when they left a girl in the lurch."

"What do you mean?" asked Audrey, feeling a hot flush creeping over her.

"Dark stories, wicked stories."

"Like what Ma?" Mr Chidlow said.

Granny Chidlow leaned forward in her chair and tapped the side of her nose. "Let me put it this way," she said narrowing her sharp eyes, "if a Yankee had made a lot of cock and bull promises to his English girl and then were wanting to get shot of her and back to America, there's one way of doing it that'll make sure she never follows him: he gets one of his pals to deliver sad news to her that her sweetheart Yank has stopped a Jerry bullet or that his plane's gone down.

How's an ordinary girl to know otherwise, or ask questions - especially if she happens to be in the family way... don't look at me like that, I've heard it was done to more than one poor unsuspecting girl..."

"Audrey – why whatever's the matter – quick, Dad!"

Audrey had keeled over off her chair suddenly onto the caravan floor. Mr Chidlow and Nellie knelt down and helped her up, Mrs Chidlow fanning her vigorously with a tea towel.

"Oh I'm so sorry," said Audrey, "I don't know what came over me."

"Probably a bit warm in here with the stove and all," said Mr Chidlow opening the caravan door to let in some air.

"Perhaps it was to do with what I was saying," murmured Granny Chidlow, "not a cheerful subject, I didn't mean to upset you dear."

"Not at all, why would it upset me?"

"Get her a glass of water Dad," Nellie ordered while dabbing Audrey's forehead with her handkerchief. "You fainted that's all."

Audrey breathed heavily, "Yes, that's all, I'm alright now, just a little dizzy."

Nellie looked at the clock, "It's time we were going anyway Mum, it's past seven and we're on the early shift tomorrow." Nellie picked up Whillan and hugged him tightly to her. "I'll see you in a couple of days love," she said kissing his cheek, "You be good."

"I always good Mummy," he said planting a wet kiss upon her cheek. Nellie laughed, "I know you are Will, and a cheeky one, too." She put him down and he ran off and began playing with a large wooden toy truck at the far end of the caravan.

Audrey thanked Nellie's family and stood in the doorway as Nellie kissed her mother, father and grandmother goodbye.

As they were about to leave Granny Chidlow beckoned to Audrey, "Here a minute love." Audrey went over to the old lady. "Give me your hand," she said. Audrey held out her hand obediently. Granny Chidlow covered it with her own and stared straight into Audrey's eyes. "You been hurt girl, shed many tears, it be all right from now on, things getting better. A man from overseas, dark past, careful of him, not everything what it seem to be."

Audrey could not turn from the woman's fixed gaze, the dark flinty eyes bored into her own, holding her captive in their spell.

Then the old woman smiled, let go of Audrey's hand and the spell was broken. Audrey let out her pent up breath in a sigh.

"You come again, my dear," Granny Chidlow said "You always welcome here."

As they were leaving the fairground Audrey stopped amid the throng by a stall full of teddy bears and rag dolls. The toys filled the stall to overflowing, big bears, small ones, fluffy ones, smooth ones, dolls with smiles sewn on, serious looking figures, funny ones, all shapes, all sizes, all colours and shades.

"All made by me own fair hands dearie," said the old lady on the stall smiling to reveal several gold teeth. "Sew a bit of love into each and every one of 'em I does."

Audrey picked up a small doll from the front of the stall. Her yellow woollen pigtails, her lovely smiley face and the pink knitted dress reminded her of Margaret. The tears began to form. Audrey wiped her eyes. "How much is this little one please?"

"Penny the small ones, tuppence the middle ones and... Hello Nell didn't see you there."

"Hello Auntie Lizzie, " Nellie greeted the old lady, "This is Audrey, a friend of mine."

"Have her on me." The old lady displayed her gold teeth again then frowned. "What's the matter dear, why you sad?"

"Audrey what's wrong?" Nellie asked in concern seeing the tears, and put a comforting arm around her friend.

"I'm being silly." she replied, "but this…this doll…"

"What about it, love?"

"It reminds me - " As if speaking of some terrible, awful thing, which to her it was, Audrey struggled to form the words: "It reminds me…of my little girl."

Now it was Nellie's turn to be surprised. "What? I didn't know you had a child."

"I didn't want anyone to know," stammered Audrey in an undertone, looking about her guiltily, fearful that others would hear her. She need not have worried; the crowd was one and all too intent on their enjoyment of the fair to notice one quietly weeping young woman. "I gave her up, for adoption, I gave her away Nellie," Audrey sobbed, "like you I fell in love, with an American, he was killed, never knew about Margaret.

I ran away, wanted to forget the pain of losing her…but it will never go away, never, never I realise that now." She threw herself on Nellie's shoulder, the tears coming in great bursts now.

"Take her home Nellie," Auntie Lizzie said kindly, "And you be alright dearie; the dolly, she will keep you safe."

Returning to Drayton Terrace Audrey made her excuses to Nellie and went straight to her room. She wanted to be alone, to think back on the day and try her best to make some sort of order of things in her mind. Visiting the fairground had been a remarkable experience for her - enthralling and magical, and Nellie's family equally wonderful, showing her such kindness, what good people she thought, a far cry from her own.

Sitting quietly on the bed, the curtains still open, the room lit only by the faint glow from the moon, thoughts of dear Molly and her family now returned to Audrey, of the same wonderful kindness they had shown her; how she wished for those days back again – and to, for Martin to be in her arms, and of course, Margaret…"But it cannot be," she said aloud to herself. Fate had decreed. And now she had a new friend in Nellie, who had heartache, difficulty and was fighting through. I must do my best to be a good friend in return, thought Audrey, and not think simply of my own pain and loss.

Taking the little rag doll from her handbag she kissed its sweet smiling face. "That's for you darling Margaret," she said, and leant the doll against the small mirror on the chest of drawers. "I'll never forget you now, never.

Audrey closed the curtains and as she slipped off her clothes and got into bed murmured softly: "Nor will I forget you Martin my darling." As she did so, the face of Granny Chidlow appeared startlingly before her. The old woman's eyes were like glowing coals, and Audrey remembered the words she had spoken, the strange, unsettling words that had so disturbed her in the fairground caravan, and were now doing so again.

CHAPTER ELEVEN

June 1946

Gladys Townsend strode decisively into the ward and marched up to Audrey. "Matron wants you in her office," she rasped. "Now!"

Audrey with a look of alarm dropped the blanket she had been carefully folding. "Why?" she asked nervously.

"Never mind why," said the nurse acidly. "Get along at the double, and pick that blanket up before you go, we're supposed to be sterile in here."

"Yes, right," said Audrey flustered. Gathering the blanket up hastily she saw the other woman smile now, not a pleasant smile but a triumphant sneering one, a smile that said: 'You're in for it now.'

"I hope I've not done something wrong," ventured Audrey.

Nurse Townsend's eyes narrowed to cruel slits, "Why, got a guilty conscience?" She gave an authoritative wave of her hand, "better look sharp about it, don't want to keep Matron waiting do we."

Her pulse racing Audrey straightened her cap and smoothed out her apron. She knocked on the office door. "It's me Matron, Nurse Stephenson."

"Come," called a voice from within.

Audrey entered and found the matron looking at some papers on her desk. She was frowning. Audrey's heart sank.

She began, "Is there...." She swallowed to clear the tickle in her throat, "anything the matter? With my work, or..."

Audrey heard the clock ticking loudly as she awaited a reply.

Finally the matron looked up and smiled. "Nothing my dear, in fact you are an asset to the Regent Trust. Your work is exemplary, a good nurse."

"Oh - so why am I here?"

Matron Stringer took an envelope from the desk draw. "It's regarding this letter. Someone is looking for you."

Fresh anxiety gripped Audrey: who could be looking for her - surely not her parents after all this time? Perhaps they wanted to repent, make up, take her back? If so what would she say? Then she thought: suppose one of them was ill, or worse...?

And then there was that business with Elsie and the police and the death of Mrs Skillycorn – suppose Elsie had confessed and implicated her, suppose the police were even now on her tail? Aghast she thought: I can't go to prison! Audrey felt a rising panic, a desire to run from the room and escape, away, away, away...

"Yes, someone seems determined to find you," continued the matron putting on her spectacles, "this letter appears to have been doing the rounds. She handed Audrey an envelope, on which had been written several times 'Not known at this address.' "Whoever it is has finally tracked you down."

With trembling hands Audrey opened the envelope and read the contents. "It's from St Angelina's adoption agency," she said.

"The one in Liverpool?" asked the matron.

Audrey nodded staring at the letter. Haltingly she said, "Someone...wants to adopt Margaret."

"I rather suspected that might be the case."

"They want me to contact them. Oh - Matron what shall I do?"

The matron took off her spectacles and looked at Audrey thoughtfully. "Well," she said, choosing her words carefully, "Much as I might wish to offer advice, I must state what appears to be the obvious I'm afraid."

"Meaning?"

"Meaning that it's rather up to you my dear."

Audrey bit her lip, tears beginning to prick at her eyes. "How have they found me, I left no address, I didn't even know where I was going myself...."

"There are ways and means," observed the matron. "But as to your decision, you must think carefully and weigh up the implications either way of whatever you do decided to do – practical and emotional."

She rose from the desk and placed a conciliatory hand on Audrey's shoulder. "Listen why don't you go home, my dear, you have my permission to take the rest of the day off from the hospital. You need solitude and quiet before making your decision. It is not an easy one."

Audrey thanked Matron Stringer and walked back to the ward. Deep in thought and ignoring both Nurse Townsend's fierce scrutiny and Nurse Withers' curious glances she went to the staff room put on her coat and headed for the door.

As she did so she ran into Nellie who was just coming in to begin her shift. "Hello Aud," Nellie said, "Going home already? What's up, feeling queer?"

"Oh Nellie – do you remember me telling you about my daughter, Margaret – well I've had a letter, someone wants to adopt her, what do I do?"

Nellie took her arm and guided her back into the staff room and sat her down at the table. She poured out a cup of tea from a freshly made pot.

"Drink this," she said "Good for shock."

Shivering now Audrey sipped the hot brew. "Oh Nellie," she said, "I never thought this would happen, I never meant it to be permanent, just until I got back on my feet. I just thought Margaret would always be there, waiting for me."

Nellie sucked in her lips pensively. "Trouble is time don't stand still Aud," she said sagely. "Kiddies grow up – I mean, don't think I'm unfeeling," she lowered her voice, "but this was bound to happen sooner or later – you put her up for adoption...."

"Oh don't rub it in Nellie, I don't need reminding of that," Audrey replied bitterly, "the question is what do I do now."

"You do what you think best love for you and your girl."

"It's alright for you Nellie, you've got your child..."

Nellie's features hardened. "Oh poor Audrey," she said sternly, "just listen to yourself, you did have a choice."

Audrey began to cry. "But I didn't, I didn't," she wailed, "I couldn't manage, that's why I gave her up, so she could have a better life than I could offer her..."

"All right I'm sorry pet," Nellie put her arms around her, "It's not my place to judge I know, me of all people, I'm sure you did do what you thought best at the time."

Audrey nodded, "I suppose so," she whimpered, "but Nellie it's so hard, so very, very hard now – oh if only I could turn the clock back..."

"Look why don't you telephone them, see what they have to say," Nellie said, "Find out some details first, like how long you've got to make your choice – it might give you a breathing space to really think deep down and clearly about whether you want Margaret back or not. Ring them tomorrow, ask them for more time if need be, but for now, go home and get some rest."

Audrey wiped her eyes and nodded. Nellie's suggestion seemed a good plan – the only one she had at the moment. She hugged her friend gratefully, left the hospital and walked slowly back towards her lodgings.

On her way, turning a corner she noticed a red telephone box. She stopped, stood stock still for a few seconds then walked quickly over and entered the phone box, fumbling in her bag for some coins and the letter matron had given her. Steadying her hand she dialled the number.

"Hello," said a soft voice, "St Angelina's, can I help you?"

Audrey pushed her penny into the slot and pressed button A.

"Hello, my name is Audrey Stephenson and I would like to speak to someone regarding…" she paused and sucked in a deep breath, "regarding the adoption of…my daughter…Margaret."

CHAPTER TWELVE

"Come back to bed Mary," Joe murmured sleepily. "Its only....." He opened one eye and squinted towards the alarm clock. "Well it's barely light anyway."

Mary turned from the window. She had been awake all night, worrying about what the coming day was about to bring. She and Joe had been summoned to appear in the great St George's Hall in Liverpool. Also summoned, for some unspeakable reason had been Margaret's 'mother'. Where little Margaret was concerned, Mary already found it difficult to say or even think the word 'mother' in relation to anyone other than herself; in her mind she and Margaret had already become one, mother and daughter, in mutual loving harmony. This other person referred to by the courts, this shameful, faceless unnamed woman, who had given the poor child away and abandoned her so cruelly had absolutely no business interfering now.

For although Mary and Joe had spent less than a quarter of an hour with the sweet child introduced to them as Margaret at the St Angelina's Adoption Agency, Mary had been instantly smitten with love and compassion for the little girl they found dangled over the railings of her cot, looking up to them with such soft innocent eyes and the dearest cherubic smile. Mary had been seized with an instant longing to take her away there and then, carry her off to her home and her heart, and there hold her safe and secure and loved for always.

The urge had not subsided in the intervening days, but rather grown stronger, more insistent and ever more clamorous in her breast. Joe was naturally more sanguine in his manly reserved way, but she sensed through this a certain glimmer of feeling in him on seeing both the child, and how moved his wife was by the experience. As they had left St Angelina's did she dare to perceive in his thoughtful countenance an equally fond, nay fervent hope that their house would soon be blessed with the sound of that little child's laughter? He had been quieter than usual on their way home from the adoption agency, and Mary had taken this as a sign of hope, which quickly became for her an affirmation, the affirmation that little Margaret was as good as theirs.

And soon she was, for what was called a trial period. Arrangements were made and Mary and Joe went post haste back to St. Angelina's. Mary, weeping tears of joy and gratitude scooped little Margaret into her arms and away they all three went together back to the house, "your new home Margaret," Mary had said kissing the little girl tenderly as they went in.

Then the letter had arrived. Seeing the official looking envelope Mary's face had lit up with the expectation this was now the stamp of approval telling them all was legally signed and sealed regarding their permanent adoption of Margaret. On reading the contents as she sat back down at the breakfast table her features dropped: the letter gave a date and stated that on that day they had to attend the court in Liverpool's St Georges Hall.

"Why?" Joe had asked, staring open mouthed and lowering a slice of toast he had been about to bite into. Like Mary he had assumed they were now simply awaiting completion of formalities before the adoption was confirmed. The word 'court' had immediately sounded a note of uncertainty, and for Mary struck fear into her heart.

"They say the..." Mary had faltered as she read, "the...mother of the child...has been asked to attend."

"What?" Joe's face had crinkled slightly. "But she's miles away by now surely?"

"I'd imagine so love, at least I hope so – or what I mean is..."

Joe had known exactly what his wife meant, and nodded his head sympathetically. For Mary, dark thoughts - of complications, stumbling blocks, rules imposed and unnamed people barring her path to happiness and shattering her desires rose up, and with these thoughts a lurking fear of bitter and desperate disappointment over her cherished dream of having a child in their lives at long last now began to haunt her.

And now the day of the court appearance was about to dawn. Mary parted the bedroom curtains and gazed at the faint grey light beginning to appear over the chimney pots. Desperately she tried to banish expectation, anticipation and most especially, the sight of little Margaret's sweet face from her imagination but it was impossible; despair she could endure, it was the hope that now seemed like torture.

The questions went round and round in Mary's head: what if Margaret's so-called mother did turn up today? What was the problem now, what was to be resolved? Why had she been called for anyway? Perhaps it was just another formality, thought Mary trying to calm her fears. The woman has to be sent for, it was the rules, the council, the government, the adoption people, or whoever decided these things had to follow the rules, that was all it was. When it was all over and done with today she and Joe could come back with Margaret, back to their home and laugh about it all. The image brought tears of joy to Mary's eyes – along with a deep, nagging anxiety in the pit of her stomach.

"Stop worrying Mary, and lay down for goodness sake," Joe's gravely voice cut into her thoughts. He reached out an arm and stroked her back. "We'll find out everything tomorrow, what will be will be."

"It *is* tomorrow," blurted out Mary. "That's just like you Joe," she turned on him angrily, "You don't care, you never have. Just like your mother, you never wanted Margaret here, I was a fool to think you did, well I do. Do you hear me? I do and…" She put her head in her hands and sobbed.

Joe sat up and put both his arms around her, and drew her close to him. "Shush, don't want to wake her now," he nodded towards the silent cot in the darkened corner of the room. "It'll be all right, you'll see. Margaret's our girl now and no one's going to take her from us. Now lie down and get some rest, you'll do no good fretting about it."

"Not yet Joe" she sniffed, wiping her eyes and pushing his arms from around her, "I'm going down for a cup of tea, settle me down that will."

Mary closed the bedroom door and went downstairs. Opening the kitchen door she felt on the wall for the switch and the room filled with light. Removing the guard from the hearth she poked the dying embers of the fire, which burst into life, then quickly subsided again to an amber glow.

On the table, the official letter telling them to be at Courtroom Number 3 in St Georges's Hall on the 26th June at 2pm rested against the sugar bowl. Mary picked up the letter and pressing it tightly between her palms knelt down on the floor. Closing her eyes she raised her closed palms heavenwards and in a whisper began to pray.

"Please, God…I've never asked for much in this life, but please I beg of you, let her turn up today… let her come yes, but…oh forgive me Lord…let her…not…want Margaret back…."

By half-past one it was raining heavily as Mary and Joe, carrying Margaret in his arms and shielding her from the downpour beneath his raincoat climbed the long flight of timeworn stone steps that led up to the huge doors of St Georges Hall. Like many people, though each of them had passed by the imposing, iconic edifice countless times before on their way to and from work, neither of them had ever ventured inside. Other than idle curiosity they had had no reason to do so, not until today

Entering the huge, echoing antechamber Mary gazed up in awe at the vast ceiling, the towering columns and the softly gleaming marble and woodwork, every surface a feat of craftsmanship, each square inch a testament to Victorian splendour and civic pride at its finest. As Mary shook out her wet hair Joe whispered something to an official, who led them down a long corridor to a door marked 'Courtroom Number 3.'

"Name?" asked a rather officious smartly attired young woman sat at a desk.

"Mary and Joe Lawson," Joe answered, "Here about…"

"I know why you're here," interrupted the woman looking at Joe over her half moon glasses with faintly veiled derision. "Follow me." She got up, opened the door of the courtroom and stepped in. Joe, still holding Margaret under his coat followed with Mary close behind.

"Sit here."

The woman, still with a slight sneer in her voice indicated a long, hard polished wooden bench behind a desk down at the front of the court. Mary took Margaret, settling her down between the two of them. Save for the woman from the corridor who had brought them in, now busily arranging papers on a high mounted desk opposite, presumably where the judge sat, the room was empty.

Mary looked across at the judge's desk, with its carved ceremonial chair like a throne, for a king presiding over his subjects. The whole atmosphere of the chamber like room with its lofty ceiling and echoing castle-thick walls felt cold and forbidding – a place where life or death, where liberty or incarceration was determined, and where today one unemotional, calculated decision about a little girls future would be decided. Suddenly the hairs on the back of Mary's neck stood up as the door swung open with a bang.

"Sorry I'm late…"

It was Miss Quinn from St Angelina's. Mary breathed a mild sigh of relief as she and Joe slid along the bench to make room. "I had to go over the papers…again," puffed Miss Quinn still out of breath as she squeezed in beside them.

"Why? What's wrong with them?" Mary asked, glancing over at a series of official looking people who were now entering the courtroom.

Miss Quinn gave Mary a reassuring smile, "There's nothing wrong with them, it's just routine, to make sure…" She patted Mary's hand gently.

"Is…she here?" Mary asked scanning the people taking their seats. . "No," Miss Quinn shook her head. "There's still time of course but that doesn't mean…"

"All rise!"

The usher's voice resounded around the room; instantly everyone stood. From a side door appeared a tall, stern looking figure in wig and robes. "The judge," whispered Miss Quinn. The judge's feet clumped ominously as he mounted the wooden steps and took up position.

Joe took hold of Mary's hand. "This is it love," he whispered. "Looks like the moth…the other one isn't going to show up."

Mary's eyes searched anxiously among the faces in the courtroom again then looked enquiringly at Miss Quinn. Miss Quinn shook her head. Mary felt herself relax a little.

Joe squeezed her hand. "Yeah, it's a no show all right love," he murmured. "Our little Margaret, will soon be ours for keeps."

The great steam train pulled slowly into Lime Street station and with a clang of pistons came to a gentle stop at the buffers. Up and down the carriages doors opened and passengers poured out forming a rapid milling crowd on the platform.

Audrey, clasping her small overnight bag peered up at the station clock: she was already five minutes late. Pushing through the throng she headed for the exit and once on the street, hurried across the road to St George's Hall.

"Court room three please," she said breathlessly to the young woman on the desk, and after following directions along the corridor was greeted outside the courtroom by another woman.

"Miss Stephenson?" Miss Jenkins asked.

Audrey nodded anxiously, "I'm not too late am I, the train was late, its not over, can't be...."

"You're in time," Miss Jenkins smiled. "The case is just being heard. I'll let them know you're here, then wait until you're called, it won't be long now."

Audrey drew in a deep breath and tried to compose herself. It was no easy task; Margaret, her darling little girl was just beyond the closed door, a few yards from her - as were the two people who wanted to take her away, forever. During the journey from London she had agonised over what she would do and say, trying desperately to search her soul and make her clear and firm decision, but now she was here she had more idea what that would be than when she had first been contacted and told about the proposed adoption. With only minutes to go before the final yes or no, the point of no return, the torment raging within her was almost unbearable.

The door to the courtroom opened suddenly. "Miss Audrey Stephenson?" the usher called. Audrey began to shake. "I can't do this," her voice trembled, "I can't do this..."

She turned to retrace her steps back along the corridor but stopped as Miss Jenkins touched her arm. "Come along dear," she said kindly. "It will soon be over."

In the courtroom Mary started as she saw a young woman being led in. So she had come. She watched as Audrey crossed the room and stepped up into the witness box. It was at this point the two women's eyes met. For a split second it felt to Mary as if an electric current passed between them, before breaking as Audrey's eyes strayed towards Margaret seated quietly on the bench between Mary and Joe.

Even at a distance Mary could perceive a desperate fear and longing in the other young woman's eyes. Mary drew in her breath in shock; this was not what she had expected.

"Miss Audrey Stephenson," announced the judge turning towards Audrey, "do you here today, finally and irrevocably give up your child, the child known to you as Margaret Audrey Stephenson, for adoption by the two persons you see present with her on the bench."

There was silence in the room, not one person moved, all eyes on the woman in the witness box. The clock on the wall ticked audibly. Ten seconds later Audrey her face drooping to the floor emitted a sort of whimper. "I do your honour," she said. A low murmur went round the room. Mary closed her eyes and gripped Joe's hand.

Then the judge spoke again. "Miss Stephenson, I ask you a second time, do you give up the child known as Margaret Audrey Stephenson for adoption."

Again the silent pause, followed by Audrey's voice: "I do your honour."

"Now Miss Stephenson, I come to the final time of asking, you may change your mind if you feel the child would be better off with you. Do you stand by your decision to give your child up for adoption?"

Audrey now looked out across the room and met Mary's eyes staring straight back at her. This time Mary felt a kind of searing heat from the contact; she saw the young woman's lips move, forming the words: "Look after her."

Audrey momentarily closed her eyes, sighed, turned to the judge and spoke aloud now: "Yes your honour, I give up my child for adoption, and all my rights to her. I will never see her again." Then with tears streaming down her face she stumbled down from the witness box and ran from the courtroom.

Only when outside the building did she stop running, and on the steps of St Georges Hall fell against one of the great marble columns, gasping for air.

"Are you alright Miss?" enquired a concerned looking porter. "Would you like to sit down? Come inside I'll fetch a chair."

Audrey stared at him with an almost crazed expression, "No! No thank you," she faltered. "I'll...I'll be all right...in a moment."

"Being in there affects some people, and who can blame them," he motioned towards the court, "not nice places, them. Where you going to now Miss?"

Audrey shook her head vaguely, "Don't know really, I just need a minute, a minute..."

"There's no rush, you just take your time," he said kindly, "I'll fetch a chair out here for you if you..."

Behind them at that moment the huge oak door of the hall opened. Audrey turned and saw the couple that had been on the bench. Cradled in the man's arms was Margaret. Audrey froze against the column then tried to slide around it out of sight.

"Miss? Miss? Are you sure you don't need a doctor..."

"I've got to go..." Panic now flooded Audrey's features, "got to leave..." She ran full tilt down the stone steps and headed towards the railway station. As she approached however, she switched direction and went into the bus terminus.

"Jericho Road," she said to the clippie boarding a double-decker just starting up.

As the bus ploughed out of the city centre Audrey gazed from the window at the once familiar sights. She could feel no distinct emotion now, but rather a confusion of vague despondent thoughts; she wanted the journey to go on forever, the gentle rhythm of the engine lulling her into insensibility.

Arriving on the corner of Jericho Road however she rose automatically and alighted onto the pavement. The pictures and memories hit her with combined force; the grimy brickwork, the squat, identical houses with their neat rows of windows, the obligatory step-polishing woman here and there, cries of the rag and bone man, a pair of skulking children playing truant. Though nothing had visibly changed it felt like she had been away for years, and that this was a scene from her distant childhood; then she remembered it was only a couple of months ago she had stood on the very same spot. The Feathers was exactly as it had always been – the gently swaying sign with the white three feathers, the frosted windows etched with the brewers' insignia, the smell of stale beer and tobacco wafting out.

Walking down Jericho Road Audrey felt sick with apprehension, as if someone might at any moment point an accusing finger or shout something horrid. But no one so much as glanced at her; she could have been invisible. Approaching the front door of number 112 she stopped opposite, recalling the dark winter night she had first turned up on Molly's doorstep distraught and homeless. Molly, and the house, the whole community had been her haven in a storm, and it was here she had shared much laughter and sadness, countless hopes and shed many a tear of regret; it was a place that would always remain resonant with memories for her.

But despite appearances everything was now changed; number 112 was no longer her home but that of some other family, and now her beloved Martin, with whom she had eaten fish chips and danced with in that little front room, and her dear childhood friend Moll and Bill were with all with the angels. And her own child, little Margaret, whom with Mother Sarah's help she had borne in the tiny room opposite was in the arms of strangers.

Fighting back the tears Audrey turned away. Jericho Road was the past yet its ghosts had never felt so alive for her. Retracing her steps she made her way back to Lime Street and the train for London.

CHAPTER THIRTEEN

"Mornin' Nurse!" The young man at the top of the ladder, paintbrush in hand flashed Audrey a cheery smile from the second storey

window. "Mind that door it's still wet, don't want to spoil that lovely uniform."

Audrey returned the smile briefly as she skirted the ladder then threaded her way through several tradesmen coming and going through the main entrance of the Regent Trust building. The door was propped open wide and glistened with newly applied red gloss paint. Entering the lobby Audrey stopped and looked; within the building similar scenes of activity were underway – decorators and cleaners working at the window and door frames, skirting boards, ceilings, floors, desks and tables – sanding, painting, varnishing, polishing and dusting, every surface being attended to with gusto, all under the keen and watchful eye of the clerk of works, who was pacing up and down inspecting progress, pointing out a crack or a stain here, a flaking piece of woodwork or chipped handrail there. Clearly the whole hospital was being smartened up, and not before time Audrey thought.

Arriving on the ground floor ward however she found nothing had changed at all. There were the same rows of shabby, rusting beds, peeling paintwork and ill-dressed homeless people moping, quarrelling or asleep, the same atmosphere of gloom and squalor and despondency. Oh well, perhaps the workmen would make their way to here next she thought. Now where was Nellie?

Not finding her, Audrey walked through the ward and towards the door that led to the upper floor. Once in the corridor she mounted the stairs, which she noticed had been cleaned and polished, and there was the same smell of fresh paint as in the lobby. As she turned the corner onto the second floor landing she stopped. Further down the corridor Nurse Townsend was stood in a doorway, locked in deep conversation with two men. They spoke in undertones not wishing it seemed to be overheard. Audrey withdrew into the shadows and watched. What made her most curious was the men's appearance; they looked decidedly unsavoury characters, muscular, hard faced types in grimy clothes and heavy boots - hardly the sort of people she would have thought Gladys Townsend would wish to be seen consorting with.

Though she could not decipher the words, the tone of their voices suggested some kind of argument or tense negotiation was taking place. Then Audrey saw Nurse Townsend proffer something. One of the men put whatever it was quickly in his pocket whereupon he and his cohort disappeared quickly down the back stairs leaving Nurse Townsend alone. Audrey straightened her uniform and made her way towards her.

"What's going on Gladys? " she asked casually, "all the painting and cleaning downstairs?"

Gladys started momentarily on seeing Audrey then snapped, "Nurse Townsend to you. Do you walk around in a dream girl? Mr Oliver Regent is coming here next week, that's what, so roll your sleeves up and get to work, we want this place spotless."

"Mr Regent? Oh, yes, right," said Audrey, "I'll start on the ward it could do with..."

Nurse Townsend interrupted her, "Never mind that, take a broom down to the courtyard - his car will be coming in that way." Then narrowing her eyes she leaned close to Audrey and said, "By the way my girl, just in case you were wondering, those two men I was talking to – they were decorators, I was giving them instructions about the work."

"Oh I see. They didn't look like decorators," replied Audrey affecting innocence. "I mean they didn't have overalls or anything like the other men downstairs..."

She tailed off, unnerved now. Gladys Townsend's face had darkened. Fixing Audrey with glinting eyes she hissed, "Are you questioning my authority?"

Audrey, her heart palpitating said as spiritedly as she dared, "What authority may I ask? I wasn't aware you had any, you're just a nurse like myself."

"Why you little hussy," snarled Gladys. "You want to be careful what you say to me."

"Why?" brazened Audrey, "you don't seem the sensitive type."

Gladys breathed out heavily through her nostrils. Audrey recoiled from the blast of suppressed rage, along with a strong whiff of nicotine from the woman's nostrils. She also noticed now that her fingernails were stained brown. Through curled lips Gladys said, "Why you little Miss high and mighty! You obviously don't know who you're dealing with – I could have you sorted out at the drop of a hat."

"Exactly what do you mean?" demanded Audrey, standing her ground despite the fear now rising up in her.

"I know people, the sort of people that would think nothing of taking a proper little madam like you by the scruff of the neck one dark night and..."

"Nurse Townsend!"

Audrey and Gladys both turned to see Matron striding down the corridor towards them.

"Oh, Matron," began Nurse Townsend, "I was just instructing Nurse Stephenson here about preparations for Mr Regent's visit..."

"Concern yourself with *your* duties nurse," Matron interrupted. "And why are you skulking about here in the corridor? There are patients to attend to."

Gladys visibly livid with chagrin muttered in a surly tone, "Yes Matron," as she turned on her heel. Audrey, giving a sort of nervous curtsey hurried off in the opposite direction.

It wasn't until Audrey reached Drayton Terrace that night that she realised she must speak to someone about her encounter with Nurse Townsend in the corridor. She had made studious attempts to avoid the woman all day, yet the curious not to say unsettling exchange had not stopped playing on her mind. Once inside her lodgings she went straight to Nellie's door and knocked.

Nellie greeted her warmly. "Audrey! Come on in duck, want a brew?"

Audrey shook her head. "No thanks," she replied, "Nellie, tell me what you think of Gladys Townsend?"

"I can't do with the woman, you know the reason. Why you asking, she been havin' a go at you?"

Audrey frowned. "Well yes, I suppose you could call it that."

"What about? I'll tell her what for Aud don't worry."

"Oh don't do that Nellie, thanks awfully but I would tread carefully if I were you."

"I'll do that all right, all over her stuck-up face!"

"Listen Nellie," Audrey said intently, "I saw her at the hospital today talking with two men - very seedy-looking customers they were. They seemed to be arguing and as I watched I thought I saw Gladys hand something to one of the men who put it in his pocket, and then they left. Afterwards Gladys told me they were decorators, and when I questioned this she became quite unpleasant with me, and from what she said appeared to be threatening to set these men or some other ruffians on me. It was all most strange and I have to say I felt quite distressed by her behaviour."

Nellie looked incensed. "The cheek of it – how dare she try and put the frighteners on a pal of mine! Don't you worry though Aud, no one's going to harm a hair on your head while I'm about, and if snotty-nosed Townsend thinks she can bring hired muscle against us they'll have the lads at the fairground to deal with first – and let me tell you when it comes to helping friends and relations, fairground folk don't muck about, mark my words."

"That's very sweet of you Nellie, but I wouldn't want to start any unnecessary trouble."

"Start trouble?" Nellie's fire was up now, her eyes blazing with righteous indignation. "We'll be the ones finishing it, and no mistake!"

"But I don't understand Nellie, what's got Gladys so rattled, and who were those men?"

Nellie knitted her brow for a moment then exclaimed, "Tom!"

"Who's Tom?" Audrey looked bemused.

"I heard about this a couple of months ago, thought the cops had hit a dead end."

"What are you talking about Nellie?"

"Tomfoolery," Nellie laughed, "sorry, Tom's tomfoolery - jewellery, rhyming slang see, it's just our way of speakin'."

"Oh I see," said Audrey, "or rather I don't, where does jewellery come into it?"

"A couple of months ago, we had a little visit from the old bill – the police over some jewellery thefts. They said jewellery gangs were working in the east end. They searched the main ward but found nothing. Matron was questioned; of course she didn't know anything, but the whole business made her ill."

Audrey looked thoughtful. "I would have thought all the patients at the Regent Trust Hospital were too poor to have much in the way of jewels, or valuables of any kind."

"Not all those poor souls at the Regent are – or at least weren't at one time – as poor as they might look to you and me."

Audrey looked intrigued. "What do you mean Nellie?" she asked.

"I'll tell you, but first let's make sure we're not disturbed, and put on the kettle for that brew. I bet you could use one now?"

Audrey nodded, "Yes I am rather thirsty to be honest."

Nellie went to the door of her room and bolted it, then drew a thick heavy curtain across the door tucking it in carefully at the edges. "Walls have ears Audrey, and so do doors sometimes especially when Ma Goldstein's on the prowl."

"Mrs Goldstein?" said Audrey, "our landlady you mean?"

"Yeah that's right." Nellie took two cups and saucers from the little shelf above her sink and set them down on the table. "Remember I told you the rumours, about her being a fence? Well they say there's no smoke without fire."

"Tell me more," said Audrey eagerly.

"Well," said Nellie, "a lot of the poor souls turned up at the Trust during the war; folk that had been bombed out of their homes in the Blitz. They had nothing some of 'em, only what they stood up in, their houses completely gone, others evacuated from their homes, grabbing what they could carry.

But there was plenty with lots of brass – gents with grand country homes they couldn't get to when the bombs dropped on their gentlemen's clubs. The debutante girls too with big fat allowances, coming back from up West in a taxi and copping it when the Luftwaffe come over. Same story, they all get brought to the Regent.

The Trust gladly took them in, and promised to look after them. All the jewellery and valuables were put into boxes with their names on and they all signed the register, names and address, all written in this book. Everything was always locked away in the filing cabinet. But one night the boxes were stolen. It had been a particularly busy night, the bombings were endless and Gladys and a couple of the others nurses were on duty. Gladys was in charge, so she was responsible for booking the folks in and registering their property. She insisted she locked the filing cabinet but the key was never found. I think she gave the key to someone. The next day the old bill was called but no signs of a break in, nothing out of place."

"Gladys may be many things but not a thief surely."
Nellie sniffed indignantly, "You think what you like, she did threaten you, and for no apparent reason by the sounds of it."

"That's true, "Audrey agreed thoughtfully "She was rather cross with me."

"I'll keep a close eye on her," Nellie said "And you do the same but keep your distance, don't get involved with her. She's crafty that one."

At that moment the kettle came to the boil on the little gas ring and let out a piercing whistle startling the two girls.

"Tea?" said Nellie

"Tea!" replied Audrey and both girls burst into relieved laughter.

CHAPTER FOURTEEN

June 1946

"He's here!" Matron marched briskly into the ward and began clapping her hands repeatedly. "Mr Regent's here. Come on please, chop-chop girls, smarten your uniforms and stand to attention."

Almost the entire staff had been summoned onto the ward to await Matron's announcement, and she now began chivvying them into a straight line. Audrey, endeavouring to find a place next to Nellie found herself shoved instead between Gladys Townsend and Nurse Withers. Gladys gave her a haughty sideways glare.

All the other girls were exchanging excited looks. The buzz of anticipation surrounding the impending visit of the celebrated industrialist and founder of the Regent Trust for the Homeless had increased tenfold as the morning wore on, and now, for the first time ever for most of them, they were about to see the great man in the flesh.

"What's he like?" Audrey whispered to Nurse Withers.

"Never seen him."

"American isn't he?"

"No English originally I believe – though his businesses are mostly over the pond now – still likes to do his bit for Blighty though they say, give something back – hence this place."

"What a wonderful gesture," said Audrey.

Hearing this Gladys Townsend remarked, "He's a wonderful man." Staring dreamily and as if to herself she murmured dreamily, "The blackest silkiest hair you ever saw, and the darkest of eyes."

Nurse Withers nudged Audrey, "How would she know, she's never seen him either."

"I have seen his photograph," Gladys retorted primly, "and what's more I have spoken with Mr Regent in person on the telephone – a transatlantic call."

"Wanted some laundry done did he?" tittered Nurse Withers.

Gladys rounded on her angrily, "I'll swing for you one of these days Withers, so help me if I don't..."

"Quiet everyone!" hissed Matron in a stage whisper, holding the door open a crack and peering along the corridor, "Mr. Regent is approaching!" She took up her position at the head of the line of nurses just in time. "Good morning sir." She bowed her head obsequiously.

Flanked by two hard-faced, thickset men in overcoats, with to the rear a Mayoral looking gentleman in chain of office accompanied by assorted dignitaries and their wives and two men in dog collars, a tall, elegantly dressed figure, had swept into the ward.

All eyes watched as with dramatic deliberation he removed the black overcoat from his shoulders and handed it to one of the bull necked aides. "Welcome to our ward Mr. Regent," said Matron, "This is indeed a privilege. We would consider it an honour," she gestured to the attentive line of girls, "if you could spare a moment to meet some of our nurses."

Oliver Regent held out his hand towards her and they shook. "Thank you Matron Stringer, the honour would be mine." His voice was resonant, deep, with a beguiling transatlantic accent. "Please, lead the way."

"Isn't he tall," Nurse Withers whispered, "And so beautifully dressed. How old do you think he is?"

Audrey made no reply but watched as Matron accompanied the VIP and his entourage along the line, introducing the nurses in turn. Well he *was* tall as Withers had observed, thought Audrey, and that dark grey impeccably tailored suit was so becoming. As to his age it was hard to tell, but there was certainly 'something' about him, a presence, an indefinable aura and magnetism, which, as he smiled at them and spoke so intimately, in such rich honeyed tones, seemed almost to render the girls beyond the power of speech.

The entourage had now reached Audrey. "And this is Nurse Stephenson," Matron said. "She has recently joined us."

Audrey looked up at the visitor and smiled. This time the smiled was not returned. Unnerved, the smile faded on Audrey's face, as she continued to gaze nervously at the man staring back at her, his dark eyes narrowing, penetrating her own.

"Nurse Stephenson," he repeated, as if turning the name over ruminatively in his head. "What may I ask is your first name?"

Audrey's nervousness intensified. He had not questioned any of the other girls, why her?

"Audrey - sir." Her voice trembled.

"And where are you from?"

Audrey hesitated then stammered, "Crosslands…Liverpool."

At this Oliver Regent drew in his breath, and for a split second his demeanour seemed to slip. Then he nodded, smiled at her and moved on.

When the ward visit was concluded the entourage followed Mr Oliver Regent towards the door. Here he paused, turned and stared directly back at Audrey. Matron looked at him enquiringly, "What would you like to see now Mr Regent?"

"I think I've seen enough for today thank you Matron," purred the VIP. "More than I expected in fact."

As soon they had left the ward Nellie came up to Audrey. "He likes you!" she said excitedly. "See the way he looked round just then? Couldn't take his eyes off you."

"Don't be silly," Audrey laughed. "He's an old man, and any way…."

"Get back downstairs Chidlow!" In the absence of Matron, Gladys Townsend had lost no time in seizing authority. "And you Stephenson, do the job you're paid for, not that you're worth it."

"What's up with her?" Audrey asked

"Jealous cow that's what," Nellie laughed. "I saw her looking all doe-eyed over him, pathetic, as if he'd take a second look at the likes of her!"

Audrey shook her head. Gladys Townsend had no reason to be jealous of her. Yet Mr Regent had seemed to take some strange interest in her. And she was the only one he had spoken to, and that look from the door! It was all most peculiar. If he had taken a shine to her it was flattering, but surely she thought, at his age, he must be married – wasn't he? If so perhaps he was one with an eye for the ladies still… Oh, what am I thinking these silly foolish things for, thought Audrey, and set busily to work on a stack of blankets that needed folding.

Yet even as she bent to her task, the dark eyes of the visitor continued to burn in Audrey's imagination, and she had the tingling, excited and unnerving feeling that, for reasons as yet beyond her understanding, this had not been her last encounter with the famous Mr Oliver Regent.

CHAPTER FIFTEEN

July 1946

Sitting at the ward desk Audrey opened the leather bound patient register and turned to that morning's page. Reaching for the fountain pen she began carefully to enter the date: 9th July 1946. Suddenly she froze and dropped the pen as a searing pain seized her heart: it was Margaret's birthday. She thought: oh what is my little girl doing, where in the world is she? The pain intensified and she felt tears pricking at her eyes – oh, Margaret…!

"Have you finished?" She looked up. It was Gladys. She snatched the register from beneath Audrey's hands. "Don't take all day about it. Wasting time again as usual I suppose. Dear me what a mess you've made," she said loudly, and taking a piece of blotting paper made a great show of dealing with the trail of ink on the page.

"Sorry Gladys…Nurse Townsend…"

"I should think so, now look sharp and finish checking the entries, it's nearly 8 o'clock." With that she thrust the register back on the desk and stomped off. Audrey swallowed hard, and trying to avert her eyes from the date traced her finger down the list of patients' names.

"Nurse Stephenson." Nurse Withers had just entered the ward. "You're wanted."

"Oh - " Audrey looked up. "I'm just doing the register…"

"I'll finish that for you dear – best not keep him waiting."

Audrey looked mystified. "Who?"

Nurse Withers seeing Gladys peering at them from the other end of the ward leaned over and whispered conspiratorially, "The big man himself – Mr R."

"You mean Mr Regent?" gasped Audrey.

"Shush…"

"But what does on earth does he want with me?"

"Haven't a clue, but I dare say you're about to find out – he's in Matron's office waiting for you now." She held the ward door open. "Best of luck," she smiled, "and don't worry about the register."

Pausing for breath outside Matron's office, Audrey straightened her uniform and knocked on the solid oak door.

"Enter."

Audrey turned the brass knob and went in. Matron was sat at the desk, and stood looking out of the long arched window, dressed in an elegantly tailored dark blue suit was the tall, imposing figure of Oliver Regent.

For a moment he remained quite immobile, his hands clasped behind his back, then turned silently and gazed impassively at her, his face an inscrutable mask. Unnerved Audrey looked down at the floor and cleared her throat self-consciously.

Matron Stringer beckoned her towards the desk. , "Sit down Nurse Stephenson." Audrey sat on the edge of the chair. Matron smiled, "You have been summoned here as Mr Regent has a proposition for you."

"How would you like to work for me?" Oliver Regent's voice was smooth as honey, the mask replaced by an expansive, smiling countenance.

Audrey stared. "Oh?"

"It is a good opportunity for you Audrey," Matron Stringer smiled encouragingly, "an exceptional one in fact - if I may say so sir."

She turned her head respectfully towards Mr Oliver Regent, who acknowledged her deference with the faintest flicker of an eyelid.

"You will work from my head office here in London," he announced, "alongside my other permanent staff and answer directly to me. In fact you will have your own office, and your post will be unique, your duties at a much higher level than anyone else in the Regent Trust."

Audrey's mouth fell open. "Goodness," was all she could say.

"You will meet and talk to the press, government ministers, our large financial donors, titled people, and from time to time members of the royal family. From what I know – from what I have seen of you, I feel confident you are more than capable of fulfilling this role with style, charm and self assurance."

Audrey's nerves had intensified. She felt anything but self-assured.

The whole atmosphere, Mr Regent's measured authoritative tone suggested the matter was already decided. How could she, how dare she refuse him? Gripping the chair she said, "Thank you for your confidence in me Mr Regent, I am flattered, overwhelmed really, especially as you barely know me. But am I obliged to accept right now? Could I perhaps have time to consider your...very kind offer?"

Regent pursed his lips a moment then replied slowly, "I would prefer to have your decision now. Without wishing to force your hand Miss Stephenson, I must emphasise that this is not merely a job of work and a modest increase in salary we are talking about. I am offering you a chance to better yourself, your income will rise considerably and you will I feel certain do well from this proposition. It will elevate you – or perhaps I should say re-instate you - in society. From what I gather you have, forgive me, come down in the world, am I right?"

Audrey's eyes widened in surprise, but she could make no reply.

Regent continued: "If you are concerned about losing contact with the friends you have recently made here at the hospital, there will be no need to sever yourself in that respect – no 'burning of boats'. If you find your new situation disagreeable you will be free to return to the life of an ordinary nurse. But frankly I do not think you will wish to."

Audrey looked perturbed now, her mind working frantically: precisely how much had Olivier Regent discovered about her past – and how?

"But...but why me?"

Regent smiled. "Matron tells me you are a good worker, not afraid of strenuous labour, and as I say, I believe that in the past you have enjoyed privileges and a lifestyle which your colleagues have never known. Such a transition suggests character – nay it *forges* character Miss Stephenson – I should know. I need someone with just such exceptional qualities at the heart of my organisation. And if you should entertain any feelings of guilt about the privileges you will once more enjoy, just imagine all the less fortunate people you will be helping - in a quite different, far more effective way."

Audrey breathed out and looked searchingly about the room as if seeking some sign to guide her. "Thank you Mr Regent," she said at last, "I'm quite taken aback I really am, and most grateful. But if you can forgive me I fear I cannot possibly give you an honest yes or no immediately. My head is a whirl. If your kind and generous offer is still in place first thing tomorrow morning I would be most grateful to give you my answer then."

Oliver Regent's eyes narrowed for a second then he smiled. "Of course my dear. But I warn you, I don't take no for an answer." Both he and Matron laughed.

"Thank you Mr Regent, Matron - may I return to the ward now please?"

Matron Stringer looked to her employer. Oliver Regent nodded and turned again to face the window.

"Yes Audrey," said Matron, "go back to your duties."

As she was about to open the door Oliver Regent, his back turned to her said, "And don't mention what we have spoken of - to anyone."

Audrey paused and nodded silently, then closed the door and headed back to the ward. She was reeling. What a bolt from the blue, what a proposition – to work closely with Mr Oliver Regent himself! How could she say no? This was her chance to make something of her life at long last.

Back on the ward Gladys greeted her with a snide grin. "You for the chop then?"

Audrey stared at the woman, how shabby she looked – and how pleasing it would be to be away from her, in every respect.

"No," she replied simply, walking over to the ward desk. "Quite the opposite if you must know."

"What do you mean by that?" Gladys growled suspiciously. Audrey turned. She had had enough of this vulgar woman's jibes and sarcasms. She looked her up and down and with a wry smile murmured, "Wouldn't up like to know Gladys, wouldn't you just like to know!"

It was raining heavily. Audrey buttoned up her coat and headed for the bus stop. The battered umbrella she had borrowed from the communal stand in the hallway of Drayton Terrace had seen better days and as she opened it one of the spokes tore through the black fabric rendering the contraption useless.

She lifted her collar and shielded herself from the downpour against the wall.

Her shift had officially finished over an hour ago but Gladys, true to her overbearing self had found some last minute menial jobs for her to do. She would have been there now if Matron had not intervened and sent Audrey home, which had angered Gladys enormously. Audrey had again steered clear of the woman as much as possible during the day. On the odd occasion their paths had crossed it had been Gladys that had avoided conversation, only barking orders at her when within Matron's hearing. What a peculiarly unpleasant piece of work the woman was!

Twilight was fast approaching; in the distance Audrey heard the church clock chime ten. A moment later she saw a red double-decker bus grinding through the grey London fog towards her. The bus was almost empty and climbing the stairs she sat and gazed out at the drab streets.

"Where to dear?" The conductress smiled down at her.

"Drayton Terrace please." Audrey searched her handbag for the right change.

The clippie handed her the cream coloured ticket and Audrey settled down for the half hour journey. She thought of Gladys, and of what Nellie had said the previous evening. What was going on there? Whatever it was she resolved to stay well clear of it. But what of Mr Oliver Regent and the strange, astonishing offer that he hade made to her? I will have to sleep on it, she thought, and who knows perhaps tomorrow I will wake and find it was all a dream!

She smiled to herself as she climbed the familiar steps of Drayton Terrace and thought: my life is nothing if not full of surprises. Oh well.

Inside all was quiet save for the gently beguiling notes of the clarinet from the room opposite. The light was subdued, the low lamp casting soft shadows on the walls and stairwell.

Suddenly Audrey's foot collided with some unseen shape. Thrown off balance she toppled over the obstruction and fell onto the hall table sending a large china vase crashing to the floor. The music stopped abruptly and a door opened.

In a narrow shaft of light Audrey saw a figure coming towards her. "Are you hurt ma-am?" It was a young man.

Audrey froze. His voice sounded strangely familiar, who…?

"Let me help you."

"I'm fine, thank you," Audrey replied getting to her feet, "didn't see the suitcase that's all."

"How could you in this poor light. Who could have left it there?" He moved towards the switch. The hallway suddenly became brighter.

Audrey stared at the tall physique, chiselled bronzed features and neatly parted hair of the man stood before her. "Are you American?"

"No ma-am, I'm from Canada – look you've dropped your things, please allow me to assist."

As they both bent down to retrieve Audrey's handbag and gloves, suddenly their eyes met. They held the look, the man's dark brown, lustrous eyes boring into hers. Audrey could feel her cheeks reddening.

Taking her hand gently they rose as one. "I'm Richard Neame." He smiled warmly.

"I'm…Audrey," she stuttered. What was it about him made her feel so strange, yet so familiar? "Thank you…for your help." She was feeling distinctly flustered.

"Any time ma-am."

Nodding shyly Audrey hurried to her room, closing the door behind her.

"Sit down love" Nellie bundled Audrey to the armchair, "You look all bothered; tell me what's up"

It was later that evening, and unable to settle down Audrey had knocked on Nellie's door.

"Where do I start?" Audrey sighed heavily

"At the beginning, preferably." Nellie smiled "You sound as if you've got the weight of the world on your shoulders. What *is* going on?"

"I've been offered a job."

"Who with, you're not leaving are you?"

"No - not really – not as such, look Nell don't breathe a word of this to anyone as I'm sworn to secrecy, but Oliver Regent has offered me a position, working directly for him in his offices."

Nellie's eyes widened, "*He's* offered you a job? I told you he liked you," she laughed, "I knew it!"

"No, no it's nothing like that Nellie – at least I hope not." Audrey's brow furrowed. "It's a proper, very important sounding sort of job, talking to press people, to MPs - he even mentioned royalty."

Nellie gave a low whistle. "Sounds like you've landed sunny side up there Aud. Royalty! Who'd have thought it? Mind you, not being funny love but you've got class everyone knows that, and class will out. Hope you'll still talk to us!"

"Oh of course Nellie," she took her friend's hand fondly, while her brow tightened further with indecision. "The only thing is, I've got to let him have my decision tomorrow. Oh, Nellie what do I do?"

"What do you want to do? It's that simple really."

"I suppose it is," she sighed again, "I suppose it is."

The kettle whistled on the gas cooker, Nellie spooned the tealeaves into the teapot and poured on the water. Stirring the brew noisily she then poured it out into two china cups and handed one to Audrey. "Well its all happening for you now Aud." Smiling archly she added, "And I believe you've met Mr Neame tonight too."

Audrey blushed, "Oh - yes, so silly, fell – in the hallway – he helped me. How did you know?"

"Heard the clatter, walls have ears. Bit if a dish, that one." She flashed the cheeky smile again.

"Is he, I hadn't noticed" Audrey's colour deepened and she blew on her steaming teacup with exaggerated vigour.

"By the look of your face lady," Nellie smiled, "I'd say you've done more than notice."

That night lying in her bed Audrey tried to empty her mind of all the events of the day. It was the early hours of the morning before she finally fell into a restless sleep, filled with dreams, disturbing and wonderful by turns; she saw herself with Margaret back in her arms, with her father and Oliver Regent all laughing and convivial together, then a terrible scene of drowning, people screaming, a gunshot, pursuit, separation and despair, only to end in smiles and happiness once more and Margaret gurgling on her knee. Whatever did it all mean?

When her alarm clock rang stridently out as the first shafts of daylight were filtering through the threadbare curtains she buried her head beneath the blanket. All she wanted now was sleep. With an effort she rose, washed and dressed and made her way downstairs.

Passing the closed door of Richard Neame's room she paused, and felt a strange, unaccustomed tingle in her stomach, and, it was not unpleasant. Walking on she noticed someone had tided the hallway. Perhaps it was him.

The sun was shining as Audrey opened the front door on Drayton Terrace. A milkman called out a cheery "Good morning" to her. "Good morning!" she replied and beamed back at him. She had made her decision.

At the corner of the street she saw a bus for the Regent Trust pulling up. Climbing aboard she felt an extraordinary sensation began to fill her soul. Light as air she glided to the upper deck and began to hum a happy tune. As the other passengers turned and smiled, an elderly lady turned to her husband and said: "Sounds like someone's in love!"

CHAPTER SIXTEEN

September 1946

Audrey?"

Miss Erskine put her head round the door of Audrey's office. "Sorry to intrude, but Mr Regent would like to see you later this morning, he says he'll call through in about half an hour." She pointed to the large black telephone sitting prominently on Audrey's desk.

Audrey looked up from the file she had been studying. "Oh dear – nothing wrong I hope?"

"Hardly," smiled Miss Erskine – you're the golden girl around here now. He probably wants to make sure you're settling in all right. You've been with us a month now and he likes to know everyone is coping all right – especially newcomers to office life."

"Oh but I used to help my father in his business in Liverpool before the war..." began Audrey eagerly. Then, remembering her family and the happy times they had known together she fell silent.

"Don't worry," Miss Erskine was chirruping obliviously, "I'm sure Mr Regent has every confidence in you – like I say, you're the golden girl." A person of naturally high spirits and human goodness her words flowed entirely without guile or envy.

"You're very kind, but I hardly deserve the title, " sighed Audrey. "I simply can't make head or tail of these financial reports - a lot of the figures just don't tally. I mean last month alone there was about two thousand pounds in donations that seems to have disappeared from the Regent Trust bank account..."

"Oh heavens," exclaimed Miss Erskine looking suddenly perturbed. "I was supposed to clear those files out before you arrived, Mr Regent gave me strict instructions. You see this was previously his chief accountant's office, but he's left now."

Coming over to Audrey's desk she reached over and gathered up the documents she had been poring over. "I'll take all these out of your way now," she said, and began bundling up a stack of other files from the shelves. "Not something you want to bother your head about, your job's to be public relations, that's what Mr. Regent said."

"Oh - thank you," said Audrey. "But I don't seem to have been given anything to do in that line either since I arrived. I thought the least I could do was try to tidy up the books while I'm sitting around here twiddling my thumbs, although I seem to have failed in the attempt. I always thought I was good at accounts and what have you, but the Regent Trust is obviously a more complicated organisation than I realised."

"Oh don't worry, believe you me I don't understand half of it myself – oh dear these are all out of order now."

"I'm awfully sorry," apologised Audrey, "I was only trying to help."

"Never mind I'm sure it'll all come out in the wash. You see before, we had Mr. Leeming, he was the accountant, to do all that."

"Oh – yes. So why did he leave?" asked Audrey, putting her finger on the string Miss Erskine was tying round the bundle of files she had stacked up.

"Suddenly called away, a family matter so Mr. Regent said. Disappeared on the Friday afternoon and we never saw him again. Hey ho. Thank you my dear, I'll take these along to Mr Regent – he says he's going to look after all the accounts himself from now on. How he'll find the time I don't know, but then that's Mr. Regent all over; the work of the Trust always comes first with him."

Despite Miss Erskine's assurances Audrey was convinced she was in trouble. In the month she had been working at the Regent Trust she had been given almost no work to do, and now she had interfered and messed up the bookkeeping. It did not bode well. She tapped nervously on the door.

"Enter," came the authoritative voice from within. "Ah Miss Stephenson," Oliver Regent was wearing a white silk shirt beneath an exotically patterned waistcoat, his black collar length hair, tinged here and there with silver glistening. He stubbed out the large cigar he had been smoking and rose from his leather chair. "Please sit down."

"Mr. Regent, before we begin I just want to apologie about the files - " Audrey's words gushed forth in an anxious torrent. "As I explained to Miss Erskine I've had no real work to do since I arrived here, and I thought perhaps you were waiting for me to show some initiative so I decided to have a look through the accounts and see if I could tidy them up, and although I have some experience I got in rather a muddle as I couldn't seem to balance the figures, and you'll think me awful…"

"Silence," Oliver Regent held up his hand. Audrey tailed off and looked at him awkwardly. "It is I who must apologise."

"You…?"

"Firstly for neglecting you since your arrival; I have been unexpectedly busy the last few days and haven't had time to welcome you to the Regent Trust's London headquarters. Secondly, I am sorry your office was not prepared properly. The accounts need not trouble you Miss Stephenson; your talents would be wasted on such trifles. As I told you before I have grand plans for you. Drink?" He rose from behind the desk and opened a cabinet filled with bottles of expensive drinks. "Brandy and soda, a glass of champagne perhaps? Just a little aperitif."

"Aperitif?"

"Yes, I've a table booked for lunch at the Savoy Grill."

"Oh - then I mustn't keep you from your guests…"

"But you are my guest Miss Stephenson – one of them. The others are Lord and Lady Emerson and Sir Richard and Lady Carlisle – oh and Admiral Duncannon and the Bishop of London. We have a lot to discuss about the Trust. Here let's open the champagne – after all we must toast your future with us mustn't we?"

With a flourish Oliver Regent popped the cork and filled two shimmering glasses with golden foaming champagne. He handed one to Audrey. "Here's to you – and the Regent Trust."

Audrey raised her glass. "Oh, - yes –" she said uncertainly. She noticed Oliver Regent staring at her intently.

"Whatever is it Mr. Regent?"

"Forgive me," he sat on the edge of his large desk and took a large swig of champagne. "Now listen before lunch I'd like to sort one or two things out."

Audrey nodded blankly, her mind still trying to catch up. "Firstly, I would like to offer you a promotion."

"But from what? I haven't done anything yet."

"Its not what you've done Miss Stephenson, it's who you are – your character…and…your pedigree shall we say. Yes. The fact is I would like you to be my personal assistant."

Audrey stared at him in amazement. "Mr Regent - I'm even more flabbergasted - why?"

He crossed to the window and looked out. "Isn't London wonderful?" he said. "Britain is wonderful – a great country, and set to be greater. The Regent Trust is going to play a big part in its future believe me. I need someone I can trust Miss Stephenson. There will be a significant increase in your salary. What do you say?" He turned from the window to face her.

"I don't quite know what to say sir. I'm already honoured to be working here – I don't know what more I should rightly expect."

"As I told you before I am aware you have had hardship and sorrow in your life, yet you came through. I like spirit, and you have that. So how would you feel about taking this position?"

Audrey fingered the stem of her glass. "I'm sorry Mr Regent, I can't believe all this, it's too good to be true. Why would you want me, you don't even know me."

Oliver Regent's smile was strangely cold, then, he said, "You would be surprised what I know Audrey. I'm offering you a chance to get out of the gutter, to get back to where you belong, to give you the life you should have had. Don't bite that hand my dear, it won't be offered again."

Audrey did not reply, did not dare look at him, but could feel him staring at her, awaiting her answer.

Refilling her glass he asked, "Tell me my dear, do you like where you live at present, Drayton Terrace I believe?"

"It's not so bad," Audrey replied lowering her eyes.

"You don't sound so sure. Is it really that luxurious?"

Audrey sighed, "Well the room is small, the bed is in the sitting room and the kitchen is behind a curtain. Its very clean though and Nellie lives next door, but it's not…."

"Not what you've been used to?"

"I didn't say that."

"No, I did. Do you trust me Audrey? Because I trust you."

Audrey nodded, "Of course I do sir."

"I have within the Trust a residential property, which I would like you to consider.

With your new salary you would be more than able to afford it, and it would be much more in keeping with your new position, should you wish to accept it of course."

"Well I suppose it would be nice to have more space than my present lodgings...."

"This would hardly be described as 'lodgings' Miss Stephenson. It's an apartment in Somersby House, Kensington. I'll take you to have a look at the place, if you don't like it then by all means remain at Drayton Terrace, but today Miss Stephenson I will have your decision. But first – to lunch!" Draining his glass Olivier Regent took his homburg from the hat stand and bowing gallantly to Audrey, opened the door.

"Is this alright Miss?"

The chauffeur had brought the sleek black limousine to a halt a few doors down from Drayton Terrace. Audrey had directed him to stop short of her lodgings, not wanting Mrs Goldstein to see her arriving in such unaccustomed style. It was going to be hard enough telling her she was leaving; there would be questions.

"This is perfect, thank you so much."

The chauffer stepped out and opened the door for her. Thanking him she waited till he had driven off then walked to Drayton Terrace. Her head was whirling, spinning. A short walk she hoped would settle her mind.

Lunch had been a dream like affair, the assorted dignitaries asking polite questions about her previous work at the Regent Trust Hospital, and about her family, Audrey managing to answer the latter with a carefully selective degree of truthfulness. Oliver Regent, after telling them how 'Miss Stephenson will be a great asset to the Regent Trust' had spent much of the time in conversation with the Bishop of London about matters of finance. After lunch he had taken her in the limousine to see the apartment in Kensington; Audrey had found it magnificent - spacious, modern, light and airy and more besides - all that Drayton Terrace was not. On the way back in the limousine she had agreed to take both the position and the apartment.

Opening the front door now, the familiar, haunting sound of the clarinet greeted her; Richard was at home. Lingering for a moment she listened to the music, till suddenly it stopped. Not wishing to bump into Richard she made her way quickly up the stairs, then hearing the front open and close she presumed he must have gone out.

She was about to open her door when she heard a familiar voice from the hallway below. Moving closer to the banister she leaned cautiously over, just enough to spy Mrs Goldstein deep in conversation with Gladys Townsend. What on earth was Gladys doing here?

Leaning over the banister as far as she dared Audrey strained to catch what was being said. Gladys was handing Mrs Goldstein a parcel: "This is the last lot they tell me till you paid up."

"You mind your step Gladys Townsend," hissed Mrs Goldstein, "ain't a good idea threatening me."

"It's not a threat Bessie. I'm just telling you what they said - the money, or god help you what they'll do to ya' - and another thing, you gotta sort out that Nellie, she seen me with 'em the other day, nosy cow, asked a lot of questions till I gave her a flea in the ear – don't want her blabbing on to Matron."

"You're getting careless Glad," retorted Mrs Goldstein, "that's the posh one and now Nellie seen you, its you what wants to be careful."

"Stephenson's out of the way now, got a new job up west with Mr Big," Gladys sneered. "You just sort Nellie out, you know what to do?"

Mrs Goldstein snorted, "Is the Pope Catholic?" she gave a hollow laugh. "Now come in and I'll sort you out for the last lot and shut your gob. Everyone knows Ma Goldstein pays what she owes fair and square."

As the two women disappeared into Mrs Goldstein's Audrey's eyes were wide with fearful speculation: what did they mean by 'sorting Nellie out'? She had to find out, she must warn Nellie at all costs to be on her guard.

Her heart thumping loudly in her chest Audrey slipped off her shoes and descended the stairs. On reaching the bottom step she tiptoed softly towards Mrs Goldstein's room, when all of a sudden the door opened slightly.

In horror Audrey shrank back into the shadows; she realised it was too late to return back up the stairs for they would see her instantly. She could hear their voices, scraping noises, they would see her any second - what excuse would she have if Mrs Goldstein found her lingering outside her room? Whatever was she to do? Then she heard the clarinet; the only way of escape was Richard's room.

Darting down the hall she grabbed the handle hoping it was not locked. To her relief it opened and she almost fell in and closed it swiftly behind her just as Mrs Goldstein emerged.

"Well I...hello again!" Richard, his fingers frozen on the keys of the instrument was staring at her in bemusement. "Kind of you to drop in."

"I'm so sorry...I..." Audrey panted, "...didn't think you were in...and..."

"You didn't hear my wonderful rendition?" he smiled ironically, indicating his instrument. "Or maybe you thought I've just been playing gramophone records all this time?"

Suddenly there was a loud knocking on the door. "Gee I'm popular this evening," quipped Richard, "did I throw a party and then forget that I'd sent the invitations?"

As he opened the door Audrey dived behind it out of sight. Through the narrow slit of the doorjamb she could see Mrs Goldstein's hatchet face. She tried desperately to quieten her breathing.

"Everything alright Mr Neame?" Mrs Goldstein's hard, nasal voice oozed suspicion.

"Why wouldn't it be Mrs Goldstein" replied Richard pleasantly. "I have a wonderful apartment with the most up to date facilities, and a landlady so concerned for my well being, can surely have no cause for complaint."

The irony was not wasted on Mrs. Goldstein. "Very amusing I'm sure," she wheezed, "but they'll be complaints from me if I find you flouting the rules of this establishment - by entertaining women in the room."

"My only love is my music Mrs Goldstein," he smiled.

"Thought I smelt women's perfume in the 'all," she sniffed the air noisily, "and in here..." Mrs Goldstein moved closer into the room. Inches away behind the door Audrey squirmed.

"All sorts of aromas drift in off the street Mrs Goldstein, I like the window open," Richard said airily, barring her way. "I know and respect your rules Mrs Goldstein and no there is no woman in my room, now, if there is nothing else - "

Mrs Goldstein turned away and Richard closed the door. Turning to Audrey he said, "So - what's going on? And who owned the black limo you got out of earlier? My window faces the street."

"I'll explain," said Audrey panting now after holding her breath. "Though it may take some time."

"Then why not let's relax," he indicated a sofa. "I'll make some tea. I'm getting quite proficient at it after six weeks in your wonderful country."

As they sat together on the sofa and drank tea, Audrey, blurted out all about the great Mr Regent's amazing offer of a new life, the lunch and the limousine, about the jewellery gang working out of the hospital and the alarming conversation she had just overheard in the hall concerning her friend Nellie. Then realising that she knew absolutely nothing about this man she gathered her thoughts and headed for the door. "I'm sorry Mr Neame, please forget what I have just said."

Richard grabbed her hand. "Where are you going?"

"Away from here." He put his arm around her and guided her to and armchair. "Sounds like your pal Nellie could be in trouble – and you were too nearly."

"That's why I dived into your room – I'm so sorry, I was so frightened of what Mrs Goldstein might do if she caught me eavesdropping on her and Gladys."

"I know how you feel," Richard shook his head. "She scares the pants off me too to be honest – creepy lady. And call me Richard."

Audrey gave a rueful smile. "So you were my saviour. I don't know how to thank you."

"I have one idea, said Richard tentatively.

"Yes, anything at all," Audrey realised their arms were touching, and that she felt no inclination to pull away.

"Well seeing as you're leaving here for your swanky new apartment in a couple of days, maybe a kiss from a pretty lady will suffice." He pointed to his cheek.

Audrey felt her legs go suddenly weak. It was a long time she had kissed a man, not since Martin. Her heart racing she replied, "All right," and moved slowly towards kiss his cheek.

Just as she was about to place her lips there, Richard turned his head, their eyes met and they held each other's gaze momentarily. The next second her open mouth found his, his arms were around her and the couple were locked in a desperate and passionate embrace.

CHAPTER SEVENTEEN

"This is more like it Aud!" enthused Nellie casting an admiring eye over the interior of 22a Somersby House. "And in Kensington too - ain't we posh now! Oh sorry no offence dear, 'cause I know you are, or you was, or at least..."

"Let's have a drink Nell, to celebrate," said Audrey seeing her friend's embarrassment.

"Oh, lovely yeah – but hey aren't you going to wait for your fancy man – sorry I forgot his name, Mr music feller...?"

"Richard," smiled Audrey, "Yes I suppose we should wait for him, I'll put this back in the refrigerator."

"That's it Richard, from Canada you said. Well if you're sure – blimey where did you get the bubbly?"

Audrey was holding an expensive looking bottle of champagne. "Mr Regent sent it over – for my house warming he said. Honestly he's been so generous, I can't think what I've done to deserve it, all of it – this marvellous place, the salary increase, the job. I just hope I can live up to his expectations."

"Don't knock it Aud," counselled Nellie, "and I'm sure you're worth every penny to the Trust, and more besides. Here, listen I don't want to play gooseberry with you and Richard tonight...I mean if you and him are – well if you want a - how shall we say 'romantic evening' I don't want to be in the way."

"Not at all Nellie, he knows you'll be here, this is to be a housewarming and I wanted you both to get to know one another – after all you both share a hallway at Drayton Terrace, but he says you've never yet met?"

"Only through his music," sighed Nellie. "Oh - any man what can play the clarinet like that – well, he must have romance in his soul, know what I mean?"

"I do indeed," beamed Audrey.

"Well you just tip me the wink when you want me to be alone and I'll...

"Oh - that'll be him!" cried Audrey as the doorbell chimed. She went into the hall and pressed the intercom button. "Hello – Richard?"

"At your service," crackled a voice from street level.

"Come on up – the champagne is waiting – and so am I!"

The evening had begun in good spirit, with introductions for Richard and Nellie, followed by a hearty toast to Audrey's new home. She had prepared a fish pie with fresh vegetables from Kensington market, and made an apple tart with cream to follow.

Nellie, tipsy on the champagne, had been loud and merry throughout the meal, but Richard had remained strangely quiet. When the dessert was eaten he had made polite excuses and bade them both goodnight. Audrey, who had been hoping for some mention of meeting again, was left feeling both deflated and baffled.

Nellie blamed herself: "I shouldn't have come Aud," she lamented as they sat sipping brandy by the high living room window of the flat and gazing out at the lights of London. "I shouldn't have drunk so much, I know I act stupid when I've had a few, especially on the old fizz, oh dear me."

"No Nell it wasn't you. I realise I don't know Richard - one fumbled kiss when I burst into his room and start making all sorts of assumptions."

"Oh so he's kissed you!" Nellie's eyes lit up, "what was it like?"

"Heavenly if you must know," sighed Audrey. "But perhaps that's as far as it will go. I suppose he just accepted my invitation tonight out of politeness." She sighed more deeply.

"Well if so it's his loss," said Nellie. Strange chap if you ask me, gorgeous, yes, but very strange, after all what sort of a man plays a *clarinet*!" They both laughed.

"I do like him though Nell – that kiss meant something, its been so long, and for a man to hold me in his arms like that and do what he did – well, I'm a woman after all."

"Then don't wait for him to do the chasing – let him know you're interested. I'll put in a word if you like."

"But I'm afraid, Nell – its all so scary, the possibility of falling in love."

"Who mentioned love – a kiss is just a kiss, why not enjoy more of them? By the way, how come you were in his room in the first place?"

"Oh my goodness!" Audrey's hand flew to her mouth. "I forgot to tell you Nell, Mrs Goldstein and Nurse Townsend they're up to no good – now listen carefully, you've got to be on your guard..."

It was almost midnight and Nellie had left for Drayton Terrace. Audrey's warning about Mrs Goldstein's sinister intentions towards her had been gratefully received. Nellie though was made of strong stuff and not easily frightened, and she assured Audrey she would 'give Goldstein and her tomfoolery cronies what for if they dared try it on' with her.

Audrey had gone to bed but could not sleep, her mind too full of the amazing new turn her life had taken.

She mused on the fact that just two weeks ago she had been confined to a rundown room in Drayton Terrace, not even daring to think of the future, and now here she was living in a beautiful apartment in an affluent and fashionable part of London.

Arriving with her few clothes and possessions in her small suitcase, the rag doll she had been given by the old lady at Nellie's fairground tucked in her pocket, Mr Regent had proudly shown her the large wardrobe, filled with expensive clothes and shoes; what was more, everything fitted her - how he had known her exact size was a mystery, and she had been too grateful and overwhelmed to dare to ask.

Who was this great and magnanimous man from America, who had so inexplicably taken her under his wing and given her back the kind of life she had known so long ago? Don't dwell on the reasons Audrey she said to herself – just be grateful for what you have been given.

But her restlessness persisted, and she knew the reason for that only too well: Richard. His reserved demeanour tonight had surprised her. Maybe it had been Nellie's presence that had held him back. From the man who had held her and kissed her that evening in his room at Drayton Terrace he seemed to be a different person. But how could a kiss that even now burned like fire on her lips be ignored, forgotten? It was impossible. Oh how she ached for those lips on hers now, her whole being yearning to feel his hands on her body...Richard...oh Richard!

The early morning sun streamed though the bay windows of the lounge as Audrey surveyed her reflection in the large gilded oval mirror above the mantelpiece, straightening a loose strand of her raven black hair.

The clock on the sideboard chimed eight. She peered from the window; the car was waiting to take her to work. Gathering her handbag and matching gloves she looked once more in the mirror: perfect. She smiled, pleased with what she saw.

"Good morning Miss Davenport." Audrey said breezing airily through the front door of the Regent Trust offices. "Is Mr Regent in yet?"

"Yes Miss Stephenson. I believe he is in a meeting at the moment. Arrived with a lady - well dressed she was too according to Reg."

Audrey raised an eyebrow, "Reginald should concentrate on looking after the front door here rather than gossiping."

"He's on his tea break."

"Already?" Audrey couldn't help smiling. "Well I'm sure Mr Regent won't mind my looking in on his meeting." Lowering her voice she added playfully, "Then I can report back on this mysterious lady."

Miss Davenport gave an arch look, "Now who's the one for gossip?"

The two women laughed as Audrey turned along the corridor. As she approached Oliver Regent's office she could hear voices from within. She was just about to knock and enter when something made her stop dead in her tracks; it was the voice of the lady. No, thought Audrey incredulously: surely not - it couldn't be - could it? Pressing her ear to the door she listened intently: there was no doubt about it: the voice was that of her mother Clarissa!

"…So, you're on the run again John - what is it now, fleeced another poor widow out of her inheritance? What name did you use this time?"

There was a momentary pause then Audrey heard Oliver Regent laugh: "Ha -two women actually, one unfortunately died, got in the way."

"Just like dear old Kitty eh?"

"Kitty was unfortunate, pity – if things had been different she and I might have settled down by now, made me an honest man."

"Hell would have to freeze over first John Bamford."

121

"Don't use that name around here dear sister, and keep your voice down, walls have ears. The New York police had nothing to go on, but a change of scene for a while seemed prudent. Besides I missed London – and you; we're flesh and blood after all, and I care about you believe it or not."

"You care about nothing but yourself - that and money."

"How bitter you are Clarissa - life not been good to you lately?"

"My life John, has been hell," snarled Clarissa vehemently. "And all because of you, yes, you owe me John."

" I can't see how you work that one out, I asked you to come to America with me years ago but you refused. You preferred to stay with that abominable bore Marcus."

"How could I leave? James was a little boy and Audrey was just a baby – god knows where the unfortunate child is now..." her voice tailed off.

"She's here."

"What?"

"Audrey, your daughter is here."

There was a deathly silence. Audrey, her heart in her mouth bent and pressed her eye to the keyhole of the door; then she gave out an audible gasp: caught in the small semi-circle of light she saw the face of her mother. Clarissa looked haggard, ancient almost. She was staring open-mouthed at Oliver Regent.

"You're lying – you mean here, with you?"

"By pure chance," replied Regent. "She was working at the Regent hospital, nursing. I knew it was her as soon as I saw her, she's just like you dear sister – before you...matured."

"Like me!" Clarissa gave a mirthless laugh, "Like me, how could she possibly be like me? She's Marcus's daughter – naïve, sentimental and foolish. You and I John are two of a kind; single minded, clear sighted and we neither of us suffer fools – we know what's what and how to get it. Anyway I hope at least you're looking after her, teaching her how to survive and look after number one at last."

Oliver Regent walked to the window. "Clarissa I have a great deal of wealth, some I've made honestly and the rest...but you know all this. Well let's not beat about the bush, I'm assuming that's why you're here - you want some money?"

"John, you took everything from us. Braeside was the last straw; it broke Marcus's heart, he loved that house, not that I care a jot about that now. I cannot find any sympathy – his own weakness brought him to this pass. He is ill and the business is failing. I want to leave him but I need money. And you owe me John."

There was another, longer pause then Oliver Regent said: "How much?"

"Twenty thousand pounds will do for a start."

"And what if I refuse?"

"I think you know what."

"Is that a threat my dear? I don't take kindly to them." There was menace in his voice now. "I advise you to think carefully; remember what happened to Mac – and to Kitty."

"That too is a threat," replied Clarissa, "and I too am not easily threatened. You should know this: I have lodged certain papers with a firm of solicitors, papers containing facts about Mac and Kitty Mason – and about the Regent Trust. If anything untoward should happen to me, the solicitors are instructed to hand the papers over to Scotland Yard."

"Interesting," replied Regent coolly. "Which solicitors?"

"You really thing I'm that stupid?"

"Very well, I'm sure we can arrange twenty thousand."

"Think of that as a down payment."

Regent's tone of voice shifted almost imperceptibly, "Be careful not to push your luck sister," he purred, "it can so easily change."

"I must go John. I shall call for the money in a few days – be sure to have it ready – unmarked banknotes."

"Wait Clarissa, there's something else."

"What?"

"Don't you want to see your daughter?"

"Audrey? Why on earth would I want to see her?"

The keyhole suddenly became a blur as Clarissa marched towards the door. Audrey in alarm took to her heels and ran headlong back along the corridor to the main door. Passing Miss Davenport she panted, "Emergency – I have to go home at once – oh and would you be an absolute angel and tell Mr Regent you haven't seen me today?"

CHAPTER EIGHTEEN

Audrey was too upset to go back to the apartment. The associations of the place with Oliver Regent, revealed now as her uncle John Bamford, the villain wanted for the murder of her dear uncle Mac and Kitty Mason just as the sinister rumours she had heard since her childhood had related was too much to bear.

After wandering the West End streets for a while, her mind in turmoil, it occurred to her to take the bus to Drayton Terrace. Nellie would be at work, and in any case she did not particularly want to share the dramatic events that had just transpired with Nellie, not yet at least.

In fact she positively did not want Nellie to be there, and for a good reason as her thoughts instead had turned to Richard, and she felt gripped now by an overwhelming desire to see him. After that passionate kiss did he really like her, and been constrained on their last meeting merely by Nellie's presence? She hoped fervently this was the case.

His impetuous advances that afternoon aside, Richard seemed level headed and shrewd – she felt sure he would listen calmly to what was a lengthy and quite incredible story, and be able to offer her some kind of advice, some reassurance. And to be alone with him again would hardly be unwelcome; even now she could feel again the tender, yet insistent caress of his lips on hers.

As the bus ground along Kensington High Street Audrey crossed her fingers that she would find him home. It was only then she realised she had no idea whatsoever what Richard did for a living, or why he had come to London.

Pressing the button marked 'Flat 3" Audrey prayed Mrs Goldstein was not around she had simply left a note for her when moving out of Drayton Terrace, and certainly didn't want to run into her now and face the inevitable interrogation about whom she had come back to visit. With relief she heard the crackle of Richard's voice: "Who is it?"

"Richard, it's me Audrey, can I come in?"

With no further reply the front door buzzed open and a minute later she was sitting on the sofa in Richard's small neat front room. Without ceremony she began to tell her story as clearly and concisely as she could. When she had finished Richard stretched his hands above his head, raised his eyebrows and said simply: "Wow!"

"But you do believe me," pleaded Audrey, "You don't think I'm making it up?"

"My dear," he replied stroking his chin, "I don't think even Charles Dickens could make up a plot like that – Edgar Allen Poe maybe, but even he'd be pushed. It must have come as quite a shock to suddenly find out that not only is your boss, the great do-gooder Mr Oliver Regent – both a fraud and your long lost uncle, but also a cold blooded killer on the run – and then into the bargain your estranged ma turns up out of the blue and blackmails him – it's a wonder you didn't faint with horror!"

"I nearly did," quavered Audrey, "and I might yet - if I do you will pick me up won't you?"

He gave Audrey a look that spoke volumes. Then reaching towards her took her firmly in his arms.

"Oh Richard – I've been so afraid you didn't like me after all...that night at the apartment, Nellie prattling on, I'm so sorry I..."

"Shush," Richard placed his lips gently on hers and they kissed. Audrey felt a spear of fire go through her as his tongue probed her mouth. She responded, arching her back in rapt surrender, her fingers gripping his hair. They kissed for some time then sat up and gazed at one another. Audrey whispered, "I must go Richard."

He nodded silently.

"May I come again?"

"May you?" he stared at her in awe. "My darling girl, I am yours to command. But you're right, let's not spoil this moment, let's just hold it, as we have held each other. Tomorrow evening I'll come to your apartment, if you will allow me."

"Allow you? Why Richard I..."

"I mean, or rather I don't mean – well, you know, unless..."

She put her hand gently to his lips," You're right, we mustn't spoil it, we must go slowly, though goodness knows how - "

"We'll be alright," he took her hand in his and kissed it. "Go now," he said softly, "– and don't worry about anything else, the stuff you told me. I can help - I have friends in London we can sort this mess out. But hey – don't open your door to anyone but me – and be careful if you go out. Try to get some sleep."

That night back in the Kensington apartment Audrey sat up at the dressing table and looked in the mirror. She had put on only the table lamps, trying to blot out the fact of where she was. All she wanted now was the oblivion of sleep but tired as she felt it would not come, there was just too much to consider, to decide and plan. Richard had said he would help, that he would come to her the following evening, but much as she ached for his presence she wondered what he could realistically do. This was a police matter, and she must go to the police; surely that would put an end to the matter.

But suppose it wasn't so simple as that? Bamford, or Oliver Regent was a respected figure, with friends in high places; what he was alleged to have done, had taken place a long time ago. Would anyone now even recognise Regent as Bamford? Her mother would certainly not testify, not if he paid her off, as she had demanded. And it sounded as if her poor father Marcus was in a bad way – could he be relied on to identify Bamford, and if so, would he, now a failed businessman in ill health, be believed? And what proof did she have of what she had overheard between her mother and Bamford?

Gazing at her reflection Audrey recalled the sinister story dear Jack had told her about John Bamford; well, now she knew it was no fairy tale. And horrific as it was to contemplate, Bamford's sister, her own mother was in it up to her neck, aiding and abetting a murderer and a fraudster. Any buried hope Audrey might have nurtured of some kind of future reconciliation had in that moment of eavesdropping surely been utterly destroyed.

Tears now welled in her eyes at the tragedy of this estrangement from her mother; worse still, she could see how the sins of the parent were already being visited on the child – her mother's rejection of her when she found out about the baby had culminated in Audrey being forced to abandon her own little girl. Then a more horrible possibility occurred to her: would Margaret grow up to despise and pity her, as even now she despised and pitied her own mother? Almost choking with anguish Audrey fell on her bed and wept bitterly.

When the storm had passed she lay very still and quiet and allowed her mind to clear. She realised now of course why Oliver Regent had been so generous towards her ever their meeting; he had known immediately who she was – she recalled the momentary flicker of shock as his eyes lighted on her at the hospital.

126

Clearly he had been deeply disturbed at the possibility of Audrey discovering his true identity, and crucially that he had murdered her Uncle Mac; and as the saying went: keep your friends close, but your enemies even closer. Audrey, potentially John Bamford's most dangerous enemy was being drawn so close she would ultimately be a party to whole criminal…must think of a plan. Should she simply go to the police first thing in the morning and tell all she had heard between Oliver Regent and her mother?

Perhaps there was another way. John Bamford was a callous and despicable man but also clearly a very clever one, who had constructed a new and respectable identity for him self and profited handsomely from it.

He would not give that up easily. If a young woman in his employ, one with a history of immorality who had abandoned her child no less were to publicly accuse him of murder and deception, there would be an outcry not against Olivier Regent, but against the wretch who dared make such vile accusations. He had friends in the police force, in government, among the Royal Family itself, and she feared they would not hesitate to help him. She stared at her reflection again; she had never realised how like Clarissa she was. Then she smiled; "I won't fall into that trap, John Bamford, I *will* play you at your own game; but I will write the rules."

Audrey left the Westminster and London Bank and hailed a taxi. One pulled up immediately. "Kensington High Street please."

As they bowled off she sat back, closed her eyes and breathed out. Opening an account in her own name had been easier than she thought; no awkward questions, and it would all be done in a few days the manager had assured her. The first stage of her plan was in place. Now came the more unnerving part. She had already telephoned to arrange a meeting that morning with 'Oliver Regent.' She rehearsed in her head what she was going to tell him; whatever her words she knew at all costs she must sound relaxed, unhurried and completely oblivious to his real identity – as if everything were 'normal' in fact.

Arriving at the Regent Trust offices she paid the cabbie and trotted quickly up the steps. "Good morning Miss Davenport," she smiled at the young receptionist on the front desk as she passed by. Taking the lift to the first floor she looked at her watch: 9.30am, perfect.

Pausing a second outside the large panelled door, she took in a deep breath, knocked firmly twice and waited.

"Come in - my dear girl!" Oliver Regent, smiling expansively rose from his desk as Audrey entered. "How are you feeling now?"

"Feeling?" replied Audrey.

"I understand you had to leave yesterday – I assumed you were unwell. You should have told me, I'd have arranged a car to take you home."

Audrey felt a moment of panic: so someone had told him she was in the building yesterday. She would have to be careful from now on.

"I didn't want to be a nuisance, just a little under the weather that's all…"

"Of course, of course, you're obviously working too hard." He guided her to the chair in front of his desk and resumed his seat. "Shall I have tea sent up?"

"No, thank you sir." Audrey shook her head. "The fact is I haven't really been working at all – maybe that's what tiring me out, if you see what I mean."

"Yes, yes of course you said," he nodded, "that's just it, you're a firebrand like myself dear girl, can't abide sloth, the devil makes work for idle hands after all. Though come to think of it the most successful criminals are highly industrious about it - so they say." He looked across the desk at her now, his eyes suddenly intense, boring deep into hers: "Why, perhaps you and I are long lost relatives – what do you think!"

Audrey stifled a gasp. "Ah, um, yes." She clutched at her throat and said in a strained voice. "Well yes its true I am restless without sufficient to occupy myself…"

"Ha, ha, ha!" His laugh was deep and guttural, the laugh of a triumphant dictator or demigod. "How – elegantly you put it."

"Thank you sir." I must come to the point, thought Audrey; I must carry this through now… She focused her eyes at the wall immediately behind him and spoke carefully and clearly. "The reason I asked to see you sir is that I would like to make a proposition – a suggestion at least – for the Regent Trust, for how I might contribute, and do something to, …to earn the very generous salary you are paying me."

Oliver Regent spread out his hands and leaned back in his chair. "It all sounds intriguing my dear, you have my full attention – well?"

"Well – um," Audrey cleared her throat, "When I came here from Liverpool, I had no plans or even any idea of what to expect. I had seen the poster for the Regent Trust in a hotel lobby near Lime Street station and on an impulse I decided to come and find you…"

"Find me?"

"The Trust, of course. When I arrived at Euston station, alone in London, I felt I had perhaps been foolish - if it had not been for the Regent Trust in Butter Lane – well the rest is history."

"What were you running away from Audrey?"

"Nothing, Mr Regent," she said uneasily. "Nothing at all…"

"It is not for me to pry – forgive me. Now, your proposition."

"It concerns the Regent Trust premises in Butter Lane, sir – at present it is a drain on our resources – I have seen the books."

"Agreed – and?"

"I think it can be improved and thereby attract government funding, even become a going concern. There is also an adjacent property which with a modest investment could be turned into a profitable hotel, the income from which will greatly enrich the Trust."

Audrey paused, noting the momentary glint in Oliver Regent's eyes. "Enabling us do even more good work for the poor," she continued quickly.

Oliver Regent pursed his lips and looked long and hard at her. "You are a young woman of considerable imagination," he said at last. "But how exactly would you go about this scheme?"

"I would engage architects and builders, seek the best professional advice, supervise the whole project, I would put my absolute all into it sir you would have my word on that."

Oliver Regent was looking very thoughtful. "Hmm, yes, I see. Of course the adjacent building would have to be purchased first, do you know who owns the property?"

"No but I can find out," replied Audrey, "I can do all the necessary research and negotiations, it needn't trouble you a bit, I know how busy you are with the running the rest of the Regent Trust." Audrey sat like an eager puppy that has fetched a stick for her master and now wanted approval, a pat - a reward. Inwardly however she was palpitating with anxiety.

"Very well," he said at last, rising decisively from the desk. "You have my full permission to begin this project at once. You'll probably encounter some objections from some of the senior management at the hospital over the refurbishments – but from now on you will have ultimate responsibility, and complete authority over the staff – all right?"

Audrey could not suppress a broad grin. "As you wish sir – of course - "

"Well what are you waiting for young lady? A luxury hotel won't build itself – I suggest you begin by finding whoever owns that property and making them an offer." He smiled at her, "And now you must excuse me, I'm lunching at the Ritz with Lord Bradbury. Shall we walk down the corridor together?"

The next morning Audrey arrived at the Regent Trust Home early. She made a beeline for Nellie, who was in the ward kitchen making a pot of tea.

"Hello Audrey," Nellie smiled, "what brings you back to the front line - had enough of office life, or did you just miss my tea?"

"Both to be honest Nell!"

"Come on then, get this down you girl." She handed Audrey a large china cup of steaming tea."

"Ooh, saved my life," said Audrey appreciatively, pulling a chair to the table and sitting down. "Now listen Nell, I've got a proposition for you."

"Sounds worrying," replied Nellie pouring some hot tea from her cup into a saucer and fanning it with her cap.

"No - it's really exciting," said Audrey eagerly, "I've been instructed by Mr Regent himself to undertake a complete renovation of this hospital and the home, and, next door we're going to make into a marvellous luxury hotel, and raise absolutely heaps of money – and, you're going to help me."

Nellie stared at her open mouthed. "Me?" she exclaimed, " You want me, to help you, what can I do?"

Audrey laughed, "Be my eyes and ears when I'm not here for one thing – Nell, I know how much you really care about the people who come to us for help - you helped me remember? That's why I want you Nellie, I need you - please say you will?"

Nellie laughed and shrugged her shoulders, "All right – I don't know what I'm letting myself in for, but all right. Where do we start?"

"The medical ward."

Nellie whistled, "Gladys won't like that Aud…"

"That's exactly what I'm hoping for," Audrey smiled assertively. "Now come on Nell, let's get started. Together we're going to turn this place around. Gladys Townsend, and the Regent Trust won't know what hit them!"

CHAPTER NINETEEN

November 1946

After the predictable resentment and murmurs of protest, instigated chiefly by Gladys Townsend, Audrey and Nellie had made good progress with the improvements. While Gladys muttered veiled threats and tried her utmost to enlist the Matron against them, the pair had stood firm and Audrey had got briskly on with the task in hand – reorganizing shifts, arranging relocation of the patients with care and consideration, and briefing the decorators to now bring the whole hospital up to the immaculate standard of the recently refurbished ground floor.

She had also written to the land registry enquiring as to the ownership of the empty property next door, and put an architect and a builder on standby for a conversion; in the meantime they were to draw up plans for knocking down some of the walls in the hospital itself, thereby providing airier and more spacious facilities for staff and patients.

Together with the decorating firm, the builder and architect had put in estimates for the requisite work. Audrey then went away and promptly sent her own hand-written note to Oliver Regent's secretary, asking for a payment to be made to the special 'Regent Trust Improvements' account that had now been set up, for which she was sole signatory. The figure she requested however was precisely double the combined quotes of all the tradesmen. She told no one of this discrepancy – not even Nellie. The secretary made the payment to the bank that same day – "Miss Stephenson's instructions are to be followed to the letter," Oliver Regent had told her, "whatever she wants."

Nellie had proved herself an efficient and loyal assistant to Audrey, tackling each task set her with willingness and pride; Nellie's confidence had subsequently grown and together they now constituted a formidable and respected team around the hospital.

With the work progressing well, Audrey told Nellie they both deserved a treat of some kind. She proposed that without telling anyone, they take the afternoon off, hail a taxi to the West End and there have a slap-up meal. Nellie, who rarely travelled in a taxi, was agog at the daring extravagance of such a plan, and full of giggling excitement. Audrey however had another reason for wishing to visit the West End, which she did not reveal to Nellie.

"This place looks OK," said Audrey as they alighted from the taxi. "The Olde English Ale House – Luncheon served 12 till 3."

"OK?" marvelled Nellie gazing at the quaint half-timbered pub nestled between a fusty looking tailors shop and the grand stone columns of the Westminster and London Bank. "I could do a three hour 'luncheon' in there any day! Oh but will they serve unaccompanied ladies though Aud?" Nellie had been refused entrance to hostelries before, and was always wary of 'snooty' managers.

"We're paying aren't we?" smiled Audrey. "Which reminds me I have to do some banking next door first – why don't you go in and look at the menu – ask for a wine list – oh and the plat du jour."

Nellie looked blank, "Plat du what?"

"Dish of the day – I'll only be a few minutes."

The Westminster and London Bank was not busy. A cluster of city gents conversing by the door tilted their bowler hats politely as Audrey entered; since her promotion she had invested in some fine new clothes, and looked once more, every inch the 'lady.'

At the counter she wrote out a cheque from the 'Regent Trust Improvements' account, and together with a short accompanying note handed it to the clerk.

"Could you please pay this into my personal account – these are the details."

The young male clerk scrutinised the cheque and said hesitantly, "I might have to get this approved by the manager, given the amount…"

"Oh I don't think there's any need for that," replied Audrey demurely, "I'm Miss Stephenson, I'm in charge of the Regent Trust improvements - you remember me I think, from when the account was opened?"

The young man, who remembered her very well, smiled self-consciously, "Oh, yes indeed - certainly Miss Stephenson, anything to oblige."

As he rubber-stamped her cheque and filled out a payments slip, Audrey added, "Oh and could you be an absolute angel and let me have some cash today? Ten pounds should be sufficient."

"Ten pounds? I...of course, delighted Miss Stephenson..."

"You're so very kind and helpful whenever I come in here, I don't know what I should do without you, you make banking a real pleasure."

The young man blushed. "Happy to be of service, Madam – Miss...um..."

Putting the ten pounds in her purse, Audrey leaned towards the counter, the fragrant aroma of her perfume wafting through the brass grill that separated them. "Do you know, I think I shall have no hesitation in recommending you for a managerial position Mr -?"

"Cotton," spluttered the clerk quite overcome, "Ernest Cotton."

"Well Mr Cotton, Ernest, goodbye - or perhaps I should say 'au revoir?'" And with a flutter of her eyelashes Audrey left Ernest Cotton gazing glassy-eyed as she made her way to the door.

In the 'Olde English Ale House' Nellie was at a cosy corner table drooling at the menu. Audrey took a seat beside her and winked conspiratorially, "Order what you like Nellie," she whispered, "Lunch is on me."

Nellie was stood drinking tea with the builders. They were all laughing. Gladys was not happy. In fact her face was like thunder. Nellie had just issued Gladys an instruction to remove some dozen or so broken beds, as a delivery of brand new ones was expected. "Could arrive any time Nurse Townsend, so if you wouldn't mind pushing these old ones into the corridor when you get a moment..."

Of all the nerve, simmered Gladys – trying to get me to do a porter's job!

Nellie and the builders laughed again, Gladys felt sure they were talking about her. Just then Matron walked in. "Why are these old beds still in the way?"

"Oh, Nurse Townsend's dealing with them Matron," said Nellie.

"Very well, what are you waiting for Nurse Townsend?"

Gladys gave a truculent stare, "Begging your pardon Matron, but shifting beds is porters' work."

"The porters are busy elsewhere." She turned to the builders, "perhaps these fellows could assist -"

"Oh sorry Matron," interceded Nellie, "the boys are busy with the new window frames – they've got to get them in by tonight or the patients will freeze - this is the first tea break they've had all day." The builders mumbling in agreement hurriedly drained their mugs and picked up their tools. The last thing they wanted was to be seconded to 'Grisly Gladys.'

"And I've got a meeting now," added Nellie quickly, "with Miss Stephenson and the architect.

Matron raised her eyebrows but made no comment. Turning back to Gladys she said, "I'm afraid it's a case of all hands to the pump during these refurbishments Nurse Townsend – so if you could see to it personally that these beds are shifted I would be grateful."

"But Matron - I really must protest…!" began Gladys.

"And *I* must insist," said the Matron crisply. "You have been given an order, please carry it out. Any more insubordination and I shall be forced to reconsider your position at this hospital."

When she had left Gladys cornered Nellie at the door. "You'll pay for this lady," she hissed, "I'll make sure you do."

Nellie returned the hard stare, "Better get shifting beds Gladys Townsend – or you'll be outside with a begging bowl."

"I don't beg from no-one," snarled Gladys, "least of all a fairground tart like you – you'll get what's coming to you - mark my words!"

Nellie said no more and left the ward with a defiant stride. Inside however she could feel herself shaking.

Richard Neame put the key in the latch then froze. He had just returned from Charing Cross Road with a rare second-hand biography of Mozart, and was looking to relaxing over it with a glass of wine in his apartment at Drayton Terrace, when he heard the authoritative voice behind him: "Just a moment sir."

Turning he saw a thick-set moustachioed man in a trilby hat and trench coat, accompanied by two uniformed London 'Bobbies.' Drawn up at the pavement was a large unmarked Humber. "Might I ask who you are sir?" asked the man in the trench coat.

"Richard Neame, I'm a Canadian citizen staying in London on business – who the hell are you?"

"Inspector Collier, we're here on business too sir – police business. I would advise you to wait outside, this won't take long – all right lads follow me."

As they mounted the steps the front door opened to reveal Mrs Goldstein. Ignoring Richard she said, "Upstairs, second door – she won't give you no trouble."

Inspector Collier touched his trilby, "Much obliged Mrs Goldstein."

A moment later there came shouts and a woman screaming from the first floor, then Nellie appeared on the stairs, her arms pinioned by the policemen, and struggling frantically. "Let me go you brutes, I haven't done anything...let me go I say, I'll have the law on you...!"

"We are the law."

"I'll swing for you if you don't let me go now!"

"Now, now, that's enough of that," advised Collier calmly, "you can tell us all about it down at the station." Turning to Richard he said, "Sorry about that sir, you can go in now."

"Just a minute," said Richard barring their way, "what's the charge against this young lady?"

"Theft sir."

"Well what proof do you have?"

"This for a start." Inspector Collier held up a gold bracelet. "Found in her room – the owner reported it stolen yesterday."

"How do you know it's this one – this could be her own property...?"

"There's an inscription look: RB - now if you don't mind sir we'll be on our way. I suggest you go in and check you have nothing missing."

Mrs Goldstein, who stood triumphant in the doorway, curled her lip. "Yeah, no trusting fairground rabble like that, I knew she was a wrong 'un soon as I clapped eyes on her."

Nellie, still writhing in the strong arms of the officers was hauled down the steps to the waiting car. One then produced a pair of handcuffs and secured them about her wrists. As they were about to put her in the car Nellie threw back her head and cried out plaintively to Richard: "Tell Audrey, the bracelet's mine, I swear on my mother's life...for god's sake please...tell Audrey...!"

It was just past 6pm when Richard reached Audrey's flat. The taxi had made good time through the early evening traffic

Audrey opened the door, a wide smile appearing as she soon as she saw him. "Richard, what a wonderful surprise," she exclaimed. "To what do I owe this honour? Do come in and have a drink- why Richard you look so serious, whatever's the matter, is something wrong -?"

"Nellie's been arrested."

"Arrested? But why, when…"

"This afternoon – lets sit down and I'll explain."

They sat down together on the sofa, Audrey's expression anxious, desperate for information. As Richard described the scene he had witnessed outside Drayton Terrace less than an hour before, Audrey's face grew ashen.

"Well, what do you think," he said. "Is Nellie guilty?"

"Of course not," gasped Audrey in disbelief, "How could you think such a thing, there's obviously been some ghastly mistake."

"Look, how well do you actually know her – she's from the fairground right?"

"What difference does that make? You said she told them the bracelet was hers, and that she swore so on her mother's life - what more do you want? Unless you're saying all fairground folk are thieves and liars!"

Richard said ruefully, "I'm sorry, that was a bad assumption – but the police seemed pretty sure – they said the bracelet found in her room had been reported stolen."

Really – by whom?"

"They didn't say."

"There you are then."

"Meaning?"

"Meaning there's more to this than meets the eye – and besides, how did the police go straight to Nellie?"

"I guess someone tipped them off."

"And you said Mrs Goldstein was there?"

"Yeah – seems like she was in on the arrest."

"I might have known!" Audrey clenched her fists, "she's the crook – you remember I told you about her and Gladys Townsend?"

"The rumour about fencing stolen goods?"

"Exactly – I saw them in the hall that day at Drayton Terrace, furtive as a pair of ferrets, and Gladys has had it in for me and Nellie for a long time – I'll bet my last farthing she's behind this."

"Ok," said Richard slowly, "but what can we do?"

"I don't know, oh, I don't know," said Audrey biting her lip. She began to pace the room, "There must be someone we can call, someone we can talk to...there must be a way we can help Nellie, but I just don't how -"

"I hate to point this out Audrey," said Richard, "but why would Nellie be the rightful owner of a bracelet inscribed RB?"

Audrey halted in the middle of the room and stared distraughtly at Richard: "Oh gracious you don't suppose she really did steal it?" She tore at her hair, "Oh my goodness what am I saying! ...I don't know what to think..."

"Come on Audrey, get your coat." Richard stood up decisively.

"Why, where are we going?"

"To the fair Richard, I've got to see Mrs Chidlow."

CHAPTER TWENTY

"I wish I were bringing you happier news Mrs Chidlow."
Audrey's expression was solemn as she spoke these words to
Nellie's mother.

At Richard's suggestion they had hailed a taxi to Hampstead
Heath, and were now sitting in Nellie's mother's cosy caravan
having told her the events of that evening.

"We thought we ought to speak with you first Mrs Chidlow
before going to the police," said Richard, "we wanted to hear it from
you that Nellie's no thief."

Audrey looked anxiously at Mrs Chidlow; she had tried to
warn Richard beforehand that such a question about her daughter
was unlikely to be well received.

"Don't look so scared," said Mrs Chidlow observing
Audrey's nervousness, "I won't bite his head off. You done right Mr
Bream."

"Neame."

"There's many a thief among those what calls themselves fair
folk."

"So I understand Mrs Chidlow, so forgive me- "

"But we are true Romanies – we speak honest and we do
honest, by one and all. So hear this – my Nellie's as straight as a die,
it's the way we was all brought up – isn't that right mother?"

"Aye" In the corner armchair Mrs Chidlow's mother bared
her gold teeth and screwed her features into an expression of deep
and inscrutable wisdom.

Audrey and Richard exchanged a glance. "So Mrs Chidlow,"
began Audrey carefully, "This bracelet of Nellie's – the police say
someone has identified it as belonging to them…"

"Then, they're a cursed liar!" glowered Mrs Chidlow jabbing
her index finger at Audrey.

"Aye – a cursed liar!" repeated the old lady.

"That's just what we said," retreated Audrey, "wasn't it
Richard?"

"Oh absolutely. So tell me, where did Nellie get the
bracelet?"

"Given to her when she was sixteen years old as a good luck
charm by old Ruby Barrett the palm reader."

"RB - " chorused Audrey and Richard immediately.

"Solid gold it is – worth a tidy sum, that's why she don't wear it."

"Would this Ruby be prepared to come down to the police station and testify to that?"

"That would be difficult," sighed Mrs Chidlow.

"Aye, difficult," repeated her mother.

"Seeing as how she's upstairs."

"Upstairs," Richard looked nonplussed.

"Passed over just before Christmas, two years ago now."

"Oh, sorry," chorused Richard and Audrey.

"Ruby never liked coppers when she was alive, gawd rest her soul, and I don't suppose she feels any different where she is now. No, I'll come down to that police station me self, and tell 'em the bracelet hers fair and square and to let my girl go – I'll get me husband to take me there tonight, he's out doing a bit of tottin' at the moment, but soon as he's back we'll go, just give us the address."

"We would gladly take you," frowned Richard, "but sadly Mrs Chidlow I fear your testimony alone may not be enough."

"You mean the coppers will say a mother's bound to stick up for her daughter, whether she's guilty or not?"
Richard nodded and stared intently into the glowing coals of the stove, deep in thought. "What we need is a plan – one that will free Nellie, and lead the police to the real culprits."

"What kind of a plan?" asked Audrey.

"Aye," wheezed old Mother Chidlow her gold teeth glinting in the glow of the stove, "what kind of a plan?"

"Gladys?"

"Who is this?"

"It's Mick – from the fairground, remember? You and me walked out a few times when you was a barmaid at the Jack Straw's…"

"I'm sure I don't know what you mean," declared Gladys imperiously. She had been on the ward when Matron had called her away to the 'phone. Now alone she gripped the receiver and pushed the door closed discreetly with her foot.

"You've got a nerve," she hissed, "haven't you got enough to do running that crummy boxing booth of yours instead of bothering me like this, I've got responsibilities here, a respectable position, I want nothing more to do with the likes of you, do your hear."

"Don't be like that Glad, I know you gave me the elbow but there's no hard feelings. The thing is, I always look after me friends, and I've got a little proposition for you."

"What are you talking about?

"Something as might benefit you, in a manner of speaking."

"Such as?"

"Some nice bits of jewellery, look lovely on a beautiful girl like you, or you might want to sell them to some friends, worth a fortune."

"What's your game?"

"Don't give me that Glad – we both know you're still in the old tomfoolery lark, and this stuff's class believe me, and you can have it all for a snip - bring you in a lot of folding, know what I mean."

There was a lengthy pause then Gladys said guardedly, "All right, supposing I might be interested?"

"I'll come and see you…"

"No – not here – listen, I'm off tomorrow afternoon, I'll meet you at the Jack Straw's, 3 o'clock. It'll be quiet in the snug."

"All right - oh, and be sure to bring Mrs Goldstein with you."

"Eh? Ma Goldstein? What do you want her there for?"

"She's got an eye for quality."

"No – she'll want a cut, no…"

"She's also the best fence in London – she'll get you top money, it'll be worth your while cutting her in, she knows the right people and they'll pay handsome – knock this lot out and you could be live like a queen and never have to work again."

"All right, I'll bring her, but we'll not pay over the odds for anything mind."

"You always did drive a hard bargain Glad, in business and pleasure – but you was worth it girl!"

"How dare you! What are you implying?"

"Nothing, nothing."

"Good, I want no funny business, just be at the Jack at three sharp."

"Oh and Glad, would you wear that dress I always liked, you know the one with the…"

Gladys blushed, "I've got to go." She said smiling and put the phone down.

The Jack Straw's Castle was festooned with Christmas garlands hanging from the oak wooden beams and stretching across the small bar. A tall fir tree, adorned with baubles and tinsel stood proudly in the corner of the snug by the window filling the space from floor to ceiling, with the Christmas fairy bending forward at a very precarious angle.

It was, as Gladys predicted, quiet in the pub. By 3pm the dog walkers from Hampstead Heath had downed their drinks and departed, and aside from a solitary grey haired old gentleman, dozing over the Times crossword, the snug was deserted.
Gladys and Mrs Goldstein, entering stealthily through the side door found Mick, the fairground pugilist already arrived, his overlarge powerful frame filling the chair, his pockmarked features and variously broken nose the telltale legacy of the ring.

"Gladys -" he rose, towering over the table and held out his ham-sized arms, "what about a kiss for old times' sake?"

"This is business," said Gladys curtly, "We'll get straight down to it if you don't mind." She and Mrs Goldstein sat down.

"At least let's have a drink?"

"Port and lemon."

"Same," said Mrs Goldstein, lighting up a Woodbine.
As Mick returned with the drinks and a glass of stout for himself, Gladys retreated into her headscarf, wary of the barman's gaze.

"Oh, you're safe here Glad," assured Mick, "they don't like talking to the law, gets the pub a bad name."

"Surprised they even let you in," Gladys remarked.

"They're pleased for the trade while its quiet – 'sides I've got me best whistle and flute on," he ran a hand over his ill-fitting tweed jacket.

"Ooh, quite the gent aren't we," sniped Mrs Goldstein joining in the sarcasm. "Call that a suit? I've seen better rags on a scarecrow."

"Here, here," said Mick, "I've a good mind to take my bit of tom elsewhere…"

"Keep your voice down," hissed Gladys, then patted his hand and gave him an oily smile, "We were only having a bit of fun, weren't we Bessie?"
"Yeah, only a bit of fun," croaked Mrs Goldstein, her ash laden cigarette waggling up and down in her mouth. "No need to take on."

"That's all right," smiled Mick, "Glad always did like a laugh. Now then ladies, to start us off, feast your mincies on this." From an inside pocket he drew something out and placed it carefully on the table. It was a gold bracelet. Gladys examined it. Suddenly she emitted a strangulated cry.

"What's your game!" she snarled flinging the bracelet back at him.

"Eh – what do you mean?" Mick stared at her innocently. Under the table Mrs Goldstein nudged her. "Let me have a look Glad." She scrutinised the bracelet for a few seconds then turned to Mick, "Where'd you get this?"

"Let's just say it came into my possession,"

"Well we won't be retiring on this Glad," said Mrs Goldstein.

"There's a lot more where that came from ladies."

"Well we'll give you five quid for the bracelet," said Mrs Goldstein."

Gladys stared, "Are you out of your mind Bessie? That's..."
Mrs Goldstein once again nudged her to be silent. "I think Gladys and myself would like to confer in private, would you mind?"

"I can take a hint," said Mick. "Ding-ding, seconds out - I'll take me stout and sit in the sunshine for five minutes, let you girls battle it out."

When he had gone, Gladys jerked her head towards the old man in the corner of the snug, "What about him?"

"Don't worry, he's out for the count," said Mrs Goldstein. The old man's snoring was indeed now audible.

"So what we going to do?" said Gladys. "That bracelet's 22 carat, worth fifty quid at least. How come he's got it now?"
Mrs Goldstein shrugged, "A bent copper sold it to him, who knows?"

"I don't like it – it's too much of a coincidence."

"So what - we can get it back for a tenner and still be in the money, and the girl's in chokey. And you wont be chancing your arm trying to get it back down the nick."
Gladys breathed out hard, "All right, if you're sure it's worth what you say."

"I can get fifty for it tomorrow."

"Shush, here he comes."

Mick was peering round the door. Mrs Goldstein beckoned to him. Slipping a ten-pound note under a beer mat she pushed it across the table.

"We've agreed it's worth ten."

"Hmm, how about fifteen?" said Mick.

Gladys was about to retort: "Take it or leave it" when someone else spoke: "Now don't be greedy young man."

The two women span round aghast to see the grey haired old gentleman in the corner rise from his chair, and with surprising agility stride towards them.

"Besides you're supposed to be performing this little drama in the interests of justice, not for personal gain."

Before the astonished eyes of the women, the old man then carefully peeled off his moustache, followed by the grey mop of hair. The elderly figure in the armchair, had transformed into a sharp eyed, fit looking middle-aged man stood before them.

Mick grinned up at him. "Just waiting for you to make your move guv – I was beginning to think you'd really nodded off there for a minute! Ladies, may I introduce Inspector Collier of the CID. This is Bessie Goldstein, fence extraordinaire, and Gladys Townsend her accomplice."

Gladys and Mrs Goldstein who had sat open mouthed and staring during this extraordinary scene now began to speak.

"I don't what you're talking about," blustered Gladys, "I'm just out for a quiet drink with my friend…"

"That's right," spat Mrs Goldstein, "you can't pin nothing on us," she jabbed a finger at Mick, "this feller's been pestering us, trying to sell us hooky jewellery, I demand you arrest him."

"The only ones being arrested today are yourself and Miss Townsend – for theft, deception and receiving stolen goods."

"Where's your evidence?" snapped Gladys, her eyes darting and unpredictable like those of a vicious, cornered animal.

"I heard quite sufficient from that armchair."

"That's just your word against ours -"

"As did these good people." Inspector Collier coughed loudly. From behind the bar rose Audrey, Richard Neame, Mr and Mrs Chidlow, and last of all Nellie.

"Cor it ain't half dusty down there," Nellie said brushing herself down as all four shuffled out and came into the snug to join Inspector Collier. "Don't fancy your old barmaid's job back Gladys? Oh no, you're off to chokey aren't you, shame."

Gladys sprang to her feet, "Why you little tart – I'll swing for you yet."

Grabbing Mick's beer glass she brought it down violently on the table smashing off the end, and aiming the jagged edge at Nellie's throat lunged towards her. Quick as lighting Mick's arm flew out and held Gladys's wrist in a vice-like grip. "Now, now, no rough stuff Glad, someone could get hurt."

Inspector Collier called out, "All right." Two uniformed constables marched through the door and handcuffed both women. "Take them to the station," ordered the Inspector, "I'll be along shortly." He turned to Nellie, "Well, you're free to go young lady, I'm sorry about what we put you through."

"All's well that ends well," sighed Nellie taking her bracelet.

"Though I know what Ruby Barrett would have said," muttered Mrs Chidlow, "bleeding coppers don't know their a…"

"Shush," cautioned her husband.

"As a matter of fact," smiled Collier, "I do recall one thing the real Madame Ruby told me all those years ago at Margate – she said that I would one day come into some money."

Taking Mrs Goldstein's ten-pound note from the table he held it aloft. "Strictly speaking this money is the proceeds of crime and I should confiscate it – however, I think an unofficial award for gallantry in assisting a police officer is in order – on the strict proviso it is donated to the fairground children's benevolent fund, of which I understand you are the custodian young man."

He handed the ten pounds to Mick, who nodded gratefully, while Nellie, Audrey, Mr and Mrs Chidlow, Richard and the barman, who had just reappeared broke into spontaneous applause. Nellie and Audrey hugged one another tightly.

"And I suppose," mused Collier taking out his wallet, "that since I made such a frightful mess of this case in the first place, I had better try to win back your respect for 'coppers' by making this my round." Then raising his eyes aloft he added, "And one for you too, Madame Ruby."

"Hear, hear!" they all chorused. "Now we can have a real good Christmas."

CHAPTER TWENTY-ONE

September 1947

"Well?" asked Audrey.

Nellie shook her head, "No, it's a sight for sore eyes and nothing more Aud – and to think we actually lived there!"

The newly painted 'For Sale' board outside Drayton Terrace had the effect of making the old Victorian terraced house look even more dilapidated. Mrs Goldstein and her partner in crime Gladys Townsend, found guilty on multiple charges of theft, receiving stolen property and demanding money with menaces, were now beginning their fifteen year sentences in Holloway prison. It had then been discovered that Mrs Goldstein during her time as landlady had run up large accounts with a number of local traders. To meet these debts the judge had decreed that her property must now be confiscated and put on the market.

Audrey, fired by the success of bringing the nefarious pair to justice, and clearing Nellie's good name, had immediately come up with the idea of buying the place for the Regent Trust. She and Nellie were now stood outside on the pavement considering the matter; or more precisely, Audrey was trying to convince her friend of the good sense of her plan.

"A lick of paint and some flowers in the window - that's all it needs."

Nellie gazed up at the crumbling stucco and the pigeons nesting in the rusted gutters. "How about a stick of dynamite and steamroller?"

"Oh Nell, don't be like that."

"Sorry," Nellie gave a rueful smile. "I just thought you'd be glad to see the back of this dump, now you're in clover. And we've got our hands full as it is with the hospital and the hotel conversion."

"That's the whole point," replied Audrey.

"Eh?"

Audrey turned to her friend, "Because the house is a dump as you put it, we can get it for a good price. Our builders will be finishing the hospital alterations in a few days, and the hotel is coming on splendidly." She waved a hand towards the old house they had once both inhabited, "Drayton Terrace can be our next acquisition for the Regent Trust."

"What are we going to do with it though – another hotel?"

"Proper homes for working people," said Audrey, "not a slum or a workhouse but spacious, comfortable accommodation."

"I could do with that myself," sighed Nellie, "it's nice to be with Whillan of a night time, but Mum and Dad's caravan's feeling a mite crowded since I left this old place."

"Oh Nell, I said you could stay with me in Kensington," protested Audrey.

"I know, but like I said before I couldn't impose."

"In that case we'll convert the top floor here straightaway, put in a kitchen and bathroom and allocate it as Regent Trust management staff quarters – that means you Nell – if you wish of course."

"Really?"

"You won't recognise the place, you'll have room for Whillan to stay too, and you can be in charge of converting the rest of the building."

"Well, I wouldn't say no to that," Nellie beamed.

"Consider it done," smiled Audrey.

"Oh but what about your Richard, where's he going? Sorry, when I say 'your Richard' I didn't meant to imply, that is I wasn't um…." Nellie tailed off sheepishly.
Audrey laughed out loud, "No need to apologise," she said cheerily, "Richard's already gone…"

"Oh Aud I am sorry, and you were getting along so well, me and my big mouth…"

"No, no, I mean he's moved out from here. "He's taken an apartment near mine. And yes, he is 'my Richard. At least I think he is, if having dinner together and walking hand in hand along the embankment on a number of moonlit evenings means something like ownership. I can confirm we are courting yes, though I know I mustn't count any chickens," she sighed.

"Oh I'm so glad." Nellie gave her friend a spontaneous hug.

"Now," said Audrey briskly, we must get to work," and taking out her diary she wrote down the name of the estate agent.

"The estimates for the refurbishments sir." Audrey smiled as she placed the paperwork on Oliver Regent's desk, "You said you wantcd to see them?"

"Hmm? Oh yes, thank you." Regent put on his spectacles and scrutinized the columns of figures. "It seems rather excessive." He looked at Audrey carefully. "Double what I would expect. Is your architect doing his job? And what about the clerk of works?"

"Clerk of...? Oh, we um, don't exactly have one of those sir."

Regent raised an eyebrow. "Maybe I should be overseeing things-"

"NO!" Audrey's heart missed a beat. "Sorry, I mean - Mr Regent - it's not that I wouldn't welcome your assistance, its that your time is far too valuable - the work has overrun, we had some problems, which should have been resolved beforehand, it's my fault, I'm sorry..."

Regent raised a hand, "I wasn't questioning you my dear, simply saying that if you need help – "

Audrey lowered her eyes. "I am sorry Mr Regent, I feel I have let you down."

Oliver Regent rose from his chair and came around the desk. Placing his hand under her chin he gently lifted her head.

"Nonsense my dear," he purred. "Life is full of unforeseen events. We all of us, make mistakes. But how we learn from them is what counts. You are learning every day, and I am very pleased with all you are doing for the Trust. As a man sows, so shall he reap, isn't that what the Bible tells us? What you are doing on the Trust's behalf is an investment, I am very well aware of that, and in time it will reap rich rewards for us, enabling us of course to do even more good work for the unfortunate of this world." He looked lost in thought for a moment then said, "Shall I let you into a little secret my dear?"

Audrey felt a stab of fear. What was he about to say, which of his terrible deeds was he about to admit to? And why to her, why now, what was coming? She stared into his eyes, two mesmerising pools of black behind which there seemed only impenetrable space, the eyes of a dead person. She shivered as if all the blood had suddenly left her body. "If you – if you think it...wise sir," she whispered almost inaudibly.

He nodded slowly, as if coming to some momentous decision. There was a pause that seemed to Audrey to last a lifetime.

"Well," he went on at last, "don't breathe a word of this to anyone my dear, and I know I can trust you, but a certain shall we say 'little bird', one who sits on a very high tree in this great country of ours, has told me that one day quite soon, people will be calling me: 'Lord Regent'. What do you make of that?"

Audrey stammered, "How very – nice that would be sir."

Olivier Regent smiled like a fiendish schoolboy who has pulled off a clever prank, "Yes, wouldn't it." He turned and began pacing the room now, warming to his theme. "It would be in recognition of all the good work the Regent Trust has achieved of course, and with my ah, elevation - your contribution to the even greater successes of the Trust will not go un-rewarded, of that you have my promise."

"Oh – really sir, I don't think - "

"Nonsense, don't be so modest. Now run along – but remember, not a word. Oh and keep this Saturday evening free, there's a ball at the Grosvenor House, the cream of London society will be in attendance, and I would like you to be there too, as my guest. It will be an ideal opportunity for you to tell people all about our latest plans for the Trust. There are many more wealthy sponsors who I am sure would be glad to help us."

Audrey made a sort of awkward curtsey and murmured, "Very good sir."

As she was about to leave the room, Oliver Regent opened his diary and without looking up said, "Oh and I would like see all the accounts for the work you have paid for so far - I don't need to remind you that every penny has to be accounted for. Would you fetch them for me now please?"

Audrey, putting a hand to her face, which had suddenly gone scarlet stuttered, "They're – with the accountant at the moment - "

"Oh you've appointed an accountant? I knew you were sensible. All right, well get everything to me as soon as you can. That's all. "

Half an hour later Audrey was in the back of a taxi threading its way through the murky back streets of Whitechapel. "Did you say Leeming and Holt miss? It's just on your left here." The driver pulled over by a grimy Victorian building. "Four and eleven pence please."

Audrey climbed the narrow stairs and knocked on the office door.

"Come in please."

A thin middle-aged man with receding grey hair was sat behind a desk piled high with folders. Seeing Audrey he rose awkwardly.

"Good afternoon madam, how may I help you?"

"Leeming and Holt?"

"I'm Mr Leeming – my partner Mr Holt is at lunch…"

"Good, it is you whom I wish to see Mr Leeming. I am Miss Stephenson."

"Stephenson, Stephenson…" Mr Leeming scratched his head, "the name rings a…oh – the Stephenson Trust?"

"Yes, I wrote to you asking to prepare accounts in that name."

"I've sent them to you, every month, next one will be posted to you shortly, to the Kensington address as usual? I hope everything was in order, I received your cheque for the work."

"Yes quite thank you."

"Well, what can I do for you?"

"I wish you to make up a new set of accounts."

"Oh – yes by all means, glad to oblige. If you'd care to take a seat Miss Stephenson and give me the particulars." He removed a stack of ledgers from the only other available chair.

"The items," said Audrey as she sat down, "you already have. All that needs to be changed is the name on the accounts – and the figures pertaining to each item must all be – adjusted."

"I'm sorry I don't quite understand – the Stephenson Trust has changed its name - and the figures need to be adjusted? Could you explain why? This all sounds somewhat irregular if you don't mind my saying so."

Lowering her voice Audrey said, "You were previously engaged by the Regent Trust."

Mr Leeming paled, and she noticed him swallow hard before replying, "What about it?"

"Your services were dispensed with rather abruptly I believe."

He eyed her suspiciously. "What's this all about?"

"You found discrepancies in the Regent Trust accounts."

Mr Leeming went paler still. "Did I?" he said guardedly, "perhaps I did, perhaps I didn't - how would you know?"

"Because," said Audrey leaning closer, "I found them too. Serious discrepancies, we're not just talking about a few pennies short, but thousands of pounds of charitable donations over a number of years, huge amounts of money given in good faith for the Regent Trust's work among the poor - money that apparently just vanished into thin air. This is what you found Mr Leeming. It is the reason you were sacked, and why you're nervous about talking to me now."

Leeming, agitated got up and moved to the door. "Look I'm afraid I don't know what you're talking about – I'm sorry I have an appointment..."

"No Mr Leeming, you do not. Please sit down. You have nothing to fear from me. What passes between us will go no further." He was breathing hard. "Look, all right, there were some gaps in the accounts, great holes you're right – I brought it to Regent's attention and the next day I was told they no longer needed me. On my way home someone followed me, a big man, not the sort of man one likes to get entangled with. He cornered me in a dark alley and told me to keep my mouth shut or else. You can understand my reticence."

"Of course," said Audrey. "Regent is a powerful man, and a dangerous one.

Leeming nodded grimly. "So, what exactly do you want from me?"

"Your help."

"To do what?"

"To take Oliver Regent for every penny he's got."

Audrey knocked boldly on the oak-panelled door of Oliver Regent's office and waited to be summoned.

"Come in"

With a polite "Good morning sir," she strode up to his desk and set down a green, leather-bound ledger. "The accounts as requested. I think you'll find them in order."

Mr Leeming had worked swiftly since their meeting in Whitechapel; the thick plain brown parcel had been delivered that morning to Audrey's apartment. A quick glance through showed he had also done a thorough and convincing job, every expenditure itemed with invoices and receipts for services and materials exact copies of the originals, right down to the signatures; all that was different were the typed figures.

Oliver Regent donned his gold-rimmed spectacles. He smiled and nodded courteously, but said nothing. Having not been invited to sit down, Audrey remained standing. She watched anxiously as he opened the ledger and began to study it, his keen eyes scanning each entry, checking and re-checking the columns meticulously, comparing every item against every item, figure against figure, reciting his calculations to himself in a soft whisper like a medieval monk reciting some sacred text.

Audrey waited with beating heart, not daring to comment or attempt explanation. At one point his expression changed, his eyes narrowing with suspicion, turning the same page back and forth again and again. Audrey's fingers gripped the folds of her skirt; had Mr Leeming made some fatal error? Or perhaps he was playing a game with her, pretending to spot a discrepancy to see how she reacted, hoping she might betray her deception…she must be calm, calm…

He closed the ledger, took off his spectacles and looked at her, his features immobile, unreadable.

After a moment Audrey could bear the silence no longer. "I trust everything is to your satisfaction sir?" Her voice seemed to her inaudible, subdued to a faint murmur, lost in the muffled heavily carpeted room with its ancient imposing panelled walls. Oliver Regent tapped his spectacles rhythmically on the desk, setting her nerves further on edge

"Well, now that I've seen this," he gestured to the ledger, "The question is, what do I do with you?"

"Is – is there a problem Mr Regent?" asked Audrey as nonchalantly as she dared, her voice again dropping away to the faintest murmur.

"Of course there's a problem." His face was hard, tense with thought.

"I'm sure any…oversight in the accounting can be rectified…"

"Oversight? There's no oversight – no, no there's nothing wrong with the accounts, in fact I've rarely seen such exemplary bookkeeping – and the property acquisitions, which were your idea will make the Regent Trust a fortune in due course. No you've proved yourself a shrewd businesswoman and an admirable administrator my dear. It is therefore imperative your talents now find a higher expression. Hence my problem."

She did not know whether to laugh or cry with relief. A second later however she had quite forgotten the dilemma, for his next words made her mouth fall wide open in astonishment.

"Audrey my dear how would like you to go to America?"

CHAPTER TWENTY-TWO

"All aboard that's staying aboard – all ashore that's going ashore!"

The embarkation officer, bellowing his command pushed his way through the throng of passengers, relatives and friends saying their last goodbyes on deck.

Audrey and Nellie were among them. Audrey's trip to America on behalf of the Regent Trust had been arranged at a giddying speed. Oliver Regent had issued no specific brief other than that she was to travel as a 'goodwill ambassador' for the Trust. He would be unable to accompany her due to demands on his time with the Trust in London, but assured her she would be escorted and looked after both on the voyage and during her stay, which was to be for two months.

"Going ashore madam?"

"Ooh heck that's me," said Nellie as the officer brushed past her again. "Though I wish I was staying aboard. Sailing on the Queen Mary! Me mum wouldn't half be impressed!"

"You've still got time to change your mind" said Audrey squeezing her wrist, "I'm sure if I tell the Captain you're on an urgent mission with the Regent Trust and I need you desperately he would find you a cabin."

"I'd love to Aud, but someone's got to keep an eye on Drayton Terrace and the hospital, and besides, me go all the way to America? I'd get awful seasick"

"How do you know?"

"Took a boat out on the Serpentine once with Whillan's dad – went green as a pea - he couldn't stop laughing bless him!"

Audrey smiled then said, "You must miss him awfully – oh gosh sorry Nell, I didn't mean to- " She saw the sadness now in her friend's eyes.

"Don't mind me - "

"All ashore that's going ashore...!"

"Look I'd better get down that gangplank, or I'll be sleeping in a lifeboat tonight."

"Oh Nell, I'm going to miss you," said Audrey as they flung out their arms and held each other in a tight embrace.

Nellie stood back and wiped a tear from her eye, "Go on with you, you'll have a whale of a time, and you deserve it too. Say hello to Roy Rogers for me, and Mr Rockefeller, and send us a postcard."

"I certainly will – go on Nell, quick, they'll be sounding the hooter in a minute."

"Be good Aud, and if you can't be good be careful!" Giving her friend a last peck on the cheek Nellie joined the jostling line of people now queuing to descend the gangplank.

Audrey stood wrapped in thought for a moment, then on a sudden impulse she ran to the ship's rail. Her eyes searching among the waving crowds, streamers and bustling porters she cried out, "Nell! Nell, remind me! What's your husband's surname?"

Nellie was halfway down the gangplank. She turned, straining her eyes back towards the huge vessel, its engines now running, the hooter blasting. Then cupping her hands to her mouth she called: "Westby! His - name - is - Curtis – West-by!"

It was a smooth sailing from Southampton docks. On a calm sea, beneath the blue skies of an English high summer the Queen Mary steamed majestically out of port, funnels billowing and her crew busy about their tasks. A sprinkling of passengers remained on deck watching the coast grow smaller, or, looking seaward, transfixed by the myriad little buds of foam that danced and bobbed all the way to the horizon. Others were already below, in high spirits and partaking of a celebratory drink in one of the lounges, or settling into their accommodation, the rich in their finely appointed state rooms, the not so rich in more basic accommodation, and those who had scrimped and scraped to travel 'steerage' on the world's most famous liner, working out the best way to fit their trunk and themselves into their small cabins on the lower decks.

Audrey gazed back towards the land until the chimneys of Southampton were but tiny splinters. Lost in thought she felt excitement but with it a degree of trepidation, wondering, not for the first time since the trip had been proposed, just what the great continent of America, so huge and amorphous and unknown to her held in store. Her exodus from Liverpool had seemed a large and daring enterprise, but in London she could easily and at any time have stepped on a train and returned within a day.

This was different; she would soon be on the vast Atlantic Ocean, and there was no turning back. Exactly what Oliver Regent expected of her though, and more importantly, how she might now use this distant excursion to her own advantage, Audrey had as yet no idea.

She felt a sudden intense desire to see Richard; they had spent a wonderful weekend in London prior to her leaving for Southampton; dinner and the theatre, and then a late night drink in a discreetly romantic candlelit bar. Richard had offered to postpone his business meeting the following day to come down and see her off, but Audrey had urged him not to; a more private au revoir here she insisted, was preferable to a snatched kiss on deck in broad daylight. Outside on the pavement their conversation faltered, Richard offering to see her home, both trembling with unspoken desire, fearful of spoiling the moment. After a passionate kiss Richard had whispered softly, "I'm going to miss you, be careful out there," and they had gone their separate ways.

With a stiff sea breeze getting up, the deck was by now almost deserted. Feeling the need to be among people Audrey made her way below. Passing an open door she heard the sound of children's laughter. In a spacious room the Queen Mary's nursery was already in full swing, with smiling tots, watched over by nannies and mothers, rode merrily aboard their own little toy boats and rocking horses. Audrey glanced nervously in, her eyes lighting immediately on a little girl. "Margaret...?" Hearing the stricken voice one of the nannies came over, "Have you lost your little girl madam?" Audrey felt the words as a dagger plunged into her heart. Unable to speak and clutching her throat she hurried away blindly down the companionway, stopping only when she could hear the children's voices no longer.

Trying to steady herself she made her way on, and came across a small lounge in which a few other passengers sat reading or in quiet conversation. A woman looked up from her book and surveyed her over her lorgnettes. Audrey nodded politely, the woman returned the solicitude and lowered her gaze again. Taking a newspaper from the rack Audrey settled into an armchair and closed her eyes, breathing slowly.

"May I get you anything madam?"

Opening her eyes she saw a steward stood to attention. "Oh, um thank you, a pot of tea please," she replied, "and perhaps some scones?"

"Certainly madam – jam and cream?"

"Yes – oh but wait, the sea's not likely to be rough later is it?"

Another voice provided the answer, "Don't worry Miss Stephenson the forecast is calm right the way past Land's End – it'll be like a mill pond out there for the next few hours at least. You could eat a horse if you wanted to and be fine – not that we serve horse of course, ha, ha!"

Audrey stared up at the affable, handsome young man in blue flannels who had just appeared. "No of course – look I'm sorry I have..."

"No idea who I am? Forgive me, Johnny Oxford, passenger liaison and entertainment officer. I've been asked to..."

"Entertain me?" said Audrey surprising herself at the playfulness of her tone; the experience at the nursery seemed to have rendered her slightly hysterical.

"Well, I'll do my best. My orders are to look after you while you're on board."

"You think I might get up to mischief?"

The young man put his head on one side. He smiled a rueful charming smile, a mischievous schoolboy's smile. "The Queen Mary is a big ship Miss Stephenson...."

"And I might get lost?"

"With a great many passengers; my job is to introduce you to the right ones, and to ensure your stay aboard is to your utmost satisfaction. You are travelling first class and I have seen to it your luggage has already been taken to your stateroom."

"You are most kind." Audrey said just as Briggs the steward arrived with the tea and scones. "Would you like some tea?"

Johnny shook his head, "Thank you but no, I won't intrude long. The Captain asks if this evening you would do him the honour of being his guest at dinner."

Hearing this the woman looked up from her lorgnettes again.

"How exciting!" exclaimed Audrey, feeling the hysteria again, and a sudden gay abandon, – she was on the Queen Mary with dinner at the Captain's table, a charming young officer to look after her – it was all quite too exciting, like being a little girl again given a surprise...oh! - but she must not, must not, must not think of Margaret...

"You can speak to me at any time, just mention my name to any of the crew and they'll send for me in a jiffy."

"Thank you Mr Oxford," said Audrey mildly, fighting down the calm.

Leaning over he said discreetly, "Please, call me Johnny – oh and by the way Mr Regent cables his best wishes. Dinner's at seven thirty in the First Class Lounge." With a polite salute he was gone.

Desiring to see her accommodation now Audrey finished her tea, and realising she had not touched her scones, took a napkin and with a furtive look round tucked the cakes into her handbag. She did not notice the woman in the lorgnettes peering discreetly from behind her book.

"May I introduce our distinguished American guests - Sylvester and Dilys Boothroyd, John and Mabel Fotheringay, Monty and Grace Walters," Johnny Oxford bowed towards Audrey, "Miss Audrey Stephenson, of the Regent Trust."

Audrey shook hands politely with each of her dinner companions. "Thank you Johnny," she smiled, "and thank you everyone, and please do all sit down again, you're really too kind."

"You sit down too honey," drawled Dilys Boothroyd, an imposing and ample figure in sequined black evening dress and pearl necklace, "it's so lovely to meet a real English aristocrat, and one so normal and homely with it, which I mean as an absolute compliment my dear – why some of the English nobility are quite without manners, which in South Carolina where I was brought up were the first requirement of any person expecting to be considered a lady or a gentleman. Here this is your place, next to me, we don't go in for the strict boy girl boy seating rule."

"Forgive my wife," said Sylvester Boothroyd; "she does go on sometimes - welcome aboard the Queen Mary my dear, if I may have the honour of saying so, and welcome to our table – which in the absence of the Captain I think we may refer to it..."

"Now who's going on?" broke in Dilys.

"There's nothing to forgive I assure you," smiled Audrey, "and if you'll forgive me – " There were gales of laughter.

"Whatever for?" asked Sylvester.

"For not being an English aristocrat, or any kind for that matter, my father was – is – in trade."

"That's what I mean about going on," nodded Mr Boothroyd, "I know more about you than my wife does, she will always get the wrong end of the stick."

"Oh but how refreshing to hear you say that," exclaimed Mrs Boothroyd to Audrey, "so many nonentities these days claiming this or that birthright or pedigree – I admire your honesty and straightforwardness my dear, and let's not forget that trade is what made both our countries great."

"And I'm going to drink to it," rejoined her husband, raising a glass of whiskey enthusiastically.

"Gracious!" exclaimed Johnny Oxford, "I quite forgot, the Captain sends his apologies, he's been detained on the bridge, and will join you all as soon as he can."

"You're sure that's not playing bridge Mr Oxford?" remarked Mabel Fotheringay archly as they all sat down, "I hear he likes a rubber or two."

"No, no, he's just checking the course, make sure we make the best time – the Queen Mary has her Blue Riband record to live up to don't forget."

"Oh to hell with the Blue Riband," said Monty Walters, "the best part of going between London and New York is being on the Queen Mary, and amongst such wonderful people - who wants to rush, I mean we all just love good conversation, good wine and food, and what better place to enjoy it than this incredible ship…?"

"Tell me, how much do Cunard pay you to shoot that line all night Monty?" The person who had interrupted was a mean faced man who had just sat down, rather unsteadily at the table. His dinner jacket was crumpled, his bow tie awry.

Monty smiled wearily, "Audrey dear this is George Fairweather the Fourth."

"Please forgive Mr Fairweather," apologised Mrs Fotheringay, "he's still finding his sea legs."

"Yes he's spent some time looking for them at the bar," quipped her husband.

George's expression became even harder. "At least the company's better there," he slurred sourly. "Decent, honest people, not the type to shoot you in the back if you know what I mean."

"George likes to joke," said Monty. "He has what they call a dry sense of humour."

"That's about all that is dry about him," chipped in Sylvester. There were more roars of laughter. George said nothing and cast a rheumy eye around the group.

"Well we all think the Regent Trust does a marvellous job, and that Mr Oliver Regent is an absolute hero," declared Dilys to warm murmurs of approval.

The Captain then joined them and shook hands with Audrey. As the meal got underway a series of separate conversations began around the table. Dilys turning to Audrey asked, "I understand you're travelling alone my dear?" Audrey nodded. "And you haven't a pooch in your cabin by any chance?"

"A dog? Goodness me no."

"Then you obviously enjoy scones as much as I do." She raised a pair of lorgnettes to her face and smiled.

"Oh my goodness," exclaimed Audrey, "it was you in the reading room earlier on..."

"I'm a great believer in the doggy bag myself, but I've never seen an English lady indulge the habit, congratulations."

Audrey was about to explain the 'habit' had been acquired when destitute in Jericho Road, the daily struggle for survival making every crust of bread count. Instead she said, "Well you see, at the Trust we value thrift..."

"How does thrift square with travelling First Class on the Queen Mary?" butted in Fairweather from across the table.

"Ignore him dear." Dilys advised.

"I'm so sorry I didn't recognise you from the reading room," said Audrey, "you look so different."

"I like to dress down during the day, can't wear too much makeup, plays havoc with the complexion, oh, and do try to avoid Mr Oxford."

"Johnny?"

Dilys nodded. "He's adorably cute," she whispered, "but will insist on talking endlessly at whoever he bumps into, and a frightful gossip, worse than a woman, I wouldn't be surprised if he were – you know what." She narrowed her eyes meaningfully, "many sailors are they say.

And you mustn't take any notice of George," she nodded in the direction of Fairweather, now staring moodily at his dessert, "he's not been the same since he lost all that money."

"He robbed me of it," snarled George.

"George your hearing is too acute for polite company – and your stories repetitive, as well as slanderous."

"Who does he mean by 'he''?" Audrey asked.

"That swine Regent," said George.

"It was a game of cards," said Sylvester leaning over, "George lost and Oliver won. Simple as that."

"How do all of you know Mr Regent?" enquired Audrey.

"We've been over England to do some business with him, for the charity of course."

"He never mentioned anything to me," said Audrey.
Sylvester smiled but did not reply.

"And its not just robbery," George continued, more loudly now.

"Oh?" murmured Audrey casually.
As George sat up to say more, John Fotheringay got swiftly to his feet,

"Miss Stephenson would you care for this dance?"

"Oh…thank you – but the band hasn't started yet -"

"They're about to."

Sure enough at that moment the bandleader waved his baton and the opening bars of 'Slow Boat to China' struck up. Half a dozen couples were soon up.

"Well yes, all right thank you," smiled Audrey, "if it's all right with Mrs Fotheringay."

Mabel Fotheringay waved her hand towards the dance floor, "You go ahead my dear, John always says I have two left feet – besides I want some more of that delicious trifle!"

"Thank you for a delightful evening," said Audrey as they all left the First Class Lounge.

"The pleasure was ours my dear." Mrs Boothroyd blew a kiss as she rejoined her American friends. "We'll see you in the morning I expect – a game of quoits if you're feeling the need for exercise, or perhaps a swim, the pool is heavenly, and heated. Sleep tight honey."

Audrey waved back then began to make her way below. Passing a half open cabin door she heard someone hiss.

"Hey sister – fancy a nightcap?"

Leaning in the doorway was George Fairweather. She was about to bid him a polite goodnight when something made her change her mind.

"Thank you Mr. Fairweather, that's most kind."

"No wise guy business you understand…." Beckoning her in he lurched across to a cocktail cabinet and poured out two glasses of brandy. "We're both alone, but I'm old enough to be your father – I think though we could both use a little company. Here's mud in your eye – its what we say in America – sit down- " he gestured to an armchair then flopped on the bed.

"Mud in your eye it is then," said Audrey raising her glass.

George was staring at her now, his face thoughtful, as if trying to come to some decision. "The fact is, I asked you to join me, because I want to tell you something – what I was trying to tell you before that heel Fotheringay decided to play the gallant gentleman – gentleman! That's a joke – those bums wouldn't know the meaning of the word. Oh they fool everyone with their money and their repartee and their fancy clothes…"

"What was it you wanted to tell me Mr Fairweather? Was it something about Mr Regent?"

George looked at her again, studying her face. "I think I was right about you sister. You're 'cute, real 'cute – that means smart on my side of the pond by the way. The fact is Miss Stephenson, that fine upstanding Mr Oliver Regent, business tycoon, philanthropist, friend of senators and statesmen and all round noble fellow, is a cold blooded killer."

Audrey regarded him steadily for a moment then replied, "That's a very serious accusation Mr Fairweather; on what grounds do you base it?"

Calmly George replied, "The fact that he murdered my wife." Audrey's face remained immobile for a few seconds then she replied, "Say that again?"

George's eyes were closed. His body had slumped down the bed, his head to one side, his brandy glass drooping on his chest.

"George - " Audrey rose and took the glass. "George?" she shook his shoulder. It was no good; George, full of dinner and fine wine and brandy and snoring heavily, was oblivious to the world. Audrey placed the brandy glass back on the cocktail cabinet and looked around the cabin. There was not much to see, a copy of Life Magazine on the bedside locker, and on a stand in the corner a suitcase. Audrey felt a sudden compulsion to open it and took hold of the catches. Hearing a faint noise outside from the companionway she froze then tiptoed to the door. Opening it cautiously she looked out. There was no one to be seen.

With a last glance back at the snoring George she closed the cabin door and made her way swiftly along the companionway. Halfway along, hearing footsteps she hesitated and turned to see a man in an evening suit, suddenly appeared from nowhere coming up behind her, his head lowered. As he squeezed past her Audrey drew in her breath on glimpsing his face; which bore a long scar ran diametrically from the left cheekbone to the top of the mouth. Murmuring, "Excuse me," on an impulse of curiosity she then hurried after him. But when she turned the corner he had vanished.

The next morning Audrey woke early, her mind full of the previous evening's events – the effusive Americans, George's dramatic accusation against Oliver Regent, and the sinister scar-faced man in the companionway.

Over dinner the American party had all of them seemed entirely dismissive of George, writing him off as a fantasist – at best a mildly amusing drunk, at worst a slanderous bore. Yet it was this very consistency of their attitude that only made Audrey more intrigued – that and the conversation she had overheard several weeks previously between her mother and Oliver Regent – John Bamford to be more precise.

George's words replayed over and again in her head: He murdered my wife…If a man could kill once he could kill again, and if he had something to gain from disposing of poor George's wife, then he would surely have little compunction in doing so.

Audrey also realised that suddenly out of the blue she had a potentially crucial ally; someone, assuming George could be believed, with knowledge of Bamford's evil. But she had to find out more, and somehow try to keep hold of George – but how? She must speak to him alone when he was sober she decided, obtain his address in America, gain his trust and establish some kind of agreement or secret alliance with him, which at some point could be called upon. How this would work in practice, and what exactly she envisaged doing when the time seemed right she could not as yet envisage, but one thing was clear in her mind: one way or another, legally and openly, or through some other means she would break him, and George could be a vital weapon in her armoury.

After breakfasting in her cabin she washed dressed, and pulling on a broad brimmed hat, went up on deck. The hat was a deliberate disguise; she wanted if possible to avoid the Americans till she had first located George. Passing a cocktail bar she peered in; sure enough George was sat on a stool conversing with an amiable looking middle-aged man in club blazer and slacks.

"Why hello," George greeted her, taking her hand and kissing it ostentatiously. "Harry this is Miss um…"

"Miss Stephenson," said Audrey, "How do you do?"

"Oh you're English," said Harry approvingly, "I don't feel so outnumbered, though George is splendid company, we're both on the hair of the dog – are you alone? May I buy you a Singapore Sling?"

"Thank you it's a little early for me – but perhaps a tomato juice."

"Make it a Bloody Mary!" suggested George.

"If you insist," Audrey relented.

"I do!" Harry smiled, "A Bloody Mary and two large G and Ts over here…"

While Harry bantered affably with the barman Audrey turned to George, "Listen I've got to speak to you about last night…"

"Yes, I must apologise -"

"No need – but you must tell me everything you know about Oliver Regent, about what happened to your wife."

George's expression narrowed. "Not here." Emitting a sort of cough he shot a look towards the back of the bar. Audrey followed his eyes then gave a start; sitting in the corner was the scar-faced man she seen the previous night in the companionway.

"Who is he?" she mouthed.

"That's just it," murmured George, "I don't know..."

"Mind if join you?" Johnny Oxford, beaming and glowing with health had just breezed in. "Orange juice please Jack, and make it a small one."

"Go easy on that stuff young man," Harry joshed. "Don't want you drunk in charge of the dance troupe."

"Chance would be a fine thing," returned Johnny enigmatically. "I do hope you enjoyed your first evening with us Miss Stephenson?"

"Very much, thank you."

"Marvellous I'm so glad, well if there's anything you need just ask for me – oh here's Dilys and Sylvester, with Mabel and John - *would* you excuse me, I simply must talk to them about the seating for the last night, if one doesn't organise these things well in advance its utter chaos – you'll be with us at Captain's table for the grand New York arrival dinner of course?"

"Oh, um yes I...suppose so," said Audrey vaguely.

"I'll put you down – in the best possible sense of course!" chortled Johnny, his full laugh showing off perfect, gleaming white teeth. "See you on deck later I expect."

Harry had by this time got into a discussion with an elderly military type about the Burma campaign, and the bar having now filled up Audrey and George were hidden from the corner of the room by an eagerly conversing throng. Audrey took her chance. "George, let's go somewhere - we need to talk, in private."

George looked thoughtful for a moment then rose from his stool.

"All right, but not together – wait two minutes then come to my cabin. I'll have some lunch sent down – you like spaghetti, red wine? Good, and remember, two minutes and make sure to leave the bar by the port side door."

Audrey sipped her Bloody Mary and looked at her watch. She felt conspicuous in the bar now as she seemed to be the only unaccompanied woman. When two minutes had ticked by she picked up her handbag and made for the port side exit as George had instructed. Reaching the door she felt a hand grasp her wrist. It was Mabel Fotheringay.

"Audrey my dear, you must give us your advice – Dilys and Sylvester are considering buying a house in London but just can't decide where– would you offer your wisdom?"

"I'd be delighted Mrs Fotheringay – perhaps over dinner this evening...?"

"Oh no, come and join us now, we'd so appreciate your company – besides we can't let you wander about this great big ship all alone after that Bloody Mary I just saw you put away my dear, who knows what might happen to you?" Mabel Fotheringay wore a fixed, tight-lipped smile.

"Well I - " stammered Audrey, feeling the other woman's grip tighten on her wrist.

"In fact we simply can't let you leave," said Mabel, still smiling as she steered her back into the bar. "It would be most impolite of us."

"Ladies and gentlemen – the good Queen Mary – and all who sail in her!" Sylvester Boothroyd lifted his champagne flute. It was the evening before the ship's arrival in New York, and the last night dinner in the First Class lounge was in full swing.

"They usually say that before they *launch* a ship dear," pointed out Dilys.

"Well I'm saying it now," insisted her husband, "and it's a toast, which means you should all be upstanding – those that can." He cast a sideways look at George, who was staring into space.

The assembled diners stood and raised their glasses in salute: "The Queen Mary!"

As everyone sat down again the conversations resumed where they had left off, while the waiters came around with coffee and brandy. Audrey glanced over at George, now deep in thought and tapping his coffee cup meditatively with a teaspoon.

Since the day of the lunchtime cocktails when Mabel Fotheringay had intercepted her plan to speak to him alone, she had simply been unable to find another opportunity; either one of the American posse, seeing her and George in proximity to one another had politely but forcefully waylaid her, or the mysterious scar-faced man had appeared out of nowhere, prompting George to put his head down and scurry off. It was all most peculiar and frustrating, and now they were almost at the end of the voyage, and she was no nearer finding out anything more about George, or his dramatic allegations against Oliver Regent.

"Johnny – oh Johnny darling!"

Hearing Mabel's summons Johnny Oxford strode up. He beamed obligingly, "At your service Mrs Fotheringay, how may I help?"

"Oh Johnny would you be an angel and bring the ship's photographer over, we simply must have a picture of us all with dear Audrey to mark this wonderful voyage."

As the photographer set up his tripod, Mabel leaned over and whispered in Oxford's ear, "We can't have George in the picture – see to it."

Oxford nodded and spoke discreetly to the photographer, who adjusted the angle of his camera slightly. "All right everyone ready? OK, say cheese."

"Cheese!"

At that moment the Captain took the rostrum, "Ladies and gentlemen, I am pleased to announce we will be arriving in New York Harbour in just over six hours." There were loud cheers of approval. "In the meantime the bar is open, and our crew and entertainments staff are on hand to entertain you till the small hours. Please, enjoy yourselves!"

The band immediately struck up a rousing chorus of Yankee Doodle Dandy and the whole room erupted in a melee of even louder cheering, hugging, handshakes and kissing.

Amid all the excitement Audrey felt something pressed into her palm. Looking up she saw George. He winked at her quickly then headed towards a rotund lady resplendent in pearls and twin set waiting on the dance floor. Written on the piece of paper in Audrey's hand was an address in New York.

CHAPTER TWENTY-THREE

October 1947

Audrey stood on the deck of the Queen Mary and gazed out at the shimmering vision arising above the Hudson River. This was it, New York! The Empire State Building, the Statue of Liberty, the tightly packed rows of skyscrapers like huge stalagmites glinting in the early morning sun as it cut away the fog. Tugboats hooted, harbour men shouted, all was noise and excitement as the great ship was brought to berth. She had witnessed scenes like this in countless films and magazines and now she was part of it! She could almost hear The Star Spangled Banner, quite smell the hot pastrami on rye! But wait a moment surely that actually was music...?

She looked down over the ship's rail to see a colourfully attired ensemble on the quayside playing God Save the Queen. As the gangplanks were lowered the musicians segued effortlessly into a jaunty medley of American tunes, Alexander's Ragtime Band, Yankee Doodle, New York New York.

"It's from On The Town – a sensation on Broadway."

Audrey turned to find Mabel Fotheringay on her way to the First Class disembarkation point. "Oh – yes, it's very jaunty."

"Now, you must come with me my dear, John and I have all the arrangements in hand for you – now where's he got to – ah John, here she is..."

Audrey, feeling somewhat overwhelmed by the clamour followed her escorts down the long gangplank. Alighting on the quayside she happened to catch sight of George. While the Fotheringays' backs were turned she made her way towards him. Before she could get near however, Mr and Mrs Boothroyd appeared suddenly and bustled him off towards a waiting car. Audrey ran forward. As the vehicle passed slowly by through the swelling crowd, George peered out of the rear window and gave a surreptitious wave of the hand.

"Oh there you are Audrey, I thought we'd quite lost you for a moment!" Mabel and John Fotheringay, both looking relieved were stood beside her, now accompanied by a tall, elegant young redheaded woman. "Audrey your luggage is being taken straight to your hotel, it's all taken care of. Now may I introduce Miss Bernadette O'Grady?"

Miss O'Grady flashed a confident smile and shook Audrey's hand with some force. "Welcome to New York Miss Stephenson, I'm very honoured to meet you. I am here to show you the headquarters of the Regent Trust here in the city – its on the way to your hotel, so we thought you might like to look in and see the office we have assigned for you right away – I hope that's all right?"

"Oh yes, quite all right thank you," said Audrey, "and do please call me Audrey."

"As you wish Miss Audrey."

"Well we'll leave you in Miss O' Grady's capable hands dear." Mrs Fotheringay kissed Audrey's cheek. "We'll be meeting up again soon, and I can hardly wait," she gushed, "its such a pleasure to have you here."

"Whenever you are ready then Miss Audrey your car is over here, the blue Cadillac."

The Regent Trust New York Headquarters were located very high up in an extremely tall and modern office building in Manhattan. "Goodness," exclaimed Audrey dizzily as they came out of the lift and passed a huge picture window through which the whole city seemed spread out below them, "we must be on the top floor."

"Almost Miss Audrey," said Miss O'Grady. "The next floor is the very top, the penthouse, Mr Regent's private apartment when he's in New York."

Fifteen minutes later, after smiles and handshakes with the Regent Trust staff and offering approving comments on her office, Audrey was back in the luxurious interior of the chauffeur driven blue Cadillac bowling through Manhattan.

"Well, what do you think of our city?" asked Miss O'Grady.

"Everything seems so – big," replied Audrey, peering up at the unending blocks of concrete and glass. "Oh and what's this place with the flags outside, it looks very grand."

"The Waldorf Astoria."

"Oh - isn't that a very famous hotel?"

"I guess so," smiled Miss O'Grady. "It'll be even more famous in a few moments."

"Oh, why?"

"Because the famous Miss Audrey Stephenson is about to check in, and I mean that with the greatest respect Miss Audrey."

The Cadillac turned into the forecourt beneath the flags. A doorman in gold braided uniform stepped forward and saluted.

"You mean you've booked me a room here?" said Audrey.

"Not exactly Miss Audrey – you have a suite, Mr Regent insisted."

Audrey's hotel suite, like her office, afforded a magnificent view of New York. After Miss O'Grady, with solicitations for "a wonderful stay" had left her, she stood at the window and gazed out at the breathtaking panorama for several minutes till she felt slightly giddy. Kicking off her shoes she lay down on the bed. The upholstery like everything else in the suite was the last word in comfort. She looked around – at the high ceiling, the deep soft carpets, the rich velvet embroidered curtains, the elegant Tiffany lamps. It was, she reflected, a long time since she had been surrounded by such luxury. Crosslands and Braeside had been very finely appointed properties certainly, but the Waldorf's attention to detail, the sheer quality of the furnishings and fittings was clearly second to none. The Grand Hotel Liverpool, a hotel she had been familiar with, was of course charming, and grand in a very English sort of way, but here – well, this was splendour on a wholly different scale.

Closing her eyes, she fell quickly and blissfully into a sort of half slumber, and dreamed of Crosslands, of Molly and Joe and Jericho Road and the simple, heart-warming Christmases she had spent there. Then into her dream stepped Martin, and cradled in his arms was little Margaret. Audrey awoke with tears streaming down her cheeks - her whole being inexplicably filled with hurt and loss.

The unhappiness and the loneliness she felt seemed impossible to heal; there was nothing she could do, not even, the "famous Miss Audrey Stephenson,"

She went to the window and looked out again. Somewhere in this vast country she thought, are Martin's parents. Wouldn't they like to know they have a little granddaughter? It might yet even be possible for them to know her, take her to their bosom. And then there was Curtis, Nellie's husband; he too was out there somewhere. Why should they not be brought together –Margaret and Martin's parents, Nellie and Curtis and their son Whillan? Audrey drew herself up to her full height. "Yes, I am the famous Miss Audrey Stephenson," she said quietly to herself, "and if I set my mind to it I can achieve extraordinary things."

The afternoon sunlight glinted on the tops of the skyscrapers. There was much to be done, and first she must speak to George. She picked up the bedside phone. "Yes Miss Stephenson, what number do you wish to call?" Audrey hesitated. "No – it's…all right…thank you," she then put the receiver down again.

There was a knock on the door, which made her start. Opening it she saw a porter. He was young and pimply and looked Italian. "Your suitcase Miss Stephenson, it was brought straight from the steamship, sorry for the delay, there was a lot to unload I believe."

"Oh, thank you that's quite all right." The porter deposited her case inside the door. Audrey fished in her handbag and handed him a three-penny piece, which he looked at curiously. "Oh - I beg your pardon," she delved again and produced a five-cent coin from a stash of American currency Johnny Oxford had supplied her with. "Well thank you Maam," the porter touched his hat and smiled.

When he had gone she put on her jacket and shoes and went down to the lobby, out of the hotel and across the street. Finding a call box she pushed some coins into the slot, and taking out the piece of paper George had given her dialled the number written beneath the address.

A croaky voice came on the line. "Well hello Ms Stephenson, how's the Waldorf?"

Audrey hesitated, "How did you know it was me?"

"I don't get many callers sister. And you looked pretty keen to talk down at the harbour. And I know you're at the Waldorf "cause that's where always take them."

"They?"

"The Fotheringay mob – anyone they want to impress they put them up in the Waldorf. Dirty money gets cleaned not only in Chicago sister. Now get in a cab and get over here while you can."

"You want me to come to your apartment?"

"It's clean enough little lady, and I got plenty of Scotch."

"Yes I'm sure you have, " Audrey felt suddenly apprehensive. Why was he so keen to get her alone now? She knew he carried a burning grudge against Oliver Regent, but in doing so he might not be willing to believe she was on his side – seeing her as the emissary of Regent, suppose he was plotting to exact revenge on her by proxy? Strange things went on in New York, that much she had heard. In the privacy of an anonymous apartment building, with sirens wailing in the streets and amid all the noise and bustle of a big city, who would hear her cries for help?

"We'll meet in some public place George– Central Park perhaps?"

There was a throaty laugh. "Don't you trust me little lady?"

"As much as you trust me George."

George laughed again, "OK Central Park it is, by the lake, the third bench from the hot dog man."

"Third bench, all right –Tomorrow morning, ten-thirty."

"All right," he said then the line had gone dead.

Returning to the Waldorf Audrey passed a solitary figure standing on the street corner reading a newspaper. His collar was turned up and his homburg hat pulled down over his face, yet something about him struck her as familiar.

Reaching the hotel entrance she remembered: the man with the scar! She turned quickly and looked back, but he was already gone.

The next morning Audrey found the lake easily. The taxi driver had dropped her at the nearest point and directed her to the hot dog seller's usual location. Now she was sat on the third bench, watching the New York world go by; businessmen, ladies with dogs, nannies and mothers with prams, young couples arm in arm. It was Saturday fortunately, and she had the whole weekend to herself before a hectic round of meetings and engagements for the Regent Trust began on the Monday. She had studiously ignored several messages left at the hotel by Mabel Fotheringay, inviting her to lunch, dinner, and a "soiree" over the next two days.

"The park look's lovely in the sunshine doesn't it?" George had sat down unobtrusively beside her on the bench.

" - George, - good morning, why yes, yes it does."

"This was Bella's favourite spot."

"Bella…?"

"My wife."

"Yes, of course," Audrey said,

"We used to come here most mornings, just to sit. We never said much to each other, but we didn't have to – that's the wonderful thing about love – it can be quiet."

"Yes, yes that's true."

"So can hate."

Audrey gave a little gasp. "You mean…?"

"My hatred for Mr Oliver Regent, that's right. But let me tell you how it began. Bella and me were married for ten years, then Regent turns up and everything changed. Bella divorced me and six months later married Regent. He told everyone Bella chased him, but I know different. He wanted her for one thing - her money,

"But Mr Regent has his own fortune, he has long been a wealthy man."

"Young lady, Bella was ten years older than him. She was going through a difficult time, losing her looks so she thought. This English charmer waltzes in and tells her he's in love with her. She's insecure, she believes him, goes a little crazy – well, loses her goddam mind to be truthful. But I can see it all – she's vulnerable, and I think to myself, she'll see the light, she'll wake up and realise what a class A idiot she's made of her self and when she does, I'll be waiting – that's what love does, though maybe you're too young to know these things."

Audrey said nothing, just nodded gently.

"Anyhow, next thing I know I read in the paper there's been an accident – Mrs Bella Regent drowned in Malibu – can you imagine what it felt like to read that, about my Bella, in a goddam newspaper on the sidewalk, on the front page her picture as a young girl with every bum from here to Hoboken drooling over it?" He put his head in his hands.

Audrey laid her palm gently on his arm. "I'm so sorry."

They were silent for good minute, then Audrey quietly, "You'll hate me for saying this, but do you not think it was just an accident – a terrible, tragic accident?"

George turned to her, his face sombre. "Sister listen to me; Bella was a high school swimming champion, she represented her state in the national galas – and she was in perfect health, as fit and strong an athlete as she had always been."

"Perhaps there was a current that day…"

173

"I've checked the meteorology and oceanic reports, the water was calm on that beach all day."

"Had she been drinking?"

"My Bella was teetotal, took the pledge. The newspapers said she couldn't swim a stroke, how about that?"

"But there must be records somewhere?"

"I checked the press corps – all the articles about her swimming championships have been erased – ain't that peculiar. Regent killed her all right, she had a legacy coming from her brother, he owned a steel mill, Regent knew the brother was sick, and as soon as he heard the man had passed away, that's when he killed my Bella, on that beach, held her under the water I guess, no marks on the body...oh god – oh god I'm sorry- " His head sank into his hands again, his shoulders beginning to shake.

"No," said Audrey, "I'm sorry for bringing this all up, you don't want to be reminded."

George suddenly sat bolt upright again, his eyes blazing. "That's where you're wrong sister – I need to remind myself everyday of what that man did, "cause that keeps my hate alive, and that's how I'm going to finish Regent."

"But how?" lamented Audrey, "Is there no one that will testify Bella was a swimming champion?"

George shook his head, "She was an orphan you see – and besides, people don't like to get involved – especially when they're fearful, fearful of the powerful, fearful who might be watching them, following them."

Audrey shivered as she remembered the scar-faced man.

"But there's something they don't know about - something I've got."

"What?"

"Why should I tell you?"

"Why not?"

"So you can tip off Regent? Christ, you work for the man!"

George shook his head vigorously, "ah, I've said too much -"

"On the contrary," said Audrey, "it's what I've wanted to hear for a long time – that someone else knows that the great Oliver Regent has feet of clay."

George turned to her, "You're saying you already knew the man's a crook – how?"

Audrey sighed, "Never mind now. George I'm with you all the way, but what evidence do we have."

"There's an investigation here in the U.S. going on right now – why do you think he didn't come with you?"

"Well then we must go to the authorities and tell them all we know."

George's face darkened. "If only it were that simple."

"What do you mean?"

"It's knowing who to got to – who Regent hasn't paid off in City Hall and the FBI. He's keeping clear till the dust settles."

Audrey sighed heavily. "And we're no nearer bringing him to justice."

George said quietly, "That's where you're wrong. I do know someone."

"Who?"

"A senator; a good man, who it just so happens is a friend of your British Prime Minister - if we get the evidence to him he'll do the rest believe me."

"That would wonderful – but what evidence?"

"About Bella." George leaned towards her. "Her medals - my Bella's beautiful shiny silver swimming medals – some she won for seniors races, when she was already over fifty years old, and her American lifeguard's badge, all authenticated. Seeing those, it'll be hard for anyone to believe she drowned on that calm day."

Audrey gazed at him. "Where are these medals?"

George cast a look around him. In the distance the hot dog seller was talking to a customer, a workman in overalls. On the next bench sat an old lady sat feeding the pigeons. He lowered his voice to a whisper, "Right here in Manhattan, in a safe deposit box."

"Then why don't you get them right away and take them to the senator?"

"Because I think Regent may have someone watching the bank, waiting for me to show up. No one can access the box without the key, and there's no name, just a security code and the key number. That's where you come in – take this."

Keeping his eyes fixed on the lake he pushed his clenched fist along the bench towards her and released an envelope containing a small hard object. Audrey covered it with her hand and slipped it deftly into her handbag.

George got up. "I'm going to take a stroll now little lady." He tipped his hat to her. "It's been nice talking to you. Ain't often I get the chance to sit with a pretty girl in the park. You know what to do, call me when you have the goods." Giving her a brief but charming smile he walked briskly off.

Audrey opened her handbag discreetly and without taking it out, looked in the envelope George had given her. On the back were scrawled six digits followed by a sequence of letters and other numbers. She snapped her handbag shut. She would go to the bank on Monday; strike now against Regent while the iron was hot. Fired with a mixture of adrenalin and apprehension she rose and smoothed down her skirt. George had said the bank was here in Manhattan so she could probably slip over there from the Regent Trust office in her lunch break. Which bank had George said? She couldn't remember.

She opened her handbag again and examined the envelope, inside and out. There was the key and the security details but no name or address of any bank. She looked across the park; George was now out of sight. Never mind, she would telephone him from the call box again later and find out about the bank. Holding her handbag tightly, she walked quickly towards the park exit. As she did so, the workman in overalls, who had a long scar down one cheek, followed her at a discreet distance.

Back at the Waldorf Audrey found another message from Mrs Fotheringay. This time she decided to return the call, and accepted an invitation to dinner at a nearby restaurant for that evening.

Mrs Fotheringay was in even more ebullient mood than usual, basking in the reflected glory of introducing Audrey - "Mr Regent's right hand person in England, and a leading light in London society..." - to a crowd of New York hangers-on, and generally playing Grande Dame to all and sundry.

At 10pm, as Audrey thanked her hostess for 'a wonderful evening,' Mrs Fotheringay beamed magnanimously. "Not all my dear – after all what would Mr Regent think of us if we didn't look after his prized new asset – where Oliver Regent leads, other men strive to follow." Audrey couldn't help smiling to herself as she wondered what Mrs Fotheringay would have to say when she heard Oliver Regent had been convicted as an embezzler and a murderer. If George was right about Bella's medals, and his friend the senator, that moment might not be far off.

Alighting from her taxi at the Waldorf she crossed the road to the call box and dialled George's number. After listening to the ringing tone for several minutes she hung up.

Back in the hotel Audrey sat on the bed and thought over the events of the day. It seemed almost incredible – George coming out of the blue as an ally, someone who could testify to Oliver Regent's wickedness, expose him as the evil fraud he was. It was also frightening, especially if George was right about Bella's past being erased in the press records.

But how had Regent been able to do that? Surely the United States was the land of freedom and justice, people couldn't just go around falsifying public information? Then she recalled something someone else had once said to her: in America money talks, it was a country run by criminals, criminals who spoke politely and wore smart clothes and went to church on Sundays – what they did the rest of the week would make your hair stand on end. Audrey shuddered as the image of the scar-faced man rose up before her. She had to do something, tell someone, find out where this bank was and get the evidence against Regent without delay. But whom could she tell? She felt suddenly very alone and frightened. Then she remembered; of course, there was someone she could tell.

The street was quiet when Audrey, her heart beating rapidly, slipped out of the hotel again. She looked up and down. To her relief there was no one about. She entered the phone box and dialled the operator. "I'd like to place a call to this number in London please." She gave the number. Several seconds went by before a voice said,
"Hello?"
Audrey almost collapsed with joy, "Oh Richard, thank God, is that really you, you sound different?"

"Audrey? Yes its me, but its rather late here, or should I say early, I was asleep - "

"Oh Richard, I'm sorry I quite forgot about the time difference."

"That's all right I was due to get up anyway – well, in an hour or so I guess - "

"Goodness! It's the middle of the night?"

"Um, coming up to 5 a m – but listen, its good to hear your voice - how is the great city of New York?"

"Strange, incredible, bewildering – and I'm scared Richard…"

"Whoa what's wrong honey, look where are you - should I call the cops -?"

"No, I'm all right Richard, I've just come back from a dinner engagement with Mrs Fotheringay and her friends, it's just past midnight and I'm outside in a call box -"

"Midnight, in New York, and you're in the street alone?" He sounded incredulous.

"But I'm all right honestly, the hotel is just opposite, but I can't phone from there in case someone's listening in – Richard the most bizarre thing has happened."

"What?"

Audrey shot a quick glance left and right along the street, then lowering her voice went on, "You remember what I told you about Oliver Regent?"

"Sure, how could I forget?"

"Well I've met someone who can corroborate my story – or rather he has a story of his own, a man called George, he was on the Queen Mary coming over with the Fotheringay set, they all treat him as a drunken bore with a stupid grudge but and he swears Regent murdered his wife, or his ex-wife rather, who then married Regent, who killed her to get her money, but George has proof that Bella was a champion swimmer and has her medals in a safe deposit box in a bank and gave me the serial number, and now I have to go there and get the medals because Regent's men will be watching out for George…"

"Whoa, slow down honey – that's one heck of a lot of information - and what's the swimming got to do with it?"

"Sorry, yes, Regent made out Bella drowned because she couldn't swim, but that wasn't true, she was a champion swimmer…"

"Hence the importance of the medals, I get it. But listen Audrey, sweetheart," Richard's voice was deadly serious now, "assuming all this is true, then on no account must you go to that bank, it could be extremely dangerous, you hear me?"

"But I've got to -"

"No – please, I absolutely forbid it," he replied gravely.

"Well, yes, I suppose you're right, it might be risky, though I can't do anything at the moment in any case because George forgot to tell me which bank, and there must be hundreds in Manhattan, and now he's not answering his phone."

"Oh?" Richard hesitated for a moment and she could sense him thinking hard. He then said, "Ok, in that case, listen Audrey, I want you to give me the serial number that George gave you."
Audrey opened her handbag and read out the number.

"Ok," he continued, "I'm going to contact someone from here, someone in authority and see if they can find out which New York bank these medals are in, and take charge of the matter from there. Meanwhile if you do manage to contact George, ask him the name of the bank, and as soon as you have it ring me. Meanwhile tell George to stay put, and that someone you know and trust and is on his side is dealing with the matter. What is his address in New York by the way?"

"I don't know, he never gave me that."

"Ah – ok read me out his phone number."

"Yes," Audrey gave the number. "I think they'll be another number at the beginning if you ring from England."

"Right. You've don well honey, I'll take care of things from here."

"Yes, yes I will, oh Richard thank you, its so nice to hear your voice, I have missed you so, I didn't realise how much till now, its been such madness here."

"I'm missing you too honey, everyday. Now get yourself back to your room and get to bed – and honey, lock your door. I'll call you at the hotel tomorrow, the Waldorf right?"

"Right."

"If you're not there I'll leave a message. Goodnight sweetheart."

Richard Neame replaced the telephone and poured himself a whiskey and soda. Drawing the curtain back a few inches he surveyed with a thoughtful expression the London skyline beginning to appear in the grey light of morning. Then he picked up the receiver again and dialled.

"Mike? This is Dick Neame - hi feller, sorry for the early morning call but there's been an urgent development regarding Mr Regent. Remember George Fairweather? - That's right, well the heat's back on – yeah he's turned up again, and this time he's talking about evidence. I want you to get on to our boys in New York Mike, have them find him, and fast - now take these two numbers down." He read out George Fairweather's New York telephone number and the deposit box number as Audrey had recited them. "Oh and Mike, there's a girl mixed up in this too, yeah, an English broad, she's over there now. I've cooled her out, told her the matter's being taken care of. Her name is Audrey Stephenson, we'll deal with her later."

CHAPTER TWENTY-FOUR

The next morning was Monday, and Audrey was due to report for work at the Regent Trust offices. A car would be calling for her. After breakfasting downstairs in the hotel she went to the ladies" room, checked the security box key in her handbag then slipped discreetly out to the call box and rang George again. Still there was no reply. Returning to the lobby she gave a start. Sat opposite the reception desk, a black leather briefcase on the table in front of her was Miss O'Grady. She was flicking through a copy of Life Magazine, in between glancing at her watch.

"Why good morning Miss O'Grady," breezed Audrey, affecting a nonchalant air. "You're early."

Replacing the magazine and picking up her briefcase her aide stood smartly to attention. She switched on a robotic smile, "I believe our schedule was to collect you at 9 am Miss Stephenson. It is now one minute past. Mr Regent likes his staff to be punctual at all times, but then of course you would know that." The smile like a warning light flashed again. "I have a full list of your appointments for this week," she tapped the briefcase. We can discuss them on the way to the office."

"Of course," replied Audrey, "I am at your disposal."

"On the contrary Miss Stephenson, I am at yours. You are our guest here in New York City, and if there are any alterations you wish to your schedule, such as the time you begin your day, I will be most pleased to accommodate them, where possible of course. You only have to ask."

"Hmm, thank you," said Audrey. She felt somewhat at a loss with this unnervingly efficient woman, who seemed to be being both obsequious and snide at one and the same time.

"And if there is anything you require here, in the hotel for example, you may simply speak to the manager or any of the staff. Your comfort and enjoyment whilst here are their priority, as well as ours. There is also no need to leave the hotel unaccompanied at any time of the day, or night. Did you find what you were looking for just now?"

"Just now?" Audrey looked baffled.

"I noticed you crossing the street."

"Oh, yes I see." Her visit to the phone booth had clearly not been as discreet as she thought.

"Oh I just went out for some fresh air"

"Fresh air?" Miss O'Grady echoed the words as if they had been uttered in a foreign language.

"That's right," beamed Audrey, adding with a hint of defiance now, "we quite often do that in England you know. Well, shall we go? Mustn't lose the Regent Trust reputation for punctuality now must we!"

From the back of the big limousine Audrey gazed out at the streets. The city seemed busier today, lots of other big cars, honking their horns, cab drivers shouting from their windows. On a street corner a busker in battered clothes was playing a battered saxophone, collecting dimes in a battered hat. As the car drew level in the crawling traffic Audrey saw that the man was wearing military attire. Peering more closely she gave a little gasp, for, though the material was torn and faded, she realised it was a U.S. Air Force uniform, a uniform just like the one Martin had worn.

"Are you all right Miss Stephenson?" Miss O'Grady was staring at her.

"Yes, yes, - just that man with the saxophone," she murmured as the car pulled away.

"It's a scandal isn't it," said Miss O'Grady, "that so many of our brave servicemen, who did so much for the country are reduced to vagrancy. But it is a scandal the Regent Trust is determined to address, just as in your own country Miss Stephenson. That is all part of your mission here in the United States to spark debate and spread awareness of the pressing needs among so many sections of our communities, on both sides of the Atlantic. Our hostel in Brooklyn, which you'll be visiting on Friday is doing wonderful work…"

Audrey stared out of the window. She thought, if Martin were one of those men out there somewhere, I would find him - destitute, stood on a street corner with a battered saxophone, homeless and hungry and lost, I would find him, somehow I would find him. Craning forward she began to scrutinise every street corner as they passed, studied every tramp and hobo, every shambling underfed busker shuffling along, cap in hand, Martin could have been one of them, he could be, he could be, he must be, if only she thought it intensely enough she could surely summon him into life.... Martin's face rose up before her, dancing in her memory; Martin smiling, laughing, holding her as the band played Red Sails in the Sunset, his body pressed against her, his lips touching hers. Oh this is madness, she thought, madness...

The limousine had picked up speed now, her pulse likewise quickening as the buildings and sidewalks flashed by. Where was Martin, where was he? Dead of course, dead...but could he not just as easily be alive, if only she could will it with her imagination, with her love? She pictured flinging herself out of the moving vehicle and running to him, his arms outstretched towards her, his face lit up with joy as he saw her coming, as she told him about Margaret – Margaret...! She closed her eyes as the tears arose.

"I do hope you're feeling a little better now Miss Stephenson."
Daisy Meadows, the young secretary at the Regent Trust Manhattan had entered with a tray. Audrey was lying on a couch in her office with the blinds closed. Daisy had been told that Miss Stephenson had been a little travel sick in the limousine on the way over. "Miss O'Grady said I wasn't to disturb you, but I peeked round the door and saw you looking so sad I thought you might like some coffee and pastries."

Audrey sat up and looked at the girl. She must only be about eighteen years old, she thought: what a sweet thing. "How awfully kind of you, that coffee does smell good, and those cakes look divine."

"They're bagels, with fresh cream, which I hope you like." She set down the tray. "It puts on weight, but I always say a little of what you like is good for you."

"I agree with you," smiled Audrey. "Its Daisy isn't it?"

"Daisy Meadows yes, we were introduced when you arrived last week - but goodness however did you remember so many names?"

"I'll let you into a secret," said Audrey conspiratorially, "I didn't!"

"Well how could you possibly? But thank you for remembering mine."

"A pleasure," said Audrey biting into a pastry, "as are these."

"Oh goodness," said Daisy suddenly, "I hope it wasn't an upset stomach you had, in which case these cakes were not a good idea on my part -"

Audrey shook her head, "No, these are doing me the world of good, sheer indulgence, just what I need. No, between you and me this morning was more an emotional upset."

"I could tell you had been crying," said Daisy, then looked awkward, "that is, I mean, I hope you don't mind my saying?"

"Not at all, I was just having a silly sentimental moment that's all. You see, I lost my fiancée in the war, and on the way here today I saw a veteran wearing a similar uniform. My fiancée…was in the U.S. Air Force. We met while he was stationed in England."

Daisy's hand had flown to her mouth, "Oh my gosh I'm so very sorry Miss Stephenson, I had no idea, please forgive my intrusiveness."

"You've not been at all intrusive." Audrey smiled. "I should not be burdening you with my problems."

"There is no burden Maam…you must still suffer great sorrow in your loss, I'm sure."

"It comes and goes," said Audrey. "This morning it came with a vengeance."

After a few seconds silence, Daisy said gently, "This may be impertinent of me Miss Stephenson, but if during your stay in New York there's ever any time you want to talk, or just someone to hang out with for an evening, or away from the office and…and without - " she hesitated.

"Without Miss O'Grady breathing down my neck you mean?" ventured Audrey.

Daisy looked down, "Oh no, well not exactly, well ok yes - "

This made Audrey laugh, "She's quite a lady isn't she?"

"Oh sure – and I mean, no disrespect she's very good at her job, it's just she can be a little, I don't know - "

"Overbearing?"

Daisy laughed too now, "That would be the word, oh but I hope you won't -"

"Mum's the word." Audrey tapped her nose.

"Pardon me?"

"Sorry, its means, your secret's safe with me, it's a peculiar English expression, we have a lot of them."

Daisy laughed again.

"Listen," said Audrey, "help me out with these bagels," she passed her the box of cakes.

"Are you sure? Well then thank you. Hmm, these are the best."

"And do tell me what is it you do here exactly? I never had the chance to ask when we met last week.

"Hmm - I work in tracing," said Daisy through a mouthful of cream.

"Tracing what?"

"Lost relatives – there's a lot of displaced people in America, in New York alone come to that, especially since the war. We try to find them."

"How fascinating," said Audrey, "and what a marvellous thing to be doing, especially when you are able to tell someone you've found their loved one."

"Yes, it can be. Though that part can be a little nerve-wracking."

"Ah, if it turns out the loved one is dead?"

"You got it in one. Or worse."

"What could be worse?

Daisy lowered her voice, "Some cases I've dealt with have been like something out of a movie."

Audrey looked interested, "Really?"

"I'll give you an example. There was this lady came to us, a friend of her husband's had been to see her in 1946 and told her he had been reported missing in action. Well she never received official confirmation of where and how he died, and so she asked us to look into it."

"And?"

"We found her husband living right here in New York, but he denied all knowledge of her. After that he vanished again, and this time without leaving any trace. The wife had a child by him too. It seemed he had just wanted to get away from them, and got his pal to fake his death – maybe he did the same for the pal who knows. I guess the war changed a lot of men, after what they went through they didn't want to settle back down with their boring little wives and have to support them working on an assembly line, you'd be surprised how many similar cases we found, poor ladies who'd been grieving …oh my goodness Miss Stephenson, I've gone and done it again, me and my big mouth, you don't want to hear about this! I am the most tactless person, how can you ever forgive me - "

"There's no need to apologise," said Audrey, "I know my dear Martin would never have done such a thing. He was a hero through and through. And he loved me."

"Talking to you Miss Stephenson, I have absolutely no doubt of it. Well I guess I'd better get back to my typewriter, the other girls will think I'm angling for promotion or something. I hope the coffee's helping, and thank you for sharing your bagels with me."

"It's been a pleasure."

"I meant what I said by the way, if you ever need a friend in this big old city - "

"Thank you Daisy you're the first person since I arrived in New York that has said anything like that to me, it means a lot."

"In a few minutes time, if you're up to it, Mrs Boothroyd and Mrs Fotheringay are due in to finalise the details of the charity auction at the Radio City Music Hall next week." Miss O'Grady, her master diary held like a holy text, was now sat with Audrey in her office.

"What do I have to do at the charity auction?" asked Audrey, now sipping her third cup of coffee since the one brought by Daisy earlier that morning. "Hmm, this coffee is divine, Italian I imagine, its quite perked me up."

"You will be the auctioneer, it will be quite a treat for everyone, they're looking forward to seeing a real English lady."

Audrey winced slightly. "Oh, well all right, I expect it will be rather fun."

"Tomorrow you have a 1pm lunch appointment with Rupert and Marjorie Evans-Smyth. That's an important one, they are among the wealthiest families in New York and we must be sure to encourage them to next week's auction. They have recently become benefactors to the trust, and we must look after them accordingly. They have asked to meet you particularly. Mrs Fotheringay will also accompany you to the lunch, after which we have a meeting back here with the heads of department and the people from City Hall to discuss..."

Audrey held up a hand, "Please re-arrange that Miss O'Grady. I shan't be able to think straight after lunch if Mrs Fotheringay's there – she always presses me into drinking enormous amounts of wine, and I shan't be able to concentrate one bit."

"Might I suggest you stick to coffee? This meeting has been arranged for several weeks," said Miss O'Grady firmly. "It takes a great deal of organisation to get all the relevant parties together."

Audrey smiled. "And might I suggest, or rather insist, that you all manage without me. Besides I'm sure the items on the agenda would be mostly above my head and I should simply be in the way. You did say I could make alterations to the schedule, if possible?"

Miss O'Grady expression stiffened further. "As you wish Miss Stephenson," she said coldly, and made an amendment in her diary. The intercom buzzed and Daisy's voice was heard: "Mrs Fotheringay and Mrs Boothroyd are here to see Miss Stephenson."

"Thank you Miss Meadows," Miss O'Grady clicked the switch back. "Your first appointment Miss Stephenson," she said then rose and marched briskly out.

The rest of the day was one of irksome forced smiling and general nonsensical chitchat Audrey was glad when it was time to leave the office. The limousine was already waiting at the front door and she slumped thankfully into the back seat. Fortunately Miss O'Grady, her nose no doubt still slightly out of joint since Audrey had challenged her sacred schedule, had chosen not to accompany her, and the drive back to the Waldorf was conducted in silence.

On alighting she remained in the lobby until the car was out of sight then crossed the road to the phone booth. She had to contact George now at all costs. She dialled and waited. What was he up to? Was he ill, or gone on holiday? Surely not, he had said specifically he would be waiting for her call. Nothing could be done about retrieving the evidence against Oliver Regent without the name of the bank, and if George had got cold feet she could only hope Richard managed to get the wheels in motion from London, though how he proposed to do this she could only speculate. Richard was something of a mystery man in his own right.

As she stood there listening to the dialling tone, she had a sudden stab of horror: suppose George had been sent by Regent to trap her? Panicking slightly now she was about to put down the receiver and run back to the hotel when a woman's voice said. "Hello, can I help you?"

Audrey stumbled for a second, "Oh – yes…um, is George there please?"

"No I'm sorry," said the woman politely. Audrey recited the telephone number. "That's this number yes Maam – I can see it on the telephone here. I'm the maid from the agency, just cleaning up for the new tenant."

"Oh," said Audrey nonplussed, "and you're sure there's no one called George lives there – George Fairweather?"

"Fairweather did you say?"

"Yes that's right."

"Oh well in that case you would be right Maam…"

"Thank goodness!"

"Because I was talking to the lady down the hall just now, and she told me Mr Fairweather had to go away unexpectedly just yesterday."

"Oh I see - and what forwarding address did he leave please?"

"There was no forwarding address apparently, I'm sorry."

Audrey walked quickly back to the hotel, She felt uneasy, the suspicion of conspiracy still playing on her mind, and an ominous sense that something unpleasant was about to befall her. Richard had warned her to be careful, perhaps she should get away for a while, get out of New York. But how was it to be done?

CHAPTER TWENTY-FIVE

Audrey slept fitfully that night. Two things were troubling her. The first was the mysterious disappearance of George, and what dread consequences this might imply for her own safety. If either Regent's men were onto him, or he himself had been sent to trap her, they might come for her at any time. The euphemism chilled her. She tried to convince herself her worries were unfounded; she was an Englishwoman in a smart hotel in a big city, with a policeman on every street corner, what harm could possibly befall her? But the image of the scar-faced man would not go away.

She was also haunted by the rekindled memory of Martin, with which had returned all the raw pain of her abandonment of her daughter. She realised now that Margaret was far from a closed book in her mind, and neither was Martin. Both were gone from her life, yet not gone, and like a reopened wound, the agony was acute. The past could not be undone, but if there were only some action she could take to in some way lay to rest her ghosts, and to honour both Martin and Margaret, whose life was yet to come, to bring them together and at the same time say a final goodbye, she might find some measure of peace in her soul.

Lying awake in the long dark night, she felt called upon to enact a final gesture towards her loved ones, perform some dignified and selfless duty in their names. Yet what it was she did not know. Fear now preyed on her; I must leave, she thought, escape this hotel, this city and disappear - but where on earth to, and how? Unable to find a solution, sleep finally overcame her as dawn broke over New York.

It was 8.30 am when, still bleary eyed, she telephoned the Regent Trust office and left a message at the switchboard that she was running a little late and would be making her own way in by taxi and not to send the usual car. Showering and dressing quickly she then went down to the breakfast room; she did not want Miss O'Grady calling her back with insinuating questions, those could wait till later.

At the office however Miss O'Grady murmured only a perfunctory "Good morning," and promptly disappeared into her own office. Audrey felt relieved.

At midday she joined Mrs Fotheringay at a nearby Italian restaurant for the scheduled lunch with Mr and Mrs Evans-Smyth. To her surprise she found the occasion enjoyable, and the Evans-Smyth's far from stuffy, even rather jolly, their company mellowing Mrs Fotheringay, who herself seemed unusually relaxed and unpretentious.

The couple asked about England, the royal family and Buckingham Palace, and were delighted when Audrey described witnessing on a state occasion the King and Queen riding down the Mall in their gilded carriage waving to the crowds.

After the meal, over coffee Audrey got on to the subject of Daisy Meadows" and her work in the Regent Trust's family tracing department. Mrs Evans- Smyth was clearly fascinated. It was then that a vague, as yet unformed idea began to glimmer in the back of Audrey's mind.

"Yes, I think it provides a very valuable social service, which at the moment, sadly, goes unrecognised by many in the trust" she said. "I would very much like to gain some experience in that department while I'm over here, so that I can try to expand its work. Though between ourselves I doubt that would be possible."

"Why would it not be possible?" asked Mrs Evans-Smyth with interest.

"A question of funds I suppose," said Audrey. "There are so many more visible demands on the Regent Trust's resources."

"Well," smiled Mrs Evans-Smyth reassuringly, "that's something we need to talk about, isn't it my dear."

"This is all most irregular Miss Stephenson." Miss O'Grady was struggling to contain her ire. "Missing an executive meeting, albeit an important one, I can overlook, but this proposal of yours will mean you're away from the office for..." she put on her glasses and reread the internal memo which Audrey had sent her that morning, "a whole month?"

"That's right," replied Audrey calmly. "The idea is for me to gain direct experience of our family tracing work, so I can organise training and enable us to take on more staff."

"You are aware that Miss Meadows handles our missing persons enquiries?"

"Yes, I've already spoken to Daisy- "

"Oh you have, have you?" snapped Miss O'Grady, her tone distinctly sarcastic now.

"Yes, and she's run off her feet dealing with floods of enquires as it is, and simply hasn't time to follow up the ones that require going out and about physically – following up clues, tracking down friends and acquaintances who might lead us to the missing person."

"Following up clues!" sneered Miss O'Grady. "This is not the Pinkerton Agency Miss Stephenson."

"I'm aware of that," said Audrey retaining her composure, "but looking for missing people inevitably requires a certain amount of detective work."

"If you must know Miss Stephenson," said Miss O'Grady, "I was not in favour of this so-called family tracing unit being set up in the first place. If a man deserts his wife she's better off without him-"

"Oh but those are not the only cases," protested Audrey. "There are missing sons, shell shocked veterans, fathers who may have had breakdowns or be ashamed they cannot support their families and see no other option but to disappear, they deserve our sympathy not our judgement..."

"That may be your opinion, and you have every right to it." Miss O'Grady held up her hand authoritatively. "Meanwhile we have far more urgent work to do among the sick and the deserving poor in this great country of ours. And that is why I am afraid I must veto your request to take leave from this office."

Audrey said, "But if you'll forgive me Miss O'Grady, Mr Regent did say I was to gain a broad range of experience while I am here ..."

"And if you'll forgive me," Miss O'Grady retaliated, "I am in charge of staffing here, and it is in that capacity that I regret to decline your request in this instance, since, as I repeat, we have far more pressing priorities for our resources." She flashed a satisfied smile and pushed Audrey's memo back across the desk.

Audrey nodded. She thought: right now for the big guns. "You know, that's just what I told Mrs Evans-Smyth."

"What?" Miss O'Grady looked at suspiciously again.

"About resources - which is why she sent me this, I received it this morning."

From her pocket she took out an envelope and handed it over. Miss O'Grady scrutinised the contents and Audrey saw her jaw drop. "As you see the cheque is made out to the Regent Trust, and Mrs Evans-Smyth specifies in her letter she will also pay all my expenses for a month, and make a further donation to the trust, providing I am allowed a free rein to develop the family tracing department."

Miss O'Grady laid the letter and cheque down. Through tight lips she said, "I don't have to go along with this, my authority in the matter is final."

"I see," Audrey said slowly. "In that case, do you wish to telephone Mr Regent and explain that the lady who has donated the largest single amount to the Regent Trust so far, is to be denied a small request as to how some of the money is spent - or shall I?"

Miss O'Grady breathed out hard. Her teeth gritted she muttered, "Well, all right, I suppose, after due consideration of these special circumstances...Miss Stephenson, I am... that is...very well, your request is granted."

"Well done Miss Stephenson!" Daisy smiled at Audrey in admiration.

They were sat drinking coffee in Frankie's Deli and Diner, a little Italian café around the block from the Regent Trust offices. It was late afternoon and the place was quiet save for two old men playing chess, and the owner singing a soft Neapolitan serenade behind the counter while slicing onions.

"You should have seen the look on Miss O'Grady face!" whispered Audrey.

"I can imagine! Ok listen, I got the information you asked for, both addresses – and guess what, Curtis is living right here in New York."

"Really? Well that certainly makes that simpler – gosh you're a miracle worker!"

Daisy looked pleased, "I wouldn't say that, but I did work on it overnight – well this is rather a special case."

"Bless you," she squeezed Daisy's hand conspiratorially.

"I thought it best not to use the office for phone calls either, less chance of Ma O'Grady finding out."

"Yes, good thinking – if that woman gets wind I'm actually on a personal mission here she might still scupper things."

"You're also going to need a driver."

"No need, I can go by train or bus," said Audrey blithely.

Daisy gave a horrified look, "Alone? No way Miss Stephenson, America is a great country but there's some animals out there, and I don't mean the four legged variety."

"Then what would you suggest?"

"I've already spoken to Miss O'Grady and she's agreed you can use one of Regent Trust men."

"Oh – but won't that be risky – suppose he finds out I'm using the family tracing service partly for my own ends, and tells Miss O'Grady?"

"She's agreed you can use Conrad."

"Who?"

"Your chauffeur."

"Oh you mean the chap who usually collects me in the limousine every morning? I didn't know his name."

"There's something else you don't know about him."

"Oh - what?"

"He's my fiancé."

"Oh how sweet, well congratulations Daisy, when is the happy…"

"Shush." Daisy put a finger to her lips and looked around the diner anxiously. "Please, we're keeping it a secret at present. Miss O'Grady doesn't approve of relationships between the staff, thinks it undermines morale or something.
Anyway Conrad knows the score with you, what you'll be doing, so there'll be no problems. He'll look after you too, he's ex-US Marines Corps, Special Forces."

"Gosh, well thank you, Daisy," said Audrey, "and of course I won't breathe a word about you and Conrad. Now, how about Martins family, you said you had found them too?"

"Yes, though I'm afraid they're a lot further away, New Orleans."

"Well, I have a whole month of leave, thanks to Mrs Evans-Smyth."

"Look," said Daisy, looking concerned now, "Are you sure you're going to be OK with this?"

"Yes, if Curtis is in New York I can go and see him straightaway, tell him that Nellie still loves him and wants him back, and that Whillan needs his father, after that its up to him. I'll pay for his passage to England out of my own pocket, if that's what it takes."

"OK, but, I was thinking more about when you go visit Martin's family?"

"They have a right to know about their granddaughter."

"Sure, but do you not think it might be better to write to them, in the first instance at least?"

Audrey sighed, "I suppose the truth is I'm also really desperate to see them - it's a way of connecting with Martin again. I'm thrilled by the prospect, and terrified, but I definitely want it to happen – it has to happen. I'm worried that if I write first they might simply reply with a thank you, and say they prefer not to meet me."

"So you want to just turn up, make it a - what do they call it – a fait accompli?"

"Is that so terrible?"

Daisy looked thoughtful, "Hmm, I guess I'd do the same in your shoes. Forgive me for this though," she continued tentatively, "and this will be hard, but you will try not to make any, how shall I say, assumptions, before you've met them?"

"I know what you mean," nodded Audrey. "Martin's family won't really know me from Adam, and arriving out of the blue – well it'll be a surprise I suppose."

"To say the least." She looked searchingly at Audrey.

"There's something else on your mind, I can tell."

Daisy sighed, "Again, tell me to butt out on this but…"

"Go on please, I value your advice."

"Well, these people are southerners."

"And?"

"I imagine they will be God fearing folk. They may wonder why…"

"What? Spit it out Daisy, please."

"Why – I'm sorry – why you gave away your child – their son's child. I only say this to prepare you for -"

"The worst – their anger, their rejection?"

"Both – I mean, you tell them they have a granddaughter, and then that they can't see her…that even you can't see her…Oh dear God, I'm sorry - " Daisy's eyes shimmered now with tears.

194

"Don't be," Audrey rested a hand on her sleeve, "I know the risks - this is just something I have to do. First though, I have to go and see Curtis. I'd like to do that as soon as possible."

Daisy nodded, "I'll speak to Conrad. He'll have the car ready to take you up to Harlem first thing in the morning."

CHAPTER TWENTY-SIX

"So this is Harlem."

Audrey gazed out at the long row of brownstone houses. Along the sidewalk strode smartly dressed couples; the men in sharp suits, two tone patent leather shoes and fedora hats, their lady folk in elegant vibrantly patterned dresses and high heels. "There's not a white person to be seen in the whole street."

Conrad smiled at her in the rear view mirror. "That's about to change. We've arrived Miss Stephenson, but don't get out just yet, and keep your window up till I come back"

He slowed the limousine and pulled up opposite a ramshackle looking building. Two young men clad in vests and dungarees, their feet bare, were sat on the steps. They looked up as Conrad emerged from the vehicle. He took off his peaked chauffeur's cap and nodded as he approached them."

Eyeing him suspiciously one said in a languid voice, "You lost brother?"

Conrad looked up at the number on the door behind them. "Don't think so, though maybe you can help me from here on in."

The men looked at one another and grinned. The second man said, "I'd say you is well and truly lost. You're in Harlem boy."

"Yes I know, and pleased to be here," smiled Conrad.

The second man sprang suddenly to his feet, his eyes glinting angrily, "Don't you get cute with me white boy – I say you're in the wrong place, so take that fancy motor and your little rich missy in the back and hi-tail it out of here – unless you is tired of living boy!"

"Hey, steady now Joshua," his friend said, "That ain't no way to treat a stranger. I'm sorry about my companion here - he gets a little hot blooded. You see the only white folk we get coming down our street is mostly cops, and they usually ain't friendly. Now I don't think you're no cop, but I'd say you've seen some service, the way you carry yourself."

Conrad nodded, "Marine Corps. You?"

"Five years in the US Army." The man narrowed his eyes, "I got some good memories of those times – and then I got some real bad ones. I seen some things, I done some things, and I had things done to me that I don't care to think back on, but they haunt me just the same. You know soldier, if we both was still in uniform, you and me wouldn't be talking like this; colour of our skin an all.. I'm kinda surprised we're talking now to tells you the truth."

"So why *are* you talking to him?" demanded his friend, "he must want something bad to come to down this street with a white lady in tow, and I say tell him to go to hell!"

"Calm it down Josh, let's hear the man out."

"Well yes, I am looking for something, someone to be precise," said Conrad. "And as one soldier to another I'd like to ask for your help in finding him."

"And who would that someone be?"

"An ex-serviceman like us man, name of Curtis."

The man immediately put a hand on his friend's arm, "Easy Joshua. And why might you be looking for him mister?"

"That's kind of personal. We have a message for him."

"From where?"

"England. From another lady, a white lady."

The man's eyes flickered for a moment. He said, "And just how would this Curtis know a white lady in England?"

"I'd rather he heard the message himself, its kind of personal you understand."

"Tell the man to go to hell, before I -"

"Josh, hold it down. Listen mister, what makes you think this Curtis lives here?"

"The Regent Trust found an address, I work for them, as does the lady in the car."

"I've heard of Mr Oliver Regent. They say he's a good man, do anything for the poor people, black and white. Some folk say that he was sent by God- you believe that mister? I thought it was only Jesus Christ that was sent by God. How do you work that one out, is he an impostor what do you think?"

Conrad placed one foot on the bottom step, leaned against the railings and scratched his chin. "I guess the only person who can rightly answer that would be God."

The man smiled and nodded. "I guess you're right there mister. We'll just have to wait for judgment day."

"Anyhow, we just want to give this message to Curtis," said Conrad. "Then we'll go. He might be pleased."

"Well, you won't have to wait for judgement day to find that out."

"Oh?"

"I'll tell you whether Curtis will be pleased or not."

"You do know him then?"

"You're looking right at him. You'd better step inside the house mister, and bring the lady with you."

Several pairs of eyes stared, some in wonder, some with mistrust, as Conrad and Audrey were ushered into a crowded kitchen hung with pots and pans.

Audrey slowly glanced around; there were three women, Curtis and an old man, and several children, ranging from about 6 years of age to 13, who had just appeared, the two smaller girls now peering at the visitors from behind the table. Joshua, who had followed them in from the street, stood in the doorway, observing the proceedings warily.

"Will you have some coffee Miss, Sir?" said the older of the women, whom Audrey took to be Curtis's mother, as they sat down at the table. "That is, if you're not here to try and take my son to jail, in which case- " She lifted a large cleaver from beside the cooker and gave a meaningful look.

"And that means you won't be getting no coffee either," said Curtis and gave a sudden roar of laughter. Audrey laughed rather nervously.

"We'd appreciate coffee Maam," said Conrad.

"Excuse my manners," said Curtis, "this lady that is handy with the meat axe is my mom, as you can tell, and these two fine looking ladies and my two sisters, Delilah and Rose, and hiding under their skirts there," he grinned, are their beautiful, mischievous children."

The boys and girls all giggled self- consciously. "And that lazy good for nothing brother of mine Joshua, holding up the doorway, you've already met."

Joshua scowled.

"And your father Curtis?" enquired Audrey, "He's out at work I take it?"

There was a second of silence in the room before Mrs Westby said, "He's resting honey. Resting in God's care. Struck down with a fever five summers ago." She pointed to a framed portrait on the wall, adorned with passages from the scriptures. "The Lord have mercy on his soul, Amen."

"Amen," chorused Rose and Delilah, making the sign of the cross.

"I'm so sorry," said Audrey.

There was a further brief silence then the old man spoke.

"Curtis said you was in the service?" he said to Conrad, "what unit would that be?"

"He was in the Marines granddaddy," said Curtis. "And he and this lady are from the Regent Trust."

"I'm just a driver sir," explained Conrad. "Miss Stephenson is – well she'll tell you in a moment."

"Oh," said Mrs Westby with interest, as she filled two cups from a steaming coffee pot, "you gonna give us a new house? I heard the Regent Trust give people new houses, with bathrooms and curtains and proper heating…"

The old man guffawed, "Oh that's for white folk Salina, no one gonna give us nothing, and we don't need no new house we got a fine house right here thank you, yes siree."

"The Regent Trust aims to help everyone, regardless of colour, we could probably help you with a bathroom, and improve your heating,"

"Really?" beamed Mrs Westby, "well tell me Miss, who do I talk to about that?"

"I'll be pleased to put you in touch with our housing department here in New York."

"I say we don't want no fancy new bathroom," protested the grandfather.

"Who's we?" retorted Mrs Westby.

"I am the head of this household," said the old man and banged his stick. ""And I say no new bathroom."

"God, is the head of this household excuse me father…" Curtis held up his hands, "Could we get down to business here please? Now this message you have for me from England, what is it?"

Audrey cleared her throat and looked round at the expectant faces, "Are you sure you wouldn't prefer to talk in private?"

Curtis shrugged, "This is my family; there ain't much private goes on here."

"Very well," said Audrey. "The Regent Trust is a foundation established by Mr Oliver Regent for the welfare of people. We also provide a tracing service for families and individuals to find missing relatives. This has proven to be on the increase especially after the war." Audrey paused momentarily and stared directly at Curtis. The young man met her gaze then lowered his head.

"I have come here to establish if you Curtis are who I am looking for and with that I have several questions."
Curtis sat in silence contemplating the situation.

"What do you want to know miss?" Mrs Westby asked.
Audrey sighed. "The questions are for Curtis, he must answer them."
Curtis lifted his head, "Ask them," he said looking directly at her.

"Very well," Audrey said, "Curtis, were you in the US army stationed in England during the war."

"Yes" he nodded, "I was."

"Where was that?"

"Just outside London." He replied, "In the country, not exactly sure where, but I remember it was close to the river. "

"Do you remember a fairground on Hampstead Heath."
Curtis momentarily closed his eyes then nodded, his face impassive, "I do, and I remember Nellie, is she's what this is all about Miss?"

One of the little boys laughed, and Mrs Westby shot him a reproachful look.

"Yes," said Audrey. "She wants you, and Whillan needs a father."

"Whillan," Curtis shook his head and smiled, "so she named him after that river, that's just what she said she would do."

"He's growing up fast," Audrey said "and he's started asking questions."

"What?" Mrs Westby looked agog at her son. "Who, is Whillan"

"He's your grandson," Audrey said kindly, "Curtis's little boy."

"You have a son in England, son?" Mrs Westby asked him, "Why you never tell me this?"

Curtis sighed heavily, "You know what happened over there, mama. My wife, she was carrying a child."

Mrs Westby and her two daughters began to talk amongst each other excitedly, while the old man banged his stick and muttered; "Well, well, well," shaking his head in wonder.

Finally Mrs Westby called, "All right hush now," and turning to Audrey said, "So this lady loves my boy?"

"She and I are good friends. I know she does, and she'd welcome him back with open arms. But she fears you may have forgotten her Curtis."

Curtis began shaking his head and smiling wryly. "Women," he said.

"What do you mean?" asked Audrey.

"They all love a happy ending - especially for other folks. But what makes you imagine that, curiosity aside I still carry any shred of concern for the lady I left behind?"

"Because you haven't denied it."

"Denied what?" Curtis spread his hands out in a gesture of defiance.

"That you still love her," said Audrey boldly. "Do you deny it?"

He shook his head, "I have never forgotten her, she was beautiful and I loved, and love her still, that's why we married. We used to meet secretly by the river where I was stationed." He smiled at the thought. "They were strange times Miss. I hoped one day if I survived the war that I would go back for her, but the military put pay to that. They took me back to the camp that last night. I was beaten and put into solitary confinement until we were shipped out. I tried to write to her but the army put pay to that, ripped up all my letters. After the war I came home and thought about contacting her again, but it had all seemed a dream. Life here is hard and we would never have survived," Curtis, deep in thought sighed again. "And from what I know Miss, England's the same as here in America with regard to Negro people. White folk don't take kindly to us living in the same street, let alone sharing a bed."

Mrs Westby gave the children another stern look to forestall any giggling.

Audrey said, "Nellie's a fairground girl, they take people for what's in their hearts, not what they look like or where they come from. You'd be welcomed by one and all amongst them. And something tells me you'd be a wonderful father to Whillan."

There were amazed intakes of breath around the room. All eyes were on Curtis. He turned to Audrey, "This has been a shock for me, lady, I don't mind saying. I did often wonder what happened to Nellie, and the baby."

"She's managing, and she's doing her best for Whillan, he's such a sweet little boy," said Audrey misty eyed, "but she thinks about you, and misses you terribly, I know she does."
Mrs Westby looked wistfully at her son, "England's a mighty long way."

"I'm sure he'd come back and visit you when he could." Audrey said, "Curtis, I can't expect you to answer right away. But I'll arrange a passage to Southampton on the Queen Mary, with all your expenses paid."
Mrs Westby and the two sisters sat open-mouthed, staring expectantly at one another and then at Curtis.

Finally he said, "If the answer be yes, it would not follow that I can up and leave my mama and sisters and granddaddy with no one to support them. My wage from the night shift at the garage is all they got right now""

"You gotta do what your heart tells you son," said Mrs Westby. "If you go, there'll be a place in my heart that feels real empty in one way, but mighty full in another, 'cos you'll be with the lady you love and the little child you're gonna love soon as you set eyes on him. We'll be all right here - Joshua can get a job."
Joshua, looking suddenly horrified pointed an accusing finger at Audrey and Conrad and spluttered, "I knew these two were trouble!" The rest of the family erupted into mirth.

Curtis stood up. "If I do go back to Nellie, and I say if, it won't be on charity ticket either. I'll pay my own way to England, either that or work my passage."
Mrs Curtis threw her hands up, "That's just plain stupid son..."

"Maybe." Curtis then gestured to Audrey and Conrad "I want to thank you two people for coming here to see me today, whatever I decide."

"Here's the number of the Waldorf Astoria," said Audrey handing him a card. "You can call me there collect. Let me know by tonight if you can? The sooner the better, for you and Nellie."

"And Whillan," said Mrs Westby, wiping a tear from her eye.

Curtis ushered Audrey and Conrad to the front door. "Thank you for coming here Miss and I will think about what you have said. It's all been a bit of a shock that's for certain. I will think about it but I can't promise I will come back, may be it's all to late."

Audrey touched his arm, "It's never too late Curtis,"

Curtis sighed and looked at the card Audrey had given him. "It may be for us Miss, too much time gone on since then," He squeezed her hand gently. "I'll say goodbye now and thank you again." He said and hastily closed the door.

Back at the Waldorf Audrey thanked Conrad and said goodnight. She watched the big limousine sweep away up the avenue. At the hotel entrance she stopped, turned back and crossed the street to the call box. She dialled Richard's number, but there was no reply.

Replacing the receiver she gave a start. A few yards down the street a man was walking towards the call box, and as he drew nearer she saw, beneath the homburg hat the long scar running across his cheek. Her heart pounded and for a few seconds she felt paralysed. Then with an effort she ran out, seeing from the corner of her eye the man increasing his pace towards her. At the edge of the sidewalk she leapt back as a huge shape roared up.

"You OK Miss Stephenson?" It was Conrad in the limousine.

"I saw that man watching you so I turned back." He got out.

"Here, let me escort you over the street."

Safely inside the hotel lobby Audrey; still breathless with fright said, "I can't thank you enough Conrad. I can't think what might have happened if you'd not been there."

"Best not think about it, but in future I advise not leaving the hotel unescorted, especially at night."

"Yes of course, thank you again."

Audrey ordered a late supper from room service. There was no message from Curtis. At 11pm she got into bed and turned out the light. Tomorrow, she thought, I shall set out for New Orleans, and Martin's family.

CHAPTER TWENTY-SEVEN

"What a lovely room, but is it always this hot?" Audrey took off her straw hat and mopped her brow with her handkerchief.
The bellboy set her suitcase down by the wickerwork dressing table.

"You're in Louisiana now Maam," he smiled, "I'll put on the breeze." He pulled a cord and the ceiling fan whirred into life.

"Oh that's wonderful, thank you," said Audrey lifting her face to the cool air current as she proffered a quarter.

The bellboy touched his cap appreciatively; "Thank you Maam, and I wish you a pleasant stay at the Belmont."

Audrey had been somewhat awestruck during the journey down, aware for the first time now of the sheer scale of America, and of its diversity of landscape and people. In New York, true she had observed real poverty in Harlem, and in Manhattan too, where hobos starved watching limousines bowl by. Entering Louisiana she found it harder to assess the situation – did the fly blown homesteads and frail looking agricultural workers on the roadsides signify rural deprivation, or merely a simpler way of life? If the crops failed or were washed out by the heavy rains, there were, unlike New York, very few passing millionaires from whom to beg, nor the multiplicity of restaurant garbage bins in which to forage.

New Orleans itself was somewhat different, a little more like New York from what she had seen as they drove in, but more mysterious and exotic, the grand old houses in the French style rich with the aura of faded splendour. She wondered about Martin's family; were they poor subsistence farmers living on the outskirts, or more prosperous city folk? She could not recall him telling her much about them. All that Daisy had tracked down was an address.

"Come in," said Audrey, answering a knock on the door.

"Is your room to your satisfaction Miss Stephenson?" It was Conrad.

"Perfectly thank you, now that the fan's on."

"Does get sticky in these parts doesn't it? I've had a word with the Maitre D" here, and it turns the place we're looking for is just around the corner."

"Oh, gosh…how fortunate." Audrey felt suddenly on edge.

"It's 4pm now, so if you wish, when you've freshened up we can go right on round there and you can meet these people."

"Now you mean?"

"If you wish, I am at your disposal Miss Stephenson."

Audrey breathed in. She said decisively, "Give me half an hour."

"I would prefer to go in alone, if you don't mind Conrad."

They were sat in the limousine down a side road. Opposite was a slightly ramshackle looking motel.

"I'll be right out here Miss Stephenson, keeping an ear out. You just shout if you need me."

Audrey got out of the limousine and immediately stopped in her tracks. By the entrance to the motel a young man, his back to her, was applying an oilcan to the hinges of the gate. Her eyes fixed with incredulity on the figure by the gate. She could see the down at the back of the young man's neck, his close-cropped hair, the, oh so familiar shape made by his wrists and arms as he bent to his task. 'Oh Martin is that you.?' her thoughts raged. 'What if he didn't die after all? And, what would she do if this was him.'

Her heart was thumping, her throat gone dry. 'The past has altered, the whole world has changed I must get out of here.... But what if it is Martin...I must find out............'

As if in a surreal dream which had engulfed her thoughts she carelessly stepped out into the road and walked more slowly over towards the gate, feeling that at any moment the earth might explode around her. She could feel those emotions deep within her surging to her breaking heart.

Suddenly the front door of the house opened, a little girl ran towards him.

"Daddy, Daddy," she called; the man picked her up and held her in his arms.

Audrey froze, she couldn't move. She didn't see the lorry round the bend hurtling towards her. It was only when the driver jabbed loudly at the horn that brought reality rushing back and she stepped out of its way just in the nick of time.

Sobbing she turned to go back to the limousine, she heard the little girls voice, "Did you see that lady nearly got run over!"

The young man straightened up and ran towards Audrey.

"Martin..." she murmured weakly swaying out f conscientious and fell limply into his arms.

The autumn sun was low in the sky, casting a golden, late afternoon light over the fields as Audrey sank into an armchair on the veranda at the rear of the motel.

"Are you feeling a little better now?" the young man asked her as he poured out the mint julep into a tumbler and handed it to her. Audrey lifted her head and took the glass. The man, a young woman and the little girl were staring intently at her. Conrad who, having run out from the limousine when he saw Audrey faint, had also been invited in, stood by the door

"Yes, I'm fine now, thank you" she said sipping the liquid, "It was just a shock...seeing...er ...the lorry coming towards me" She looked at the young man, how like Martin he was - but it was not him.

The young man smiled, "You were very lucky Miss, are you sure you are OK."

She nodded and turned to Conrad, "We should be going; I've taken up too much of their time."

Conrad smiled, and helped her to her feet. "Thank you for your hospitality." She said to the couple, "You've been very kind."

"Glad to help Miss but, tell me...before you passed out you called out a name, Martin, my brother's name...?"

Audrey reached for the arm of the chair to steady herself.

"Sit down Maam" the young man, said helping her back into the chair "Hearing Mart's name like that on the mouth of a stranger, no offence ma-am."

She smiled weakly, "None taken,"

The young man smiled, "Yes, I'm Brian, his younger brother, this is my wife Joan and our daughter Charlotte, but tell me how do you know him."

Audrey sighed heavily, closed her eyes, tears were forming, pricking her eyes. Martin felt close to her, in this house that was his home.

"We met in Liverpool in 1944," she said her voice breaking as she remembered those heady days when they had danced and fell in love. "We courted for a few months but then he was to leave. Before he went he sent me a ring, an engagement ring. He told me to arrange the wedding, he would be back in three months and we would be married but he didn't come back to me."

"My son was killed in action in Italy in '44" An older woman had appeared in the doorway,

"Come and sit down Mother," Brian said, "This is Martin's girl."

"Audrey," She said kindly ... Martin wrote about you. Oh my dear it is so good to see you, to meet you. He was so looking forward to making you his wife."

Audrey eyes filled with tears again.

"I understand your shock, Brian does look awful like his elder brother now." Mrs Corbett continued. "You had to come – to see if he was really gone. I know. I hoped one day, that if you truly loved him you would find a way to come to us."

"I've a great deal to tell you," she said, "You see, we…Martin and I have a child, a little girl… Margaret."

Martin's mother closed her eyes and clasped her hands in silent prayer. "Oh how Father would have loved this news.
He died shortly after Martin, couldn't come to terms with his death and just faded away. Martin was so full of life and we all miss Martin every day that goes by. We know what pain you must have lived with Audrey – and to have borne your child through all that…" she shook his head sorrowfully. "But out of tragedy comes new life – Martin lives on in your daughter! We have another grandchild!"

Mrs Corbett looked mistily now at Audrey, "Oh, tell me dear, when can we see the little darling? Charlotte would love to meet her –We're all longing to meet her!" She squeezed Audrey's hand excitedly, "Does she have your eyes, or Martin's, is she - oh my - do you have a picture of her?"

"I – I'm afraid not, there were difficulties you see -"
Mrs Corbett frowned, "Difficulties?"

"That's what I must explain," said Audrey. Oh but what on earth do I tell them she thought despairingly – Daisy was right, this is the very situation she warned me about…

Her voice unsteady she began, "When I had received the news about Martin…I didn't know what to do with myself…"

"Of course dear, of course," said Mrs Corbett gently.

"Money was short, and I gave - I asked, someone to look after Margaret."

There was an awful silence as Audrey felt their eyes on her. Taking a deep breath she continued, "I hadn't even a roof over my head you see, because well, to tell you the truth my family had cut me off – disowned me -"

"Why?" demanded Brian incredulously

207

"Hush dear," said his wife, "give her a chance."

"That's a very long story, which I'll tell you one day I promise. The upshot was, I was on the breadline, and I had to do what was best for Margaret."

"Till you got back on your feet," said Joan.

Audrey nodded vaguely but did not look at her. "I took various menial jobs, then went to London and worked in a hospital, and that's where I was taken on by the Regent Trust, who sent me to America, and right now I'm working for their family tracing department."

"And you thought quite rightly that charity beginning at home, you must start with us," beamed Mrs Corbett.

"Well, yes, I suppose..."

"And now here you are and we're a might pleased to see you. And you young man," Mrs Corbett turned to Conrad, "how do you fit into this tale?"

"Oh I'm an employee of the Regent Trust, a driver Maam," said Conrad, "tasked to escort Miss Stephenson on this mission."

Mrs Corbett ruminated on these sudden revelations. "So now you've found us, and being estranged from your original family you have no ties in your home country, you are free to settle here. She and little Margaret would be most welcome,"

"Oh, we should want nothing better," said Joan looking imploringly at Audrey. "Why, you can stay right now, this very night – carry on your work for the Regent Trust here in New Orleans, you too Mr Conrad sir, there's a mighty lot of poor folk would praise the Lord to have you here amongst them, I'll have a bed made up for you right away, you can have Martin's old room, if you feel comfortable with that - "

Alarmed, Audrey interjected, "Oh but its not as simple as that, you see –"

"No I'm sure," agreed Mrs Corbett, "Let's not jump ahead of ourselves. Audrey will need to report back to the Regent people, first, tell them what's happened, that she's been reunited with her in-law family and that she now intends to live here from henceforth on with her daughter, our granddaughter."

"No no, you don't understand -" pleaded Audrey. "Margaret – you see she's in England -"

"Now don't you worry about that," advised Brian, "we'll pay to have her brought over, or if you prefer to travel back and come on over with her, we'll cover all the costs."

"Oh but I'm sorry, you see it would be impossible -"

Mrs Corbett raised an implacable hand, "Nonsense. We are by no means wealthy folk, but the motel's been doing well, we've got money put aside, and what better way to spend it than bringing Martin's girl and granddaughter to our home and to our hearts."

"But it's not the money -"

"I understand it will mean a big adjustment for you, but let me ask you this my dear, do you like what you've seen of America?"

"Yes but..."

"And do you think this would be a loving family and a fine home for a young child and her mother?" She spread his arms to take in Brian, Jeanie and young Charlotte, who had just come into the room and was looking at Audrey with an affectionate, doe-eyed expression.

Audrey bit her lip, "Of course," she said querulously, "of course, but there's more I have to tell you -"

"I tell you what, it can wait," Mrs Corbett stood up decisively. "Will you stay the night? You can tell us more in the morning, you must be dog tired, and you Conrad."

"That's very kind of you sir," said Audrey, "but we couldn't possibly impose at the drop of a hat like this, we are booked into the Belmont Hotel, and I have to head back for New York first thing in the morning." This was not strictly true, but she felt desperate now to escape. "I will write to you from there."

"We understand," smiled Mrs Corbett, "you need time to make your arrangements – bringing a little girl all the way across the Atlantic takes some planning! And listen dear if you really feel you'd rather not settle here just yet awhile, then in the meantime we can always come to England to see you and Margaret - Matt here will look after the motel, after all its going to his and Joan's when I'm not around. We'll stay in a hotel when we come to England Audrey, we wouldn't be any trouble to you, but we'd be happy to look after Margaret if you need to go away with your good works my dear...."

"You've all been so very kind," stammered Audrey, feeling herself about to cry. She got up, "And I'll explain everything in my letter, I promise."

"There's nothing to explain dear, really," said Mrs Corbett breathlessly. She came forward and wrapped her arms tightly around Audrey, "but you must send us that photo of Margaret, you promise now, I so look forward to holding her in my arms, just like I'm holding you now. Oh - it's a miracle, nothing less than a God given miracle!"

Back to the Belmont Hotel Audrey lay restlessly on the bed, her thoughts agitated, her emotions raging. After a while however her mind grew calmer, and she began to have an idea.

"Richard -"

"Audrey, Darling – how are you? I've been worried about you."

It was Sunday evening and Audrey was stretched out on the bed in her room at the Waldorf, a large cocktail in one hand, the 'phone in the other.

"I'm sorry Richard I had to go away for a few days."

"Yes I know."

"Oh – how?"

"Ah, well, I 'phoned the hotel, they said you were out of town."

"Oh. I've been to New Orleans."

"Quite a trip."

"Yes, in more ways than one – I was all right though, I had an ex-Marine with me."

"I see!"

Audrey laughed, "Nothing like that I promise – he's engaged to Daisy, but don't breathe a word, they're keeping it secret."

"Who's Daisy?"

"Works for the Regent Trust, awfully sweet."

"Right. What's the weather like there at the moment?"

"The leaves are turning golden."

"You'll enjoy autumn in New York, though I wish I could be there to enjoy it with you."

"You will, or rather, we'll see autumn in London together - I'm coming home Richard."

"What? Well that's great, but I thought you were scheduled to stay out there for six months?"

"I was – but a lot has happened in the last few days, and well - I have to come back."

"What about the Regent Trust?"

"I've told them. They can't complain, I've brought in a large sum of money already in sponsorship."

"So, when do you leave?"

"I sail on the Queen Mary tomorrow."

"Well, I'm bowled over, but naturally I'm delighted. I'll book tickets for the opera, and we'll have dinner together as soon as you get back -"

"That's very sweet Richard, though I'll be rather busy for a few days – I have to see a solicitor, and then I might be going away for a couple more days."

Where to?"

Audrey hesitated, "I'll explain when I see you."

"You are a woman of mystery, you never cease to surprise me."

"Not really," said Audrey, "mysteries and surprises just seem to surround me that's all."

"I'll agree on that one. Which reminds me, any news on - that other matter?"

"George Fairweather?" Audrey lowered her voice, "no, I've heard had no word from him, what do you make of it?"

"I'm not sure. We'll talk more about that when you get back. Well Bon Voyage my dear, and I look forward to seeing you."

"Thank you Richard, likewise, I'll call you as soon as I arrive in London, and we will have dinner I promise."

The following day, Audrey was on the deck of the Queen Mary. The sun glinted off the waters of the New York harbour as the other passengers filed aboard. Daisy and Conrad had come to see her off. Now all three of them were straining their eyes towards the quayside, looking for Curtis.

"Did he definitely say he was coming?" asked Daisy.

"He didn't definitely say anything," sighed Audrey. "It's my fault, I only sent him the telegram yesterday."

Since the visit to New Orleans, Audrey had done everything in haste; the telegram to Curtis, appealing to him to accompany her back to the arms Nellie, and to his son had been a last minute impulse.

"I just thought if he doesn't come now he never will – I just know those two are made for each other, I know it, and I told him his ticket is all paid for – oh where is he!" She began jumping up and down to see over the heads of other passengers now crowding the rails.

Daisy and Conrad exchanged a look. "I do hope you have a pleasant trip Miss Stephenson," said Daisy, "its been so nice meeting you, and I hope everything works out for you back in England." Audrey turned to her, "It's been nice meeting you too Daisy," she smiled, "more than nice, oh," she sighed wistfully, "you don't know the half of it, what you've done for me- "

"New Orleans," said Daisy.

"Yes?"

"Has it - "Daisy hesitated, "Has it something to do with why you're going home so suddenly?"

Audrey looked awkward for a moment. "You're sharp Daisy - "I…" she tailed off.

"You don't have to say any more – and look, it's not my place to give advice, but please, whatever you do, be careful- "

"Thank you -"

Audrey's next words were drowned out in the hooting of the ship's horn.

"All ashore those not sailing," bellowed a steward.

"Well this is it I guess," said Daisy. "Will you come over for our wedding if you have time?"

"I'd be delighted," beamed Audrey.

"I can't wait to see Miss O'Grady"s face when I tell her!"

"It's the only reason she's marrying me," said Conrad drolly and they all laughed.

The ship honked again. Audrey bit her lip, "It doesn't look as if Curtis is coming."

Conrad reached out and shook her hand. "You can't win them all Miss Stephenson."

Audrey and Daisy embraced, then Daisy and Conrad made their way to the gangplank. Audrey squeezed herself a place at the rail and looked down onto the quay. Suddenly she noticed a commotion, raised voices, scuffling.

"Trying to jump ship eh! Get the louse out of here!"

"I tell you man I got get aboard…"

"   Call the harbour police."

"Let me through!"

"You're going nowhere, you no good…"

Audrey caught her breath as she saw, struggling to evade the clutches of two burly stevedores and a harbour official, the desperate figure of Curtis. She leaned over the rail and yelled for all she was worth, "Let him aboard, I have his ticket…"

The wind, whipping over the deck carried her voice away, lost in a tumult of ships' horns and shouting passengers.

In desperation Audrey watched as Curtis was dragged back. With tears in her eyes, she was about to turn away when she saw two other figures enter the scene on the quayside: Daisy and Conrad. She watched breathlessly as Conrad stood calmly and spoke with the harbour man, pointing up towards the ship. Audrey waved frantically and a moment later Curtis, released, ran like an Olympic athlete up the already rising gangplank, and on to the Queen Mary.

CHAPTER TWENTY-EIGHT

November 1947

"Nell – come in come in this minute, oh I'm so happy to see you!"

Audrey had thrown open the door of her apartment with such force Nellie stared as if the hinges might buckle.

"I can see that, well welcome back."

"I've a present for you," said Audrey breathlessly, "and I can't wait for you to see it!"

"Oh, you shouldn't have bothered - " began Nellie, as Audrey, breathless with excitement pulled her friend into the apartment, almost dragging her coat from her and hanging it up.

"But first – first - come and have a drink, a large one – come on, come on…!"

"My, you *are* glad to be back."

"Glad to see you, my dear – gin, whiskey – no champagne, this evening it's got to be champagne -"

"Champers? How'd you -"

"Don't ask questions," burbled Audrey, producing a large bottle of champagne, "and I'll tell no lies."

"Who's the other one for?" Nellie said, seeing Audrey set three glasses on the drinks table.

Audrey's eyes sparkled mischievously, "My butler."

"What?" Nellie exclaimed.

"Except he's not going to be my butler much longer, just doing me a favour – he's cooking dinner right now, roast chicken in white wine, and vegetables, with lemon sorbet to follow -"

Nellie shook her head in bewildered amusement, "Oh I see, cook's night off is it?" she said sardonically. "Butler indeed! Have you taken leave of your senses since you got off that boat Audrey Stephenson?"

"Never call the Queen Mary a boat Nell, the sailors don't like it," said Audrey.

"Oh, excuse me," chuckled Nellie.

"No, she's a ship, a great lady- just ask my butler." Audrey reached to the mantelpiece and shook a small brass bell.

"That's right, she's a great lady," said a man's voice, "but not as great as you."

Nellie spun round, her mouth fell open. Swaying slightly, she stared towards the kitchen, where framed in the doorway stood Curtis. He was wearing a smartly cut dark blue suit, and was smiling. "You're the greatest lady in the world."

Nellie gaped. "Curtis?" she whispered.

"Don't tell me I've changed that much," he grinned, "apart from the suit, which your friend here insisted on buying me."

"What the…" Still gasping Nellie shot Audrey a look, "Oh - you're a crafty one – but, oh my eye…tell me this is a dream…butler eh-?"

"Well, I can open that bottle there at least – that's if we have something to celebrate – do we Nell?"

Nellie looked fit to burst, "You bet we do" she laughed "Come here you!"

The next second they were locked in each other's arms, tears rolling down Nellie's cheeks. Audrey, gesturing to Nellie, retreated to the kitchen and closed the door behind her.

A few minutes later she peeped tentatively out. Nellie and Curtis were sat on the sofa holding hands and gazing serenely at one another.

"I was just waiting to hear the pop," said Audrey. The champagne was unopened.

Nellie looked up, her eyes still luminous with tears. "Your butler's neglecting his duties. He was telling me how everyone on the boat – sorry ship – kept taking him for a waiter."

"Yes, it wasn't easy being the only black passenger," said Audrey, "apart from that appalling snobbish African Padre who was the worst of the lot, and everyone staring as if he shouldn't be there. Poor Curtis was remarkably sanguine about it all."

"You forget, I've had that treatment from white folk all my life, present company excepted."

"Well you'll have no funny looks on the fairground – we're one big happy family, and you're going to be a very welcome part of it. Oh, I still can't believe you're really here!" She squeezed his hands tightly and leaned her head affectionately on his shoulder.

Curtis looked thoughtful, "What have you told Whillan?"

"Not much really, I told him you were away over the ocean, but you loved him very much, which he seemed to quite like – you're already a hero in his imagination."

"I hope I don't disappoint him in reality!"

"He'll be made up, believe me. I knew it wouldn't be long before I had to answer more and more awkward questions."

"Well, I hope I can answer them," sighed Curtis.

"Just get to know him – he'll love you, I think secretly he's been waiting for this moment, I think we both have." They turned to each other again.

Audrey coughed discreetly, "Look, why don't I leave you two alone for the evening- "

"No, no- " the couple cried in unison. "If it wasn't for you I wouldn't be here," said Curtis, "besides I'm the butler – for tonight at least."

"Then get that bottle open," laughed Nellie.

"Yes Maam!" Curtis stood up and saluted.

The champagne, along with much excitable conversation flowed, and a delicious supper was served. An hour later the three of them were sat around the table sipping brandy.

"You know Miss Stephenson…" began Curtis.

"For the last time, I'm Audrey."

"Sorry - Audrey, well I think that meal was better than anything we had on the Queen Mary."

"You cooked it," Audrey raised her brandy in salute.

"With a little help."

"It wasn't all you cooked up tonight the pair of you, was it," said Nellie. She gazed fondly at her husband, "You know I'm still thinking this is a dream and I'm going to wake up any minute."

Curtis patted her hand, "I feel the same way too honey, but here we are, together, and it's all thanks to Miss – to Audrey. We owe you a mighty big debt – and my ticket on the Queen Mary, along with this here suit too -"

Audrey held up her hand, "Stop there, we're friends, and if I hear any more about debts and money and what's owed we shall stop being friends."

"I wouldn't argue with her," advised Nellie. Curtis smiled and shrugged his shoulders in resignation.

"Well its been a lovely evening," sighed Nellie, "a bit of an understatement I know, but now I suppose it's time I took my husband home – think you'll be all right love?" She turned to Curtis with a look of concern.

"I guess tonight's as good a time as any, though I won't pretend I'm a might nervous about meeting your folks again after all this time – and my boy too."

"Whillan'll be abed by the time we get back to the fairground," assured Nellie, "me mum tucks him up if I'm late. You'll see him soon enough in the morning."

"I'm so pleased for you both," said Audrey. "And now I have just one more announcement to make." She rose from the table and put on the wall lights, casting a soft glow over the room.

"Gawd, what now?" Nellie gave a mock grimace, "Nothing could top this little surprise!" She nudged Curtis playfully.

Audrey turned towards them and said in a clear precise voice, "I've decided to take Margaret back."

There was a deathly silence for a few seconds. Then Curtis said, "That's your daughter right, the one you told me about on the voyage?"

"Yes."

"Oh Aud- " Nellie was looking shocked, uncertain how to respond.

"What? Is that such a surprise?"

"No – yes – sorry, I just never expected, from what you always said – so the couple that took Margaret in, they want to give her back?"

Audrey paced to the window then stopped. "This – is my decision"

"But I mean, have you told anyone?"

"I'm telling you," said Audrey, her voice on edge now, "my best friend. I'm sorry -" she put a hand to her temple, "perhaps this was the wrong time, but I just, wanted to share it with you, especially now you two are…" She made a gesture towards them both.

Curtis was looking embarrassed. Nellie's face was creased with bewilderment and concern. Audrey continued pacing. Finally Nellie said, "I don't think its right."

"I beg your pardon?" Audrey stared at her.

"You can't just go and demand Margaret back after all this time. There's two other people to consider – they've been looking after her, loving her – they're her parents now – it's not fair, not fair on them or Margaret."

Audrey looked at her aghast, "Excuse me, but Margaret is my daughter – you don't even know her -"

"You gave her away Aud, to two people who love her-"

"How do you know they love her?"

"All I'm saying is, she's theirs fair and square now-"

"This is not some country auction we're talking about -"

"Exactly – it's a child."

"My child."

"Not any more."

"We'll see about that."

"You might not be able to, there's laws you know, you signed her away, that's what you told me, it'll be legally binding I'll warrant."

"How dare you try to lecture me about what I can and can't do, I'm Audrey Stephenson, and I shall decide what will be regarding my own daughter! You've got your son, and now thanks to me your husband back. What right have you to tell me how I should conduct my affairs? Besides, don't you think I have feelings too?"

"I'm sorry for you love, believe me I am, but you can't go back on what you did, not where a kiddie's concerned. Its too late."

"Aghh!" Audrey pulled with both hands at her hair, her voice strangulated with anger and exasperation.

"I did what I thought best for my child at the time - pardon me for making for making a mistake, now I intend to rectify it. When I want something, I take it - there are ways, whether it be money or other means. I will do this believe me."

"I can't believe it," said Nellie shaking her head in sorrow, "you're a Stephenson all right, you're turning into your mother from what I've heard of her."

"You know nothing of my family, nothing about me," Audrey was almost shrieking now, "you're just a, just a -"

Nellie said briskly, "I know what I am, a poor working girl, and proud of it. I know what's right and wrong too. Perhaps it would have been better if you hadn't told me this Aud, not tonight of all nights – its rather spoiled things hasn't it."

"No, no you've spoiled things," Audrey rounded on her spitefully, "with your selfish, high-minded ingratitude. Oh why did I ever tell you!"

"I think it's time we were going Curtis." She got up and went to fetch her coat, Curtis shuffling after her awkwardly. As they were leaving she turned, her face sad, she said quietly, "Thank you for bringing Curtis back to me."

"Oh get out," snarled Audrey, "Get out, get out get out!"

Audrey drew back the sitting room curtain and looked out across London to see the streetlights already glimmering. The nights were drawing in. Nellie and Curtis had been gone almost half an hour, since which time she had paced relentlessly up and down, the walls of the apartment seeming to reverberate with the violence of the quarrel. Her thoughts raged this way and that, her mood obstinate and bitter. Suddenly the phone rang.

"Richard! Oh heavens - no of course I hadn't forgotten," Audrey stammered, "yes I tried to call...only the train from Southampton was delayed, there were simply no empty phone boxes and I had someone with me, and - something to arrange for them this evening, a surprise...what? - Oh, it's not important, although I wish now I hadn't bothered.... Yes, oh yes I'm absolutely fine, apart from this little upset, which doesn't matter except it's left me rather – drained I'm afraid ...yes I'm so looking forward to seeing you too, but look as I'm so awfully tired now could I call you tomorrow...of course, I promise...yes you too, goodnight darling."

Pouring another glass of brandy Audrey gazed from the window. After a moment her face began to shine with resolve. She reached for her diary, picked up the phone again and dialled.

"Mr Leeming?"

"Who's this?" the voice on the other end was suspicious.

"Audrey Stephenson."

"Oh -"

"I'm sorry to call you so late."

"That's all right, not at all, you were lucky to catch me in the office though, I'm working on your latest accounts as it happens, the um, you- know-what."

"Is there someone with you?"

"No, Mr Holt's gone home."

"Good, now listen I need your help, I want someone traced."

"Eh?"

"And when you've found them I shall need a letter drafted, a legal letter."

"I'm not a solicitor-"

"Never mind, just make it sound legal, if it's on your headed notepaper I doubt they'll know the difference."

"They?"

"I'll explain all the details tomorrow. Will you be in your office at around lunchtime?"

"Yes, but look I'm not a missing persons bureau."

"Use whatever means you have to, if it takes money I'll provide it." " "Its not just a question of money, I don't want to get involved in anything dodgy-"

"What do you think you've been doing up to now?"

Mr Leeming hesitated, "What do you mean?"

"Your accounts for the Regent Trust refurbishments make a wonderful work of fiction,"

"Now hold on -"

"Though I don't imagine you'd like them read out before a judge and jury."

"But that was your idea, to pay back Regent, he put me out of a job for no good reason, we both know he's a crook."

"So are you now."

"But I only followed your instructions -" protested Leeming.

"Then we're as guilty as one another aren't we," cut in Audrey, "we can share a taxi to the trial, though I'd rather it was Oliver Regent's day in court not ours, wouldn't you agree?"

"Look I'm afraid I shall have to reconsider our arrangement -

"It's too late for that, expect me at noon."

CHAPTER TWENTY-NINE

"I must confess I'm surprised."

Oliver Regent, leaning back in his leather chair and stretching his arms behind his head smiled a thin, amused smile and stared inquisitively at Audrey. It was the sort of look a cat might give a mouse, waiting for it to move again before pouncing on it.

"Surprised sir?" Audrey gazed back at him over the large desk that separated them, her eyes wide and innocent looking.

"I receive a series of telegrams saying how much you're enjoying America, then the next moment you're back. Thought you would have stayed for the Christmas Holidays."

"I just felt I'd done enough there, sir, for the time being," Audrey said earnestly. "And learned a great deal too, about how they do business in America, and how the charitable foundations benefit so hugely – I was inspired in ways I never expected, and what I learned there has given me so many new ideas that I think I can make greater strides for the Regent Trust here in England now."

"And you couldn't wait a few more weeks to start putting those ideas into practice?"

Audrey gave a sheepish look, "I suppose that's it in a nutshell, I know its not what was agreed regarding my trip, but I'm afraid patience was never my strong point when it comes to having ideas sir."

Oliver Regent laughed, "I admire your forthrightness. And I must admit," he waved a letter on his desk, "I am impressed by this donation, the largest single sum we've ever earned, which you seem to have conjured up by magic."

"They were just very nice people," she said, nevertheless beaming with pride, "and they have an awful lot of money, some of which they would far rather give to good causes than pay in taxes to the United States government. It just needed someone to show them how."

"And you were that someone," he grinned. "I spend years on the other side of the pond and I get little more than a few dinners and promises. I suppose I just wasn't as charming or as smart as you."

"Oh I don't know sir," said Audrey, "I believe you had difficulties of your own in America, it couldn't have been easy to-"

"Difficulties?" Regent's expression had hardened. "To what are you referring?"

"Oh, just what I overheard about your time in America, and what I took to be common knowledge, not that it's any of my business..."

Audrey stopped awkwardly but when he made no reply she went on, "I merely wished to point out that, shall we say, obstacles in one's personal affairs can have a bearing on success, in business dealings. I was fortunate in having no ties, or distractions, during my trip, so..."

She was floundering, and sensed him watching her do so with grim satisfaction.

There was an agonising silence before he said quietly, "I wouldn't believe all you hear about me Audrey. You might think this arrogant, but those who walk tall in this world tend to get shot at from time to time."

He swung his arms down and stood up, his mood lightened again.

"Well," he smiled, "I think we can consider your US mission accomplished Miss Stephenson. What do you propose to do now that you're back?"

Relieved, Audrey sat up and looked businesslike. "Well the refurbishment work on our Drayton Terrace premises is now complete -"

"So you and - what's her name – Nellie, will be celebrating."

"Well, as far as I'm concerned she can- " Audrey broke off then sniffed rather haughtily. "That area of responsibility is out of my hands now, the staff must take over the day to day running of the new hospital, and the hotel."

"I see, well from what I saw when I was over there last week the hospital is transformed, a real showpiece, and the hotel will make good money. And now you've something else in mind?"

"Well I've been thinking sir, about where I started this journey – how I got involved with the Regent Trust."

"And?"

"Liverpool."

"Liverpool?"

"Yes – that's where it started, where I first saw your poster, and I was inspired to come to London."

"And you've done great things here."

"Exactly sir, London is important, the poor and needy are here for all to see certainly, but those kinds of needs aren't just here in the capital. I know Liverpool well and I've seen how some people are forced to live. I know the trust has already done a lot of work there, but I want to build on that now, to make sure the people of the north are not forgotten."

"Hmm," Oliver Regent looked at her through gimlet eyes. "And what do you think you can do in Liverpool, that our staff and volunteers who are there at present cannot?"

"Perhaps what I did in America, I still know some influential people in the city, who feel a connection to the place, and a sense of responsibility to those less fortunate. I'm talking about rich people." She watched his expression carefully as she spoke these last words.

Regent put his hands together. "Hmm, very well, Liverpool it is. When are you proposing to leave?"

"As soon as possible Sir, thought this would be a good time to find the property and start the project in the New Year, new beginnings…?"

Regent smiled, "Very well my dear, you'll keep me closely informed, you understand?"

"Yes sir, and thank you." Audrey smiled; her plan was falling nicely into place.

That evening, and Audrey was in her apartment on the phone to Mr Leeming.

"Did you have any luck?" she asked.

"As a matter of fact yes."

"Excellent – how did you manage it?"

"Well it was quicker than I thought. I remembered an old army pal of mine who's now a reporter on the Liverpool Echo. I rang him up and he went in and had a chat to the caretaker at the St Angelina's adoption place you mentioned. Slipped him a few shillings, and got the information."

"But how would the caretaker know," asked Audrey.

"Oh he's the driver too – when one of the kid's gets adopted, he drives them to the new family."

Audrey said dubiously, "Hmm, sounds like a suspiciously good memory – how much did your chum give him?"

"Ten bob he said, but it's all correct, he looked it up in the book."

"Book?"

"They record all the adoptions in a book apparently, names of all parties involved, dates and where the children are sent to. The book's kept under lock and key at St Angelina's, but the caretaker got hold of the key when the nurses weren't about and had a look."

"So she's somewhere in Liverpool?"

"Yes, and the date matched the name you gave me, Margaret. Yes, unless they've moved since, you'll find her in Liverpool all right. Now take this down...." He dictated an address. "Got that? I've done the letter you asked for too."

"Good work," said Audrey. "Have it delivered to me first thing tomorrow at my apartment, I must leave for Liverpool by the 10 o'clock train at the latest."

"There won't be time."

"Bring it over in a taxi, I'll pay for everything."

Leeming gave a worried sigh, "All right - though I tell you again I'm not at all happy about all this, cooking up phoney letters and whatnot, there's law against deception you know," he muttered. "Is this child really yours?"

"Of course, why else would I be doing this?" snapped Audrey. "Besides it's really no business of yours."

"It will be if there's any comeback."

"There won't be. Be sure to get that letter to me by the morning."

Audrey put the phone down. Her brow furrowed. She had still not called Richard.

CHAPTER THIRTY

The train had not been crowded; few people it seemed were travelling north. She had shared the first class compartment with an elderly vicar and an even more elderly lady reading a detective novel. Once or twice she had caught the vicar gazing at her in the curious way men of the cloth were wont to do, trying to guess perhaps at the quality of a person's soul, the sins one had committed, and the things left sadly undone.

Regarding the latter, Audrey felt as the train sped on, she was more determined than ever not to succumb. Her daughter Margaret would soon be in her arms once more, and would have all the things she had once despaired of being able to give her.

Arriving in Liverpool she had taken a taxi to the Adelphi Hotel and arranged her stay. Leaving her suitcase to be taken up to the room, without waiting she had then summoned another taxi, giving the driver the address supplied to her by Mr Leeming.

"Number twenty-two, to your right madam," said the driver. It had now begun to rain, as they had pulled up halfway along a terraced street. Telling the driver to wait Audrey got out, pulled her coat collar up and unfolded an black umbrella while several children gathered around to scrutinise the smartly dressed woman with the small expensive looking handbag. She smiled at the children, who laughed happily then ran off again chasing their ball. She had never been to this part of Liverpool before, though it reminded her very much of Jericho Road and she felt a sudden surge of nostalgia, half expecting to see Mollie appear at any minute. Her heart was beating fast. Steeling herself she breathed in deeply and knocked on the door of number twenty-two.

When it opened Audrey stood face to face with a man who looked to be somewhere in his thirties or perhaps early forties, dressed in a clean white shirt, trousers and braces. Audrey lowered her face, she remembered him. He though clearly did not remember her, for he smiled broadly, "Hello, is it about the Sunday school for our daughter?"

Audrey smiled nervously back, "It's about Margaret - yes, but -"

"Then come in, come in, out of the rain, my wife asked at the church and they said they'd send someone round, we'd like to enrol Margaret of course, she's ever such a good girl, and we want her to learn all about the Bible – Mary!" he called up the stairs. "Folk think it's ever so funny us being Mary and Joseph, not that you should blaspheme mind – Mary! Oh there you are love, this lady's from the Sunday school."

Audrey saw again the pretty young woman she had seen on that fateful day. Now she wearing a floral apron as she came down the stairs. She was carrying a young child in her arms. Margaret! Audrey's pulse quickened as she fought the urge to reach out her hands.

"Hello I'm Mary, I was just getting Margaret up from her nap, they say its good for them to have a sleep in the afternoon, even though she's just a few months over two now, and a big girl, aren't you darling?" She nuzzled the little girl's tousled hair with her nose. Then, looking more closely at Audrey her expression altered, "Have we met somewhere before?"

Audrey had a swooning sensation. "Yes, yes I'll explain, perhaps I could come in?"

Joe, oblivious, was beaming at Margaret, "She's a good girl too."

"Where's your manners Joe," said Mary, her eyes now fixed on Audrey, "take this and show the lady into the front room."

Joe grabbed the umbrella from Mary's hand, and drew a chair up to a small drop leaf table for Audrey. Mary set Margaret down on the rug then sat opposite Audrey. Joe stood by the window and Margaret chattered softly to herself, "...five, six seven, eight, nine..." Joe smiled. "We're teaching her numbers," he said proudly, "getting on well aren't you sweetheart."

Audrey, her stomach tightening, said. "I suppose I had better get to the point." Joe nodded expectantly, while Mary stared even harder at their visitor. "I am here about Margaret, but I'm not from the Sunday school." She lowered her voice to a whisper and leaned towards them, "I am Margaret's mother."

There was silence, broken only by Margaret's innocent murmuring on the rug. Joe seemed robbed of the power of speech. Mary said in a strained voice, "Joe, please take Margaret into the other room."

Her husband picked up Margaret and carried her out. When he returned a moment later his face was like thunder. "Right, now you listen to me, you've no right to be here, now please leave." He pointed his finger at Audrey then the door.

Mary held up her hand, "No Joe, let's hear what she's got to say – then she can go."

"I'm so sorry," began Audrey, "I want to do this with as little fuss as possible, I didn't come here to cause any trouble -"

"Do what? And how could you not cause trouble," fumed Joe, "turning up out of the blue without so much as a by your leave, you've no right, visiting is against the rules once the child is with us, you must know that."

"I realise," said Audrey trying to keep her voice steady, "that this must be a great shock for you, but a principle is at stake, and a child's future, a child whose welfare must be our paramount concern. I have taken professional advice." She opened her handbag, took out the letter that Mr Leeming had composed, together with a bulging envelope and placed them in front of her on the table.

"And I'll give you a piece more advice," snarled Joe, "leave us alone, for everyone's sake."

Mary, who had been sitting very still said quietly, "I knew it was you the minute I clapped eyes on you. You were there that day, the day you gave Margaret up - they asked you to say it. You look different though." She ran her eye over Audrey's elegant attire, her fine shoes and bag.

"My circumstances, have changed somewhat," said Audrey slowly.

"Well," said Mary plainly, "what do you want now you're here?"

"Oh I see what this is about," intervened Joe waving his arm at Audrey, "you gone up in the world and think you can come and interfere with what's rightfully ours."

"Let her speak Joe," said Mary.

"I came here today, you are right, to find my daughter."

Joe glared. "Well you've found her, now you can go."

"Hush Joe," said Mary, "Margaret will hear and get upset – let her have her say."

Audrey cleared her throat and unfolded the letter. "This sets out my legal claim to the child, my child. If you choose to contest it, we will go to the High Court in London to settle the matter, which will cost you a great deal of money, money I doubt you have. I am now in a position to give Margaret a materially improved upbringing, much improved in fact, and to raise her in the kind of society from which she will substantially benefit."

"Are you going to sit there and listen to this Mary?" Joe's face was turning purple with rage. Mary had begun to shake visibly.

"This envelope contains £500 in cash as reimbursement for your trouble -"

"Why I've a mind to swing for you!" Joe was almost apoplectic now. He moved towards Audrey, a threatening glint in his eye.

"Joe!" said Mary abruptly, jerking her head towards the door. Margaret was stood there, her face full of curiosity.

"Mummy. Hungry, want milk?"

Mary leapt from her chair ran towards the little girl and wrapped her arms around her, "I'll fetch you some bread and milk, and a rosy read apple off our tree in a minute or two dear - this lady's – visiting us darling."

Margaret smiled and looked wide-eyed at Audrey. "Nice lady" she said.

There was a deathly stillness in the room. Audrey laid both her hands over the letter, not daring to return the child's gaze.

"Joe love," said Mary, "why not go and get Margaret's bread and milk, we'll talk to the nice lady for a minute." Joe, his fists clenched tight, slid out. Margaret, spying one of her picture books in the corner of the room, ran over, buried her head in it, and began chattering away cheerfully to herself.

Mary, tears in her eyes turned to Audrey and said, "All I can do is tell you is this, we don't need your money and we don't want it. We do all right here, Joe's got a steady job and we've a bit of garden out back. We get by just fine. Margaret's making friends in the street, we look after each other, we're happy. As for what you said about our 'trouble', we've had none. Joe and me couldn't have kids of our own - Margaret wasn't 'trouble', she was a gift from God and we love her beyond words. If you want to take that gift away badly enough, I daresay you'll find a way. It'll break our hearts that's all.

"Here we are princess!" announced Joe, his voice brittle with forced jollity as he came back in, "Mummy's special bread."

He set a plate of crusty buttered bread, a cup of milk and an apple down on the table. Margaret ran over and bit off a chunk of bread, "Hmm...lubbly." Then sidling up she draped her arms affectionately round Mary's neck, looked into her eyes and said softly, "Mummy lubbly."

The two of them stayed like that as if they were frozen in the space, Mary's head bowed, locked into one another. Joe's face as he looked on was filled with tenderness, then as if the spell had broken, he turned to Audrey.

"So you want to take her away from us do you?" he shouted, "Well, you can't, she's our daughter and here she stays. Take us to court with your fancy letters and lawyers, we'll fight you, somehow and we'll win.... you'll...."

At that moment Margaret began to cry, "Daddy not shout," she sobbed, "Not shout..."

Joe instantly picked her up in his strong arms; she buried her head in his neck.

"It's alright darlin'" he cooed and kissed her head, "I'll not shout any more." Then turning again to Audrey he whispered, "Now see what you've done Madam, I think you'd better go."

Audrey stared at her daughter in the arms of this man, he loved her, as did Mary, she could see that in their eyes. How could she take her from them? It would break their heart. She knew that pain all too well, and she had come here to inflict it on these poor innocents. Margaret was happy, she could see that, she was not her daughter anymore, barely recognised her, she had already forgotten.........

Without saying a word Audrey picked up the letter she had brought, tore it into small fragments and threw it onto the fire. Then, leaving the envelope of money on the table, she slipped quietly out of the house closing the front door behind her.

Back at the Adelphi Hotel she went as if in a trance into the lounge and ordered some coffee. She felt utterly exhausted, saddened from the experience and numb.

Setting down the tray the concierge proffered a newspaper. She was about to shake her head when something caught her attention. "Wait, yes might I see that please?"

Staring at the front page her eyes dilated. Beside a photograph of her mother, printed in bold type, but appearing to Audrey as a pronouncement etched in fire were the words,

CLARISSA,
WIFE OF PROMINENT BUSINESSMAN
MARCUS STEPHENSON
DIES
IN TRAGIC CAR CRASH.

A maelstrom of thoughts and emotions surged through Audrey. Inextricable from the shock, horror and disbelief lay a pungent, unmistakeable shot of pure glee. Like a hound taking the scent her mind raced forward, searching out the consequences – and the possibilities - that this bizarre and freakish twist of fate might now unleashed for her. Her face a mask of repose she read the details of the funeral, sipped her coffee and made her plans.

CHAPTER THIRTY-ONE

The car stopped at the arched iron gates and Audrey stepped out. The procession of mourners was filing slowly into the church. Waiting till everyone had entered she made her way through the gates, along the path and slipping quietly in, took a seat in the back pew. It was however impossible for her to be inconspicuous.

Heads began turning discreetly, curious about the stunningly beautiful woman in the tailored black suit who had just arrived. Those who thought they recognised her whispered to others, who themselves turned and peered. Audrey adjusted the delicate close fitting veil on her hat. The soft notes floated from the organ. She peered through the congregation at the polished oak coffin that stood, almost majestically, on trestles below the altar. It was hard to believe that the woman who had brought her into the world was now lying lifeless in that odd shaped box. A large spray of red roses lay on the top.

Then Audrey saw her father, seated in the front pew, his shoulders hunched in grief. An intense pity gripped her; this man that she had loved and respected, who had cared for and protected her, and on whose wisdom and love she had once so depended, seemed now but a frail shadow. Would she go to him after the service, could she find it in her heart to do what her heart now urgently pined for – to forgive, and be forgiven? Or would that be weakness, an error - a disastrous, perilous mistake?

The reverend, prayer book in hand stood before the coffin and began his address. Audrey closed her eyes, the image of her mother with Oliver Regent, or John Bamford as he really was, the day she had seen them together, a brother and sister locked in hatred. Blackmailers, as Audrey knew her mother had been, walk a dangerous tightrope, particularly when their victim is dangerous. In that same conversation Audrey had overheard with her own ears her uncle's gloating confession to murder. Few details of her mother's death had been published. How certain could anyone be that it had it been an accident…?

The pallbearers were hoisting the coffin onto their shoulders and begun their sombre deliberating tread. Marcus, leading the mourners out, glanced briefly at her as he passed. Only when the last person had left did Audrey move from the pew.

Standing on the church steps, she watched the slow procession over to the far side of graveyard, the reverend's solemn incantations carried faintly on the gentle breeze. Buttoning her coat Audrey drew a deep breath and followed on.

At the graveside Marcus, tears now visibly flowing, crumbled a handful of earth above the coffin as it was lowered, watching the soil dolefully as it fell, as if with every grain the strength and will to go on were leaving his soul. Then he saw the flower. It had landed on the coffin. Bending closer he gave a look of recognition. Audrey knew it too. It was Love Lies Bleeding, the cutting he had brought from Braeside and planted in the garden at Crosslands. He glanced up and saw Audrey again. His mouth fell open slightly, his features drooping, pleading. She returned his gaze for a few seconds then turned away and walked quickly back to the waiting car.

Crosslands please," Audrey instructed the taxi driver, "146 Whindolls Road."

On returning to Adelphi Hotel after the funeral she had felt not a change of heart about seeing her father, so much as a cautious sense of not wishing to leave anything undone. She would see him, talk for a few minutes, offer some kind of polite condolence and then leave. Surely there could be no harm in that? Onerous and awkward as it would be, she would have performed her duty. She had tried telephoning him from the Adelphi, but the line had been engaged. She had dined at the hotel and had an early night. It was now the next day. She stared out at the streets. Oh but what *would* she say to him?

Brushing past the maid who opened the door, Audrey strode into the study to find her father sitting in the armchair by the fire. It was as if nothing had changed in all the time she had been away, and an intense sadness gripped her.

"Clarissa?" Marcus looked up, "you've come back to me?" There were no lights on in the room, and Audrey realised he had been sleeping. She moved forward out of the shadows, into the light of the fire. "Father, its me Audrey."

"Audrey..." he sat up slightly, squinting towards her. "It was you at the funeral." She nodded. "Oh Audrey...!" he held his hands out towards her imploringly.

232

"Father, I…" Fighting the wave of empathy rising up within her Audrey pressed the hands briefly then pulled away. The bitter memory of the leaving the so-familiar room, ordered no less from the house, left the overriding impulse to recoil from his touch. The pity she felt now was mingled inextricably with disgust at his abjectness, his hypocrisy. Her jaw clenched tight she sat down opposite him wondering what to say, whether or not to go.

"Father what happened to her?"

"Run down by a car, the driver didn't stop," He shook his head in sorrow, continuing to murmur vaguely. "Your mother and I had been living apart, she was living in the apartment in the centre of Liverpool, that's where it happened, hit and run they called it."

"Had you…seen her recently?" she asked cautiously,

"No but she telephoned two days before," he answered, "She said she had got something important to tell me and she was about to come into a great deal of money."

"How did she seem to you?"

"Happy, joyful, like the Clarissa I first met." Marcus smiled, his eyes gentle in the fire's amber glow.

"Did she mention Uncle John?"

"I heard he'd come back," Marcus looked awkwardly at Audrey and smiled timidly, "But not from you mother,"

"Daddy what happened all those years ago?"

Marcus drew back momentarily, "That is all in the past Audrey, too painful to discuss; but what of you? Where have you been all this time - sweetheart?"

The endearment seared Audrey's heart. "London, America," she replied flatly.

"America?"

Audrey nodded, she realised her Father had decisively and intentionally ended the discussion,

"Yes," she said "But I came back to Liverpool to take Margaret back."

Marcus stared uncomprehendingly, "Margaret?"

"My daughter."

"Your daughter – take her back? But I thought you…that that was why you left home - "

"Why you threw me out you mean, you and Mother, cut me off."

"Audrey, please -" his face creased with pain.

"Can't you bear the truth? I struggled for a while, and eventually took Margaret to St Angelina's adoption agency, then moved to London. After you disowned me I had no money to look after her, I was forced to give her up."

"So you blame me."

"Of course." There was a devil in her now, and it would not spare him.

There was a long silence as Marcus stared into the fire. At last he said quietly, "I understand. I don't deserve your forgiveness, even now. But - where is your child – you said you had come to take her back?

"In the end I couldn't, the people she was with loved her, I could see that."

"I'm sorry."

"Don't be, it was the right decision, she belonged with them and it was too late to turn back the clock. It's too late in so many ways. When did Mother walk out on you?"

"A few months ago, the business had been going downhill you know – look Audrey, I know I can't ask much of you, but will you do me one favour?"

"What?"

"Go to see Jack."

Audrey sat up, she had barely thought about Jack in months. "Does he still live at the beach – I mean, is he all right - "

"Yes, and no, at least he needs help, he can't really look after himself out there now, exposed to the elements all year round, he needs a proper home, care. I visit him now and again, and I've tried to talk him into coming here, but he won't hear of it. He always liked you, he might listen if you were to suggest something – the veteran's hostel up by the docks perhaps, they look after them well there."

"I'll go at once." She got up.

"Now? But it's late, almost dark, stay the night at least."

"I know the way to the beach like the back of my hand, you forget, this was once my home."

She was already in the hall. Marcus had risen and was following. "Audrey, there's something I have to tell you, Audrey wait, please, it's important -"

The maid was opening the front door for her. "I'll write to you," she said not looking back, "now I must go to Jack."

As she strode out into the gathering dusk Marcus called after, "Audrey, the belt, I found the belt, ask Jack about the belt…"

"Jack?"

Audrey knocked harder on the door of the old hut. Although night had descended a three-quarter moon cast a soft light over the beach throwing up the outlines of rocks and casting strange shadows over the driftwood. The air was still, the waves breaking in a gentle, even rhythm. Audrey had a sudden image of Jack lying dead inside the hut, that in this mission too, she had come too late. But a second later the door eased open and she blinked in the sudden flare of a lantern.

"Audrey!" Jack said at once. "Why, your father was talking about you only the other day – come in, come in."

Audrey was greatly relieved; Jack seemed just as she had always remembered – almost.

Though his mind was sharp as ever, she noticed him limping markedly and wheezing noisily as he moved with some effort around the hut, heating milk on the stove and bringing out his customary offering of cheese, bread and brandy.   When he had laid out the little table he looked at her and said hesitantly, "You've heard the news then?"

"About my mother? Yes. "

"I'm so very sorry."

Audrey tossed her hair back petulantly. "I wish I could be," she said, then screwing her features up, "or do I? Well I am of course, I must be, she was my mother – I'm sorry I expect the shock has yet to take effect, to sink in or whatever they say -"

"Have a nip of brandy girl," said Jack gently proffering a glass, "it'll warm you at least."

"Thanks Jack," she squeezed his hand, "oh I'm so sorry I haven't been to see you for so long!"

"You're young, you've got to live your life, not waste your time with shrivelled old soldier like me," he said grinning.

"Trouble is," she sighed, "I've not been living my life very well."

Jack wagged a parchment-like finger, "Remember, the person who never made a mistake, never made a thing. And you've never had it as easy as people think girl – a silver spoon can be a curse as easy as a blessing. I don't mean to pry but what happened to your little girl?"

"Its all right, she's all right at least, she's been adopted by two very loving people. I'll get over it, or get used to it." The pain seared through her; she sipped the brandy.

"If you must know I thought your father wronged you sorely the day he turned you out Audrey," said Jack, "and though one shouldn't speak ill of the dead, your mother too. I can only think they were not in their right minds. Its too late for her to try to make amends, Marcus on the other hand -"

"I can't forgive him." Audrey's features were set in a hard stare. "I'd like to, but too much has happened, too much..." Tears began to fall down her face.

"There there," said Jack. He poured a little more brandy into her glass. "We'll talk of other things -"

"Jack," Audrey sat up now, her expression alert, thoughtful.

"Yes?"

"What is 'the belt'?"

"Who told you about that?" Jack said warily.

"Just now, as I left the house, my father said he had something important to tell me. He said, "Ask Jack about the belt" – what did he mean?"

"Ah," Jack put down his glass and leaned closer. "Well, before your mother left him, your father was rooting through some things in the attic there, boxes that had lain unopened for years. That's when he found the photograph."

"What photograph?"

"Of her brother."

"John Bamford?"

"The same, and in the picture he was wearing the belt, the one the police found at Braeside, the day Kitty Mason was found shot dead in the house, and your Uncle Mac's drowned body was pulled from the Loch."

Audrey was staring wide-eyed. "Good God," she breathed, her pulse quickening. "Look has my father told anyone else?"

"Not so far as I know, " said Jack. "I'm not sure he can think straight enough at the moment."

"But this is evidence," said Audrey excitedly, "we've got to take it to the police."

"That's what I told him."

"And?"

"I think he wanted to, but Bamford being your mother's brother, he felt torn. When she walked out on him, he was going to ring the police then, but again he put it off – thought she might come back maybe, probably he still loved her."

"Well now she's gone for good."

"True."

"I'll go back to Crosslands tomorrow and ask him for the photograph, I'll take it to the police myself."

Jack shook his head. "I've already tried to do just that."

"He said no – why?"

"Either he's afraid of Bamford – and no one could blame him for that – or he wants to keep a hold over him."

"A hold?"

"Your father is short of money Audrey, and I know for a fact that his biggest regret next to disowning you was the losing of Braeside. I'll warrant John Bamford has a great deal of money by now, and they do say that he lives under an assumed name.

Marcus has a crazy idea of getting Braeside back. After all that's happened, it would be like getting his life back, especially now. With that photograph he thinks he might just have the winning card in his hand. His only dilemma is knowing how and when to play it."

237

CHAPTER THIRTY-TWO

"That's good, I'm so glad – yes he's a dear man isn't he. And so good for him to be among old comrades with whom he can reminisce. Well thank you for your help Major, I'm most grateful for your intervention, and please assure Jack I'll come up to see him again, just as soon I am able to get away from London. And tell him not to worry about – anything. Goodbye."

Audrey, who was in her office at the Regent Trust put the telephone down and breathed a small sigh of relief. The retired Major who ran the veteran's hostel in Liverpool, after receiving Audrey's telegram had lost no time in seeing Jack, and persuading him to accept an offer of accommodation. It was a weight off her mind to know her old friend henceforth would be dry and warm, enjoy regular meals, and have companionship.

Before leaving Liverpool she had intended to return to Crosslands but then changed her mind. Vital as the photograph Jack had described might be in bringing Oliver Regent to justice, she had in the end felt unable to face her father a second time, especially so soon after her mother's funeral, and concerning a matter of such gravity. I will deal with it when the time is right, she had thought, though when that might be she had no idea.

Throughout the two days she had been back in London, her thoughts had been in turmoil. The combined drama of recent events – the painful outcome of her visit to Margaret, then hard on its heels the shocking news of her mother, the strained audience with her desolate father and the revelation of the incriminating evidence against Oliver Regent, and what to do about it, had left her nerves raw, her head crammed to bursting with a hundred and one anxieties.

Since their quarrel she had not even Nellie to talk to about it all, and was feeling increasingly desperate for a sympathetic ear, a shoulder to lean on. She knew now that only one person could fulfil that role. Her love for Richard was something she had tried not to acknowledge, had not indeed had time or solitude to reflect on. He had telephoned her when she returned from America and she had put him off. She wondered now how many more times during her absence he may have 'phoned.

But now the boot was on the other foot, thrice in the past twenty-four hours she had tried to call Richard but there had been no answer. What could he be doing? He had never discussed his work with her, other than to say it was in 'international trade' and the occasional mention of business lunches. Perhaps he was just very busy right now.

Or might there be another reason he was unobtainable; that he had grown tired of waiting by the 'phone, taken her lack of response for indifference, concluded that she was no longer interested in him?

Audrey picked up the telephone and dialled his number. There was no answer. She looked at the clock, then got up and put on her coat. She must see Richard, and she must see him now. It was almost 5 pm and any business lunch must surely be finished by now. Pausing she took an envelope and notepaper from the desk; if he were not at home, she would leave a letter explaining everything, her feelings towards him included.

By the time the taxi pulled up outside Richard's apartment Audrey had filled four sides of notepaper. Even if the letter were not needed, the writing of it had greatly helped clarify her thoughts, telling about the incriminating photograph of Oliver Regent in her father's possession, and asking for Richard's advice about what she should do. She ended by opening her heart to him, with a tender expression of how much she had missed him while in America, and how she now realised just how very much he meant to her, and her fervent hope that these sentiments were reciprocal.

The sky was darkening and a few spots of rain falling as she paid the taxi and hurried to the front door of the apartments. She pressed Richard's buzzer, waited a moment then pressed again. Perhaps he was asleep, in the bath, had the gramophone on... Agitated now she rattled the locked door and buzzed for the porter but without success.

With the rain getting heavier and nowhere to shelter she took out the letter and scanned her somewhat shaky handwriting. (The taxi ride had been a bumpy one) Satisfied, she sealed it in the envelope, wrote 'Mr Richard Neame, Apartment 7 – Confidential' on the front and pushed it under the door.

The rain was coming down in buckets now. Audrey ran to the kerb, and seeing a taxi approach held out her hand. The vehicle pulled up a few yards ahead of her.

"Where to guv?"

A man sheltering beneath an umbrella suddenly stepped forward, "The Savoy Hotel please." At that moment there was a flash of lightning. As he lowered his umbrella she saw his face. "Richard…!"

The taxi had already pulled away. Audrey immediately hailed another. "Savoy Hotel," she ordered breathlessly.

Fifteen minutes later they drew up outside the Savoy, the rain still falling. Audrey paid the taxi and turning her coat collar up ran quickly over the glistening pavement. A uniformed doorman ushered her politely in.

Shaking out her wet hair she surveyed the lobby; there was no sign of Richard. She looked in the bar, and walked up and down several times before noticing the open door to the restaurant. There were several couples dining early. Then at the far end she saw him. There was another man with his back to her and the waiter was showing them to a table. From their gestures the two men appeared to be very well acquainted, and to her considerable relief there was no woman present. Audrey felt a leap of joy, and with it a desperate urge to speak to Richard now, however briefly; would he mind awfully if she were to go in and announce herself she wondered? Perhaps she could ask the waiter to hand him a note, saying she would meet him in the lobby after dinner. No, she must speak to him now, just quickly, to hear his voice, be reassured by his smile, his pleasure at seeing her. Smiling now herself at the thought of surprising him she walked boldly into the restaurant.

The surprise however was hers, or more accurately, the most severe of shocks. Richard's dining companion had angled his head slightly and she could now see his face. On doing so she froze and stared in horror then turned on her heel and ran headlong back out of the restaurant. For the man sitting opposite Richard, engaged with him in what could only be described as intimate, companionable and convivial conversation, was none other than Mr Oliver Regent.

Almost falling onto the pavement she summoned a taxi, her mind a frenzy of despair and incredulity. Now she knew the reason he had talked so little of his work: all along he had been hand in glove with Regent – as business associate, friend and doubtless partner-in-crime! And he must have long ago informed on her, told Regent everything she had said, what she knew and what she suspected, and her desire to bring him to justice. All this time he had been playing cat and mouse with her, waiting to strike, and – oh good heavens, no…! Audrey's hand flew to her mouth. The note she had delivered to Richard less than half an hour previously! It revealed the existence of the incriminating photograph in her father's possession. Regent would surely stop at nothing to obtain and destroy such evidence, as well as anyone with any knowledge of its existence. Not only would she now be in infinitely greater danger, but her father too, possibly even Jack. Oh why did she have to set it down in writing, why, why, why, could she not have waited, bided her time, been more cautious!

But it was too late, everything she had relied on was suddenly shattered to a thousand pieces, what little secure ground she had had under her feet replaced by a yawning and perilous chasm that she might plunge into at any moment, and the worst most devastating part of all was that Richard Neame, oh Richard! - whom she had entrusted with her secrets, and in whom she had until a few moments ago invested such hope - of love, of happiness, was supping with the devil and as much her sworn enemy as Oliver Regent himself. Now she was completely alone with no one to turn to. How could such utter disaster have befallen her!

In the midst of her anguish she strove desperately to think, to plan what her next move should now be. It then dawned on her a crucial part of the potential damage could be avoided; Richard had only just sat down the dinner, while the letter she had written him still lay unopened in the ground floor lobby at his apartment building. If she could somehow gain access the letter could be retrieved before he returned. She commanded the taxi driver to change course, and gave Richard's address.

The rain had now thankfully stopped. It was dark however and there were few people about outside Richard's building. Audrey squinted though the thick glass door panel and saw her letter lying in the same place on the mat. Presumably no one had passed in or out since. She tried the porter's buzzer again. This time the box on the wall crackled and a voice was came through. It was a woman:

"Yes?"

"Is that the porter?" asked Audrey.

"That would be my husband, but it's his night off, he's down the Bottle and Jug."

"Oh then perhaps you could help me, I need to get a letter I put through the door here earlier."

"Letter?"

"Yes, for one of your residents, Mr Neame, its terribly important." "Why?"

"Oh – well, there's something I forgot to mention in the letter."

There was a pause. "Then put another letter through the door. Mr Neame will see it when he comes back."

Audrey bit her lip cursing her own ineptitude. "But it's not quite so simple as that, there's…also something I have to take out of the letter you see"

"Oh."

"So could you please come and open the front door, so I can pick up the letter?"

"Can't do that madam."

"Why on earth not."

"Might be money in there, you might be a thief for all I know."

"How dare you – I'm sorry, I mean -"

"Well I don't know you from Adam let's face it. My husband never lets anyone in except residents who've lost their keys or people he knows. Mr Neame I daresay will be back later this evening, you can speak to him about it then madam, goodnight." The box crackled once more then silence.

Audrey stared again in fearful desperation at the blue envelope lying as yet harmless on the mat as if it were a bomb about to explode. She looked up and down the street. If only some other resident would appear, it would take her but a second to dart in behind them through the door and grab the letter.

After five fretful minutes spent pacing the pavement Audrey took another taxi back to her apartment. Shutting the curtains and putting on the table lamp she poured herself a drink and sat down. In another hour or so Richard would be returning to his apartment. She pictured him finding her letter on the mat, taking it upstairs and reading it. Would he telephone Oliver Regent immediately? Probably. The existence of the photograph upped the odds against Regent considerably. What would Regent then do? He would certainly want the matter dealt with swiftly. Audrey realised she ought to warn her father. She reached for the telephone and dialled his number, but heard nothing but the ringing tone. Regent might send someone to break into the house in Crosslands the very next day; she must send a telegram immediately she thought, then remembered it was evening and the post offices were closed; first thing in the morning then.

Audrey closed her eyes. She tried to think rationally and calmly, keeping her shell-shocked feelings as far as possible in suspended animation as she considered what to do about Richard Neame. As things stood neither he nor Regent had any inkling that she had discovered their alliance. If she were still intent on bringing Regent to justice (and by implication now, Richard Neame too - and she shuddered at the emotional somersault this notion required) would it not be shrewder to maintain the illusion? Like a chess player, she considered what, in that scenario Richard's next move might be. After finding her letter he would probably acknowledge it and try to string her along, playing for time with discussions about when and how to alert the authorities. Meanwhile though, what would Olivier Regent be doing? She must get that telegram to her father as soon as the post office opened. Sipping her drink her eyelids drooped. The drama of the past hour had drained the energy from her body, and within a few minutes she was sound asleep in the armchair.

Audrey was dreaming of a summer afternoon with Martin's family. The droning of bees in the honeysuckle that grew up the walls of the motel, a place she recalled in her conscious thoughts, but whose distant memories lay in her unconscious like precious jewels buried deep beneath the soil of everyday existence. The bees grew louder till suddenly her eyes were open again, and she realised it was the intercom on her wall that was making the noise. With an effort she roused herself, went over and flicked the switch to reply. "Hello?"

"Audrey I'm so glad you're there, can I come in?"

For the second time that evening Audrey froze in horror. The voice was Richard Neame's. Her heart pounding she turned off the table lamp, ran to the window and peered down. Though she was on the second floor the streetlight illuminated sharply the area around the entrance to the building. She saw two figures looking up: one was indeed Richard Neame, and with him a lantern-jawed man, a scar down the side of his face. He was, unmistakably, the same man who had followed her in America.

She shrank back from the window in terror; her only thought now that of escape. Snatching up her coat and handbag she hurried to the small rear window of the apartment, prised it open and squeezed out onto the metal steps of the emergency staircase. On reaching terra firma she ran quickly down a side alley and out to an adjacent main road where she hailed a passing taxi. "Hampstead Heath please, and be quick." Her last and only refuge now was the fairground, and Nellie.

What she did not realise was that another car was pursuing her, and that in it were Richard Neame and the scar-faced man.

CHAPTER THIRTY-THREE

Audrey, her hair still damp from the rain shivered as the taxi wove through the streets of north London. Though well away from Kensington now, she could not relax. It occurred to her she had no idea what she was going to say to Nellie when she turned up unannounced at the fairground. Perhaps this was a foolish impulse to run to her friend, whom she wasn't at all sure would greet her amicably, remembering with shame the harsh words she had spoken to her the last time they met. If Nellie turned her away she could hardly blame her. If so, she would have to go to a hotel, but then where? She couldn't go on running for the rest of her life. Maybe she should head directly to the nearest police station and tell all she knew, about Oliver Regent and how he was really John Bamford, wanted for murder, and about the photograph of him wearing the belt found at the scene of her Uncle Mac's death.

But suppose they didn't take her seriously, suppose the Chief Inspector chanced to be a friend of Regent and arrested her for slander...and then what about Richard Neame, now his known accomplice – she winced, it was simply unbearable to think about Richard, whom she had regarded of as *her* Richard, in this new and hideous light. In the space of an evening her whole world had become her enemy. She had heard about the tormented souls who, all hope abandoned threw themselves off London Bridge into the cold deathly embrace of the Thames, and as the taxi rumbled on to an unknown outcome, not for the first time in her life she understood them.

Her feverish thoughts calmed a little as they entered the leafy environs of Hampstead. Jack Straw's Castle, filling up with the evening trade looked cosy and inviting, a world of ordinary people with everyday routines and enjoyments, and beyond the trees the lights of the fairground were a comforting sight. She could hear the joyful clamorous notes of the hurdy-gurdy. Now, in a sudden burst of optimism she felt certain Nellie would welcome her with open arms! The next second any thoughts of blessed relief vanished, when she saw another car draw level, its occupants the scar-faced man and Richard Neame. The horn sounded aggressively, and an arm gestured to the taxi driver to pull over. Audrey shrank down into her seat, "Please don't stop I beg you," she quaked, "Turn right here, into the field quickly, to the fairground!"

Audrey gripped the seat as the taxi lurched past the open five bar gate and bumped across the grass. On reaching the fairground encampment she peered from the rear window to see the pursuing car pulled up a few yards away. Grabbing her handbag she almost fell from the passenger seat and ran headlong towards the caravans.

The first to see her was Mrs Chidlow, who was stood in the doorway of her caravan puffing on a pipe. "Why if it isn't young Audrey."
She called into the caravan, "Nellie – Audrey's here."

"Oh Mrs Chidlow," panted Audrey running up to her, "you don't know how glad I am to see you."

"Audrey!" Nellie had appeared, "as I live and breathe!"

"Oh Nell, I'm so sorry, you've got to help me please -"

"What the matter?"

"They're after me - "

"Those men," Audrey pointed back to the car.

"Loan sharks are they," Mrs Chidlow narrowed her eyes, "tally men? Well we'll soon sort them out."

Richard Neame and the scar-faced man were walking towards the caravans. "Audrey I need to talk to you," called Neame.

"Go away," shouted Audrey, "to think I trusted you, to think I -"

"I read your letter, you one you left at my apartment, we have to talk about it."

"There's nothing to talk about, you're in league with Olivier Regent, and you're both going to get what's coming to you, I'm going to the police."

"No, we must wait, the photograph may not be sufficient evidence." The two men had reached the caravans now.

"You heard the lady," said Mrs Chidlow firmly, "go away, you ain't wanted here."

"We can't do that I'm afraid Maam," said Neame, " I have to talk to this lady in private, its very important."

"Hang on a minute," said Mrs Chidlow, as he approached, "ain't you the feller that came here with Audrey when our Nell got arrested over that bracelet business?"

"The very same ma-am, and now its Audrey that's in trouble"

"Yes," cried Audrey, "but you deceived me, you may have helped Nellie but all along you were an out and out crook yourself!"

"No, I swear," said Neame taking her arm, "you must come with me Audrey now."

"Never! Get away from me!"

"Get your hands off her," barked Mrs Chidlow, "Nell get over to the stalls and get some of the boys here now."

"Right Mum," said Nellie and ran quickly off.

"That isn't going to do any good," said Neame.

"Not to you my lad," Mrs Chidlow folding her arms authoritatively.

Turning back to Audrey Neame said, "Look if you'll just sit in the car with me for two minutes, we can straighten this whole thing out."

"You must think I'm even more naïve than I am," said Audrey, "which is a lot, I admit it now," – oh what an absolute fool I've been." She began to shake with misery.

"Don't you fret duck," said Mrs Chidlow coming down the caravan steps and beckoning Audrey to her, "help's on its way." Nellie and a group of burley men were now advancing, with Mr Chidlow and Mick the boxer in the lead. "What's the row love?" asked Mr Chidlow, "we've got a fairground to run you know."

"Sorry to have troubled you Jesse my sweet, but these gentlemen are threatening Audrey," declared Mrs Chidlow, "and Audrey as you know is a friend of our Nellie."

Mr Chidlow's expression altered immediately. "Is that so?" he said rolling up his sleeves and squaring up to the two intruders, "Right, who's first?"

"Wait a moment sir," said Neame, "we've met before, I helped free your daughter from that trumped up theft charge remember?"

Mr Chidlow lowered his fists a moment and gave a look of recognition, "Why strike a light yes - "

"But Audrey reckons he's up to no good now," interjected Mrs Chidlow, "trying to take her off he is."

"It's vitally important I speak with her," began Neame.

"Well in that case -"

"No, no don't listen to him he's a criminal," insisted Audrey.

"Come with me now Audrey," Richard Neame stepped forward to grasp Audrey's arm once more. As she screamed in terror Mr Chidlow lunged at him. Before the blow could connect however the scar-faced man had stepped forward, caught the assailant's arm, twisted it hard and thrown him deftly to the ground. Mick and the other fairground men immediately fell upon them, fists flying, and though Neame and his companion put up an impressive defence the superior numbers quickly overpowered them.

"Take them to the stores," ordered Mrs Chidlow, "we'll hear them out there then decide what to do with them. And give this to the taxi man," she added taking a ten-shilling note from her blouse. "Poor blighter."

Battered and bruised the two intruders were escorted behind the caravans and into a faded old army bell tent stacked with tea chests, ropes and fairground paraphernalia. Nellie squeezed Audrey's arm gently in a gesture of reconciliation. "Oh Nell I'm so sorry," said Audrey meekly.

"Hush," replied Nellie, "we'll talk about it later, over a glass of beer, right now I want to find out what your Richard's up to causing all this ruckus."

"He's no longer my Richard, oh dear, this is so - " Audrey said shakily.

Richard Neame and the scar-faced man, looking battered and dishevelled were sat on a pile of tarpaulins, their captors surrounding them.

"So come on?" demanded Mrs Chidlow. "What's your business with frightening Audrey, and why are here making trouble on our fairground? You'll not be going anywhere till you start talking."

The two men exchanged a glance then nodded in agreement. "It's true Audrey is in danger," said Neame, "but not from us."

"Oh no, who then?" growled Mr Chidlow rubbing his arm.

"A man called Oliver Regent, a fraudster and murderer – so it's alleged."

"Yes, and you're his accomplice as I found out tonight!" blurted Audrey.

"What?" Neame looked baffled.

"I followed you to the Savoy and saw you in the restaurant together."

"Oh lord…"

"Yes, so the game's up for you, I'm going to the Jack Straw's Castle to telephone the police right now."

There was loud murmuring among the fairground folk, several more of who had now gathered in the tent.

"Ask for Inspector Collier of Scotland Yard, give him my name."

"You're bluffing, playing for time."

"Then call my bluff, go ahead and phone, he'll tell you I'm no crook."

"All right, I know Inspector Collier helped when Nellie was in trouble, but how do we know he's not been secretly working for Regent all along just like you?"

"I'm not!" said Neame in exasperation. "All right I guess I can't prove anything right now, so what are you going to do? Who do you trust?"

"I'm thinking about it," said Audrey.

"I guess we'd better tell them Freddie," Neame looked at the scar-faced man, who nodded. "This might sound far-fetched Audrey," he said taking a deep breath, "but the truth is I work for the FB1."

"Come again?" said Nellie, while Audrey stared in disbelief.

"The Federal Bureau of Investigation, I've been tracking Oliver Regent for two years now. Right now I'm posing as a businessman looking to invest with him, hence the meeting at the Savoy tonight." This was greeted with even louder murmuring and perplexed looks.

Audrey was dismissive, "A likely story, you're right it's far fetched, and it won't wash. You should also be aware that I know very well who this man is," she pointed an accusing finger at Neame's companion.

"Who?" said Mrs Chidlow.

"One of Oliver Regent's henchmen," said Audrey, "he followed me everywhere I went in New York, and I'd recognise that scar anywhere. Well, do you deny it?"

Neame shook his head. "No, I can't deny it. May I introduce agent Freddie Garcia, ex-Green Beret. Freddie tailed you in New York on my orders. I was concerned for your safety, Regent has a lot of enemies stateside and if he thought any one of them had got to you, you could have been in real danger. If you had found that bank and gone looking for George Weatherly's deposit box someone would have been waiting outside to put a slug in your back. Except Freddie would have got them first, he never misses. Its lucky for everyone we weren't carrying firearms tonight, or this might have turned into a real tragedy. No offence Mr Chidlow, or any of you gentlemen, you acted to protect a lady, and that was right."

Audrey was still looking sceptical. "For a start the FBI is American, you told me you're Canadian."

"Canadian by birth sure, which is why I was originally assigned to the case. There was a rumour Regent was planning to relocate to Canada, making contacts with the criminal underworld there. I know all the big hitters and their operations. In the end he came back to Britain, and I followed. Then I met you." He looked at her pleadingly.

For a moment Audrey looked ready to capitulate. Then she said, "Wait a minute though, if you're with the FBI where's your identity card?"

"That's right," chipped in Mick, "plain clothes coppers always has a card."

Neame shrugged, "You got me there," he sighed. "I couldn't risk carrying an ID badge tonight any more than a gun, not meeting Regent. If he wanted to frisk me it would have blown my cover and two years solid of investigative work."

"A convenient excuse!" crowed Audrey.

"Freddie however can show you his badge." The scar-faced man took out a small leather wallet and flipped it open.

Inside was his photograph, the scar clearly visible, and a metal badge inscribed with the words Federal Bureau of Investigation. Mr Chidlow snatched the wallet, examined it for a moment then passed it round the assembled company.

"Well Audrey," said Mrs Chidlow, "what do we do with them?" Everyone looked at Audrey while suggestions to 'turn them in to the old bill' 'send them packing' or 'give them a chance' were discussed loudly by all and sundry.

Audrey tore at her hair in desperation, "I don't know, I don't know," she cried. "I'm at my wits end – that badge could be fake for all I know - "

"Audrey."

All heads turned towards the man who had just entered the tent. "Curtis -"

"Are these men saying they're Federal Agents?"

Audrey nodded.

Curtis approached them. "May I see that badge?" Freddie handed him his wallet. Opening it Curtis held it towards the light of the hurricane lamp. He scrutinised it closely for several seconds. At last he said, "It so happens I've seen an FBI badge before, and in my opinion this is the genuine article." Further murmuring broke out.

Richard Neame said, "Well, will you trust me now?"

Audrey wrung her hands together, her expression still wary and uncertain. "What choice do I have?"

"Well, that's a start."

Curtis said, "Do you have a plan sir? The FBI always got a plan Audrey. It ain't always a good plan, but they always got one. Let's hear yours."

"Sure, we've got a plan," said Neame, "one that will bring the great Mr. Olivier Regent finally to justice. But we need Audrey's help."

"In what way?" said Audrey.

"That I am afraid, is confidential. It means bringing a dangerous criminal to justice, and my duty to the public good demands a certain level of discretion at this stage, or we cannot proceed with the plan. I will therefore need to discuss the details with Audrey in private, with your permission Maam?" He looked enquiringly at Mrs Chidlow.

"All right, these boys need to get back to the fairground anyhow," she said nodding. "I'm grateful for what you done for our Nell that time Mr Neame, and I'm going to give you the benefit of the doubt and leave you alone with Audrey – all right Jesse?" Mr Chidlow nodded his assent. "But hear this, harm a hair on her head and you'll reap the consequences, and that's a showman's promise."

"Thank you ma-am."

"Yes, thank you Mrs Chidlow," said Audrey.

"That's what friends are for." She smiled and followed her husband out of the tent.

"And we are friends aren't we?" said Audrey turning to Nellie and Curtis when the onlookers had left. "I know I behaved appallingly, and I know it looks as though I'm only here now out of desperation, but I am truly sorry for speaking to you the way I did. Can you believe me?"

Nellie took her hand. "We knew you weren't in your right mind that night," she said. "Children do funny things to people. Curtis and me have been blessed being back together again, and Whillan having his dad back, and we have you to thank for that. Did you know we were planning to come and see you tomorrow, now how strange is that?"

"Really?"

"Its true Audrey," said Curtis solemnly, "you see, we heard what happened after you went to find your daughter."

"Margaret?" Audrey looked surprised, "you heard, how?"

"You'd be surprised what fairground folk know," said Nellie, tapping the side of her head. "I'm so sorry Aud."

"I suppose it was meant to be," said Audrey, tears pricking at her eyes."

"Are you sure you want to do this?" said Nellie, nodding towards Richard and Freddie Garcia waiting discreetly at a distance.

Audrey nodded limply, "Whatever is meant to be."

"You look like you need a good night's sleep to me. Will you stay with us tonight, after you've finished talking to these two?"

"Yes, thanks Nell, I'd love to. I feel so very tired." Feeling a touch on her other arm Audrey looked up in surprise. A small, wizened figure was smiling up at her, her gold teeth glinting in the light of the hurricane lamp. "Why, Auntie Lizzie - "

"You said right dearie," said the old lady in a soft voice, "some things are meant to be. Keep your dolly safe and all will be well."

With a gasp Audrey felt in her handbag. Hidden deep in the lining was the rag doll she had been given on her first visit to the fairground. "Yes, oh yes thank you I must - " But Aunt Lizzie was gone.

Audrey turned to Richard Neame. Her expression composed she said quietly, "Now I am ready."

CHAPTER THIRTY-FOUR

January 1948

Audrey stepped from the taxi and pulled the black hat down over her head. Her thick raven black hair, lately grown longer fell like sleek, lustrous armour into position across her shoulders. She looked at her watch. It was 8pm. Oliver Regent would be waiting. The huge oak doors of the Regent Trust headquarters offices loomed above her. Entering she walked purposefully across the deserted foyer, her footsteps resounding on the polished black and white tiles.

The lights from the chandelier burned softly, throwing a ghostly light on the mirrored walls. Audrey stopped and studied her shimmering reflection. She had taken extra care with her appearance tonight, her expensively tailored red suit cut by expert hands from the finest of cloth. She turned to admire the perfection of the lines. Red; how appropriate she thought, the colour of passion, of blood; Oliver Regent and I are of the same blood, and blood they say, will always out.

The figure before her seemed to glow now, as if fringed with a demonic fire. The clothes, the posture the very image, were unmistakeable to her and now in a visitation from the grave that person, radiant and indomitable had returned. Yes, it was her mother. Clarissa, laughing, triumphant, mocking, Audrey heard her voice, a clarion call from hell itself: *Yes child just as you and I are one blood, mother and daughter, you are one blood with him, uncle and niece, there is no other way, you have a destiny. Death is nothing, I am eternally my brother's sister, and I bear him no grudge. He and I will be bound in the afterlife as we were from the beginning. You are his niece, and blood will out, blood will out, blood will out, your fate is to do his bidding, do it my child with my blessing, and the world and all the riches in it shall be yours - h-ha, ha, ha, ha...!"*

Audrey turned silently away, pulled the black hat tighter and began to climb the stairs, her mother's sepulchral laughter echoing in her ears.

On the darkened upper corridor a shaft of light was shining from a door slightly ajar at the far end. Audrey walked at a slow deliberate pace towards it, her heels measuring each step. Entering she saw Oliver Regent at the window. The blinds were drawn back and he was stood, staring motionless at the night sky. A solitary lamp illuminated a small area around the desk, leaving the remainder of the room in shadow. Hearing her tread he turned.

"Audrey – good evening," he said in a hushed voice, "won't you be seated?" Audrey sat on the upright chair in front of the desk. "So, what's all this about? What so urgent that it couldn't wait until the morning."

"I'm sorry if I have inconvenienced you sir," she said slowly. "I have a certain matter to discuss with you, a matter you may consider to be of a delicate nature."

"And you wanted privacy, I understand." Oliver Regent nodded and sat behind his desk. "Well there's no one here but the two of us, and to ensure we're not interrupted, let's switch off the telephone, and just in case my indomitable secretary decides to return and burn the midnight oil over her typewriter, which she has been known to do, we'll turn of the intercom too."

"I'm sure that won't be necessary -" said Audrey quickly.

"But one can't be too careful." He reached out and flipped two switches on the desk. He then leaned back and cupped his hands behind his head and said in a relaxed tone, "Now, let's hear what's on your mind, it all sounds very ominous. Are you thinking of leaving us, is that it? Resignations are always difficult, and thankfully I've never had to make one. I only ask for them, and getting rid of people I find quite easy, not that I actually enjoy it of course, contrary to some rumours." He grinned wolfishly, his flint-like eyes glinting in the lamplight.

Audrey said, "I have heard certain opinions of you, of course."

"That I don't suffer fools gladly? It's true, and I appreciate that some people find me unduly harsh in that respect. Which is why I thought perhaps you had come to say something of that nature, and that as a consequence you could no longer work for a tyrant?" He flashed the wolfish grin again.

"Personally I have never found your behaviour to be tyrannical," said Audrey, "and I have not come to hand in my resignation."

"Hmm, well I'm glad to hear it. And now more intrigued than ever as to why you requested this mysterious after-hours rendezvous - well?"

Ignoring his expectant gaze Audrey, with studied languor continued: "The Regent Trust has given me everything – you have given me everything." Still avoiding his eyes she removed her gloves and placed them casually on the desk by the telephone. "And the fact of the matter is Mr Regent I still feel that I have never thanked you properly."

Regent spread out his hands. "For what?"

"Why, for the remarkable opportunity you have given me – income, position, travel – a purpose in life. Ordinarily few women enjoy such privileges."

"You are no ordinary woman."

Audrey smiled modestly then said, "But I am curious, why me?"

Regent's gaze wavered for a second. He said, "I was already looking for someone to assist me with my new plans and ideas when you happened to come along. You appeared capable, sophisticated and bright, good with people too, just what the Regent Trust needed at that point, we were growing stale, I felt people were getting fed up with hearing about how much I had done for good causes, we needed a breath of fresh air. Your achievements have proved me right – the ideas, the hotel, the refurbishments, not to mention the remarkably successful American trip – scooping our biggest ever single donation - need I say more?"

"Your appreciation of my efforts is most welcome." Audrey gave a little bow of her head. "However at the outset when we met at the hospital I was just another nurse, we had not even spoken. There are many capable and sophisticated women who work and volunteer with us, several of them from good families, county people, titled in some cases. Had you appeared to have been seeking matrimony, or some romantic liaison for example – forgive my frankness – it might have explained things – so the point is…I repeat Mr Regent, why me?"

Oliver Regent stared at her, his smile fixed. "What is it you find so baffling?" He rose and crossed to the window, turning his back to her. "All right, if you must know after we had met there stirred certain feelings within me, not of any gross nature you understand, rather feelings of - a familial kind."

"I see," said Audrey.

"I have no children of my own. I saw you in loco parentis. I knew of your difficult circumstances, the rejection by your parents."

"How did you find that out?"

"There are ways – I investigate all my senior staff."

"I wasn't senior when we met, just a humble nurse lining up to meet the great man."

"Quite."

"So you wanted a protégé?"

"Is that so ignoble? I have never known the pride that comes from having an accomplished son or daughter - a young person to teach and inspire in my own image. Though we are not related, I can't deny it gives me satisfaction to see you playing something of that role in my life. I own several champion racehorses, and I like to see them galloping happily forward and winning, it makes me happy. It's the same with people – with you – if you'll pardon the comparison!"

Warming to his theme now he began to pace the room, "I also felt immediately that we were alike – bold, imaginative, unfettered by convention, free from – how can I put it - certain narrow moral restraints, visionaries even. I have always seen us as kindred spirits. I hope this revelation, if that is what it amounts to answers your question. Of course there is no need for this conversation to change our working relationship or your future with the trust, which is assured. And there is no need on your part for gratitude, it is I who am grateful."

"Thank you for telling me all this," said Audrey eagerly, "I am so glad, it is what I was hoping and praying to hear."

Leaning forward, and with a both sadness and great relief in her voice she said, "Oh I have been so adrift since the separation from my family, and other events have conspired to render my existence an isolated one. But since coming to London, to be respected and taken under the wing as it were of a person of your standing has been like a gracious gift – the gift of a new life – and more than compensation for being spurned so absolutely by my own mother and father. But you must forgive me," she continued, now assuming a solemn and prescient air, "For now it is my turn for a revelation, and of a serious nature. When you describe us as kindred spirits, there is rather more to it than that is there not?"

"Meaning?" Regent's dark eyes flickered.

"Because, you are my uncle by blood, my mother's brother. I believe you have known who I am for some time."

"What?" Regent's face puckered as if he had been unexpectedly struck. Then he began to laugh. "Why of all the - when did you dream this nonsense?"

"Please don't let's pretend any longer."

"Audrey I'm sorry if my candour this evening has temporarily unhinged your mind, I sought only to answer your question as to why you were chosen, in as honest a way as I could, and now you spout this fantasy -"

"Stop!" Audrey brought her palm down smartly on the desk. "In your own interests now, be truthful with me Uncle John."

Hearing his name on her lips his features froze, while his eyes burned like fire. He said quietly, "Go on."

Audrey's face was radiant with purpose. "I came here tonight not to confront you but to warn you. I know the reason you have been living under an assumed identity, that you fled this country as a wanted man, and made your fortune in America as Oliver Regent. I also know the authorities have not stopped looking for you. When I first discovered who you were I wanted to go to the police, but something made me wait. I could not be your judge. You have been kind to me, kinder than my own parents. I want to help you."

Oliver Regent shook his head incredulously. "I have never heard anything so preposterous...."

"Listen to me," she hissed, "there is a man called Richard Neame, he is a detective -"

"Not Sherlock Holmes?" He laughed again.

"An FBI detective," said Audrey, "he was staying at the lodgings when I arrived in London and we became acquainted. He has recently confided in me, and he is laying a trap to capture you."

"I see. Well, going along with your 'penny dreadful' novel for a moment," said Regent maintaining his amused look, "if I'm a man on the run and he knows where I am, why hasn't this great detective just come and arrested me?"

"They're waiting to collect some evidence."

"Oh?"

"A photograph of you."

"In the act of committing whatever crime I'm supposed to have perpetrated I suppose."

"You are wearing a belt in the picture. A belt that was found at the scene of the crime."

There was a long silence. Regent sat back down at his desk and tapped the blotter rhythmically with his fingers. His face now fully in the light, Audrey could see that he was no longer smiling. At last he spoke. "How much do you know?" His demeanour had altered, his voice vibrating with menace.

"I know about the murder," said Audrey quietly, "or should I say murders. My Uncle Mackenzie and a woman, Kitty Mason."

"Do you believe me to be guilty?"

"The evidence points to it. But I'd like to hear what you have to say."

"I never intended to harm either of them. Kitty was my lover, and she had started fooling around with your Uncle Mac – he was inadequate, insanely jealous, it was manslaughter at the very worst. If I could turn the clock back Audrey, believe me I would, but it happened, and I can't afford to feel guilty now. Haven't I done something by way of amends, to society at least? I've raised millions for charity."

"I know that."

"So, this photograph?"

"My father has it."

"Marcus? And why haven't the police got it yet?"

"My father has it hidden somewhere, the police know about it, but he is prevaricating about whether to give it to them or not."

"We were once, friends." John Bamford gave a wry smile.

"Yes, I know. I fear in the end they may force his hand, they're applying for a search warrant. But you could get there first – speak to him as his friend, or send a man, burn down the house, I can persuade my father to go away for a day or two – if not…"

For the first time the glint in Regent's eye returned. "I told you we were kindred spirits."

"What is Marcus to me?" she shrugged, "a pompous and now pitiful man who disowned his own daughter. You are more fit to be my father."

Regent's glint intensified, "Yes, Marcus is a sad story. But sad stories don't help anyone. Strength, daring, these are the qualities of great men."

"Yes, they take what they want!" exclaimed Audrey approvingly, "unhindered by sympathy, morality."

"Yes!" Regent slammed his fist on the desk. "Yes we do!"

"After all Bella would only have squandered that inheritance of hers, she was a foolish worthless woman, you saw an opportunity and you took it, you stopped her, and put her money to good use -"

"What did you say?" Oliver Regent glared at her.

"Bella -"

"What do you know about Bella?"

"We both know her death was no accident – she was a swimming champion, you did well to cover that up afterwards, and I think you did right, some people just can't be allowed to have so much money. It must have taken a good deal of courage to strangle her out in the open water like that."

"Now listen to me, you are not to discuss Bella -" He stood up and came around the desk towards her. As he did so he brushed against her gloves that were lying over the intercom machine. He looked down at the switch, "You've turned the intercom back on, why?"

"What?"

"I know why!" Flipping the switch off again he then sprang to the door of his office and turned the key in the lock. "Jezebel!"

"Mr Regent – Uncle John, I don't understand," pleaded Audrey, "I just came here to help you -"

"The play-acting's over, how many men are waiting out there to hear me incriminate myself eh?" He reached into his desk and the next second Audrey felt something cold thrust against her collarbone. Squinting downwards she saw the grey barrel of a revolver. "It doesn't matter they'll not take John Bamford," he snarled. "You had me there for a moment my dear, but you overreached yourself, I don't like being taken for a fool, and in doing so you've signed your own death warrant."

"Give yourself up," gasped Audrey, "all right, there are a dozen men next door, you won't get away -"

"You think I haven't planned for this eventuality?" he sneered. "True, as soon as your policemen friends hear this gun go off they'll be battering on the door. But by the time they get in I'll be out of that fire escape," he nodded towards the window, "down to the basement and half a mile away - next stop the continent."

"Ha, there isn't a basement in this building!" retorted Audrey breathless with fear.

"That's where you're wrong - I had it specially built, my little secret. I'm rather pleased it's going to be used now, thank you." As he raised the gun to her neck again Audrey grabbed his hand, pushing against it with every ounce of strength in her body. The next second there was a loud report.

A moment later the door flew off its hinges. "Audrey!" Richard Neame, accompanied by a bevy of officers spilled into the room. He rushed to bend over the figure crumpled on the floor. Feeling for her pulse he lifted her limp body towards him. "Audrey," he cried out, "dear god no, no, no...!"

CHAPTER THIRTY-FIVE

September 1948

"All rise!"

At the usher's call there was a loud scraping of chairs as the door swung open. The judge, resplendent in scarlet and ermine strode in and with unhurried ostentation took his place on the high rostrum. On their cue the assembled gathering resumed their seats. Sitting hunched at a table towards the front of the court was Marcus, his cheeks hollow, and his face pale and drawn through months of anxiety. Beside him were Inspector Collier, Richard Neame and his fellow FBI agent Freddie 'Scarface' Garcia. In the public gallery Mr and Mrs Chidlow and Nellie, accompanied by several members of the fairground community gazed expectantly down. To the left of the judge's rostrum, flanked by two policemen, his expression immobile, sat the tall, ramrod-backed figure of John Bamford. His appearance was healthy, confident and relaxed; rather than being a man about to face judgement, he looked as if he could be embarking on a luxury cruise.

The judge cleared his throat, the sound reverberating round the room. "The accused will stand," he commanded. John Bamford, his features still a blank mask, got to his feet. "Ladies and gentlemen of the jury, the man who stands before you will have already been familiar to you before you were summoned to serve here today. John Anthony Bamford, adopting the alias of Oliver Regent, spent a number of years in the United States of America where he amassed a considerable fortune. At the same time he set about the task of raising funds purportedly dedicated to charitable ends, under the auspices of an organization called The Regent Trust. The word 'purportedly' in the light of recent criminal investigations, is clearly what concerns us in this case, for the results of those investigations indicate that much of the financial wherewithal, donated in good faith by corporate and individual sponsors on both sides of the Atlantic, has found its way not into the many good causes espoused by the Regent Trust, but into the personal coffers of Mr John Anthony Bamford.

You have had some days now to study the bank accounts, witness testimonies and other evidence presented to us by the Scotland Yard detectives and their colleagues in the Federal Bureau of Investigation. These are complex and convoluted documents, a reflection perhaps of the labyrinthine means by which the accused sought to cover the tracks of his alleged financial misdemeanours. But that is for you to decide. I do not need to remind you that these charges are serious, but far more serious are those concerning the taking of two human lives.

Again, you have had time to consider the evidence presented for both the prosecution and the defence. I know that you will not have found your decision easy, and I trust that you will each have searched your conscience and weighed every detail of the facts in the balance in deciding whether the man stood before you today is innocent or guilty. You have elected a foreman to speak on your behalf?"

A grey-haired man stood up, "Yes your honour."

"And have you reached a verdict on which you are all agreed?"

"We have your honour."

"On the charge of false accounting, do you find the defendant John Anthony Bamford, guilty or not guilty?"

"Guilty." A low murmur greeted the answer.

"And on the charges of deception and pecuniary advantage?"

"Guilty." There was more murmuring.

"And on the charges that the accused did, in or within the vicinity of the Stephenson residence of Braeside in Scotland, with wilful intent and malice aforethought, murder both Mackenzie Stephenson and Miss Kitty Mason?"

There was a deathly hush as the jury foreman lowered his eyes and gave a quick exhalation of breath.

"We find the accused," he said quietly, "guilty of murder on both counts."

A collective gasp was followed by an outbreak of loud and animated exclamations throughout the courtroom. Throughout the tumult, John Bamford made no flicker of movement. The judge thumped his gavel vigorously several times. "Order, order in court!"

As the babble subsided to a hush, he declared gravely, "I shall now pronounce sentence. John Anthony Bamford, you have been tried and found guilty of the murder of Mr Mackenzie Stephenson and Miss Kitty Mason. Is there anything you wish to say before sentence is pronounced upon you?"

Bamford neither spoke nor moved. With ceremonious deliberation the judge raised the black cap and set it upon his head. "It is therefore my solemn duty to inform you that you will be taken from this court to a place of public execution, and there be hanged from the neck until you are dead. May God have mercy on your soul."

The officers, having handcuffed Bamford began to lead him from the dock. Bamford held back for a second. Turning to Marcus, his face now bore an expression, and it was one of defiance, of triumph even. Looking his adversary in the eye he said, "A good try with that photograph of the belt, but I'll appeal. Money talks, Marcus, but you'll have forgotten." He began to laugh.

As the officers forced him through the door that led down to the cells he called out, "Pity you lost Braeside," you must really miss the old place."

On leaving the courtroom Marcus was greeted by a fusillade of flash bulbs and shouted questions. "Are you pleased justice has been done Mr Stephenson?" After all that's happened you must be relieved your brother's killer has finally been brought to justice – Mr Stephenson, would you care to comment sir…?"

"No, no comment," he uttered, "I have nothing to say…" and pushing his way through the throng of eager reporters, Marcus, his face a mask of sorrow walked slowly away.

Pentonville Prison 22nd March 1949

The prison chaplain, Bible in hand stood aside. The condemned man had declined all offer of prayer. Then as the hood was brought out he once again shook his head, merely staring arrogantly at the Governor and his escorting officers. The noose was put in place. With a thud the trapdoors fell away. The body twitched momentarily on the rope and then became still. John Bamford was dead.

CHAPTER THIRTY-SIX

A Spring Day

The silver Rolls Royce seemed almost to purr as it passed smoothly along the winding ribbon of the lane. Turning a corner, the occupants gave a little gasp of pleasure as they beheld the imposing façade. They were at last at Braeside.

The Rolls scrunched to a gentle halt on the gravel. Richard Neame got out.

"You know, I've always wanted to drive a real Rolls Royce," he said, "but I never thought it would be all the way from England to Scotland – quite an experience, as is this." He gestured with his outstretched arms towards the grandeur of the mountains, the sweep of the glens, the shimmering beauty of the Loch as it sparkled in the spring sunshine. "What a truly beautiful place this is – oh, but then who am I telling!" He went round to the other side of the car and helped his passenger out.

Marcus emerged and slowly stood upright.

"Yes Richard," he said, "it's beautiful all right, and now thanks to you I've got the chance to love it all over again. And of course, it's not the only thing."

"What are we waiting for?" smiled Richard.

"What indeed." Marcus led the way to the front door and lifted the old stag's head knocker.

The heavy door slowly opened. There stood Audrey, her hair glistening in the spring sunshine and her complexion like peaches and cream.

"Hello Daddy!" Her face lit up in a huge smile, "Welcome home."

The End

EPILOGUE

November 1950

"It's a boy!" Nellie's voice rang out echoing in the lofty hallway of Braeside. She rushed into the drawing room. "Did you hear what I said," she laughed, "It's a boy, a gorgeous little boy."

Richard instantly turned from the window, stubbed out his cigarette and ran towards the staircase racing towards the bedroom where his wife had just given birth to their child.

Marcus who had been seated by the fireside now walked towards the window and gazed out across the terraced garden, which led down to the dark loch. The grandfather clock chimed, 10 am. The fog was clearing and through the misty rain he saw the mountains beyond emerging through the low cloud.

Nellie touched his arm. "Are you coming to see your grandson Marcus?"

The old man smiled, "In a little while Nellie," he said patting her hand, "Let Richard be the first to see him. I'll go up in a minute."

"You should be very proud of her Marcus."

He turned towards her; tears filled his eyes. "I am," he smiled sadly, "Very proud of her."

Nellie smiled and closed the door. Marcus turned towards the window again and looked out across the loch. "All this beauty had once been mine" he said. "How could I have been so blind not to see the deception played out before me by the two people I most loved and trusted?"

John Bamford had ripped a whole through the very fabric of his existence, tore his family apart and Audrey had been the one to suffer its consequences. His thoughts turned to that cold snowy December night at the home in Crosslands when she told them she was pregnant. How cruelly and coldly Clarissa had dismissed her daughter and how he had cast her aside and closed the door to her.

And what of Audrey's child? The little girl, he had seen as a babe in her mother's arms. She should know of her family.

He took a last look across the loch again. Audrey, his spirited, beautiful daughter had brought all this back to him. His Grandson would not want for anything, but that little girl? Now it was his turn, somehow he was going to right the wrong he had done.

Printed in Great Britain
by Amazon